CW00523676

Stone and Water

David James Buckley

This is a work of fiction. Names, characters, businesses, places, events, locales, and incidents are either the products of the author's imagination or used in a fictitious manner. Any resemblance to actual persons, living or dead, or actual events is purely coincidental.

© Copyright David James Buckley 2018

Cover design by BookBeaver.co.uk
Formatting by PolgarusStudio.com

Dedication

Stone and Water is dedicated to my wife Karyn and to my children Joe, Eddie and Annie.

ONE

Carol stared across the wintry reservoir at the spot where the face had disappeared. Iron grey water clawed at the concrete slope by the dam wall. Spiky grass sprouted from ooze below her. The power station beyond stood pale and still, but November stirred black into everything.

She held her breath in the empty air. Heard her mackintosh crinkle as she turned for help. No one. It had been too far out to see clearly. But definitely a face. A young man, perhaps twenty-five. Face and shoulders breaking the surface near the far bank, but no sound and the mouth a silent O.

Then she heard the van and ran.

*

Bill Ward peered through the dirty square of glass in the interview room door, hands in trouser pockets, pale trench coat pushed back.

'What's he in for?' said Ward, as Bible approached. The police station was in the town hall and the corridor still boasted the oak panelling of a once thriving textile town.

'The usual,' said Bible. 'Try and sound a little kinder, Bill.' Behind Ward's heavy grey moustache lurked a man unimpressed by anything.

'Want me to speak to him for you?' said Ward. 'I won't slap him too hard.'

'No. I'll deal with him.'

Jim Bible opened the door and looked at the Teddy Boy in the long red jacket with a black velvet collar.

'Impressive costume,' said Ward, and turned back down the corridor.

The youth smoking at the table glanced up. Bible heard Bill whistling *Teddy Bears' Picnic* as he walked away, his heels clicking noisily in rhythm on the parquet flooring.

'Hey,' said the boy, flicking his cigarette towards the overfull ashtray, 'he's taking the piss, isn't he?'

Bible was aware of his new suit. First time on, and already absorbing the smoke of the police station. He sighed. 'Mind the language.'

'You're fussy for a cop.'

'Sergeant Ward wanted to give you a thick ear,' said Bible.

'I'd get him struck off.'

'That's doctors, not policemen.'

'Can I have a quid?' said the youth.

'After the way you spoke to your mother last night?'

'My mum died, remember?'

Bible paused to let the anger pass through him. 'So what about your wages?'

'I've been buying my so-called Mum a birthday present, haven't I?'

Bible took out his wallet and found a ten shilling note folded in with the shopping list.

'Here. Ten bob'll have to do.'

'Thanks, Dad.'

Bible held the note above the desk out of reach.

'You know what I dread,' he said, before passing it over, 'the day you're sitting there because I have to arrest you. Here.'

He stood and opened the interview room door. His son tabbed his cigarette so the glowing end fell to the floor, and put the stub behind his ear, before rising to his feet and scraping his chair back. 'I'm jacking that job in anyway.'

Bible swallowed his irritation. 'I hope you've got Mum something nice. And don't forget your sister.'

Ricky Bible, a couple of inches shorter than his father, pushed past and strutted down the corridor, meeting Ward on his return to the interview room.

'Not got that promotion yet, Sarge? My dad says you should give up,' said Ricky.

Bible watched his son's cocky walk. A police inspector and he couldn't control his own son. Bible shouted after him. 'A bit less cheek would be nice.' At the end of the corridor a young woman was sitting opposite the reception desk.

Ricky turned and waved sarcastically at Bible and Ward.

'You have to work at charm like that,' observed Bible ruefully.

'If he were my lad…' said Ward.

'You'd sort him out, eh?' said Bible. 'That's not for me, Bill.'

'If you say so, sir. A young lady at the desk wants to report seeing a ghost.'

'Just as well. The prisons don't have room for anything else.'

The woman was shaken, but calm. Unusually calm if what she said was right. If she'd just seen someone drown. Perhaps the cup of tea Bible had told Ward to fetch had helped, though there was a tremor in her hand as she lifted it.

She was young – early twenties, he guessed. And smart, with crisply permed dark hair, a white blouse beneath her mackintosh and a black skirt. Bible was glad he had emptied the ashtray and swept away the ash Ricky had left on the table. She steadied the cup with both hands as she sipped. Bible hoped he was managing to look sympathetic.

'Are you sure, Miss Carlton?' he said. He anticipated her voice again. A soft West Country burr he found quite mesmerising. He wanted to call her Carol.

She put her cup down on the Formica topped table. Ward hadn't bothered with a saucer. Carol looked down. 'How can I be sure of something like that?'

'Perhaps you thought you saw it. With the shock, you'd be unnerved. Perhaps enough to imagine something.'

She buried her face in her hands. There was a moment before she sobbed. Once, then twice more. 'He was so sad, like he was shouting for help but could make no sound.' She took her hands away from her face and looked at Bible, her eyes full. He held out the clean folded handkerchief he always kept spare. 'Sorry,' she said, taking it from him, attempting a smile, her eyes glistening with tears. 'I didn't mean to break down.' She shivered. 'It's cold in here.'

'I'll get you an extra coat.' Bible hesitated. Why did police stations have to be so uninviting? The windows with their metal frames made the cramped room feel like a cell. The paint on the heavy cast iron radiator was chipped, as if no one who used the room cared.

'I'll survive,' she said.

'And it was no one you'd seen before?'

Carol looked down and paused. 'No. Reminded me of someone, that's all.'

'And then you saw him go under?'

'Yes. No. I don't know. His shoulders kept dipping beneath the surface. Perhaps I did imagine it.' She stood, and held out the handkerchief. 'I'm wasting your time.'

Bible liked her, didn't think this smart professional young woman was lying. What would be the point of lying anyway? Attention seeking? Perhaps. You could never be sure.

'Let's go over it again,' said Bible. 'Please.' He gestured towards the chair. Carol sat down again. 'So, you were walking by High Gill Dam at nine this morning.'

'I don't work on Tuesday mornings.'

'It's a bleak place,' said Bible.

'Not always. It was lovely in September. I like the quiet. It clears my head.'

'How do you get there?'

'The bus from town. The dam's the nearest open space. I don't like to be closed in.'

Bible was longing to ask why she was in Yorkshire. Why she hadn't stayed in Devon, or Cornwall or wherever? But it was best to stick to the facts.

'And you saw this man in the water?' he said.

'He just appeared. I'd looked out before and seen nothing. Perhaps he wanted to drown.'

The inspector was kind, but she felt he didn't believe her. His questions were direct, and Carol was embarrassed about the uncertainty of her answers.

'Was he fully clothed?'

'I think so,' said Carol. She'd no need to say think. Why was she doubting herself? Perhaps it was his name. Bible. Like he'd know the truth, whatever she said. 'Yes, he was. A jacket and tie. I suppose that rules out killing himself.'

'People like to look smart for death,' said Bible, writing in his notebook. Carol wondered how many deaths he had seen in his career. 'What about this van that chased you?'

The van. Seeing the figure, she'd been mesmerised for a moment, begun to run for help, turned back. But when she looked again, the water was like no one had been there. Just choppy lapping and cold, as if nothing had disturbed it for years. Then there was a van bouncing up the rutted track, an old green van shuffling out of the mist and frost. She'd panicked, skidding on the frozen curls of tyre track as she ran back to the gateway. She'd reached the gate as the van lurched past. The driver's flat cap was pulled down low over his eyes. He could have been anyone. Water Board worker. Farmer. No reason to think it was coming for her. She had to stop being frightened of everything.

'I'm not sure it did chase me.' The inspector's pencil paused over the notebook. She'd not given him anything worth writing down. 'I think I've wasted your time. I'm sorry.'

'Have you felt chased before?'

Carol hesitated. 'No. Just an ordinary girl. Not usually hysterical.'

'I'll send someone out there,' said Bible, closing his

notebook. 'Might go out there myself. Watch the seagulls whilst I have a sandwich.'

'So I'm free to go?'

'Yes'

For a moment she sat there, not sure who should rise first. Then Bible pushed his chair back, and opened the door. Carol gathered her handbag and picked up her cup to take it back to...she didn't know where.

'I'll look after it,' said Bible, holding out his hand.

Carol smiled as she passed him the cup. As he showed her out, she was glad she hadn't said why the van had scared her.

*

It was already dark when Carol got back to her bedsit after work. Only six o'clock – in summer she'd think nothing of it – but tonight she felt she was out late. Squares of yellow light shone through the windows of the textile mill opposite, but it only made it seem darker outside. All the buildings around her were the colour of soot. She was alone in a new city and no one knew where she was, but she felt she was being watched. At the door to the house of bedsits she glanced round. Left, right, head down to get her key out, check again like an animal at a waterhole. Her key worked smoothly, snugly. Hall light on. Up the stairs with the brass stair rods and worn carpet. Act normally. Walk naturally. Key in the door of her bedsit. Light on. A slender finger curled behind the oven, beckoning before disappearing behind it. Carol gasped, her hand frozen on the light switch, as goose pimples prickled her skin. Then her mind caught up with her eyes and she realised the finger had been a mouse's tail curling up vertically as the tiny creature flipped down the gas pipe. She slammed the bolt across, latched the Yale, sank to the floor and cried.

*

Bible looked at the water lapping the dam wall, and the stunted hawthorn at the far end, blown into a claw. It wasn't right. What had a young woman been doing out here on a bleak weekday morning? Four uniformed constables in their rain capes were each taking an area of the bank opposite. Ward was directing them, his collar up against the drizzle as it turned to sleet.

'We don't want to waste too much time here, sir,' shouted Ward. 'She said herself she might have imagined it.' A lone horse penned in by black dry stone walls galloped away when Ward shouted.

'Keep looking.' Bible was worried. The girl had been apologetic and self-doubting, but she must have seen something. He wondered if he could persuade someone from the local diving club to have a look, though no one had been reported missing.

A search of the patchy grass on Bible's side had revealed nothing. A stocky reservoir keeper with a red neckerchief knotted round his throat stood a little way down the slope.

'It all looks normal to me. West Riding normal,' grinned the Water Board man. 'Grey and wet.'

'So what goes on under the surface, where we can't see?'

The reservoir keeper stumped up the slope to Bible. His donkey jacket smelt like a wet dog.

'Water goes out over there below the off-take tower, and there's a spillway yonder by that tree.'

'Where do you control things from?'

'From t'pumping station. Don't you know owt about reservoirs?'

'Not my line of work. Have you caught any criminals lately?'

'Fair dos.'

Bible hated this verbal fencing. Two males whose tails might just start wagging when they'd bared their teeth a bit. But he'd grown up with it. It was the way things were done in Yorkshire.

''Appen you can 'elp us catch one now,' he said, falling back on the dialect of his parents.

The pumping station had a summery yellow door set into its forbidding Victorian stone, as out of place as an early primrose in a bleak spring.

'Painted it myself,' said the reservoir keeper, turning the key. 'I like a bit of colour.' The keeper's voice changed to an echo as he walked in. 'There's nowt been touched in here.'

The machinery was well kept. The valve wheel shone and the electric motor hummed. A twelve bore shotgun was mounted on polished oak brackets. A number of water colour paintings propped against the wall stood on a spotless floor, newly painted in dark red.

'They're mine,' said the reservoir keeper, waving a hand towards the pictures. 'I spend a lot of time up here on my tod. Watching, waiting.'

Bible crouched to look.

'That's what it looks like in summer,' said the keeper. 'Gorse were out when I did that one.'

The paintings were signed in the bottom right hand corner.

'Jack Turner. That you?' said Bible.

'That's me,' said the reservoir keeper. 'Good name for a painter, eh?' If there had been room to strut about, he would have done.

Bible picked up the gorse picture and looked at the image of the reservoir in sunlight beneath puffy clouds.

'More cheerful than it is now,' he said. 'You've not put any people in them.' Bible was turning it over to look at the back of the frame when the reservoir keeper took it out of his hands.

'The sort of fellas you look for won't stop still while I paint them,' he said, putting the picture back in position.

'You've seen some then?' said Bible sharply. 'Men we might be looking for?' He didn't want Turner getting too friendly.

'No, not recently, like. Just walkers in summer and that.'

'How do you get out here?'

'Motorbike. It's in the old boiler room.'

He was about to make Turner take him there when one of the searching constables appeared at the doorway.

'Sarge wants to know when you're going to let us go home, sir? It's perishing out here.'

'When we've found something, Johnson.' Bible didn't like the young constable's familiarity. And he knew Ward would stick at it whatever the weather.

Johnson smirked and looked pleased with himself. 'We have, sir. Sergeant says you'd best have a look.'

Bible bent down to inspect a brick-coloured inner tube, still partially inflated.

'It can't have been here long, sir,' said Ward. 'And that size, must have come from a lorry.'

'That'll not get you anywhere,' observed the reservoir keeper, with the cheerfulness of someone who enjoyed bringing bad news. 'That's just rubbish someone's dumped. They're always doing it.'

'I thought you walked round the bank this morning?' said Bible. 'Did you come round this side?'

'Yeah, but you find stuff like that all over.'

'There's no road here. Why something from a vehicle?'

'Kids'll have brought it for swimming. Rubber rings and that. You know, playing.'

'In November?'

Johnson was poking in the dry stone wall where the horse had cautiously approached. 'There's a bit of rope here sir.'

'It's like Cluedo, i'n't it,' said the reservoir keeper. 'With the rope and the inner tube by the reservoir.'

'Do you like games, Mr Turner?' said Bible, looking across the water to where Carol must have been standing, a lone figure dwarfed by the landscape.

*

Carol was woken by kittens bouncing on the bedspread. Early morning light shone through the gap in the curtains over the sink. The kittens' mother was supposed to live under the oak table by the front door, looked after by the old woman on the ground floor. Mrs Jenkins had started leaving a saucer of milk for the stray on the front step, and had let her in when the size of the tabby's belly showed she was expecting kittens. But in the last couple of weeks the pregnant mother had found her way upstairs and made a nest in the bottom of Carol's wardrobe, where she gave birth to two female replicas of herself, and a scraggy black tom Carol immediately christened Smudge.

Carol sat up in bed, picked up Smudge and held him to her cheek. He and his two sisters were fond of waking her up by playing on her quilt. A week earlier she'd taken them back downstairs, but the mother had caught each kitten by the scruff of the neck and returned them to their nest in the wardrobe. So Carol had accepted them. She slid her legs from under the blankets holding Smudge in one hand, gathered up the other two kittens, and gently put them back in the bottom of the wardrobe with their mother.

Carol's few clothes were arranged neatly, each garment on a separate hanger, shoes paired side by side. She took out the skirt and blouse she needed for work in the morning, and lay them on the bed. She lifted out the work shoes with the low heel. Nothing higher than two inches, she'd been told when she got the job at the bank. She liked smartness, neatness. It had helped her get the job with no awkward questions asked. She loved the cleanness of a new life. But now she worried that the kittens and their mother would make her clothes smell. It was hard to keep mess out of your life. So she took the hangers out of the wardrobe and hooked them on the picture rail that ran round the walls eighteen inches below the ceiling. Getting ready made her feel normal, prepared for the daylight when she would clip along the pavement to work with everybody else. But it was still too early to leave, so she sat with her morning cup of tea, and tried not to think of her two sisters, and the boy who had disappeared from her life.

TWO

Bible parked his Austin A30 high above the south side of the city to collect his daughter from school. Down in the centre, held in its bowl of hills, a late winter sun hit the Florentine tower of the Town Hall. Across to the north, the jutting outline of Rivock Edge reminded him of summer picnics on Ilkley Moor. It was good not to be a policeman for half an hour.

Chapel Heights Infants' School was built out of solid stone blocks at one end of a group of buildings that also housed a junior and a secondary modern. It amused Bible that the stonemason had carved *INFANTS* in relief over the entrance. He thought of the gurgling bundle he'd held in his arms six years earlier. The magisterial Victorian letters seemed a bit grand, even for the serious little girl his daughter had grown into.

Bible stood outside the iron fence and watched children pushing out of the double doors. Some of the girls wore pretty ribbons in large bows on their heads whereas the little boys made do with grey short trousers, and school caps screwed onto their heads in a variety of unorthodox angles.

'Hello, Pauline's dad,' said a six-year-old with his gabardine slung around his shoulders like a cape as he came through the gate. 'You're a policeman,' he said, before charging down the pavement, slapping his bottom and urging on an imaginary horse.

Pauline came out last, clutching her biscuit tin and looking solemn.

'You didn't have to meet me,' she grumbled.

'I told mum I could manage it.'

'Donald goes home on his own.'

In the middle of the rocky unmetalled road alongside the school, Donald had abandoned his horse and stood in a dirty puddle, seeing if the water would come over his shoes. It did.

'Oi,' called Bible. 'Get out of that puddle. Your Mum paid good money for those shoes.'

Donald walked in deeper.

'Did you hear me?'

Donald kicked, sending a shower of spray over Bible and his daughter, and ran off. Bible shouted after him. A hundred yards up the road the little boy squeezed through two blackened stone gateposts onto the path leading to Chapel Gate.

'Are you going to arrest him, Daddy?' said Pauline.

Bible let his anger subside silently. His daughter looked anxious.

'No, love. No.' He tapped the biscuit tin she was clutching to her chest. 'Tea party OK? Did they like your scones?'

'There were some Teddy Boys. They took a scone.'

Bible stopped. 'You mean they stole it off you?'

'One of them stamped his feet to frighten us and took one. They were from the big school.'

'Where were you having this tea party?'

'Miss Jobs let us take a table outside.'

Bible wondered why children always accepted the weather, whatever it was. 'But it's cold.'

'It was all right. We had a tablecloth.'

Bible looked at the small neat houses either side of Ashdale Avenue, and down the path towards the ramshackle one-storey cottages and urban small holdings of Chapel Gate. The smell of woodsmoke drifted across from a late autumn bonfire. He gently took the biscuit tin from her.

'Here. Let me hold your hand,' he said. 'I think we'd better go back and have a word about these boys.'

'I want to go home, Daddy.'

He looked down at his plaintive daughter. It wasn't fair to drag her round after missing scones or Donald's guerrilla warfare with puddle water; but it wasn't fair not to protect her either. He gripped her hand more tightly.

'Come on, let's get you back to Mum.'

When they got back to the car at the top of St Enoch's Road, the sunlight had gone from the Town Hall, wisps of smoke were drifting from domestic chimneys, and Rivock Edge was hunkering down for dusk.

*

Shouting. An army of noise in her head. Her father marching her sisters to the kitchen table. Thumping. Her head banged on to the table. You will eat your greens. Your fork's the wrong way round. Knock, knock. Barking. Waves, water. Swallowing, drowning. Wind and rain. Out in the backyard in her knickers in winter in the rain. Punishment. Knock. Knock. Let me in. Her sister pulling the bedclothes to get in with her.

Carol woke in a sweat, her hair sticking to her forehead. The kittens were pulling threads out of her candlewick bedspread. It was already dark outside.

There was a knock at the door. Why should that be frightening? Knocking at the door was normal. Other people lived in the house and occasionally called for milk, tea – the small things. It was a community of sorts, but no one ever crossed the threshold.

It was the young man from upstairs. Mid-twenties, like herself, and wearing a tweed sports jacket and flannels. She realised she'd opened the door still tucking in her blouse.

'Sorry. I was having a nap.'

'Are you all right? You look a bit flushed.'

'Too hot. I'd got under the bedclothes. Silly in the afternoon.' Her boss had let her home early, thinking she looked ill, but in truth she'd been exhausted trying to keep down the memory of the reservoir.

The young man held out an envelope.

'I think this is for you.'

She stared at the name on the cheap white envelope, its corners bent and grubby at the edges. There was no stamp or postmark.

'I'm Malcolm. I live upstairs,' he said. 'Is it not what you expected?'

No. It was what she feared.

'You look upset.'

'I'm sorry. It's nothing,' she said, and snatched the envelope out of his hand. 'Thanks.'

'If there's anything else I can do,' he was saying as she closed the door.

She clicked the latch before he could see her beginning to shake.

Carol sat at the pillow end of the bed, hugging her knees close to her. She looked at the envelope, its

edges now neatly aligned with the corners of the
mattress, and framed by the yellow bedcover. Her
mother's writing was an old fashioned copperplate,
but pinched in its execution, with the initial letter not
much taller than those following. There were only two
words on the envelope. A name. An old name. A name
she no longer wanted. Dawn Logan.

*

'Scones!'

Bible knew they'd laugh, Bill Ward and his mates,
when he told them about Pauline's encounter with the
Teds at school. But it wasn't a time to get pompous
and pull rank. His team of plain clothes men were
relaxing in the CID room, leaning back on the back
two legs of their chairs, feet resting on the piles of
paper on their desks. Sergeant Ward had his tie
undone and was clutching a mug of tea. He was closer
to the men than Bible was.

'We could put up some missing scone posters, sir,'
said Higham, a detective constable not long off the
beat who'd just joined Bible's team. 'Say we're in a
jam.'

More laughter. They shared it like a round of
drinks. Learned it from their fathers, probably.
Fathers who took their sons for their first pint. Bible's
father was dead a month before his son was born, one
of the last casualties of the Great War. His mother had
done a good job, but he'd never felt at ease with men
at their jauntiest.

'I know it's not an all forces alert,' said Bible, 'but
wait till you've got daughters.'

Too late Bible remembered Ward and his wife had

not been able to have children. The detective sergeant took his feet off the desk. 'Let's get over to that secondary school tomorrow and push a few Teds around.'

'That's not the way, Bill.'

'So what is the way, sir? They threatened that old woman on Tyrrel Street. Stole a bag in Rawson Market. And now they've bullied your little lass, poor kid. I'm sick of them combing their hair and poncing around like fairies. They need knocking about a bit.'

You could always rely on Ward for the direct approach. Sometimes Bible envied him his certainty. It was a certainty that meant you knew he would stay by your side in a tight corner.

'What if it's just lads dressing up, Bill?' said Bible. 'They're not all thugs.'

The black phone rang on Bible's desk.

'Inspector Bible,' he announced before his voice softened. It was his wife. 'Hello love.'

'It'll be t'biscuits gone now,' said Ward, but Bible glowered at him and the joke tailed off. Higham shifted uneasily.

'I'll come over and talk to her.' Bible replaced the heavy receiver. 'My wife says a man spoke to my little girl through the railings at playtime this afternoon. Promised to wait for her after school and buy her some sweeties.'

Ward released a breath. 'Who's on the beat round there?'

'PC Best,' said Higham.

'Good man,' said Ward.

'He's not the only policeman who may have seen

him,' said Bible. 'My daughter says the man was there when I collected her from school.'

*

Carol had wondered about burning the letter without reading it, but now it was open on the bed.

> *Dear Dawn*
>
> *I hope you are enjoying your new life, now you have left us. Your father is very hurt. He only wants the best for you. Your sisters are being very good. Wendy and Jennifer are busy everyday keeping the house clean. They are both going to bed early as they should. Your father will keep them safe. Love Mum*
>
> *P.S. I don't know how you could leave us like that after all your father has done for you. Do let us know your address.*

Carol threw herself at the door and slammed the bolt across, then grabbed a chair and wedged it under the door handle. Snatching at her breath she leaned over the sink thinking she would be sick. Nothing came. After a few gulps of air, she ran her fingers under the cold tap and stroked the cool water over her forehead. The window above the sink looked out onto a small backyard and the outside toilet. Below was the pitched roof of the kitchen of Mrs Jenkins' flat downstairs. Moss filled the gutter and two slates had slipped, their corners chipped like broken teeth. Could anyone get onto the roof and into her room from there? It looked impossible, but if someone really wanted to do it...

19

She tore the letter into tiny pieces, ripping across the writing one way, and then the other. No one knew her address but the bank, and now, Inspector Bible. In her shock at seeing her old name, Dawn, on the envelope in her mother's writing she'd not asked Malcolm how he'd got it and how it had found its way to her door. One of the kittens meowed at her feet. She scooped it up and cradled it to her chest.

She should have burned the letter before reading it.

*

Bible's wife was concentrating on the haddock.

'Why didn't she point him out to me?' he demanded, blocking the doorway of the small galley kitchen. He'd flushed the door with hardboard and glossed it with magnolia that weekend and a smell of fresh paint mingled with the cooking smells. 'I could have got him.' Bible clenched his fist, and then relaxed it. There was nothing to thump here.

Shirley sprinkled more Golden Breadcrumbs on the gently sizzling fish. Bible stood behind her, and kissed the back of her head. 'She'll be fine. I'll ask Best. It's on his beat. He'll know who was around.'

'I thought it was safe round here.' Shirley pushed the pan off the hotplate, and turned to face him. She fingered the lapels of his jacket. 'Your poor new suit. It already smells of cigarette smoke.'

'And now fish.'

Shirley returned to her cooking. She was brisker now, enlivened. Like when she was the girl next door who'd nursed his first wife through her final illness, and, as an eighteen-year-old, helped him cope with little Ricky at the end of the war. Three years later they'd married and made a home despite her parents' objections. The birth of Pauline had seemed to make things complete.

Shirley lifted the lid on a pan of vegetables bubbling on the gas ring. 'I'll talk to the other mothers. We'll keep a look out. Somebody must have seen him.' The words were tumbling out as she stirred pots and shuffled the fish again. 'And I'll find out if any other schools have had problems. The woman in the big house on Beacon Road chairs the local headteachers' organisation.'

Bible gripped her shoulders from behind as she stood in front of the stove and held her firmly. 'Slow down. Leave it to us.'

'Yes, us. Her mother and father.'

'You know I mean the police. This is serious.'

Shirley lowered the gas flame and turned to face him. 'Why is it that when it's serious only the men can deal with it? You trust me, don't you?'

'Of course. But you looked after me when I came back from Burma, now it's my turn to look after you.'

'I'm not the teenager next door anymore. I'm twenty-eight. I can look after myself.'

'When's tea ready?'

'Don't avoid the issue, Jim. She's our daughter, not just a police case. I can't stay at home making tea and plumping up cushions whilst there's a child molester on the loose.'

Bible picked up the newspaper from the kitchen table. 'Suez. Another bloody war.'

'They've pulled back. The Americans made Eden retreat.'

Bible smiled. 'Good.'

'I'm joining a peace group,' said Shirley. 'I heard

21

Logan looked at the inside pages. There it was, in a small column on the right.

NEWSPAPER ATTACKS STOP

Recent attacks on newspaper vendors in the city have died off, according to Exeter's vendors. Police are still appealing for witnesses to an attack in Fore Street on local seller, Alfred Scadding.

Good old police, plodding along. To hell with the witnesses. It was sorted. He looked back at the newspaper seller who gave him a slow thumbs up. It was nice to be appreciated.

Alfie shouted after him. 'I saw one of your daughters this afternoon, Mr Logan.'

Logan halted, and turned. 'And which of my daughters would that be?'

'That tall one. Thin as a bamboo pole. Running out of the picture house. She your youngest?'

Logan put the paper away. He'd look after Jenny when he got home.

Halfway down the steep street leading to the river, a boy of about eighteen appeared from the doorway of a church. His hair was moulded into a fashionable quiff and he wore a pale blue jacket a size too big for him.

'Do you think you'll grow into that, Stanley?' said Logan affably.

'It's the fashion, Mr Logan.' An unlit cigarette waggled up and down in his mouth as he spoke.

Logan put his arm round the boy's shoulders in a

crushing half embrace. 'It looks like you need a light
for that, son,' he said, digging into his jacket with his
free hand for a box of matches.

'I didn't think you smoked, Mr Logan.'

Logan released his hold, struck a match and
cupped his hands to protect the flame as Stanley
bowed his head towards it.

'Always carry matches, Stanley,' said the taller
man. 'Give people a light, and they owe you
something. Now what have you got for me?' The last
race had finished an hour before, and Stanley had
settled the bets he'd taken for Logan that day.

'Forty-seven pounds six and eightpence, Mr
Logan. I've paid out the winners.'

He pulled out a dog-eared black notebook with a
rubber band round it. Bank notes stuck out at one
end. Stanley rummaged in his pocket and pulled out a
handful of coins.

'Here's the six and eightpence.'

Stanley dropped the coins into his boss's hand. It
was twice the size of the boy's. Logan pocketed the
change and took the notebook. He pinged off the
rubber band.

'It's all there, Mr Logan,' said the boy hastily.

Logan opened the book and took out the money.
'When someone says it's all there, it makes me think
they mean it isn't.'

'I wouldn't cheat you, Mr Logan, honest.'

Logan paused, looked at the notebook with its
pencilled list of horses, odds and amounts wagered,
and ran his finger down the last page, the bets for next
day.

'I balanced the book for you, Mr Logan. Apart

from the favourite, Mortimer's Run. I laid it at three to one like you said. Everyone wants it. You'll be in trouble if that wins the big one tomorrow.'

'It won't.'

Logan put the notebook in the inside pocket of his donkey jacket. 'So what have you got to tell me?' He put his hand on Stanley's shoulder, then lifted it to pat the young man's cheek, a little too heavily to be friendly. 'You're a nice looking boy,' he said. 'Where's that father of yours got to? I'll need him back soon.'

'He's Mister Posh for a few days.' The boy grinned. 'Somewhere up north. We haven't heard from him since he went. You know what he's like.'

'He needs to remember where he comes from,' said Logan, looking at the boy without humour. 'And who looks after him. Did you see one of my daughters in town today?'

'Which one, Mr Logan?' said Stanley brightly.

'So you did.'

Stanley coloured.

'The Odeon?' prompted Logan.

'She wouldn't go to the flicks by herself, would she?'

'Who wouldn't?'

Stanley dropped his gaze to the pavement. 'I might have seen her, that youngest one of yours.'

Logan put his fist under Stanley's chin and slowly raised it, forcing his head back. 'She doesn't need protecting by you, Stanley. I protect her.'

'That's right, Mr Logan.'

He nodded. 'Good lad, Stanley.'

Stanley looked relieved. 'No takers for Sunset Cruiser ante-post, Mr Logan. You only had him at twenties'

'Her. She's a filly.'

'They were offering a hundred to one on the course. She can't win at that price.'

'A big price doesn't stop them winning.'

So Stanley had been taking his own bets on the horse, running a side book offering bigger odds, and risking payouts he couldn't afford. Logan would let it go for now. The boy hadn't known what he meant when he said the price didn't stop them winning. But Stanley would find out when Sunset Cruiser won, as Logan had made sure it would. He was completing the boy's education. And he was proud that he didn't have to use violence to do it.

Logan leaned on the parapet of the bridge over the Exe watching the quayside. A man in a stained suit and grey trilby was unloading boxes from a ferry and putting them into a van. About a hundred yards away a policeman on his beat stood with his back to the ferry, staring downriver towards Topsham. The man unloading, a distant matchstick figure, looked up, adjusting his hat brim to stop the sun getting in his eyes. Logan stared back. The man knew not to wave or nod and carried on unloading the boxes. On the other side of the river, nestling under overhanging elderberry bushes, was an old boathouse with a corrugated iron roof. It looked empty. Logan would be down there later.

When he burst through the door of the isolated terrace house marooned by wartime bombing, Wendy, Jenny and his wife Mary were standing in line, their backs against the sideboard. Beyond lay the little offshot kitchen where they had prepared his tea. He always ate separately, and they would eat afterwards, as he'd decreed. He took in their faces. There was always that look when they had something they didn't want him to find out. But he had found out. He'd make them wait. Logan sat down at the dining table where his place was already laid.

Wendy stepped forward first, pouring a bottle of beer as she'd been told, letting the beer trickle down the inside of the glass so the head would not be too frothy. Jenny went into the cramped kitchen and returned with a casserole dish she placed before him. Logan's wife spoke.

'Jenny used the rabbit you caught yesterday.'

Logan lifted the lid and let the aroma rise. Jenny was trying to buy his approval in case he heard about her illicit cinema trip.

'Very much appreciated. Wendy's turn to cook, wasn't it?'

Mary and the girls looked at each other. 'Jenny really wanted to cook it for you,' said his wife.

'As a special treat for you, Dad,' said Jenny.

Logan grunted. He'd let it ride for now.

When he'd finished he pushed his plate away. It was a signal for his pudding. Jenny produced a jam roly-poly as quickly as a magician's rabbit, put the dish on the table and began cutting the crusty end Logan loved. Her movements were anxious and quick, eager to please. She eased a spatula underneath the pastry roll, cracking through where the jam had just begun to burn onto the dish, and placed it on a bowl.

'Custard?' said Logan. The familiar white jug was not on the table.

The three women looked at each other in panic. Logan regarded them sadly. 'I can't eat it without custard,' he said. 'See what happens when you don't stick to the rota. In the yard.'

Jenny and Wendy looked at each other.

'Both of you,' said Logan.

They turned into the kitchen and towards the back door. Wendy looked at him appealingly. 'I was going to cook, Dad. Jenny stopped me.'

Logan was disappointed in them. No loyalty, even to each other.

'The yard,' he said.

Jenny opened the glass panelled door which led out from the kitchen. Logan followed his daughters into the bare yard. A chain looped out of a shed at the far end and was cemented into the high red brick walls which enclosed the concreted space. Logan himself had added the top courses of bricks to raise the wall from its original six foot height. He liked privacy.

The chain rattled when something moved in the shed, but Logan's shout silenced it.

Jenny stood facing Logan. He couldn't read her expression. He could read Wendy's. She was usually afraid. Wendy loved him and didn't like his disapproval. Jenny was the one he had to educate more.

'Wendy, up to your room.' The older girl looked relieved and slipped past him back to the kitchen door. 'I'll be up soon,' he said over his shoulder, keeping his gaze fixed on Jenny. 'You know I need to train you,' he said.

He didn't like the way Jenny stared back at him. He'd seen that look before, in the face of the missing daughter he forbade them to talk about or name.

'Haven't you something else to tell me?'

'I don't think so,' she said calmly.

'About films?'

She stayed silent. She was stubborn. She said nothing where other people would lie. She'd been like that since she was little. Now at seventeen she was the same. Other fathers would have beaten it out of her. But he wouldn't. Not personally. Not directly. He had other methods. He felt the anger rising. The power of anger. But he wouldn't let it out. He just had to let people know it was there.

'Keeper,' he called. The chain rattled again. The shed shook and a large mastiff weighing seven stone emerged. There was a spark of fear in Jenny's eye, but she wouldn't let him know any more than that.

Logan went to the dog, undid the chain from the collar and pointed towards Jenny. The dog began to growl. Jenny backed up against the wall.

'Three hours,' he said. She knew he meant it. He always meant it. Jenny would stay where she was, knowing Keeper would not touch her if she stayed still. For now she just stared at him. He knew that look. It was the look Dawn used to give him. But he knew he could always break them. Even Dawn. In the end, she'd be his again.

Logan didn't knock when he went into Wendy's room. She was sitting on her bed, waiting for him, as he knew she would be. He was known for his reliability.

'Wendy,' he said. 'You know I'm hurt.'

'Yes, Daddy. I'm sorry.'

'I have to train you.'

'Yes Daddy.'

'Why didn't you make Jenny stick to the rota?'

Wendy looked down at her slippered feet.

'You're the oldest. You should have controlled her. Look at me.'

She raised her head.

'You'll stay in this room until tomorrow morning.'

'Yes, Daddy.'

'I'll see you tomorrow. You'll be safe. I always make sure you're safe.'

Downstairs in the dark backroom Logan's wife was sitting at the dining table with a plate in front of her. She stopped chewing and looked up nervously, her knife and fork angled towards each other, her hands at either side of her plate.

'Did I say you could have that?' said Logan, leaning over her, both hands on the table. With a quick scoop of his right he flipped her plate like a tiddlywink, sending it off the end of the table leaving a mess of meat, gravy and pastry on the pretty tablecloth.

'Eat it cold with the girls in the morning if you can't keep the house in order.'

Logan's wife still held her knife and fork either side of the empty space in front of her. He quickly stepped behind her and slapped her on the back. The chunk of meat in her mouth flew out and onto the table.

'Get that lot cleaned up,' he said. 'You're not eating anything till morning.'

Logan's wife screamed at the table, at the wall opposite, at the fate of her children. 'You'll drive them away, like Dawn!'

Logan turned and hit her round the head from the back, so hard she fell to the floor with her chair.

Sometimes violence was necessary.

FOUR

An hour after reading the letter, Carol was sitting in the Manhattan Milk Bar with a strawberry milkshake she didn't feel like drinking. She toyed with the straw and eyed Malcolm who sat opposite with a frothy coffee. She felt sorry for him as he tried not to leave scum on his top lip. Coming to the Manhattan had been a compromise of mutual embarrassment. Carol could not decently invite him into her bedsit; Malcolm had clearly felt too uneasy to invite her into his. And Carol was not sure whether to trust him or not; he could be an enemy or a friend. For now, she let him call her Dawn.

'I'm not used to coming to places like this,' he said awkwardly. Two boys in school blazers with stiff embroidered badges on the breast pockets sat by the window drinking some kind of dark pop and bending over their schoolbooks. On the street outside a workman in overalls gazed up at a bale of wool in a hessian sack swinging on chains as it was hoisted up to a third-storey door in the side of Sugden's Mill.

'Nor me,' she said. But she liked the tubular steel chairs, the bright red Formica-topped tables, and the high stools at the counter. 'It's modern.'

Malcolm slurped his coffee. Her father would have hit her for that.

'It used to be called Mill Cafe,' he said, 'before they spruced it up. All pie and peas and big white mugs. It's a place for young people now.'

'Aren't we young?'

'I don't know.'

'I'm twenty-four,' said Carol. 'What about you?'

'I didn't think women liked saying how old they were.'

'Is that what you've been told?' Carol smiled, and stirred her drink with the straw. She sensed she could tease him. She was sure he couldn't be dangerous. And it was nice to feel normal for a change. 'I'd guess you're twenty-eight.'

Over Malcolm's shoulder she watched two Teddy Boys come in. Greased quiffs and long jackets. One in red, with a paper carrier bag under his arm, went over to where the schoolboys were sitting and leaned against the window. He looked familiar. She'd seen him in the police station the day before. Ricky. That's what someone had shouted after him. His friend wore a pale blue jacket with a black velvet collar, and silver buckled shoes with thick crepe soles. He strutted over to the juke box and studied the playlist.

'Hey Len, you've got the same old stuff on here. Where's Elvis Presley?'

The burly man behind the counter raised his head from the racing page and called to his wife through the plastic strip curtain leading to the living quarters.

'Marjorie. Freddie Fraser's lad's back. Wants Elvis Presley.' His voice was flat. Unimpressed.

Ricky was watching. Waiting for something.

'Cannonball,' said the boy at the jukebox. 'People call me Cannonball.'

Len called through the curtain again. 'Cannonball wants Elvis Presley.'

A peevish voice returned through the plastic. 'Tell him we've got Lonnie Donegan.'

Cannonball rolled his eyes in disgust.

Carol turned her attention back to Malcolm. He didn't look like a threat. He seemed more afraid of her.

'My name isn't Dawn,' she said.

'Oh,' said Malcolm, surprised, 'so the letter wasn't for you?'

'Yes, it was,' she said. 'I changed my name.' The bubbles on the milk shake were popping. It had sounded nice when Malcolm recommended it – she'd never had one before - but she didn't think she could drink it.

Malcolm looked awkward. 'Not my business,' he said shyly. 'Some people...' He struggled for words before mumbling, 'Some people have secrets.'

'I'm called Carol now,' she said simply. 'What's your secret?'

Cannonball's sixpence clattered into the jukebox. Malcolm jerked round in his seat, catching the boy's eye.

'Who are you staring at?'

'Nothing,' said Malcolm and turned back.

'It's a lot to pay for listening to a record once,' whispered Carol. 'When you can listen to the wireless. So? Secrets?'

'Nothing.'

Rock Around the Clock began on the juke box.

'So how did you get the envelope and know it was for me?' Malcolm looked shaken by her bluntness.

She hadn't meant to bully him, but realised she was in control of the situation. That, despite what she felt, she was the stronger one. It was a feeling she'd felt first barely a year earlier when she'd hitched a lift out of Exeter with a man delivering a batch of the evening *Express and Echo* to Whipton, and then found herself in a lorry on the A30 heading north.

'I was in the chemist's at the end of the road. A customer asked if a girl with a West Country accent lived round here.'

Her stomach began to tighten. A knot of fear she knew too well. She gripped the fluted milkshake glass tightly to stop her hands shaking. 'And you said she did?'

'No. The shopkeeper said he remembered you, and so the man asked if he could leave an envelope there.'

'What sort of man?'

'An old man. Oldish.'

She stirred her drink with the straw. Fought to sound normal. But the look of the thick pink liquid made her feel sick. 'Did he sound West Country, this old man?'

'No. Have I done something wrong?'

'Carry on.'

'When he'd gone I said I knew someone like that, so I brought the envelope. I was just trying to help.' His voice tailed off feebly.

'Have you been following me?'

Malcolm coloured. 'I heard you talking to the old woman downstairs. I knew you weren't from round here.'

Over at the other side of the milk bar there was trouble. The boy who called himself Cannonball had rejoined Ricky, and they were swarming around the two schoolboys, talking noisily.

'You're in our seats,' said Ricky.

Carol looked down at her drink. She needed the toilet, but did not want to get up.

'There are lots of other seats,' said one of the schoolboys. He was wearing Health Service spectacles and was still holding his fountain pen.

Cannonball appeared to consider. 'Yeah. True.' He leaned over the boy with the glasses. 'But they're not our seats. Our seats are filled with your arses.'

The schoolboy's friend stared into his glass, but Specs nodded his head towards Malcolm and Carol and said, 'You could go and sit with them over there.'

Carol felt herself and Malcolm become the focus of four pairs of eyes. Malcolm was frozen, studying his coffee.

'We're not going to sit near him. He's a perv,' said Cannonball. 'I hope you've written something down about respecting your elders.' He picked up the exercise book the boy had been working in and dangled it by a corner.

'Hey, gerroff it,' said the boy with spectacles.

Cannonball threw the book across the room. 'Oh dear, I've dropped it. You'd better go and get it.'

Len looked up from his paper. 'What's going on there?'

'I think we should go,' whispered Malcolm.

Carol shook her head. She was fed up of running.

Beaten, the boy with glasses left his seat and scurried in a crouch towards his book. Cannonball gave him a push with his foot as he left, and sat in the boy's seat to face the other schoolboy.

'Now who wants me to help them with their homework?'

Carol found herself on her feet. 'Leave them alone.'

Cannonball froze and stared. The bespectacled boy stooped for his exercise book and bolted out of the door followed by his friend. Cannonball's companion watched eagerly, excited by the prospect of trouble.

Carol looked towards the milk bar owner. 'Are you going to let them get away with this?'

Len, his gaze focused on his newspaper, didn't look as if he was going to do much. Cannonball sneered. 'He's not going to be told what to do by a slag with a Nancy boy.'

A black Wolseley pulled up outside the cafe. Ricky ran for the door.

'That'll be the police, Mr. Cannonball,' said Len, turning a page. 'My missus called the cops as soon as you came in.'

Through the glass of the door Carol saw the sergeant from the police station get out of the police car. The pale trench coat worked as clearly as an identity card. His foot had just touched the front step when he met Ricky running out. The policeman grabbed the boy's arm and reversed him towards the door which tinkled as it opened. He carelessly gestured the youth to one of the tables.

'Sit down there, Ricky, till your Dad comes in.' The policeman looked round the milk bar. 'So, who's been enjoying themselves in here, then?'

Malcolm spoke quietly to Carol. 'I think I'll go.'

Malcolm began to stand, but the sergeant put a hand on his shoulder and pressed him back down.

'Not so fast, Sonny Jim.'

Carol recognised Inspector Bible as he got out of the passenger seat and wearily approached the door. He was in a smart charcoal overcoat now with a matching wide-brimmed hat.

'These young men were bullying two schoolboys,' she said to the sergeant.

He ignored her and spoke to the cafe owner.

'What happened, Len?'

'It's him again.' He pointed to Cannonball. 'He was in last week causing trouble.'

Bible came in. He looked towards Ricky. 'Go and sit in the car,' he said coldly.

Ricky picked up the carrier bag he'd left on the table vacated by the schoolboys, and walked cockily towards the door.

'The car,' Bible repeated. There was an edge to his voice Carol had not heard during her interview. He didn't look like a violent man, but she wondered. The milk bar door tinkled again as Ricky left. Malcolm was not watching anything. He was staring at the once frothy scum in his cold cup.

Bible stopped near Carol's table and spoke to his sergeant. 'Everything all right, Sergeant Ward?'

'I'll get a statement off Len. You'd better talk to your boy.'

'I suppose I'd better,' said Bible quietly, but Carol could feel the anger in him as he watched his son get in the sleek police car. 'Go and see Len. I can deal with the people in here.'

Ward bent down to growl in Malcolm's ear. 'I've got my eye on you, sunshine.' He straightened, and nodded Len towards the door behind the counter. 'Stay there, Johnny,' said Ward to Cannonball as he passed and followed Len into the back room.

Bible approached Carol. 'Miss Carlton, shall we sit down?'

Carol realised she was still standing. 'Why did that sergeant threaten Malcolm?' she began.

'No,' said Malcolm quietly from his seat. 'Leave it. Please.'

'Let's go over what happened here,' said Bible. He pulled up a chair. The rubber feet on the end of the tubular steel legs squeaked on the floor. Carol let herself relax a little, and sat down.

'Malcolm lives in the same house as me. Bedsits.' It seemed wrong introducing Malcolm as if it were a social occasion, but she didn't know what else to say. And she was afraid Bible would reveal something about her earlier visit to the police station.

'I met Miss Carlton this morning,' said Bible. 'She'd found a stray dog she brought in.'

The lie was a kindness she treasured.

Bible sent Ward to wait outside when the interview with the cafe owner was done. He was by the car when Bible came out after sending Cannonball on his way with a warning.

'Why are you protecting that little queer, sir?' said Ward.

'What's he done wrong, Bill?'

'He doesn't have to do anything wrong. It's who he is. I'd like to get him in my hands and crush him.'

Bible remembered how Ward had hated it when he had once called him Willie. It was tempting to say it again.

*

'Get inside.' Bible pushed his son through the open door into the neat hallway. Ricky was still clutching his carrier bag. 'Go into the front room whilst I talk to your mother.'

'So you can ask her what you ought to say?'

Ricky had hit a weak spot. As the teenager next door, Shirley had helped his first wife look after Ricky when Bible was away in Burma. He trusted her instincts with his son more than his own.

'So I can tell her what you've been up to,' he said, as his son nonchalantly strolled into the best room and sat down. Bible had been scared of his father, but he knew Ricky wasn't scared of his. He'd tried to scarper from the milk bar to avoid the police, not because he was ashamed of what he'd done. In the Far East, when Bible knew his wife and young son were waiting back home, he'd imagined a clear future if he survived. But as he looked at Ricky lounging in the armchair, one drainpiped leg over the arm, he felt he was back in the jungles of Burma, fighting against his son, not for him.

'For Heaven's sake, look at the state of you.'

'Can't. No mirror in here.'

'You look like you're in a flipping circus.'

'My mate says you like queers.'

Bible swallowed a shout and held himself still until the urge to rush at his son subsided. It wasn't Ricky's fault his mother had died two months after Bible had been demobbed. Nor that his father had spent most of Ricky's first five years six thousand miles away defending an ammunition dump against the Japs. He looked at the cocky sprawling youth his boy had become and wished he could see it as simply as Ward would see it.

'Stay there,' said Bible.

'She's not my mother anyway.'

Bible ignored the shout and headed towards the back room. Although they were in a semi, Bible kept to the terms he knew from the terraced house he was brought up in. Front room. Back room. But when he opened the door, he realised Shirley was not alone. Standing awkwardly, silently, their backs to the leaded glass window that looked out onto a lawn scattered with damp autumn leaves, were Shirley's mother and father. Shirley sat by the fire, unravelling a pullover Ricky had grown out of so she could make a new one with the wool.

Bible nodded towards his parents-in-law. 'Hilda. George.' Both still wore their overcoats. They never took them off on their rare visits to the house.

Shirley's father cleared his throat. 'We were just going. Come on, Hilda.'

Shirley put her wool on top of the beige-tiled mantelpiece. They'd recently installed an electric fire with artificial coal moulded out of plastic. A red bulb underneath created a cosy glow. 'I'll show you out.'

'Ricky's in the room,' said Bible when Shirley returned.

'I know. We heard you come in.'

'Why were George and Hilda here?'

'I wanted to talk to them about Pauline.'

'So they don't think I'm a child molester any more for stealing their daughter?'

'I know they said some horrible things, but it would help if you weren't so cold.'

Bible shrugged. 'I'll try.'

'Good. So what's happened with Ricky?'

'We found him bullying schoolkids in a cafe. I hoped you might be able to get through to him.'

The front door slammed. With two quick strides Bible was in the hallway, but they both knew Ricky had gone. The front room door was ajar. Bible picked up the carrier bag from the side of the chair where Ricky had been sitting. He pulled out a square package in flowered wrapping paper, with a label sellotaped to it. *Happy Birthday Shirley (Mum).* Bible held it towards his wife.

'Looks like he's got you some chocolates.'

FIVE

Her father was barking. Baring his teeth. Pinning her down. His paws printing hard bruises on the soft white flesh of the insides of her arms. Malcolm was in a corner of the yard down by the river, cowering and whimpering, but even though she was the victim, she still felt she had to protect him. Like she had her sisters, who were two shivering rabbits in the hutch.

Carol's eyes flicked open and she was awake in her bedsit, with the faintly sour smell of the kittens in the wardrobe, though a dog was still yapping as if in her dream and one of the kittens was jumping on her exposed arm. More barking and a shout. She dumped the kitten on the quilt and slid out of bed. Then, feeling guilty, she scooped up the kitten again, gave it a quick kiss, set it down gently near the wardrobe, and reached for her dressing gown.

When she looked over the banister, she saw Malcolm in the dark hallway by the front door, holding it ajar, and peering through the crack at a dog barking outside. An army surplus haversack slipped off his shoulder onto his forearm as he held the door.

'It won't go away,' said Malcolm, looking up at her helplessly. She rushed back into the bedroom, slammed the door shut and put her hands to her face.

In the yard of the little house down by the river, her father's dogs would terrify her. They had been as tall as she was, first a Great Dane and then a thickset Bull Mastiff. She was usually alone with them as they paced about in the yard, because she was the more defiant one, sent out more often. Her sisters would give in to her father's demands for food, and complete the chores he demanded when he saw they were longing for rest. Whilst Exeter Cathedral stood in holiness on the hill, Tommy Logan created hell down by the river below. His house stood in isolation among rubble, the rest of the terrace destroyed when she was eight by a bomb straying from the town centre. No one approached, or knew what went on there. Her mother gave nothing away. She was terrified too. Her father smiled at passers-by as he walked out with his daughters when they were little, the two youngest on each hand, Carol as the eldest on the outside. They wore little dresses with puff sleeves in summer, knitted bonnets in winter. He'd make them stand in the yard almost naked in freezing weather, but in public he was the perfect dad.

She could hear Malcolm saying 'shush' through the door. Pleading. 'I've got to go to work.' They were both prisoners. 'Here. Sandwich.' He was giving it his dinner. Pathetic. Carol jumped from the bed and rushed downstairs before she could think, wrenched open the door, throwing Malcolm back, and shouted at the startled mongrel collie with a bark louder and fiercer than that of the dog. The dog barked back, but Carol yelled more loudly. The mongrel retreated to the gate, and barked again. Carol advanced towards it, shouting and clapping her hands. It slunk further back, and after another shout from Carol, ran off.

'Thank you,' said Malcolm. 'How did you know what to do?'

'My father had dogs. I got used to them,' she said, and went back upstairs to dress.

The bank in the town centre where Carol worked had a sober interior with dark oak panels, a rich smell of furniture polish, and, high up on the walls, heavily framed portraits of previous managers with their waistcoats and watch chains. It was, she felt, quieter than a library, and secure. She looked at the men in the paintings. They didn't look kind but they looked honest and full of money, like they knew what was what. She didn't think they'd beat their daughters or put them in a yard with dogs. The last manager before the present one looked like Eden, the prime minister, his hair slicked back, moustache neatly clipped; the sort of man you could trust.

Carol occasionally worked at the counter, but usually she was at a leather-topped desk on the administrative floor, hidden from the public behind a screen of oak panelling. Anonymous. She liked that. Since the arrival of the letter she felt safer here than in her bedsit.

Malcolm hadn't gone back to his room when they returned from the Manhattan Milk Bar. He'd walked her to the front door of the house, but then said he had to see someone. And he'd been shifty on the walk back. No. Not shifty. Shy. She knew he was hiding something and she was beginning to realise what it was. But it was never openly talked about. Her father had sometimes sounded off about perverts and pansies, angrily banging his fist as he demanded his wife and three daughters listen to his version of morality and the right way to be a man. But she'd never openly come across a...she didn't know the right word. And Malcolm didn't seem dangerous. Just frightened. They seemed to have something in common.

She'd liked Larry because he was different. He had not been frightened. He'd known her since they were little, watching from behind the counter of his parents' shop when she was sent for bread or eggs. She'd run away when he'd asked her to play. He didn't know playing was impossible in her father's house. After national service he'd turned up at the back gate, handsome in his suit and ginger crewcut. She'd sworn her sisters to secrecy, and the two had managed to meet, fearfully on her part. But one day he didn't turn up. She assumed he'd got sick of her. Sick of secret meetings in the afternoon hiding like criminals. He'd disappeared, and that was that. She'd known it was hopeless. If her father could take that away, he could take anything.

She took the call just after ten. There was a clatter on the other end, and then a posh voice. A bank manager's voice. Clipped and to the point. A voice used to giving orders.

'Southport Branch here. One of our customers, Major Robinson, will be seeing you today. Needs five hundred pounds. Should be there about eleven. The money's in his account. It's all above board.'

'I'll tell the manager.'

'Excellent. Top hole. We don't want to offend him.'

Southport Branch hung up. Carol replaced the heavy black receiver and looked at the plaited cord. She was used to managers of other branches on the telephone being abrupt, but this had been too demanding. And was Southport really that posh, wherever it was? But when she told her manager about the call, he was anxious to please.

'We have to be careful, Carol,' said Mr Menzies sternly. A precise man, he wore a pinstripe suit and rimless glasses. 'Banks work on trust. I don't want to doubt another manager's word.'

'But there was something funny about the call, sir.'

'You're a good worker, Carol, but I think I can judge the situation.'

Then she remembered why she'd felt so uneasy. 'There was a rattle, a muffled rattle.'

Menzies turned, irritated. A lightness seized Carol's stomach. A man in the early stages of anger always frightened her; she knew what it could lead to.

'A clatter. As if someone had pressed button A to let the money drop. I think it was from a call box, sir.'

*

Jim Bible was at his desk staring at the heavy black telephone sitting on a pile of manila folders, thinking about his son and daughter when he should have been thinking about work. About Carol, perhaps, and an unsolved puzzle that might or might not be a crime; or, if he'd been ambitious, how he could prove himself whilst the Chief Inspector was off ill, rumoured to have TB. But he was still trying to remember who'd been on the street when he had collected his daughter the day before. He'd taken her to school that morning but the creep who said he'd take her home had not shown up. Pauline had said he was an old man, but to a six-year-old that could mean anyone. She'd also said he was scruffy – but most men in the city wore working clothes Pauline would call scruffy.

Ricky hadn't got home the previous night until after twelve. They were both in bed, his wife looking as bonny in sleep as when he'd first met her, the neighbour's daughter helping with his dying wife and child. Bible, though, had lain awake in the dark until he heard the door. He'd gone onto the landing to thank his son for his wife's present, but dealing with him whilst wearing pyjamas had not been productive. 'I've heard of sergeants' stripes, but dig those pyjamas, daddio.' His unusually merry son had been drinking. 'Tomorrow,' warned Bible. 'We'll talk about the other things tomorrow.' But he regretted not being able to control his days like people in a regular job; tomorrow might turn out to be two days away.

Ward poked his head round the office door, his dour moustache making it impossible to tell if good or bad news was coming. Bible hadn't seen him all morning.

'Where have you been?' asked Bible.

'In the incident room, sir, waiting for incidents. And we've just got one.'

SIX

In his office at the bank, Mr. Menzies was standing behind his desk, all of a flutter.

'You don't think he'll be dangerous, do you?'

'A lot of people still have guns from the war,' said Ward lugubriously. 'Major you say? He'll have had a service revolver. Smith and Wesson. Very effective at close range.'

Menzies looked appealingly towards the two policemen who stood facing him still wearing their coats.

'It's all very well for you,' he said. 'You live such exciting lives.'

'My sergeant has a strange idea of fun,' said Bible. 'I'm sure there's no danger. If I could talk to the young lady who took the call?'

Menzies opened his office door, its frosted glass pane bearing the legend *Manager*. 'Miss Carlton. Could you come in for a minute?'

As footsteps drew nearer, Bible tried to disguise his surprise at hearing Carol's name, whilst Ward nonchalantly tried to pick his teeth with a thumbnail. Carol appeared in the blouse and skirt he'd seen her in when she came to the station. She and Bible stared at each other for a moment in mild shock and she looked relieved when Bible continued as if they had never met before.

'Miss Carlton,' said Bible when it was clear Menzies wasn't going to invite anybody to sit down. 'Your manager tells me you've been very clever.' Bible wished he did not sound as if he were talking to a child.

'I do my best.'

'Does your friend from the cafe work here?' said Ward.

It was an unnecessary dig at Malcolm. Bible was glad Carol held Ward's gaze challenging him to say more, and he was about to fill the silence when Ward spoke again. 'I'd better take a look.'

Ward went to the office door, pulled it open and scanned the clerks' floor. Women in white blouses and a few men in suits sat behind wooden in-trays and heavy black typewriters. When they talked, they spoke in hushed tones. 'Quieter than a weaving shed,' said Ward. 'Why does everyone whisper when there's money around?'

'Get them organised, Bill. Prepare the field for battle.'

'Oh my goodness,' said Menzies, putting a hand to his mouth.

A rare smile hovered under Ward's moustache. 'Right you are, sir,' he said to Bible and strode into the main banking hall. 'Gas masks on, everybody,' he announced, in a clear tone as he closed the office door behind him.

'Oh dear, is that really necessary?' said Menzies.

'It's just his sense of humour. He can't help it,' said Bible. Carol looked down at the carpet. Bible suspected she was hiding a smile.

'Oh,' said Menzies feebly. 'This friend you were

seen with, Carol. Is there a problem?'

Bible felt he had to explain. 'Miss Carlton was an innocent bystander when an incident occurred yesterday.'

'I don't like my staff involved in unsavoury incidents,' said Menzies.

Bible was irritated by Menzies. He seemed to think decent people did not witness unsavoury incidents. Well, he'd make sure Menzies became a witness over today's excitement.

'Could I have a word with Miss Carlton alone?' said Bible.

'Of course. The customer interview room should be vacant.'

'Here would be fine,' said Bible.

'In my office?' said Menzies, startled.

'If you don't mind.' It was clear that Menzies did mind, but he left them alone.

Bible gestured towards the manager's chair. It dwarfed her, though Bible noticed she looked attractive sitting in it. It didn't take her long to tell him about the rattle on the telephone that had made her suspicious. But that was not why he had sat her there. He wanted to ask her about the face in the water. He pulled up a chair and sat opposite.

'We did a search at the reservoir. I'd like you to take us through what you saw again.'

'A trick of the light, I think.' She tried to smile. 'You know, like the Loch Ness monster. Photos that turn out to be shadows and waves.'

'I think you saw something. It isn't Loch Ness up there, and I don't think you saw a monster.'

Bible waited, but Carol said nothing. He wondered if he saw her tremble. No, she was composed.

'We'll go and have another look. Anyway,' Bible glanced at the grandfather clock in Menzies' office, 'let's catch this Major Robinson character.'

Luckily there were not many customers on the chequered tile floor. High on the wall above their heads, the minute hand of the clock in its case of polished walnut jerked another minute towards eleven. Bible pretended to argue with a clerk about how much money he was depositing. Ward lurked out of sight behind the oak panels which cut off the working floor from the clerks. Bible had hidden him there because Bill Ward seemed incapable of not looking like a policeman. It was not just the moustache and trench coat. His whole manner oozed disrespect. Bible hoped he was not at that moment reclining behind the wooden screen with his feet on a desk.

The big hand on the clock on the wall above their heads ticked towards eleven. Still nothing. Menzies looked out of his office. Bible despaired. If you were to take a guess at what Menzies' expression said, it would be that he was just expecting a bank robber to come in disguised as an ex-army man to commit fraud. Bible risked leaving the counter to tell Menzies it would be best to stay in his office until something happened.

Something happened. When Bible turned his attention back to his cash problems, a tall man in a pale overcoat and narrow brimmed hat was standing in the doorway of the bank, sizing up the scene before crossing the black and white floor to the counter where Carol was now on duty.

'Major Robinson,' he said in a clipped voice. 'I should be expected.'

'Of course. I'll get the manager.'

But Menzies was out too soon. Before he had been fetched. Carol had barely turned towards his office when Menzies came out extending his hand.

'Major Robinson, delighted to meet you. I telephoned the manager at Southport...' If he had, the fraud would have been discovered, and Major Robinson knew it. He turned for the door. Bible abandoned his cash but crashed into Menzies who was still standing with his hand out. Ward was out from behind the screen and over the counter as Robinson ran into Market Street.

When Bible reached the street, Ward had caught up with Robinson by the iron gates of Swan Arcade. Beneath the Victorian façade and the magnificent white swan, Bible saw Ward turn Robinson and thump him hard in the stomach. A woman in a headscarf stepped back horrified and hustled her little boy away. The would-be major sank to the ground as Ward caught his wrist, twisted it into an armlock, and planted a foot into Robinson's armpit as he lay on the pavement.

'Not so high and mighty now, eh?' said Ward, as Bible reached them.

'A bit violent, Bill,' said Bible quietly.

'It'll do him good, sir,' said Ward, taking his foot off Robinson and pulling him to his feet. 'Does me good.' Ward pulled his handcuffs from his coat and deftly closed a link round Robinson's wrist. The fraudster tried to retain his poise.

'I trust you will allow me the wherewithal to telephone my lawyer,' he said in an unreal voice that reminded Bible of the commentator on Pathe news.

'All in good time, sunshine. All in good time,' said Ward cheerfully.

As they led the prisoner back to their car, Bible wondered if Ward realized they would have to let Robinson go. He'd taken flight before he'd asked for any money.

*

As soon as she got in, Carol went to the kittens snuggled in the wardrobe and let them lick her fingers. She took the milk kept cold in a bucket of water under the sink, and replenished the kittens' bowl. Smudge, the smallest, was squashed out, so she pulled the others away to give him a chance, and then picked him up and cradled him in her arm.

The face in the reservoir, if she'd really seen a face, had reminded her of Larry, the friend who, in a different life, could have been a boyfriend. A real boyfriend, like ordinary girls had, whom they could take to show their fathers. They'd had secret meetings, her sisters sworn to silence against a background of her mother's warnings and miserable defeated face. Larry had insisted on a clandestine trip to Exmouth, but she'd been terrified all the time. What if her father were there? She didn't know where he went during the day. But Larry had been defiant. Careless. Even though she warned him. When they'd had a photograph taken on the promenade, Larry had tried to make her have a print, but she'd said she couldn't risk having it in the house. 'I'll keep it in my wallet,' he'd said. 'Next to my heart.' But there was a twinkle in his eye which should have told her. 'And I'll get you away from that father of yours.' But then they'd had a row, sort of. More of a silent stand-off. Because he'd wanted more and was getting so insistent. They'd kissed, and she liked his kisses. He was gentle. Had been gentle. She'd liked his hand on her breast, but she'd become frightened at his insistence. She'd let him unbutton her blouse in an alley behind a teashop, but she wasn't ready for it. Didn't know what was normal. Not fit for it, after her background. She'd not seen him again. He must have been sick of her. She was sick of herself. That's when she made plans to leave.

Smudge wanted to return to his mother. Carol let him go. She would have to face this on her own. She hadn't told the police the face in the water reminded her of Larry. Or that the van was like one she'd seen her father step out of at their house in Exeter. She had denied it to save her sanity. Denied it to pretend her escape had worked. But perhaps she hadn't just imagined the van was chasing her. And there was something about the van. The colour wasn't natural. It hadn't looked properly painted at all.

The pieces of the letter still lay in the waste paper basket where she had dropped them. She went cold. Someone knew where she was. It was time to see the police again.

Carol got up from the floor, took off her work blouse and black skirt, and hung them from the picture rail. The knitted blue top with the wide sleeves and round neck felt more casual, along with the pleated skirt in navy blue. She laughed at herself for taking so much trouble to dress for going to the police station.

She looked in the mirror. Her eyes looked puffy. She poured some water from a flower-patterned jug into a bowl which sat on top of her chest of drawers, and splashed water on her face. She wondered whether to try some make-up, but she still wasn't sure how to handle it. A bit of lipstick would do. Bright vermilion always appealed to her, and after applying a touch, she pressed her lips together. The blue top didn't look quite right with it; something summery would have been better, but it was winter – anything too bright would look silly and draw attention to herself. That would do.

She took her coat down from the hook and opened the door on to the landing. Malcolm was standing there. Staring. Frightened.

*

The body looked pathetic. Small. Lying with its head in the long grass and its feet on the blue-grey shale of the abandoned open mine workings known locally as Shaley Hills. His scuffed leather shoes still looked wet from the day before, but it was more than likely he'd been through another puddle since. This was no longer the budding hoodlum who had kicked water over Bible the day before; this had been a sad little boy, a small animal who died.

Donald had been killed only a few hundred yards from his school. Bible glanced across to the low stone buildings where his daughter went every day, empty now in the winter dusk, and blackened with soot like everything in the city. PC Best caught Bible's eye and shook his head. It had happened on the constable's beat, and Bible knew he'd take it personally. Best had been the first on the scene when the body was reported, and was responsible for protecting the crime scene.

Bible left the pathologist with the body, and picked his way through the tussocks of the waste ground towards Chapel Gate where Donald's mother was waiting for news.

*

Malcolm hovered in the doorway. 'Can I talk to you?

Carol was again unsure about Malcolm. Something was not right. His story about the letter. Weak. Even if he was only desperate to please.

'I'm just going out.'

'Please.'

'If it's important.' Carol waited with the door half open. 'Go on.'

'Not out here. Can I come in?'

'I'm sorry, I need to go to the police.' Carol pulled her door shut and tried to take a step past him, but Malcolm put out his arm to block her.

'How dare you?' she said, and pushed his arm away.

Malcolm stepped back and covered his face with his hands. 'Please don't go to the police.'

Carol was half way down the staircase, on the turn where the stained glass window cast a melancholy glow over the worn carpet. Malcolm gripped the banister. He looked nervously upstairs towards the closed doors of other residents, and spoke in a whisper.

'I've been arrested.'

He sat on the edge of her bed, with his hands held palm to palm between his knees, whilst Carol made him a cup of tea.

'I was at the toilets in the park.'

Carol spooned in two sugars and gave him the blue striped mug. 'It'll make you feel better.'

'I have to go before the magistrate on Wednesday.' He cradled his hands around the mug. 'I don't know what to do about work. They'll sack me.'

She sat in the heavy armchair and looked at the nervous young man opposite. So he was a pervert. She wasn't quite sure what perverts did and felt uncomfortable if she tried to imagine it, but it was hard to see him as dangerous. She knew now why he had accepted her old name Dawn on the envelope. He had a secret life, and knew why someone else would. But she dreaded being involved in his life, just when she was cleaning up her own.

'Where do you work?' She wondered if it was odd he had not mentioned it.

'I'm a clerk at Sugden's. I check in bales of wool. Make sure the stock is OK. It means I can work on my own.'

Carol guessed that it wasn't easy being Malcolm in a northern textile mill. She remembered her father's anger whenever Liberace was on the wireless, shouting abuse at the fretwork over the speaker cover before he switched it off, warning Carol and her sisters against people like him. Not that they were likely to meet him, or meet anyone as long as their father stood between them and the door. It was hard to imagine Liberace in Exeter, walking down Fore Street in glittering sequins.

'I don't know what you can do. Take a day off work sick. If you go to prison you'll lose your job anyway.'

Malcolm's voice became barely audible. 'I don't think I could stand prison. I know what they do to people like me.'

Carol wished he didn't look so pathetic. He'd brought her an envelope she hadn't wanted, and now she felt pressured to be responsible for him.

Malcolm looked at her mournfully. 'I don't want you to go to the police.'

The truth dawned on her. 'I'm not going because of you,' she said. 'It has nothing to do with you.'

As she said it, she knew it was a lie. He'd brought her the letter. And she knew she was about to tell Bible about it.

*

A rotting post screwed to the stone wall told Bible there had once been a gate to the blackened sandstone cottage in Chapel Gate, but the overgrown patch in the front yard, and the uneven flags, made it look neglected now. But a family lived there. A family who had just lost a son.

Sometimes Bible hated his job. Sometimes it was better not to know about the way people behaved.

He looked down the lane, a dirt road dimpled with puddles and studded with the rounded tops of embedded stones. He pictured Donald in summer kicking up dust with his feet as he galloped around pretending he was on a horse like The Lone Ranger, falling into the long grass and cow parsley at the edge when he was shot. There'd be no falling into the grass on this miserable late November evening. Now was a time for going inside, a time for reckonings.

The stone roof to the single storey cottage bowed in the middle. It was probably about a hundred and fifty years old, from when the village was only connected to the city by a steep country lane winding down among fields. Then the cottage had been home to men working in the open cast mines. Now it was home to Dotty and Alfred Holmes, and, until the day before, Donald.

A policewoman was already sitting with Dotty in the small living room and kitchen. Dotty's eyes were red and her brown dress flecked with stains that had dodged her faded apron. She was probably about the same age as Bible, thirty-eight, but she looked older and worn. Alfred was ten years her senior, a wiry ferret of a man, with grey hair and a bobbing Adam's apple. He sat upright at the square dining table, hand gripped around the handle of a mug of tea, facing the door Bible had stooped to enter, but Alfred's stare was focused on something way beyond the confines of the room.

'I told him he 'ad to go to school, or else.' Dotty twisted her handkerchief around her hands, and sobbed openly, the sodden handkerchief useless against the tide of her grief.

Bible sat down. Ward lounged against the door frame, looking at the scene.

'You mean you're not sure he got to school?' said Bible.

'I kept telling 'im, the little monkey, said 'e 'ad to go,' said Dotty Holmes between sobs. 'Nothing but trouble. And now this.' She covered her eyes with the damp rag.

Through the back window, squared with six-inch panes, Bible could see an undersized white horse, a cob, tethered in the small back garden. They'd had more luck keeping hold of the horse than Donald.

'No one's criticising you, Mrs Holmes,' said Bible. 'Did Donald ever tell you what he did when he played truant?'

'Of course he didn't,' broke in Alfred Holmes from the table. 'He wa'n't stupid.'

'Take it easy, Alfred,' said Ward from his doorpost. 'We're only asking.'

Ward had been still as a statue, but Holmes was on his feet in an instant. Two strides to the door and he stared fiercely into Ward's eyes. 'Find him,' said Holmes fiercely. 'Find him, the bastard what did it.' He stalked past Ward out of the door and called from the garden path: 'Gypsy!'

An olive-brown rough-haired lurcher uncurled itself from under the dining table and loped outside.

'Was Mr. Holmes at work today, Mrs Holmes?' said Bible. Ward chuckled dismissively, but Bible concentrated on the grieving woman.

'Mrs Holmes?'

She shook her head.

'He comes and goes. Takes the horse and cart out sometimes.' She sniffed. 'He tries his best,'

'He's a rag and bone man, sir,' said Ward.

Bible waited for Ward to add more, but Ward remained silent. Bible was glad his sergeant had kept his contempt to himself, but wondered what it was based on.

It was dark and their shoes crunched on the shale as they left the cottage and walked back towards Ashdale Avenue.

'I didn't like your attitude,' said Bible quietly.

'Sorry, sir. I am what I am.'

'They're the sort of people things happen to, Bill.'

'Are you a good father, sir?'

Bible stopped and turned. A single yellow street lamp lit Ward's face. 'Don't go too far.'

'I think you are, sir.'

Bible was surprised. 'What are you getting at?'

'Did you see any toys in that cottage? Football? Toy soldiers? Meccano?'

Bible thought. No. He hadn't.

'Any sign that a little boy was ever there?'

The answer, Bible realised, was no. And apart from two cramped bedrooms, he'd seen the only room in the house. The toilet was outside and the zinc bath was hanging on a hook by the back door.

'And that lazy bastard who calls himself his father couldn't even be bothered to make him something out of a piece of wood,' said Ward. 'They killed that little boy.'

Back where Donald's body had been cordoned off, Alf Holmes was being restrained from behind by PC Best. Another uniform held Gypsy.

'You can't bring your dog in here, Alfred' said Best. He was near retirement, but strong enough to hold the wiry rag-and-bone man.

'I need to see him,' shouted Holmes. 'The dog can smell things.'

Bible stopped Ward joining in and went to stand before Holmes.

'I'm sorry, Mr Holmes,' said Bible, 'this is a crime scene.'

Alf Holmes spat at Bible. The spit caught his left cheek. He could feel it dribbling down.

Best tightened his grip as the bereaved father jerked before him trying to escape. 'Sorry about that sir.' Bible knew Best felt responsible for everybody on his beat. 'Come on, lad. You're not doing yourself any good with this carry on.'

'I'd advise you to go back to your cottage, Mr Holmes,' said Bible.

Holmes looked round and realized he was outnumbered.

'Would you like somebody to come back with you?' said Bible.

The rag-and-bone man shrugged off the relaxing grip of PC Best and turned to walk back through the wet grass. Gypsy pulled against the hand holding his collar. Bible nodded for the dog to be released and it quickly joined its master. Bible found Ward at his side.

'You could have arrested him for that,' said Ward.

Bible took out the handkerchief neatly folded and ironed by his wife and wiped his cheek. 'He's just lost his son, Bill.'

'Do you know what he did in the war?' said Ward. 'Fuck all. Tricked them he was unfit. Bad eyesight. He sees well enough in the dark with a lamp and that dog when he's after rabbits.'

A distant police voice called. 'Sir, over here.'

'And in forty-five boasted about voting Tory. He could get a job. Give that missus of his a better life.'

'Sir!'

Ward and Bible stepped through the rough grass towards where the policeman was crouching with a torch.

'He lets the side down, sir,' said Ward. 'Lets the working class down. I don't have much respect for that.'

They bent to look at what the constable had found. A flattened worn out leather football with a burst inner bladder, and a little tin of bubble gum football cards.

SEVEN

The dog walker who had found the body hadn't seen much. An overlooker from Sugden's giving his dog some exercise before he started his evening shift in the din of the weaving shed. Middle-aged. Married for twenty years. Military policeman in the war. A solid type, thought Bible, looking at the man before him in the interview room.

The overlooker wiped his forehead with his hand. 'I can't tek my mind off it. I'm supposed to be at work in an hour, but I'll watch them shuttles shooting back and forrard, and think what's the point? A little lad's just died.' He wiped his hand across his forehead again and smiled wanly. 'Good job I had a decent kip last night. I won't get any in the morning when I've done.'

Bible shut his notebook. 'We can let you go now. Thanks for coming in.'

'Sorry I couldn't tell you more.'

Bible smiled. 'It's all part of the jigsaw.'

'Like I said, there was no one else around. Which were a bit odd like. There's usually kids. And older lads sometimes. But when I found …what I found, it were just me and the dog and that poor little fella in the grass.'

Bible stood in the hectic information room, a still centre, while all swirled around him. Ward was ratcheting the dial of a phone with the fierceness of a man who saw it only as an obstacle between him and the murderer. Higham snatched the recently developed photographs of the murder scene from the photographer and pinned them on the noticeboard. A WPC kept radio contact with the squad car at the school.

The light had completely gone from the windows, leaving uncurtained squares of black. The bulb above his desk lacked a shade, broken in a station prank, and now it shone on the police photograph of the tiny damp body in the grass. The pathologist had estimated the time of death as not long after the end of the school day. The dog walker had found the body around four-thirty. Bible wondered how their muscle-bound force, with twenty-five uniformed policemen already knocking on doors around the school, would uncover the truth if the answer lay with a hundred and fifty frightened five and six-year-olds who might have seen something.

The desk sergeant put his head round the door, and jerked it back as a policewoman bustled past within inches of his nose. Bible hoped he wanted someone else, but the sergeant's darting eyes settled on him. 'That young woman's here to see you again sir.'

'What?' Bible repeated the words in his head trying to make sense of them. What young woman?

Ward interrupted him. 'The headmistress says she's waiting at the school now, sir.' Ward balanced the heavy black receiver in his hand like a gun as he waited for an answer.

'So we could go in and question the children tomorrow,' said Bible.

'They'll be frightened, sir. Word's got round. Mothers have been ringing up the station all evening.'

'Of course.' Bible felt irritated by Ward's outburst of sensitivity. He didn't like being accused of clumsiness by a man who'd thumped a suspect in full view of the shoppers on Market Street. But Ward was right. Bible knew he had been jumping at ways of taking the case forward. He thought of how his daughter would react if she saw her father in school.

Ward had been newly animated since their return from the cottage on Chapel Gate. He had organised the door-to-door, tracked down the headmistress and begun to assemble an army of policewomen to go into the little stone school. Now he realised the desk sergeant was still hovering.

'Don't you need to get back, Swann?'

'The young woman, sir. The one who came in a couple of days ago. She's at the desk.'

Bible remembered. Faced with a real body, and a threat to the children of his home patch, Carol Carlton's face in the water sounded like fantasy. He may have believed her too much. And he knew he thought about her too much.

'Can somebody else see her?'

'She wouldn't say what she wanted. Asked for you in person.'

'What shall I say to the headmistress, sir?' Ward had his hands cupped round the mouthpiece, as if he were about to reveal a frog he'd caught in the grass.

'Say we're coming now. We need to talk to the parents. Tell the children, and they'll think every man in town is going to kill them.' Bible imagined his daughter whispering to her friends about all the peculiar men she'd seen around the school. Yes, they'd need to see the parents. And he was a parent. He knew he should telephone Shirley and forewarn her that they'd have to speak to Pauline. But he feared they wouldn't be together on it.

Ward was already on the phone again. Bible looked at the desk sergeant.

'I'll come and see her now.'

Carol Carlton sat on the wooden bench opposite the reception desk. She looked forlorn, like another child he had to take care of. And he'd already let one die. She looked up at him, and, slightly too late, he forced a smile.

'Sorry to keep you waiting. Thanks for your help at the bank today.'

'I haven't come about that.'

There was a pause. He decided not to sit next to her. He had hoped he'd be able to talk to her near the reception desk, but he found himself saying, 'Would you like to talk in an interview room?'

As he ushered her into the bleak room with its Formica topped table, he wished he'd phoned his wife. They needed to talk to Pauline tonight and the little girl would be going to bed in a couple of hours.

'I hope this won't take too long.' Bible remained standing as he pointed her towards the chair.

The young woman sat, spread out her fingers and looked at her hands. 'I've had a letter.'

'What sort of a letter?' said Bible, wondering where this was going.

'A letter from my mother.'

'I'm sorry, I don't understand.' Bible did not want to be cruel. The girl had had a shock, but she'd been level-headed at the bank despite that. But now he feared his kindness had been mistaken for a greater helpfulness than he'd intended. And at that moment, he hadn't the time.

Ward rattled open the interview room door without knocking.

'*The Argus* on the phone sir. You'd better speak to them.'

'Right.' If the local paper had already heard about Donald, he had more than enough to handle without Carol's personal problems.

'I don't know how they knew where I was,' said Carol as Ward disappeared from view. Bible realised she had no awareness of Ward's interruption and seemed lost in herself. He began to rise from the table.

'They?' said Bible, and regretted opening up the questioning as he moved towards the door.

'My father will have forced her to write it. He treats her badly.'

'I'm sorry. I don't think this is a police matter, Miss Carlton,' he said as sympathetically as he could. He went to the door and held it open for her. 'I'm afraid...' Bible relented... 'It's busy here tonight, but let us know if anything else happens'

'Sorry to trouble you,' said Carol rising, but when she got to the door she stopped and turned to him. 'I didn't get on with my father.'

'These days,' said Bible, thinking of his own battles with Ricky, 'that seems to be more common than it should be.'

She stared at him for a moment, looking puzzled,

then turned to go down the corridor. Bible followed and watched her leave, relieved she had not asked him what he meant.

*

As Carol left the police station, she wondered why she had expected so much from the meeting. There had been an urgency about the place she had not felt before and Bible had seemed preoccupied. He was a kind man, she was sure, but as he'd shown her out, and she'd burbled on about her father, she'd felt she was coming over as hysterical. She'd asked him if he were a father, and he was. She imagined him in a posh house somewhere, being kind to his family. Perhaps he hadn't a clue things could be any different.

The early evening was dark. When she got off her trolleybus near the Picture Palace, the road was soaked with rain, and the sodium lights cast yellow reflections. Trolleybus wires stretched across the sky like a spider's web, and as she turned into her road she saw a bus outside the chemist's, its roof arms flailing as the driver and conductor tried to capture them with their long rods to re-anchor them on the parallel cables overhead. It was a regular occurrence, almost a local ritual, to be sitting on the bus on the top deck, hear a thump as the arms disconnected, and wait patiently for things to be put right.

Carol slowed down as she passed. A chemist stood in the doorway of his shop, watching the scene, dangling his keys and sheltering from the rain.

He hailed her as she walked past.

'A right performance, this is. Typical bloody Corporation.'

Carol smiled slightly, but increased her pace.

'Hey, just a minute love. Aren't you that West Country lass?'

Carol wanted to say 'no' but realised that was stupid; it was obvious where she came from as soon as she opened her mouth. She stopped and turned where she was, already past the shop, showing she had no intention of approaching.

'What if I am?'

'Sorry love. Didn't mean to take liberties.' He turned back into the shop doorway, rattling his keys. 'I were late locking up, like. I've got those snaps for you.'

Her stomach pitched like a boat and her face felt numb. She fought to keep her breathing controlled, too terrified to run or stay. The busmen had almost attached the trolley arms to the wires, but they were still there. And the passengers, if she needed them.

'I don't know what you're talking about,' she said, but her voice was weak.

'Hang on a minute.' The chemist bobbed back inside his shop, squeezing past a life size cut out figure that normally stood outside advertising Kodak. A black and white photograph of a smiling model in an all-in-one swimsuit.

'I used to have another of these, but it got pinched,' he said. His voice was muffled as he rummaged in the dark. Carol stepped fully into the shop doorway. A voice in the street shouted OK, and she heard the trolleybus depart with its electric wheeze. The street was quiet behind her. Why didn't the shopkeeper put a light on?

He reappeared with a packet.

'Here, love. I knew I'd got them somewhere.'

She backed away from him. One step. Two steps. A voice called her from down the street.

'Carol?' It was Malcolm. The chemist advanced towards her, holding out the yellow wallet.

'No. No. I don't want it.' She turned, and ran, shouting, 'I didn't leave a film.'

The chemist called after her. 'That young lad dropped it off for you.'

After that she heard nothing but the clip of her heels on the wet paving stones.

*

In his office Bible hunched over his desk gripping the receiver tightly. Ward stood in his trench coat, waiting.

'I'll be a couple of hours,' said Bible.

'That's way past her bedtime.' Shirley's voice. Anxious. 'It's seven o'clock already.'

Bible looked over his shoulder at the window behind him – the curtains had not been drawn for years - and saw a sky as black as a bruise. Only seven but it could have been midnight. Rain dribbled down the window, melting the glow from the billiard hall opposite.

'Read her another story. Tell her I'll read a story.'

Ward turned his wrist, pointed to his watch and mouthed 'Headmistress'. Bible nodded.

'Try and keep her awake,' said Bible into the receiver. 'I want to talk to her tonight.'

'She needs to sleep. And be safe.'

Two other phones were ringing. Higham picked one up.

'No one's going to hurt her whilst I'm her father,

love.' He wondered at his bravado, but he'd fear no one if he had to protect his daughter. And remembering Burma, when he'd not cared if he lived or died, he wondered if he feared anyone at all.

'We need you here, Jim.'

'I'll try to be back soon,' said Bible, knowing he'd be late. He looked at Ward.

'Let's go.'

'*News Chronicle*, sir,' called Higham, cupping his hand over the mouthpiece.

'Read them the statement I've given you,' said Bible.

It was national news now.

The tyres of the Wolseley crunched to a halt on the dirt road outside the school. The rain had eased and Miss Browning was waiting at the entrance, illuminated by a small electric lamp mounted under the stone carved letters which spelled *INFANTS*. Bible guessed her age at sixty. She wore a dark suit, and a black tie with pale diagonal stripes was laid neatly over her bosom. When Bible took her outstretched hand, her grip was firm.

'Inspector Bible,' she announced as if telling him who he was. 'Pauline's teacher tells me your daughter is doing very well.'

'Good,' said Bible. Shirley had met the class teacher, but not the Head. 'This is my sergeant, Bill Ward,' said Bible.

Miss Browning raised an eyebrow and nodded towards him, but did not extend her hand again.

'We could have seen you at home,' said Bible. 'And saved you waiting here.'

'I like to keep work and home separate,' said Miss Browning. 'We all need a playtime. Come to my office.'

Miss Browning led them past empty classrooms and down an echoing corridor that smelt of disinfectant. Her office was a forbidding place. Bible hoped his daughter never had to face the Head in here. The window ledges were high, like the classroom windows, preventing any distracting view of the outside world. On one of them was an ivory-coloured bust of a woman with what looked to be a nurse's hat, and a photograph of another female in a dark dress from the first decade or so of the century. High on the wall behind the desk was a painting of a woman in armour.

'I see you looking at my inspirations, Inspector Bible,' said Miss Browning with a smile. 'Do you recognise them?'

'I was never any good at tests in school,' said Bible. He was damned if he'd let her take the initiative in the interview.

'Joan of Arc, of course,' said Miss Browning. 'And this is dear Florence.' She patted the bust on the head.

'Nightingale,' muttered Ward.

'Very sharp, sergeant. And this?' She put a hand on the frame with the woman in Edwardian dress. 'All warriors, you know.'

'Mrs Pankhurst,' said Bible impatiently.

'Emmeline or Sylvia, Mr Bible?' asked Miss Browning. My God, she was annoying.

'I'll leave doing tests to your pupils. Would you like to sit down, Miss Browning?'

Ward looked amused. Bible couldn't think why. It seemed more in character for Ward to be brusque when faced with pretension.

'I think it's rather for me to ask you to sit,' said the headmistress. 'If you please...' She waved a hand towards two dark wooden chairs with curved arms, the leather seat coverings held in place by brass studs.

Bible sat when he saw Miss Browning take her study chair behind the large oak desk. Ward lounged against the cast iron radiator, thick with repainting. Bible could tell Ward was edging along to peek at what was on the headmistress's desk cluttered with a couple of photo frames and a small statuette along with blotter, books, and papers.

'Sergeant Ward,' said Miss Browning, addressing him directly for the first time, 'you don't have to stand – if you call that standing.'

Ward smirked and took the chair next to Bible.

Bible began. 'As you know we found the body of one of your pupils, Donald Holmes, at the foot of Shaley Hills in the rough ground across the road from here.' Shaley Hills were no more than a few mounds of shale, but regarded as a mountain range by local children, including Pauline.

'Your sergeant told me.' She had a stiff reserve which Bible wanted to penetrate.

'Forgive me, but you don't seem very bothered by that.'

Miss Browning looked at her desk, clasped her hands and rested them on the blotter. She pursed her lips before she spoke. 'If I may say so, Inspector Bible, nor do you.'

Bible was taken aback. It wasn't how he saw

himself. 'Emotion gets in the way of finding the killer.'

'Exactly, Inspector.' She paused. 'I care for all my pupils, Inspector, and I remember them all. Even Bill Ward here.'

Ward sat up. 'Good Lord.'

'But any weeping I do will be at home. So how may I help you with your enquiry?'

'How was Donald in school yesterday?'

'He wasn't in school yesterday.'

'Didn't that concern you?'

'Of course, but that was not unusual. He often has the day off. Sometimes I get a note from his mother, sometimes not. I cannot be responsible for feckless parenting.'

Bible exchanged a glance with Ward. They now had a whole day to account for in which Donald could have met his fate, not the narrower window of time they had hoped for.

'It's a pity you didn't inform anybody,' said Bible, opening his notebook.

'Are you criticizing how I do my job, Inspector?'

'I'm expressing a regret.'

'Absolutely pointless,' said Miss Browning briskly. 'What I need to hear from you is what we should do now.'

Half an hour later Bible and Ward were standing under a gloomy streetlight on the pavement outside the school with a plan agreed. Miss Browning was going to invite mothers into an assembly which she and Bible would address. Afterwards a team of officers assembled by Ward was going to talk to children and parents in the classrooms.

'So what do you make of Miss Browning and her warriors?' said Bible. 'I wonder what it's like for the boys. We didn't live round here when Ricky was little.'

Bible saw Ward's eyes rest on the high windows of Miss Browning's office. 'When I was six, I thought Miss Browning was the most beautiful woman in the world.' Ward kicked at a loose stone on the pavement.

'You didn't say you knew her?' said Bible.

'I didn't think she'd remember. I should have known she would.'

'Is she hiding anything?'

'There was one picture of a man in there,' said Ward. 'On her desk. In the frame with its back towards you. Bloke in Great War uniform.'

'And?'

'I think it was her fiancé. Died at Passchendaele. So my mother told me.'

Bible made a move towards the car. 'Sometimes you surprise me, Bill.'

'As far as I'm concerned, there are good people and bad people, and Miss Browning is one of the good people.'

Bible threw the car keys to Ward as they walked across the dirt road. 'You drive, Bill. Drop me off at home before you take the car back to the station.'

As they pulled up outside the house, Bible was relieved to see his daughter's light was still on. He opened the passenger door. Ward pulled a cigarette from a pack of Senior Service, and smoothed the thin white tube with his fingers. Bible hated smoke in the car and knew Ward was waiting until he got out.

'You never said what that young woman Miss Carlton wanted?' said Ward.

'She thinks her father has found out where she lives. He seems to be a bit of a tyrant. Not our business.'

'She was spot on about the bank fraud. Perhaps she wanted to tell you more.'

Bible knew Ward was right, and regretted being so dismissive of her. Perhaps she was in danger.

'And she's also very attractive,' said Ward.

'I wasn't thinking of her like that,' said Bible, knowing very well that he had been.

EIGHT

Bible tried to put Carol out of his mind as Bill drove away. He opened the double wooden gates and walked up the drive to the pebble-dashed semi he shared with his wife. The front door was locked. Good. He'd warned Shirley again and again about leaving it unlocked; now she'd realise why he said it. He stepped into the hall, folded his key back into his key case, and clicked the Yale. He could hear murmuring upstairs. It stopped and Shirley appeared on the landing. She looked worn.

'She's nearly asleep,' she said quietly.

A small voice called from upstairs. 'Is that Daddy come home?'

Shirley sighed. 'You'd better come up.'

As Bible reached the top of the stairs, Shirley held his upper arm. 'I haven't said anything, but she told me to lock the front door.'

'She's right. It should be locked.'

Bible headed towards Pauline's bedroom, but Shirley caught his sleeve again.

'Those poor parents. Should I go and see them?'

'So you've heard?'

'Winifred's been on the phone. She lives on Ashdale and her little girl's in Pauline's class. We all want to do something.'

'Leave it to us,' said Bible. Pauline's door was ajar. They always left it open so she'd know they were near.

'Don't be a policeman with her.'

'Of course not.' Bible let Shirley's arm slip away.

Pauline was lying with her eyes wide open. Bible remembered how proud she'd been of her new bed when she'd graduated from her cot. She'd also chosen the wallpaper, a mixture of fairies and woodland animals. Bible felt awkward and too large in his suit. He took off his jacket and crouched beside her. He stroked her hair. She'd been born with black hair sticking up about half an inch all round her head. Now it curled and shone.

'What did you do with Mummy tonight?'

'Played with Mr Potato Head.'

Bible looked round the room.

'He's downstairs,' explained Pauline.

Mr Potato Head had been a Christmas present almost a year ago. Whenever she was worried, she'd busy herself piercing the skin of a potato with the spikes on the plastic noses, eyes and moustaches. Pauline would be so quiet as she concentrated that they could hear the little squelch as a new feature found its place. Bible wondered what they could get her this Christmas, though he knew Shirley would have thought already. He felt guilty that he left these things to her.

His wife stood at the door and watched him. He felt he was giving a performance and had better do his best to look like a father and not a policeman conducting an interview. He continued stroking Pauline's hair.

'You know it's been a busy day at work today.' He

wasn't sure how to carry on. 'There's a nasty man I've got to catch.'

'Are you going to hang him, Daddy?'

Bible wondered what his daughter thought he did at work all day. 'No, I won't go that far.'

Shirley took half a step towards him. 'James, don't make a joke of it.'

It hadn't been a joke, Bible thought. It was because he didn't know what to say. He looked at Shirley appealingly, but she was waiting. Ready to judge. Ready to try and deal with any damage he caused. He took his hand away from Pauline's pillow and moved from a crouch to kneeling at the side of the bed.

'The thing is, did you notice anybody funny outside school this afternoon? Anybody you'd not seen before?'

'You mean the man who looked like Mr Potato Head?'

Bible smiled at her. 'If you say so.'

Pauline sat up in bed. 'He looked dirty,' said Pauline. 'And he was round.'

'Anybody else?'

'Just Mr Potato Head.'

Shirley came into the room and sat on the end of the bed. 'Daddy's going to read you a story, aren't you Jim?'

'Yes, what would you like, love?'

'Secret Seven.' Pauline picked the book from her windowsill and gave it to Bible.

'Move over then.' He sat on the bed next to his daughter, and looked at Shirley. 'Can you go and get Mr Potato Head from downstairs?'

Shirley gave him a warning look. 'I think she just

wants a story, James,' she said. 'I'll be downstairs.'

When she had gone he opened *Well done, Secret Seven* and wondered why that stuck up little prig Peter always thought he could solve things by himself when he should have gone to the police. Bible looked at his daughter in her happy anticipation. 'You'd go to the police if you saw something wrong, wouldn't you?' he said. 'You wouldn't try to solve it on your own?'

Pauline was quiet. Bible put his arm round her. 'Pauline, you'd tell me if you thought someone had been doing something wrong?'

His daughter's cheeks flushed red. 'I think Donald has been stealing sweets,' said Pauline, in a quiet voice, looking down at her pink bedspread.

'Why do you think that?'

'He was handing out penny chews. He had lots and lots of them. I think he took them from Mrs Johnson's shop.'

Bible picked up the book again. 'Time to settle down.'

'I don't like Donald,' said Pauline.

'Why's that?' Stop fishing, Bible thought. Just read to her.

'He thinks he can bully everybody.'

'Well, he won't be in school tomorrow,' said Bible. 'He's had an accident.'

'Good,' said Pauline.

When she had fallen asleep, Bible crept down the stairs and looked into the back room. Shirley was knitting, her chair pulled close to the table lamp on the bookcase. It had a fringed apricot shade and was the only light on in the room. The Magicoal glowed under the two-bar fire. It looked homely. Warm. Shirley glanced at him anxiously.

'I'll put the kettle on,' he said.

In the kitchen Mr Potato Head was sitting on the table, sporting the plastic features Pauline had spiked into his flesh. Bible sat and faced him, his hands clasped.

'Who are you then?' said Bible.

Mr Potato Head wore a green flat cap, bright yellow glasses, and a red moustache. He was bound to stand out if he turned up at school again.

*

Carol forced the door into Malcolm's face and braced her feet firmly against the floor, but she was still breathless from her flight from the chemist's.

'Carol? What's wrong, Carol?' Malcolm's voice sounded muffled on the other side of the door. 'You ran away?'

Carol leaned her back against the door. 'Leave me alone.'

She felt the pressure on the door subside. It clicked shut. Malcolm must have stepped back. She quickly turned and slid the bolt across.

'I've got the photos.' His voice was a near whisper. Like a quiet threat. It could have been a voice in her head, repeating the threats she'd heard throughout her life.

'Who are you?' she said.

'I'll leave them here on the rug,' he said. She heard a quiet flop as he dropped the envelope on the mat outside her door. 'I'm going now,' he said, still with the same whisper.

The dog was barking outside in the garden. It had been at the gate when Carol had crashed through and run up the steps. Carol flicked the bolt back and wrenched open her door. Malcolm was at the turn in the stairs before they led up to his room.

'How did you get past the dog?' she said fiercely. 'I thought you were scared of dogs.'

Malcolm looked scared of her. 'I wanted to help,' he said.

'You're creepy.'

Malcolm looked round nervously. 'Can you keep your voice down?'

'Because you don't want people to know what you are?'

'Please,' said Malcolm.

He had a point. No one ever emerged from the closed doors on the landings of the house, apart from the old woman downstairs, but Carol didn't doubt that there would be ears listening. And she didn't want people to know who she was either. Nor where she'd come from. She lowered her voice.

'Who put you up to this?'

'I was just passing. The chemist said they were for you.'

'Just keep out of my way, Malcolm.' She looked down at the yellow photograph wallet.

He started coming down the short flight of stairs. 'I'll take them back.'

'Wait.'

Malcolm paused, two steps down. His foot hovered over the one below. Carol felt herself shiver. She covered her face with her hands. 'He said a young man had dropped them off.'

'It wasn't me.'

She took her hands away from her face. They stared at each other, Carol weighing him up, and Malcolm, she thought, waiting to be accepted back into the fold. He had been in the house of bedsits before she had, so he wasn't following her. And he seemed, frankly, a bit pathetic. There was no way her father Tommy Logan would have had anything to do with whatever the right word for Malcolm was. But she couldn't trust him – not yet.

'I could stay with you,' he said.

Carol stooped and picked up the packet of photographs in a sudden movement. 'Go back to your room, Malcolm.'

She watched him retreat and heard him close his door. As soon as he'd gone she started breathing heavily and shaking. Back in her bedsit she locked the door, wedged a chair under the knob, and scrabbled the photographs out of the cardboard wallet.

When she'd looked at no more than the first few, she got into bed, still wearing her clothes, and curled up under the eiderdown. There she cried, and shook, and tried to sleep to escape. But sleep would not come.

After a while she felt soft prodding as the kittens played on the eiderdown and the pink hill her body made in the bed cover.

*

The school hall was full. Parents – mainly mothers – sat with their children in front of them or, if small enough, on their knees. Most wore thick overcoats against the northern cold, which made them look even more squashed in as they sat on the school chairs.

Some mothers stood round the sides with the teachers, firmly alert, none of them leaning against the dark wooden panelling which covered the lower few feet of the walls. This was not an occasion for leaning. Bible took his place on the shallow platform at the front with Miss Browning and the other staff.

Pauline was sitting on her mother's knee about five rows back. Shirley had tied a pink ribbon in her daughter's hair. Bible saw his wife bend her head to whisper something reassuring into the little girl's ear. His daughter had still been asleep when he'd kissed her gently on the cheek before slipping out of the house at six-thirty that morning.

A small team of constables and WPCs were trying to be inconspicuous around the edges of the hall. They had removed their helmets, but the only other plainclothes policeman was Higham. Ward was about his business elsewhere. Miss Browning stepped forward in her smart tweed suit and held up her hands for attention. The buzz quickly subsided. The woman's authority made Bible feel he was still at school himself.

'Ladies and gentlemen, boys and girls,' she began. 'Today is a sad day, a serious day but will, I hope, be a calm day. I know many of you parents will have things you want to discuss, and some of you will feel angry. But I would ask you to save your thoughts for a few moments whilst I talk to the children.'

Bible could see some of the audience were restive.

'She's no need to come over all grand,' muttered an old man who had lost the knack of whispering. He was sitting at the end of the row near where Bible was standing to one side of the platform.

'Children, something very sad has happened to one of our friends.'

She paused. One or two children whimpered. But the general silence felt decisive. A child had died and the clock could never be turned back. 'I'm sorry to tell you that Donald Holmes died yesterday and won't be with us anymore.'

There was a wail from a little girl sitting on her mother's lap halfway down the hall. Choked childish sobs echoed under the high ceiling. Mothers cuddled their offspring to them and looked at each other for explanation. Several wiped their eyes. The few men in the audience looked grim-faced.

'Tell 'em it were murder. Stop mincing your words.' It was Holmes, Donald's father, shouting from the back. If Bible had spotted him, he would have tried to dissuade him from coming in. Dissuaded? No, he'd have been tougher. Holmes was in the wrong whatever his loss.

Two of Bible's uniformed constables went towards him. Miss Browning carried on.

'Donald was a little boy always full of life. Some would say mischief, but...'

'That's right. Tell 'em what you really thought of him.' It was Holmes again. The two uniformed men moved to block his view of the rostrum.

'See, they're trying to silence me.' Bible could see the policemen weren't touching him.

Miss Browning carried on. '...but it was a sense of fun we could all enjoy.'

Holmes' shouting had stopped any further commotion, though the two policemen had now engaged his attention. Bible hoped it wouldn't be necessary to escort him outside. That would not look good.

'A sense of fun we hope Jesus is enjoying now Donald has joined him in heaven,' said Miss Browning softly to her attentive audience. The parents were looking to her for comfort from the terrors assailing them and their children. 'Now I'd like you to join me in a prayer.'

Most bowed their heads. Children put their palms together neatly. A boy near Pauline had his hands slapped away from his face because he was sticking his index fingers up his nostrils. Miss Browning waited for silence before she began. 'Let us pray. Let us pray for the soul of Donald Holmes.'

Bible lowered his head awkwardly, watching for reactions in the assembly. Holmes looked indignant for a moment, then bowed his head like everyone else, his cheeks glistening with tears, as Miss Browning offered thanks for the life of Donald. A neatly dressed elderly man seemed to be twisting his lowered head to watch everybody at the same time. Bible even wondered if he was smirking.

'Amen,' said Miss Browning. A shy Amen rumbled round the hall in response before Miss Browning continued. 'Children, I'd like you to go to your classrooms as you normally do after assembly. Your teachers are waiting for you.'

The classrooms led directly off the hall. They had doors painted blue, their upper halves criss-crossed with wood to make four panes of glass, and nice big numbers for easy reading. A couple of classrooms were in an old Nissen hut across the yard. Those were for the older children, in their last year before junior school.

Bible saw Shirley slip Pauline off her knee and

watch her walk uncertainly towards Room Four, glancing back towards her mother.

'That could have gone better, Inspector Bible,' said Miss Browning. She wasn't looking at him but gazing over the multitude in the hall as she spoke, checking that order was kept.

'He's upset,' said Bible of Holmes. 'You can't blame him.'

'We're all upset, Mr Bible.' Bible ignored the slip with his title. She sighed. 'Poor man. A tragic family, I fear, but perhaps we have to remember the spirit that won the war.'

Bible wondered what she did in the war. He thought he might try to find out.

The children had now gone into their classrooms and only the parents were left. There was a quiet murmuring in the hall.

'I'd like to introduce Inspector Bible from the local constabulary, who is going to talk to you about the police view of the matter.' She looked at Bible with an ironical twist of her lips. It was her regular expression, as if her words never quite meant what she said. 'Over to you, Inspector,' she said quietly. He wondered if she expected him to make a mess of it.

Bible cleared his throat. 'Ladies and gentlemen, parents, I won't beat about the bush. This is a very upsetting enquiry. As you may have gathered, but as we have not officially made public, Donald Holmes of Chapel Gate was found dead last night...'

'It was in the papers,' shouted a voice. '*Daily Sketch* this morning.'

'... at the base of the slag heaps across the road known locally as Shaley Hills.'

'You told the papers before you told us,' insisted the voice.

'Yes, it was in the papers, and I wish I knew who told them.' He looked round the audience. A mistake. He sensed the hostility as they felt accused of telling the press.

He flicked open his notebook, but he knew the key facts from memory. Checking was a habit. 'Donald was found at 5.32 yesterday evening, but initial reports from the post mortem suggest he died sometime in the afternoon. He wasn't at school yesterday, but his mother says she sent him off as usual, we think around half past eight. We'd like to hear from anybody who saw a little boy wandering around when he should have been at school, or anything else unusual yesterday.'

A male voice spoke from the crowd. A Yorkshire voice unused to public speaking. 'Was there any sign of molestation?'

The voice laboured over the word 'molestation' putting the same heavy emphasis on the first three syllables. Bible realised it came from the man he'd noticed twisting his head during the prayer, a man in his sixties wearing a neatly belted fawn raincoat, smart and newly shaven in preparation for this public event. Perhaps a grandfather no longer at work.

Bible ignored the shocked gasp from the crowd and responded plainly. 'There is no evidence of that as far as we know.'

Ten minutes later Bible had finished his address and his officers had their knees cramped under small children's desks around the hall as they interviewed parents. Bible had been given temporary use of the Head's study; Miss Browning seemed to see it as befitting his station. So there he was, behind the heavy desk, surrounded by Miss Browning's images of fearsome women, facing another fearsome woman who clutched her handbag before her like a miniature battlement. She wore a black tweed coat gridded into four-inch squares with woven white lines, and a red felt hat with a feather.

'I'm not saying it's not a very sad thing,' said the woman who had declared herself as Mrs Harsnet, 'but all I can say is that the Holmeses have brought it upon themselves. That child has been allowed to run wild.' She paused for effect and sat back. 'Still, I'll help if I can. A child's a child, for all that'

'That's very good of you,' said Bible, trying not to sound sarcastic. The woman was full of the self-importance of her clichés. Why would anyone begrudge giving evidence to catch a child killer? 'So where were you when the children came out of school?'

'I was waiting at the top of Ashdale. We have a semi-detached on Moore Avenue, you know.' Mrs Harsnet's tree-lined boulevard was posh to most of the people in Chapel Heights, and to Bible too, though he now lived in a similar house himself.

'And?'

Mrs Harsnet looked uncomfortable.

'I mean, did you see anything odd? Anyone you'd not seen before?'

'I'm not saying I saw anything.'

'Well, thank you for your help, Mrs Harsnet.' He stood up to show her out, aware they had a lot of people to get through.

'I thought you'd want to know about Holmes,' said Mrs Harsnet, standing up. 'He's not fit to be looking after that child.'

'Well, he won't be any more.' Bible opened the door of Miss Browning's study.

'There's no need to take that tone. A child's been killed you know.' She gathered her bosoms and bag indignantly and stepped out of the room. 'It was either Holmes, or those workmen.' She walked down the short corridor lined with pictures of rural scenes towards the school hall. Bible caught up with her. They stopped and faced each other.

'Workmen. You said workmen,' said Bible.

'There were workmen down Ashdale. I thought the police would know that.'

'Where did you see them?'

'They were in a truck.'

'A big truck? Open at the back?'

'The sort of truck a workman would use. Now if you'll excuse me.'

'Thank you Mrs Harsnet. I may want to talk to you again.'

Bible watched her go. He'd walked up Ashdale Avenue that murky afternoon after school. He hadn't noticed any workmen. Or a truck. But he could see Shirley waiting for him expectantly at the end of the corridor and he walked towards her.

NINE

'Did you hear the way she spoke about that boy?' said Shirley as Bible reached her. 'As much as called him a hoodlum.'

'I think she felt she had to be realistic. Everyone knew him.'

'Saying that, with his father there?'

Bible turned his back towards the school hall, blocking any view people might have of Shirley and hoping his wife's voice didn't carry.

'Keep your voice down love. I know you're upset.'

'I'm going to start a campaign group. Parents. We have to look out for each other's children. Some of us must have seen something.'

'Shirley, let us deal with it.' He put his hands on her shoulders.

'Why? Why should I leave it to anybody?'

'Because it's what we do. It's our job.' She'd be annoyed if he said what he thought, that it was a man's job catching criminals. 'I need you at home, looking after Pauline.'

'It's not enough, Jim. Not now you're better, and Ricky's grown up.'

'You could have fooled me,' said Bible. He let his hands drop, but Shirley's expression told him she had seen something over his shoulder.

'There you are,' said Miss Browning, striding towards them. 'If I could prey upon your time, Inspector.' She nodded to Shirley. 'Mrs Bible.'

For a moment Bible had thought she would ignore his wife. Despite the shrines to women in her office, she seemed to live in a man's world. Miss Browning gripped Bible's upper arm and guided him through a forty-five degree turn so his back was to Shirley, and dropped her voice to a loud whisper.

'I wonder if you could help me persuade these good people to leave now. I'd like to give the children as normal a day as we can manage. School is never a good place for parents.' She patted his forearm. 'I'll leave it with you.'

'I think parents should be in school more, Miss Browning,' said Shirley.

'Don't distress yourself, my dear. Pauline will be in good hands,' said Miss Browning, walking into the school hall.

'How dare she dismiss me like that?' said Shirley.

Bible hovered in the entrance to the corridor. He knew any physical gesture of comfort would be rejected. 'She has her job to do.'

'So do I,' said his wife fiercely. 'I'm going to take Pauline with me.' Shirley stalked into the school hall, heading in the direction of Pauline's classroom.

'The Head wants the children to stay.'

Shirley turned back towards him. 'And what do you want?'

'Won't Pauline be happier here with friends?' said Bible. 'We don't want her to feel anything's different.'

'She knows something's different.'

'We're putting a policeman on the main door.' Bible felt guilty for wishing his wife would go.

'And what if the man you're looking for comes in the back door?'

Bible held his hands open in a shrug of helplessness.

'Does that mean you think she's safe?' said Shirley.

Was anybody ever safe? Life was an uncertain business. His wife needed to know what he really thought. Not what the official line was.

'She's never going to be as safe anywhere as when she's with you.' He looked directly at Shirley and she returned his gaze. He couldn't read her expression. 'But she can't be with you all the time.'

'I've got to do something, Jim. I can't just sit and wait, helpless.'

'I need to address the multitude,' he said, and left her at the entrance to the corridor. He felt like a man caught in a dark net, unable to find a way out.

In the hall the constables were on the last of their interviews, but many of the parents still hung around in small groups. Their conversation was desultory. They were waiting, rather than talking. But waiting for what? Another murder? Bible stepped onto the platform and clapped his hands for attention. Perhaps he'd be able to pick up this school teaching lark if everyone became an honest citizen and the bottom dropped out of policing.

'If I could I have your attention for a moment,' he said. 'We need to clear the hall now, but I'd like to speak to anyone who collected children from school yesterday afternoon.'

Miss Browning stood by the exit door, nodding at parents as they went past. He saw her stiffen as Shirley left the hall holding Pauline's hand.

There was a wind getting up outside the school and coats were flapping as Bible organized the few mothers who met their children at the gate. 'I'd like you to stand where you were standing yesterday afternoon,' said Bible, raising his voice above the breeze.

Miss Browning had come out with Bible and was once again trying to whisper, but failing. 'Inspector Bible,' she said huskily as the parents shuffled into position, 'I find it very surprising that you have let Mrs Bible take your daughter out of school.'

'My wife doesn't need my permission to look after my daughter. And I'm worried. Aren't you?'

'I should have thought you would want to instil confidence, rather than panic based on rumour.'

'The death of young Donald isn't a rumour, Miss Browning.' They watched the small procession of parents and children disappearing from view up Ashdale Avenue, the small houses with their neat wooden fences and gardens looking cosy beneath the grey northern sky. 'Those children should be staying in school,' said the Headmistress.

'I can understand their fear. I'm a parent too.'

She looked at him coldly. 'I am not without powers of empathy, Mr Bible. When I was in London in 1940, and saw children after the bombs had hit their homes...' Miss Browning paused. Bible thought he detected a catch in her throat, but she continued. 'Well, never mind that. Let's do our best here. So, are we any nearer with this?' Miss Browning gestured towards the handful of mothers assembled on the dirt road. The council had promised tarmac, but until the road beyond the school led to something more than a few old cottages, it was unlikely to come.

'We're not all here,' said a woman in a green belted overcoat with cloth covered buttons. 'There was a man next to me in the hall said he collected his granddaughter every Wednesday, but I'd never seen him before.'

She pointed to the line of children and adults disappearing up the road.

'And some of *them* should have stayed,' said the woman. 'I've seen them waiting. Too toffee-nosed to get involved, their sort.'

Bible looked at the crowd. A couple of women were hurrying their children along as if they feared being accosted there and then. And he realised that as he'd watched the parents and children leave, he'd not noticed the elderly man from the second row.

'Can you describe the man you mean?' said Bible.

'It was that fella who asked about molestation.' She repeated the laboured pronunciation of molestation, with the accent on the first syllable. 'Smart fella. Fawn coat.'

But although he'd been there, the man and his pronunciation had melted away.

When Bible got back in his car, Swann came over the radio from the police station. 'The girl at the bank sir. Sergeant Ward says she's not there this morning.'

Bible had sent him there on foot to take statements about the encounter with Major Robinson. 'Has she telephoned in to say she's poorly?'

'No sir. The manager says it's not like her. She's never been off before.'

It might mean nothing, but Bible felt uneasy. 'Look

up her address, I'm going over.'

The car smelt stale inside as he stepped in. Leather seats and tobacco. Whilst Swann found where Carol lived, Bible removed the ashtray Ward had filled the day before and emptied it out of the car window.

The radio crackled. 'Got it sir.' Swann reeled off the address. It was near the town centre, a short bus ride from the bank. It wouldn't take Ward long to get to the house and he could leave the questioning around the school to the uniforms for now.

'Tell Bill I'll meet him there.'

At mid-morning, with faint sun catching a scrubby privet hedge, and the wind having whipped away most of the litter, Sebastopol Road was looking its best, though that best was not very good. The tall stone-fronted houses had once been grand, but now their peeling paintwork and neglected front gardens indicated that no one lived there who cared anymore. A dog snarled at them from the gate of Carol's house, but Ward pushed it out of the way with his foot. 'We'd better find out who owns that when we come out,' said Ward. 'See if we can find someone to arrest.'

Bible overtook him to walk the three steps up the drive to the front door. There were no bells for individual bedsits so he knocked briefly before opening the unlocked door. Letters no one laid claim to had been piled to one side under the hall stand. Bible touched it as he riffled through them, and found the surface was sticky. None were to Carol. He showed one to Ward. A police envelope, postmarked the day before.

'From us,' said Bible.

'It'll be to that little pansy who lives here. Higham picked him up hanging around the gents in Grange Park.'

'When was that?'

'Tuesday. After we'd finished with him at the Manhattan.'

'Poor blighter,' said Bible. 'We'd best go up. Number Two?'

'Looks like someone else wants her as well.'

A cat, an adult tabby, was purring and rubbing its back against the door at the top of the first flight of steps. The stair carpet was worn on the lip of each tread. The paint was flaking off the bottom of Carol's door. It looked cheap. Not a solid old-fashioned panel door flushed with hardboard to make it seem modern, but a flimsy replacement – nothing more than a wooden frame with hardboard tacked to it. Easy to kick through if someone wanted to get at Carol. Bible marvelled at how she managed to turn out so smartly everyday from these surroundings.

Ward knocked. He was about to speak when Bible put a restraining hand on Ward's arm.

'She knows me better,' he explained. 'Carol,' he called.

Ward put his ear to the door. 'I can't hear anything, sir.'

Bible tried the handle. The door was locked.

Suddenly they were both aware of a figure on the turn in the stairs above them. It quickly dodged back up the short flight to the next floor, but Ward was after him in three leaps, and wrestled the young man into a half-nelson at the door to a bedsit on the floor above Carol's.

'So what do you know about this?' said Ward roughly. The figure was Malcolm. Ward had him in a kneeling position on the threadbare carpet.

'Easy, Bill,' said Bible.

Ward relaxed his grip. Malcolm got up and stood looking sullen.

'You shouldn't run away from us, son,' said Ward. 'We might think you're off to the park again.'

'We're not here for that, Bill.' Bible tried to reassure the nervous young man. 'We're looking for Carol. No one else. Is this your room?'

Malcolm nodded.

'Is she in there?'

Malcolm paused and then stepped aside. Bible gently eased open the door into a neat but cheaply furnished bedsit. Carol was sitting in an armchair with a brown woollen blanket pulled around her staring at the two glowing bars of a small electric fire. Another empty chair with wooden arms faced her. Her eyes did not move towards Bible or Ward as they went in.

'Carol?' said Bible softly.

She slowly turned her head. Her eyes filled with tears. Bible was relieved. He thought she was deep in some place where he would not be able to get to her. He crouched beside her and held her hand. The rug under his feet seemed new and there was a faint smell of furniture polish, as if Malcolm had done his best to make the place seem homely.

'Carol,' he said. 'What's happened?'

'She got some photographs.' Malcolm pointed to the sideboard.

Bible let go of Carol's hand and looked at the

images laid out on the crocheted doily. Ten two-and-a-quarter-inch square black and white photographs with a white border. The sort his daughter took with her simple Kodak Brownie. They were of Carol. Shots of her walking to the bus stop to catch the bus to work. Shots of her getting off the bus and walking back to her front door. A snap of her getting her key out, taken from across the street. A view of her bedsit window. They could have been put together to make a simple animation of a boring day, except that this wasn't simple and it wasn't boring. It was sinister. Bible could see the corners of two more photos sticking out of the opened yellow wallet.

'So where did these come from?' said Bible.

Carol dabbed her nose with the handkerchief crushed in her hand. 'I don't know.'

'I collected them,' said Malcolm. 'I was passing the chemist's shop. He was calling after her.'

'I didn't leave a film,' said Carol.

'Been taking pictures of young ladies for a change?' said Ward.

'No.' Malcolm reddened. 'I was trying to help.'

'The chemist said a young man had left them,' said Carol. Ward's eyes turned to Malcolm again. 'Not Malcolm,' she added.

Bible caught Ward's eye and shook his head slightly. They'd find out more from Malcolm at the station.

'What do you think, Bill?'

'They need bagging up for forensics, sir.'

'Wait a minute.' Bible pushed back his unbuttoned overcoat and took a pair of tweezers from his jacket pocket. Gently he pinched a corner of the top photo of the two remaining in the cardboard wallet. Malcolm had come to stand behind Ward and Bible.

'We didn't look at the last two,' said Malcolm quietly.

Bible looked towards Carol in the chair. She was staring at the two-bar electric fire. She seemed to be in a world of her own, and not a very welcoming world. 'Carol didn't look at them, or you didn't?' said Bible.

'She was so upset I pretended that's all there were.'

'And the question?' said Ward. Malcolm looked blank. 'The Inspector asked if you'd seen them yourself.'

'The top one was a landscape, I think.' Malcolm retreated to near where Carol was sitting, but remained standing.

Bible pulled the photograph clear of the wallet and laid it down next to the others. This was not taken on the street. It was, as Malcolm had said, a landscape. A moorland view, grey and rain-sodden. In the foreground, water. A reservoir. And in the distance, a figure. A woman. Carol.

Bible glanced towards his sergeant. It was the reservoir they'd searched two days earlier. Ward's face was set. A man for justice, was Bill.

Bible eased out the final photograph from the wallet. The reservoir again, in duller tones of grey. And Carol was at the side of the reservoir now. She was looking across the picture towards the camera and standing on the grassy bank where Bible had stood a few days earlier. There was a dark patch on the water. Or in the water. It could have been a figure, but it didn't look solid enough. Bible looked closely.

'We need to get it to the labs, sir. Get it blown up.

Bible lifted the edge of the other pocket in the photograph wallet. 'Empty. No negatives, Bill.'

'It looks like you have a case, sir.'

Ward was respecting his seniority. In reality, they both had a case. Two cases, Donald's murder and whatever sort of case Carol's would turn out to be. Three cases, if you counted the attempted bank fraud. But Robinson was small fry.

'Do you think the Chief will let you take all this on, sir?'

'I don't need to tell him. There hasn't been a crime, has there?'

'Sir?'

'What's the crime? What crime are we investigating?'

'There's a crime here somewhere.'

'It's the ghost of a crime, Bill. Do I tell Holroyd I believe in ghosts?'

Bible walked over to take the chair opposite Carol. He needed to question her, but he wanted to do it where she'd feel most comfortable. She was staring at him. Not crying, but looking pale, and shocked. Expectant and nervous, the way he'd remembered his first wife looking on their wedding night.

'Are you all right to talk?'

Carol nodded.

'Would you rather go down to your room?'

'I feel safer here.'

Bible looked up at Malcolm. 'Do you mind waiting outside with the Sergeant?'

Ward levered himself from the sideboard he was leaning on. 'Come on then, Nancy boy.'

'No,' said Carol. 'I want him to stay.'

'I'm afraid we need to talk to you separately,' said Bible.

Carol watched Malcolm being led out. She could tell he was nervous. Why were they taking him out? He had only been trying to help. Inspector Bible looked trustworthy. He was smart. Conventional looking in his suit and overcoat. He could easily have passed for an Assistant Manager in the bank. It was odd that he looked so ordinary and yet must have seen so many things. Like she had. She was trying to look ordinary, though she now knew her life was very extraordinary compared to some. She realised she liked ordinary.

Alone with Bible in Malcolm's neat room, she felt awkward and in a strange place, though her own room no longer felt like home.

'So you're being followed?' said Bible.

She didn't answer. She wanted to pretend there was no one else in the world she would ever have to answer to. She was weary of the whole business. Perhaps she should just give in and accept her fate.

'Someone's taking photographs of you.'

She nodded. 'What was in the last two photographs?' she murmured. She remembered her escape from Exeter with her duffle bag, skulking down the side streets avoiding the pools of light from the street lamps until she'd worked her way out of the city to the A38. Then hiding by a hawthorn hedge until first light before slipping into the back of a lorry parked up at a roadside café. But it was like remembering another person. She should have known she could not escape.

Bible had still not answered her question. 'The

photos,' she said. 'The last two. I need to know.'

'Another couple of shots with you on.'

Carol looked past Bible, at a spot on the wall, as if by not engaging with the inspector's eyes she could keep the whole experience at a distance. 'There was something different about them, wasn't there?'

When he didn't answer, Carol turned her head to him. Bible was looking at his shoe, curling the toe as if examining the shine. No, she would not give in; she would not go back. 'I need to know,' she said.

Here was a man, she thought, who would stay silent, rather than lie. She'd know if he were telling the truth. 'Where was I?' she persisted.

She watched Bible hesitate, then make up his mind. 'At the reservoir.'

'The same day?' said Carol. 'The same day I came to you? Was there anyone else? Anyone in the water?'

Bible looked down at his shoes.

'You've got to tell me,' she said.

Bible looked at her. 'There was something.'

Carol gasped and put her hand to her mouth.

'Do you want me to get you anything?' said Bible. Perhaps he thought she was going to be sick.

Carol shook her head. 'I'll be all right.'

'We can't be sure it's a figure,' said Bible. 'We'll have to wait for the lab report. It could have been a branch or a trick of the light.'

'The face I saw in the water,' said Carol, 'the face I thought I saw, reminded me of a boy I knew.'

Bible sat back in his chair and waited.

'He just disappeared,' said Carol. 'I thought he'd got fed up of me.'

'A boyfriend?' said Bible. Carol reddened.

'I'm sorry,' said Bible. 'That was clumsy of me.'

'I don't know,' she said, looking away towards the mantelpiece. 'I've never had a boyfriend. Perhaps he was.'

'What was his name?'

'Larry Cole.'

She knew Bible was watching her.

'So who do you think is following you?' he said.

Carol turned her head and looked at him directly. 'My father.'

TEN

Logan's boots crunched across the loose stones as he went to the boathouse on the landlocked side. The door was old and needed painting. It looked neglected until you noticed the fresh padlock and well-oiled bolts. Four of them, spaced down the door, sporting shiny screw heads, and each held in place with a brass padlock.

Logan pulled a hefty bunch of keys out of his pocket, opened each padlock in turn, and slid back the bolts quietly. He opened the door outwards, and stepped into the dark interior. The water lapped against the posts which supported the damp wooden platform that ran round three sides of the boathouse. A small dinghy, with a canopy and outboard motor, bobbed slightly on the black water. In one corner was a tripod with a camera mounted on top. Not a good place to leave a camera, thought Logan. He'd have to stop doing that. In the other corner was a chair and on it a young man, his head slumped to one side, his hands tied behind his back, and a piece of tape across his mouth. Logan stepped towards him. The black water slapped and sucked beneath the boards of the wooden walkway. Logan peeled the tape from the mouth of the sleeping man.

'Hello, Larry,' he said. 'I've come to feed you. And then it's photograph time.'

*

Bible radioed for a WPC to come and watch over Carol as Ward forced Malcolm into the back of the Wolseley, guiding his head under the door sill. Bible had often done the same thing. He wondered why the force always thought those under arrest were more likely to bang their heads than other people.

'They tend to wilt when you get them into the station, sir,' said Ward cheerfully from the back seat. 'And this one's a flower. He'll wilt.'

They hadn't got much out of Malcolm in his bedsit. Bundling him into the car had seemed the only solution, though the bundling part had been Ward's contribution. As he pulled away he could see Malcolm's face in the rear view mirror. He was staring out of the window and looked as miserable as the city pavements.

The desk sergeant opened his leather-bound ledger with a flop as Bible and Ward gripped the young man's arm and guided him to the desk.

'Sign on the dotted line,' said Swann holding out a fountain pen, 'and a cell is all yours. Name in full please.'

'Don't worry. You're not under arrest,' said Bible. Malcolm still looked alarmed. 'It's Sergeant Swann's idea of a joke.'

Swann pulled a roll of paper from the pocket of his tunic and passed a note through the hatch to Bible. The desk sergeant had his own arcane ways of managing information, but they worked.

'Higham left this for you.'

DC Higham's handwriting was a scrawl, but the

message told him that Miss Browning had telephoned to say several staff remembered seeing the elderly man on the second row, but no one had recognised him.

'Thanks,' said Bible.

A WPC approached with reports from the house-to-house round the school. 'I don't think it's turned up much, sir.'

'We'll go through them,' said Bible.

'Cheer up,' said Swann, closing the ledger with the deliberation of a vicar closing a pulpit bible after the last lesson. 'Holroyd wants to see you.'

Bible had known it would come. The summons. Ward was standing by the hatch, still gripping Malcolm's arm.

'Look after him, Bill,' said Bible.

'We'll be fine, sir. Won't we, son?' said Ward, guiding Malcolm towards the interview room.

Bible hoped Ward would be kind. He had once shared Ward's feelings towards homosexuals, but there had been a sad young man in Burma. Winterburn, from Cardiff. Bible had been worried for him. He'd seen the misery in his eyes. The other lads were beginning to notice, smirking at the boy's clumsiness as he unloaded ammunition from the crates, isolating him from their camaraderie. When he'd dropped a stupid, useless grenade with a loose pin his death was officially an accident but Bible was never sure; grenades were easy things to handle carelessly on purpose if you'd had enough.

Swann broke into his thoughts. 'The Chief was very insistent, sir.'

'Right, Jack. I'll go up now.'

The Chief Superintendent had a smoky office on the top floor just below the Town Hall clock. Bible knocked and walked in. Holroyd was on the telephone and wafted his cigarette hand towards Bible to tell him to stay outside. Smoke signals, then. Bible stepped back into the corridor. But he didn't let the door sneck click. A petty rebellion, thought Bible, but Holroyd probably wouldn't notice.

When he was called in again, Bible found Holroyd sitting back in his chair behind a large desk which reminded him of Miss Browning's desk at the infants' school. He thought of the clutter on his own work surface. He hoped he'd never be tempted to boost himself with a big desk.

'Don't come in like that again, Jim,' said Holroyd, lighting another Capstan, 'and explain to me why you went after our pansy in the park when you have a big fucking murder enquiry on your hands.'

Holroyd's brusqueness was designed to shock, but Bible had learned how to stand his ground in the army.

'I didn't go to see Malcolm Granger, sir.'

'Is he a suspect?'

'No evidence to connect him.'

'So what the hell were you doing there?'

'I believed a young woman was in danger, sir. I was looking for her.'

Holroyd picked up a note from his desk and dangled it by one corner as if it were something nasty he'd found in his dinner. He blew a plume of smoke into the air. 'Is that what this request for a WPC is about?'

'Yes sir.'

'Is your young woman in immediate danger?'

'It's hard to say, sir.'

'It's hard to say,' mused Holroyd placing his cigarette into an overflowing glass ashtray and putting the tips of his fingers together. 'Is it hard to say whether a young tearaway called Donald Holmes has been murdered outside his school, and that the *Yorkshire Post* is hot on our heels to find out what the hell we're going to do about it?'

'No, that's not hard to say, sir.' Bible had learned to stonewall his superior's sarcasm by taking it literally. 'And Donald Holmes wasn't a tearaway, sir. He was six.'

'That's a matter of opinion. His father has the spine of a glass of water and the morality to match. So what is happening about the not insignificant matter of a child murder on our patch?'

Holroyd picked up his cigarette to listen as Bible outlined his visit to the school that morning, the questioning he'd set up, and the sighting of the elderly man no one could remember seeing before. There was also the truck he was trying to follow up.

'So what's the issue with this young woman you went to see?'

'She thinks she's being followed, sir.'

'Thinks? Is there a crime here?'

'Not yet.'

'Are you trying to be clever, Bible?'

'No harm in trying sir.'

Bible could see Holroyd's face working as the Chief Superintendent decided whether to lose his temper. Finally he leaned forward and stubbed out his cigarette in the ashtray. 'We're not here to be fortune-tellers. Request for extra police cover denied.' Holroyd tore up the note and dropped it in his bin. 'And remember you've only got this case because the Chief Inspector's off sick. Ward's a good man, wouldn't you say?' he said, putting his elbows on the desk, interlocking his fingers and resting his chin on his hands. Bible wondered where this was going. 'About time he was an inspector.'

So that was it. A veiled threat to move Ward up and put an inspector more to his liking in his place.

Bible could see Holroyd in Ward. The same impatience. The same desire for things to be straightforward. But despite that, he liked Ward, and he didn't like Holroyd. Look for the light in people, his wife had once said. Looking at Holroyd now, he wanted to punch it out. He knew the Chief Superintendent thought he was soft, too soft for a policeman. But you needed some softness.

Holroyd rose from his seat and looked out over the blackened Victorian buildings of the city. In the distance mill chimneys rose like pencils sketching smoke trails in the sky. Shops at pavement level were topped by floors of offices with ornate stone work around the windows, the ledges trimmed with droppings where starlings roosted at night.

'Come and look out of this window with me, Jim.'

They looked down at men in flat caps and trilbies in various shades of mud, and women in a uniform of headscarves or felt hats.

'Were you brought up round here, lad?'

'Yes, sir.'

'Grand place, this city. Means success. Bit of a wrench to move somewhere else.' Holroyd probably thought he was being subtle, but the meaning was clear.

'Would you like me to apply for a transfer, sir?' said Bible, aware he'd been kept standing to remind him of his place.

'I hope you're not saying you don't like it here, Jim. I might find that a bit disloyal.'

'Will that be all, sir?' said Bible.

'For now. Make sure you keep me informed. And keep your eye on the main case.'

'Of course, sir.'

Holroyd picked his uniform cap from the hat stand behind his desk. 'I think I'd better have a look at this nancy boy you've brought in. I need a bit of exercise.'

'Ward's handling him, sir. It's a delicate matter.'

'Ward? Delicate? This is something I need to see,' said Holroyd with relish.

'I have reason to believe that Malcolm Granger can throw light on the danger the young woman is in.'

'And I have reason to believe he's in the frame for the murder of Donald Holmes.'

'What reason, sir?'

'Gut instinct, Jim. Gut instinct. It's got me a long way.'

Bible strode ahead to the interview room and looked through the small glass pane. He could hear Holroyd's steel heel reinforcements clicking their way down the corridor behind him. Malcolm had his head in his hands. Ward was sitting back relaxed, his hands in his trouser pockets, but whether he'd been bullying or sympathetic, Bible couldn't tell. He tapped on the glass. Ward looked up and shook his head - a signal to Bible not to enter at that moment.

Holroyd caught up, trying not to sound out of breath. 'Are you going in, then?'

'He wants us to stay out here, sir. He must be getting somewhere.'

'Who's the boss here?' said Holroyd scornfully, pushing open the door. 'Don't get up Ward.' Ward's anger at the interruption had frozen his face into something carved out of stone.

'Sorry, Bill,' said Bible, stepping into the room. Holroyd glared at him. Bible didn't care what he thought. He had a good working relationship with Ward, and he was damned if Holroyd was going to spoil it. The Chief Superintendent took a position by Ward's shoulder. 'So what are we going to do with our little friend here?'

'Mr Granger has been very helpful, sir,' said Ward. Malcolm kept his gaze fixed on the table in front of him.

'*Mister* Granger,' said Holroyd, emphasising the mister. 'You surprise me.' Holroyd leaned over Malcolm and stared at him closely as he spoke. 'You have told him we're looking for a very perverted murderer?'

Malcolm raised his head. 'Murder?' He looked aghast.

'That's another case, sir,' said Ward. 'We've been talking about photographs.'

Malcolm appealed to Ward. 'You said you'd have a word with someone about the park incident.'

Ward put out the palm of his hand in a calming gesture. 'Later.'

Holroyd turned and walked to the door. 'Sergeant

Ward, a word.' Ward rose from his seat. 'Stay there, Inspector.'

Bible heard them arguing in the corridor outside. Malcolm glanced at Bible and looked away, a picture of misery.

'Are you offering deals, Ward?'

'He's being very helpful, sir,' said Ward, sounding unruffled.

'Helpful? He's a pervert and we're looking for a child murderer. What more do you need? Make him talk.'

There was silence. Bible could imagine the impassive look on Ward's face. The man could be stubbornly unhelpful when he wanted to be. Eventually he heard Ward again.

'Anything else, sir?'

'Look, Bill...' Holroyd said, but then his voice dropped to a murmur Bible could not make out.

Left in the silence of the room, and leaning against the heavy metal radiator, Bible resisted the temptation to smile at the young man at the table; it wouldn't do to imply they were friends or to put him too much at his ease. It was a relief when Holroyd opened the door irritably and snarled, 'Just get me a result, that's all. The public wants to see someone arrested.' Holroyd turned on his heel and walked away, coughing as he went down the corridor. Bible joined Ward outside the interview room.

'Does Holroyd want me to arrest that poor blighter for murder?' said Ward.

'I think he does, Bill.'

'I don't think he's after Carol. Needs her as a friend, more like.'

'So you believe his story? Just happened to be passing the chemist's?'

'I felt sorry for him, sir,' said Ward. 'He makes me squirm, but I felt sorry for him. I think he picked up the photographs because he's desperate to be liked.'

'Then you were right to be kind, Bill,' said Bible, pushing open the interview door.

Bible sat down opposite Malcolm. Ward remained standing.

'Has my colleague explained the position you're in?'

'Yes.' Malcolm sat stiffly upright, his hands out of sight below the level of the table.

'We're not going to make things more difficult than they need be, and we're grateful for your help.' Bible hoped Ward had not gone any further. It was best to imply they could help him rather than promise to get him off the hook.

Ward passed Bible his notebook, and pointed to an entry.

'You say a young man left the photographs at the chemist's?' said Bible.

Malcolm nodded.

'But you didn't see him?'

'It's what the chemist said.'

'You'll be pleased to know Sergeant Ward believes you.' Malcolm did not look pleased. He didn't look anything except scared. 'But my problem is, accepting the coincidence of your being at this shop at such convenient times.'

Malcolm stared down at the table.

Bible continued. 'Miss Carlton said you got the

letter she received from the same shop when an old man was asking for her.'

'It's only round the corner. I'm always walking past it.'

'There seem to be a lot of people with an interest in this young lady.'

'He didn't ask for Carol,' began Malcolm. His voice was quiet. Not much more than a whisper. 'He asked for someone with a West Country accent.'

'And you were there, and saw this man?'

Malcolm nodded.

'And his accent. Was he from the West Country?'

Malcolm shook his head. 'He was from round here.'

'Can you describe him?'

'Quite old. Neatly dressed. Looked after himself. Scarf. Fawn raincoat I think.'

'Hat?'

'No. Shiny hair. Like he combed it a lot. Put something on it.'

Bible shut Ward's notebook and passed it back to him. 'I think we can let you go now, Mr Granger.'

Bible swung the Wolseley into Ashdale Avenue towards the school. He usually let Ward drive but this time he wanted to take the wheel. He loved sighting along the ridge of the bonnet towards the silver-winged W on top of the radiator and watching it move against the background. It reminded him of target practice in the army. He'd enjoyed that, though he'd never liked firing his rifle for real, something he'd only done twice. And he'd never shot a gun whilst in the force, though he'd carried one a couple of times.

'Do you think this will amount to anything, sir?' said Ward. It was the first thing he'd said since leaving the station.

'I hope so,' said Bible. 'But it stops us getting to that chemist's shop.'

A call had come in that a constable doing the door-to-door had found someone living near the school who'd seen a truck, though this witness had called it a van. It tallied with what Mrs Harsnet had said. But van or truck? Perhaps all vans looked the same to Mrs Harsnet. There was a chance it could lead to something, but they needed a description.

'What are you thinking, Bill?' said Bible.

'I want us to get the right man, sir.'

The school was still out of sight round a kink in the road. Ward spoke again. 'Did Holroyd really want us to finger that poor little sod I was interviewing?'

'He felt he'd made a fool of himself.'

'I believed Malcolm Granger.'

Bible glanced towards Ward, wondering if he was going to reveal what Holroyd had said to him in the corridor.

'I didn't want to believe him,' continued Ward. 'I like things simple. Villains and perverts on one side, us on the other.'

'So where would you put Holroyd?'

'I wouldn't like to say, sir. He won't like it if we make Higham lose his arrest report on the poor lad.'

As they rounded the bend and had a clear view of the school, Bible heard shouting and saw mothers pulling children away from a crowd around the school gates. The gathering kept pulsing outwards, reacting to the disturbance in the centre.

'Looks like a fight, Bill.'

Bible put his foot down and the car bounced over the stones of the dirt road in front of the school. Ward had the door open before the car had come to a halt and ran to where a skinny man had pinned a youth to the ground and was hitting him in the face. The sergeant caught the older man's flailing right arm, twisted it up his back, and levered him off the youth. A few steps behind, Bible saw that the youth was his son, and the older man was Holmes.

'You can see what he did to me,' yelled Ricky through the blood on his face. 'Are you going to get him, Dad?' Ricky jumped up. Bible wheeled towards Holmes who was struggling helplessly in Ward's grip. 'That Ted killed my son.' As Bible clenched his fist and wondered what madness this was about, a jolt in the back sent him lurching towards Holmes, but Bible regained his footing, span round, and just managed to stop himself backhanding his son across the cheek. Standing between both assailants, pointing at each of them, Bible heard his voice come out in a fierce growl.

'You two, stay back.'

'Let me get this one in the car, sir,' said Ward dragging Holmes towards the black Wolseley. But Bible had to block Ricky as the boy rushed forward, aiming wild haymakers at the rag-and-bone man, and driving Bible backwards. With anyone else, Bible could have had him on the ground with a knee in his back, but not his son. Ward let go of Holmes and there was a glint of silver as the sergeant clipped a handcuff around one of Ricky's flailing wrists, twisted it round his back, grabbed Ricky's other arm and ratcheted the second cuff shut.

'He set about me, Dad,' screamed the boy through angry tears. 'What are you going to do about him?'

Bible saw the car was empty.

'I let Holmes scarper, sir,' said Bill,

'Let's go home, son,' said Bible, pushing Ricky towards the car and forcing him into the back seat. Bible sat with him. He wanted to speak to Ward but couldn't, and thumped the back of the driver's seat instead, splitting the leather.

ELEVEN

Bible didn't release Ricky until he'd opened the door of the neat semi he was proud to call home. The boy was furious, tearful – Bible didn't know what his son was capable of in this state. Shirley came from the kitchen as they entered, ready to smile, but Bible registered the dismay on her face as she saw the handcuffs dangling at his side.

'What's happened?' said Shirley.

'He got in some trouble,' said Bible, 'outside the school.'

Ricky pushed her out of the way. The shove sent her against the wall and dislodged a watercolour of Malham Cove. It was one Shirley had painted and which Bible had framed for her.

'Ricky!' Bible shouted after him, but Ricky continued up the stairs. 'We're not having that,' said Bible, and bounded up after him.

'Jim, leave him,' pleaded Shirley.

'He can't get away with it,' said Bible, leaping up the last three steps on to the landing.

'Stop it,' said Shirley. 'Leave him alone.'

Bible looked down at her from the top of the landing. A band of light shining through the oval window in their front door caught her face. Did she feel sorry for Ricky? It was easier dealing with a hardened criminal. He was never angry when dealing with villains, but his son could make anger rise to his throat in an instant.

'Are you all right, love?' he said, wanting quick reassurance so he could get to Ricky.

Shirley looked near to tears. 'No, I'm not all right. Not when you're both like this.' She wiped her face. 'You're making it worse.'

So he was being blamed? Because Ricky had a fight? Shirley might feel sorry for him, but for once, she was wrong. 'He needs sorting out,' he said, and turned to force open Ricky's door.

He was halted by his daughter coming out of her bedroom, holding Baby One-Eye.

'Go back to bed, poppet,' said Bible automatically.

'I wasn't in bed, Daddy. It's early.' Of course. It was only just after four. Anger, confusion, were making him stupid.

'I'm just going to see Ricky,' he said.

'You were shouting.' He looked at his solemn daughter, her eyes wide like a bushbaby's. Was she scared? Or was she telling him off as well?

Shirley called from the hallway. 'Pauline, come down here, darling.'

Pauline scampered past Bible clutching her doll, and ran down the stairs where her mother's arms waited to scoop her up. Shirley clutched her daughter to her. Bible felt excluded. Powerless. He pushed open Ricky's door and found himself looking at a large photograph of Diana Dors in a low cut ball gown. Ricky was lying on his bed.

'That's disgusting,' said Bible, nodding his head towards the pin-up. He'd seen it before and wondered if he should do anything about it. 'Showing everything she's got.'

'It hasn't stopped *you* looking,' sneered Ricky. Bible stepped in towards him ready to wrench him off the bed. Ricky flinched, raising his hands to his face. Bible leaned over the boy on the bed, supporting himself with a hand either side of his son. He vaguely registered the doorbell ring downstairs.

'If you ever touch your mother again...'

Shirley called from downstairs. 'Jim, you'd better come down.'

Bible angrily pushed himself from the bed. 'Stay there,' he said. 'I haven't finished with you.'

In the hallway Pauline was clinging to her mother's neck, and Shirley was holding the door half-open with her free hand. A youth in drape jacket and beetle crushers stood on the step. As Bible advanced down the stairs towards him, the boy smiled.

'Hello mate. Ricky in?'

Pauline pointed towards the door. 'He took my scones, Daddy.'

Bible strode to the door, grabbed the youth's face with his right hand, pulled him into the house with his left, and pinned him against the wall of the entry hall. The boy tried to steady himself by putting out his hands behind him, one of them pressing against the mirror on the hall stand, leaving cloudy marks that quickly began to fade.

'Jim. Jim. Stop it!'

Bible could hear Shirley shouting at him, Pauline crying, but still he squeezed the face. The boy tried to speak through his squashed mouth. Something about the police. He was saying he'd call the police. Bible looked at the face he was holding. He recognised it. The boy from the milk bar. He was younger than he'd seemed at first. If Pauline's story about scones was correct, he was still at secondary school, so no more than fifteen. But a tough guy. A leader. Stronger than Ricky. Bible let go. Cannonball was a villain and he knew how to deal with villains. No confusion there.

'Ricky isn't playing out today,' said Bible.

Cannonball levered himself off the wall and flexed his shoulders to make his jacket sit right. He pulled a comb from his pocket and adjusted his hair.

'You're mad, you.'

'Get out,' said Bible.

Cannonball sauntered towards the door, and looked back towards Pauline. 'Nice scones, love.'

Bible grabbed the youth by the arm and twisted the door handle. 'Out.'

'Get your hands off of me.'

Bible pushed him out and slammed the door shut. There was a thump as something hit it, thrown from the outside. He pulled open the door again. A clod of earth had exploded on the doorstep and Cannonball was running down the street. Bible closed the door quietly, clicked the Yale and turned to look at Shirley but couldn't tell what she was thinking. Pauline had her face buried in her mother's shoulder. 'Has he gone, Daddy?' she said.

'Yes, he's gone.'

Bible felt he'd made a mess of it. Knew he'd made a mess. And he'd wanted to do everything well. Wanted to be good. Shirley was a good woman. And she'd been good with Ricky. He'd been six when the

125

war ended. The same age as Pauline now. They'd played football with him. Helped him fiddle with construction kits at the kitchen table in their first rented house together. Taken him to the seaside. Shirley had even knitted him some swimming trunks. An only child with a mum and dad again for a few years until Pauline had come along.

Bible went to Shirley and his daughter. 'I'm sorry, Pauline. Daddy didn't mean to shout.'

He wanted his wife to look at him, but she kept her face down and turned into Pauline's little body.

'Go on, explain. What were you doing, handcuffing your own son?'

'That's not what I was going to say.' Shirley took Pauline into the kitchen, holding her on one arm as she reached for the frying pan. Bible followed.

'There was a fight,' he said. 'Here, let me take Pauline.' His daughter clambered from her mother's arms to Bible's like a monkey swinging from one tree to the next. Bible was relieved that Pauline had come to him.

'Will an omelette do?' said Shirley. 'I haven't much appetite.'

'Neither have I,' said Bible.

'I'm starving,' said Pauline in a muffled voice as she clung to Bible.

'How about a banana to keep you going,' said Bible, tickling her cheek with his index finger. The little girl nodded. Shirley picked a banana from the fruit and vegetable rack, peeled it part way down, and gave it to Pauline.

'What was he doing at the school anyway? ' said Shirley.

'Why do you say that?'

Shirley rummaged in the utensil drawer. 'People say Teddy Boys are always hanging around the school.'

'Which people?'

There was a clatter down the stairs. Ricky. He looked at them from the bottom of the banister.

'How cosy,' he said.

Bible ignored his scorn. 'Hey, Ricky,' he said, putting Pauline on her feet. 'Can we talk about what's going on?'

Shirley stooped to Pauline's level. 'Do you want to go to the shops with me?' The little girl nodded. 'Lolly,' she said. Shirley led her into the hallway to get Pauline's coat, ignoring Ricky's glare.

'That's right, run away.'

'You pushed me, Ricky,' said Shirley.

Ricky pointed at his father. 'You've always been on her side.'

'Whose side is that, Ricky?' said Bible.

'Her side.' Ricky swung his arm round and pointed at Shirley, his finger only a few inches from her face. Bible lunged forward a step, then stopped himself.

'We're both on your side, Ricky,' said Shirley calmly.

His pointing finger was trembling. 'You've never liked me.'

'You're not going to behave like this, Ricky,' said Bible, gently pushing down his son's arm.

'You were a lovely little boy, Ricky,' said Shirley. 'We used to play together. Don't you remember?'

'It's always you three,' said Ricky. He seemed about to cry. Bible looked at his son. He was seventeen but looked young. Cannonball had looked younger, but acted older, tougher. 'Why did he put me in handcuffs? I went to collect my little sister, and he put me in handcuffs.'

'To protect you from yourself,' said Bible, but realised he'd assumed his son had been up to no good when Ricky had simply gone to collect his little sister, not knowing she'd been kept off school. Look for the good in people, his first wife used to say. He hadn't even looked for the light in his own son. 'You didn't say that's why you were there.'

'You didn't ask.'

Bible sighed. 'Mum kept Pauline off school today. You'd have known if you hadn't disappeared last night.'

'So you arrested me because I got attacked by a maniac.' Bible could see his son working himself up again. He gripped the boy's arms in what he hoped was a gesture of reassurance.

'We took him away. He'll be questioned.'

Ricky pushed him off. 'But you're not going to do anything, are you? Just because he lost his kid.'

'Ricky...'

'You care more for that dead kid than you do for me.'

'Ricky, stop it.' Bible felt his anger rising again but held it down.

'That's right, hit me,' said Ricky. He turned to the door.

'Let's talk about it, Ricky,' said Bible.

'To you?' said Ricky. He opened the door, and stepped out. 'You'll be sorry when I'm dead at eighteen,' he shouted, and slammed it shut. Bible felt relieved the boy had gone. Then helpless.

'Why dead?' said Shirley.

'National Service looms,' said Bible simply. 'He was never a brave boy.'

'Do you believe him? About collecting Pauline?'

Shirley seemed hard now. Pauline was in her mother's arms again and Bible couldn't tell whether his daughter was scared, or simply asleep. He felt he ought to know.

'I believed him,' said Bible. 'Don't you?'

'He's never done it before.'

'Perhaps he was worried about her.'

'So why wouldn't he assume I'd get her?' Shirley lowered Pauline to the floor. 'Go and play in your bedroom, love. I need to do tea.'

'You said you'd get me a lolly.'

'Too late for the shops now.'

'I want to go to Grandad's to play again,' said the little girl grumpily.

Bible waited until his daughter had gone up the stairs. 'Again? What's been going on, Shirley?'

Shirley held his gaze. 'I left her with Mum and Dad whilst I went to see Donald's mother.'

'You went to see Holmes?'

'He wasn't in. I talked to his wife.'

'For God's sake, Shirley.' They stared at each other, Shirley defiant, Bible at a loss. They were supposed to be partners, friends, complementary. 'Why?'

'When is she getting any sympathy? You're all running round trying to catch the murderer and she's on her own.'

'We left a policewoman with her.'

'She doesn't like the police. Mrs Holmes says there's always Teds hanging around the school smoking when the little ones come out.'

'She never goes near the school.'

'I'm going up to see Pauline,' said Shirley and passed him to go up the stairs. At the top she turned to look down at him. 'I've got a group of mothers to watch outside the school tomorrow. And you've got banana on your suit.' If she was trying to break the ice, it didn't work; he was too angry to speak.

The telephone rang. He turned to pick up the heavy black receiver. The plaited cord was twisted and scrunched. Shirley did that when she was on the phone and anxious. 'Bible,' he said. It was Ward. Work. A relief.

'I called in to see that chemist's Granger claimed he got the photos from,' said Ward. 'Said it was a Ted had left the film for developing. So I got thinking about that character we found in the milk bar the other day. You know. Johnny Fraser. Called himself Cannonball. The one we ticked off, and then let go.'

'And my son. He was there.'

There was a pause. 'It wouldn't be him, sir. With all due respect he's as soft as putty.'

'You don't know, Bill.'

'Believe me sir, it won't be him. But that Fraser, he's a vicious article. The thing is, we've picked up some fingerprints. The owner of the chemist's hadn't had much in for processing – he does his own in the back - so he still had the spool the film came on, and the Kodak box it was in. Let's drag Fraser in and take his prints. We might get a match.'

Bible looked towards the hall mirror Cannonball

had pressed his hand against. 'You might not have to, Bill. Send a car for me in fifteen minutes.'

Shirley had disappeared into Pauline's bedroom. He could just hear her talking softly to his daughter. He slipped down the hall into the kitchen, took a tin of cocoa powder from the cupboard, and quietly slid open another couple of drawers until he found Shirley's pastry brush. Its bristles were stiffer than he wanted, but they would have to do. He went back to the hall stand, pulled open the drawer under the mirror and removed a roll of sellotape and an unused postcard of Ilkley Moor. He tilted the mirror backwards, prised the lid off the cocoa tin and sprinkled the brown powder over the spot where Cannonball had steadied himself against the mirror. He delicately dusted off the surplus with the pastry brush, peeled back a short strip of sellotape, and bit it off with his teeth. It stuck to his fingers and folded back on itself. Useless. Stop rushing, thought Bible. He peeled back another strip and bit that off more carefully, taking his time. He placed the tape over the fingerprints, peeled it off, and stuck it to the blank side of the postcard. The prints showed through clearly, as he had hoped. He placed the card between the leaves of his notebook, and put it in his inside pocket.

He could still hear Shirley's murmur upstairs. He quietly put the cocoa tin back in the kitchen with the pastry brush. Then he checked himself. He didn't like creeping about, but he didn't want Shirley to know what he was doing. This was home to her, not a crime scene. He walked up the stairs making sure his footsteps made a sound so she would hear. But it felt false, and he wanted to be honest.

He knocked on Pauline's door. 'Shirley, I'm going into the station.'

There was no answer. Ricky had left his bedroom door open. A small glass tumbler lay on the floor. He took a step in, picked it up and wrapped it in his handkerchief. He held it behind his back as Pauline's bedroom door opened quietly and Shirley stepped out. 'She's dropped off,' she said. As she turned to soften the click of the door as it closed, Bible slid the tumbler into a pocket of his suit.

'Good,' said Bible. 'Good.'

'I think it's with all the shouting. I'll wake her up for something to eat soon.' Shirley moved in close to him and straightened the knot on his tie. 'You'd better go and do your job, Inspector Bible.'

'We need you here, Shirley, Pauline and me. You don't need to work. And you don't need to get involved in this.'

Shirley pulled away. 'Not now. Let's not argue now.'

'We'll take Pauline to the park on Sunday.'

'I need to go and see someone Sunday morning.'

'Who?'

She looked at him, and pulled her hands away. 'I told you.'

'Your vigilante group.'

'My peace group, actually.'

'What about Pauline?'

'I'll take her with me, unless you're at home.'

'I'll be here.'

'Then you can take her to the park and I'll meet you there.'

Pauline called for her mum from her bedroom.

'If you can,' said Shirley as she turned to go back up the stairs.

Bible left the house without telling her about the tumbler in his pocket. He didn't want to fuel the rumours of Teddy Boy involvement in the death of Donald. Not after Cannonball's visit and with Ricky on the loose and full of anger.

TWELVE

'Definitely a match,' said Ward. 'Fraser's prints are all over them.'

Bible was sitting at his desk in the shabby office. Images of the fingerprints taken from the empty film spool and its original Kodak box lay in front of him. He levered the arms of the Terry lamp into place so it hung over the desk like a mechanical pterodactyl. He compared the prints with those he'd taken from home – Cannonball's from the mirror and Ricky's from the tumbler. Both suspects, he thought bitterly. As a policeman, you never wanted to see fingerprints of people in your family.

'No sign of your lad's,' said Ward.

That was a relief. Holroyd would have him off the case if he knew of the family connection. 'Bring Fraser in,' said Bible, standing up. He had to work at calling the boy Fraser. He thought of him as Cannonball, a sign that Ricky's involvement made Bible too close to the case. 'See if that chemist can identify him.'

'I think he'll cough, sir. He's not a hardened criminal,' said Ward.

Bible remembered the face of the boy he'd pinned against the wall. Not a hardened criminal yet, maybe. But there was something. Something that made him wary. Cannonball was a boy who could not easily be bullied. A boy who didn't care about himself in some way. A boy used to his father Freddie in gaol and his mother on the game to make ends meet.

Bible stood up. 'Where shall we find him?'

'Higham's out looking now, sir. He'll get his hands on him.'

'You have a lot of faith in Higham, Bill.'

'He's all right when he's after villains. Doesn't take any nonsense.'

'Perhaps we should send him to get my son,' said Bible. Ward looked unsure. 'You don't seem too certain, Bill.'

'We don't need to bring your son in, sir. His prints aren't there.'

'But he knows Fraser.'

'Let's leave it for now, sir. We'll know where to find him if we need him.'

*

Bible studied Cannonball through the glass in the door of the interview room. He looked at home, lounging back on his chair, thumbs in trouser pockets and his long drape jacket hanging down carelessly to the floor. He was grinning at Higham, as if nothing could be as silly as whatever Higham had just said.

'Oh dear, oh dear, sir,' said Ward standing next to him. 'It looks bad for young Fraser. Higham doesn't like being laughed at.' Bible thought Higham looked surprisingly relaxed at being laughed at, not angry at all.

'Do you want me to take him sir? Seeing as he knows your son?'

'I'll do it,' said Bible. 'See if I can wipe that smile

off his face. But only with words, Bill. Only words.'

Bible opened the door and Ward followed.

'Oh it's the doting dad,' said Cannonball. 'How's Ricky these days?'

Higham stood up respectfully. 'Bit of a joker, sir, this one,' said Higham, standing to one side. With his blond hair and crew cut he looked like an American GI.

The three policemen looked down at Cannonball.

'Take a seat,' said Cannonball. 'Be my guest.'

'All right, Fraser,' said Ward. 'Cut the funnies.'

Fraser. His dad Freddie was known to them – a dealer in scrap metal, he'd come into the frame when Bible had started as a policeman on the beat and a few garden fences had gone missing. But it couldn't just be Johnny 'Cannonball' Fraser they were after for tormenting Carol. The lad was a thug, not a chess grandmaster.

'So why am I here?' said the young Teddy Boy. 'Because of that fun in The Manhattan?'

'Could be,' said Bible. 'The owner says you broke one of his chairs.'

'We never. We were only messing about. You've no proof.'

'His word against yours,' said Bible. 'So how did your fingerprints end up on an old film spool?'

'I don't know what you're talking about.'

*

She was woken by sunlight coming through the little window over Malcolm's sink. After Bible and Ward had left the day before, Carol had stayed in Malcolm's room, frozen inside, unable to move. She had been aware of him saying things - comforting things, helpful things - but had felt powerless to answer and had slept in her clothes in Malcolm's bed. He had slept on the floor, pulling cushions off the two easy chairs to provide padding.

Malcolm had put the cushions back and was sitting reading a book. She wondered what it was; she'd not thought of him as a reader before. He looked at her and smiled when she stirred in the bed. She smiled back.

'Cup of tea?' he said.

'Please.' It was probably the first time she'd spoken since the policemen had left. Malcolm placed a bookmark carefully between the pages, put the book on his chair and went to the sink. A noisy whoosh echoed in the kettle as water hit metal.

'Do you want toast?' said Malcolm, lighting the gas ring.'

She was ravenous. She hadn't eaten since noon the day before. 'Yes, that would be nice.'

'I rang the bank. Told your boss you had a fever.'

'Thank you.'

She pushed back the sheets, lifted her legs out of bed and stood up. Malcolm was busily sawing bread. She felt dirty, but as soon as she thought of going down to her own room to get washed, the fear overcame her and she sat down on the bed again. The sun was glinting on the taps. This would be a lovely Sunday morning for people who could enjoy it. She picked up Malcolm's book from his chair: *The Catcher in the Rye*. She had never heard of it, but then she hadn't heard of many books. 'What are you reading?' It seemed like a normal question. A safe question. Any small talk to squash back the terror she felt inside.

'Oh,' Malcolm looked at her, dangling two slices of newly cut bread he was about to put on the grill. He seemed embarrassed. 'It's nothing. Just a story. American. Some people think it's a bit too modern.' He pulled out the grill tray from his miniature cooker and carefully placed the slices of bread on it. 'Young people like it. The main character's a bit confused.'

She tried to concentrate on what he was saying, but she was focused on her fear. She could hear Malcolm talking, saying something about beatniks and Americans, but it made no sense. She was aware of him working near the sink. Suddenly, a couple of slices of toast appeared. Malcolm was standing in front of her holding a plate.

'I found a bit of marmalade after all.'

She looked at him, puzzled.

'You said you wanted marmalade,' said Malcolm.

Had she said that? Perhaps she had. She took the plate, lifted a slice of toast and took a bite from one of the corners. 'The kittens,' she said suddenly. 'The kittens need feeding.'

'I'll go down for you,' he said. 'Give you a chance to get washed.'

She locked the door behind him when he'd gone. Malcolm had left a kitchen knife on the drainer with the plates from the toast. She moved them to the side and washed at the kitchen sink with a scrap of soap she found behind the taps. She needed new underwear but had been too embarrassed to ask Malcolm to search among her drawers, and realised she'd have to go down to her room herself. But as she thought of the little room that had once felt like a safe haven, she knew she could not stay there. There were other rooms, other places. She'd make herself go out, if Malcolm would go with her, and get a local paper for the 'rooms to let' column. She could hide her face somehow. 'Make yourself do it,' she said aloud, and then looked round the empty room, embarrassed. But the decision was made. Carol buttoned up her blouse and took a deep breath, but before she left the room, she picked up the knife from the drainer and put it in her handbag.

*

Logan fumbled with the camera in a dark corner of the boathouse. He clicked open the back to ease out the yellow roll of film, taping the end down to keep out the light. He wasn't proud of what he'd done. He wasn't ashamed either. The boy was crying, slumped in his chair.

'Don't worry son. It won't be forever. This is your way of helping me.'

A boat with an outboard motor ripped up the river. A strip of light glistened on the water under the riverside door as the outboard's wash reached the damp prison. Small waves licked against Logan's dinghy which bobbed in the water. He sat on an upturned orange box and waited. The boy whimpered. A few minutes later, the doors rattled and Robbo appeared. A sliver of light lanced across the dampness before Logan's man dragged the door shut.

'You're late,' said Logan, without looking at him. 'I've got a job for you.'

'You could just drop him in the river,' said Robbo from the gloom.

'Not that sort of job,' said Logan. 'I've never needed to murder.' Logan rose and walked across the damp boards. He wished he didn't have to trust other people. But he wanted the photos ready, a final weapon to flush her out and remind her of his power.

He held out the narrow spool of film. 'Get this to your cocky little friend in Yorkshire. Tell him not to do anything with it until he hears the word. Make sure.'

'You know me, Mr Logan. Gospel to the core.'

'I'll make her come back to me.' Logan looked at the boy slumped in the chair he was tied to. 'He's somebody's son,' said Logan. 'I won't hurt him more than necessary.'

'Like you said, you're not a murderer, Mr Logan.'

Robbo pushed open the door. Logan caught Robbo's arm as he stepped into the daylight.

'What I said was I've never *needed* to murder.'

THIRTEEN

'I feel I'm with a film star,' said Malcolm as they got off the bus by the canal below Hilltop Village.

'That's not why I'm wearing them,' said Carol. She had worried that sunglasses would look odd in November, but she felt hidden in them, and at least it was sunny. She pulled her headscarf forward a little, hoping it shielded her face.

'You look amazing,' said Malcolm.

'I don't want to look anything,' said Carol. 'I don't want to be seen at all.'

She was glad Malcolm had come to view the room with her, but wished he were not in such a buoyant mood. Helping her seemed to have taken his mind off his own problems.

Quarry Cottages were a row of small well-kept terraces overlooking a field which sloped down to the canal side. They shone prettily in the Sunday sun, though at the back they were dominated by a rising swell of moorland. A path tracked uphill through the dying bracken, though it appeared rarely used. Carol looked at her watch. 'It's nearly twelve. Shall we go?'

'I'll stay here,' said Malcolm, stepping on to some rough grass where a telephone kiosk with a heavily thumbed directory stood against the gable end of the first cottage.

'Should I phone and tell her I'm here?'

'Go on. You said twelve.'

Carol felt abandoned. 'I hoped you'd come with me.'

'The landlady might think it was odd,' said Malcolm. 'People can tell there's something wrong with me.' His buoyancy had gone. 'Borrow your sunglasses?' he joked limply.

'Poor Malcolm,' said Carol. She touched his arm reassuringly. 'There's nothing wrong with you.'

He kicked at some loose stones by his feet. 'They're offering me a cure. The police. They're saying I won't have to go to court if I have the cure.'

Carol didn't know what to say. He looked so sorry for himself again. And perhaps he did need a cure. She'd never met anybody with his problem before.

'There's nothing you can do,' he said. 'You'd better get going.'

'Will you wait for me?'

'You're strong enough to do it on your own.'

She hoped he was right. She'd miss Malcolm when she moved, but running away was becoming a habit and you gained more than you lost. As she walked down the lane, she took off her sunglasses.

The newly painted door of the cottage opened when she knocked. A tough-looking, powerful woman in her late fifties stood dwarfing the little hallway, but she smiled at Carol. 'Welcome to Number 12. You found it all right.'

'The bus comes quite near,' said Carol.

The woman held out a hand. 'I'm Miss Browning. Who's that dodging around?'

Carol was aware of her new landlady looking over her shoulder. She wished Malcolm would stay out of sight and not look so shifty.

'It looks like one of those Teddy Boys. They're everywhere now.'

So not Malcolm. Carol jerked her head round but could see no one.

'Oh well, times change,' said Miss Browning. 'You'd better come in.'

The small living room was as Carol had imagined it. A settee and easy chair were covered in a pretty flowered print, pink on white. The polished oak bookshelves and round dining table were in darker tones. A window with small leaded panes overlooked a rose bed at the front and the lane she'd just walked up. A smaller window at the rear looked out on to a garden which, although neat, looked bleak, the lawn strewn with damp leaves, the shrubs twiggy and grey. The sun didn't reach the back of the cottage, though it caught the top of the rising moor.

Miss Browning followed her gaze. 'High Gill Moor,' she said. 'It's quiet out here since they stopped the blasting. There's a quarry half a mile away. But do sit down.'

Carol looked round at the choice of furniture.

'Anywhere will do. I usually sit there.' Miss Browning flung an arm at a tall hoop-backed wooden chair by the dining table. 'I don't like the feeling of sinking down. But you may sink, my dear.'

Carol chose the settee, sinking down as she'd been bidden. Miss Browning disappeared and reappeared rattling a tea trolley.

'It's nice to have company again,' said Miss Browning. 'Cake?' She sat on the tall chair and pulled the trolley towards her.

Carol demurred. 'Have you had lodgers before?'

Miss Browning concentrated on pouring tea before she answered. 'I had a companion, Ivy. She died a couple of years ago. Very sad. But lodgers? No. This is a new venture for me. Milk and sugar?'

'Just milk.' It was the third cup of tea Carol had had made for her in two days. At the police station, Malcolm's bedsit, and now here. They were the first cups of tea she'd had made for her in her life.

'Sometimes oneself isn't enough, is it? And then things happen to make you re-assess.' She paused.

'It's a very nice cottage,' said Carol.

Miss Browning resumed her brisk manner and passed a cup and saucer to Carol. 'Tell me something about yourself.'

Carol had rehearsed her answer. 'I work at a bank.' She hoped her place of work implied she was from a respectable background. 'I came up here when my parents died. Fresh start.'

It was not the absolute truth, but it felt like the truth, certainly a truth she preferred.

Miss Browning smiled. 'Let's see how we get on, shall we?

*

Bible looked down at the water, holding Pauline's hand, watching a couple of sticklebacks hang still below the surface and then twitch out of sight. A few feet away, two boys in short trousers knelt on the stone blocks that curved round the lake, dipping their fishing nets into the water. At their side stood a jam jar with a string handle knotted round the rim. They'd already caught a couple of tiddlers.

Bible loved the cold, metallic smell of water. It reminded him of fishing as a child.

'How deep is it, Daddy?'

The water surface reflected the clouds and trees, the reflections broken by sunlight catching the edges of tiny waves.

'I can't see the bottom,' said the little girl.

'It's not very deep,' said Bible. 'If you look carefully you can see a branch stuck in the mud.'

He could have said it was about eighteen inches deep where they were standing, but he knew she liked the mystery of not knowing.

'Would I drown?' she said.

'No, I'd save you,' said Bible. 'Anyway, you can nearly swim, can't you?'

Bible had been taking her, when he could, to the swimming baths in Chapel Heights. He wondered if he'd been too reassuring. 'But you've always got to be careful round water,' he added. Across the other side of the pond a youth in a drape jacket was coming down the slope from the bowling green and children's playground. Bible hoped he hadn't bullied any little ones off the swings. He tensed a bit when he realised it was Johnny Fraser. Cannonball.

'Pauline! Jim!' Shirley was calling and waving as she came towards them. 'I've got some bread here.' She was with two women he knew as mothers of children Pauline's age, but there was another he hadn't seen before, a woman in her sixties with close-cropped white hair.

'Great, let's have it.' Bible turned and walked towards her, holding out his hand for the paper bag of crusts Shirley had brought.

'You must be very proud of your wife,' said the older woman, smiling. She was clutching a sheaf of papers.

'Of course,' said Bible, taking the bag and returning to his daughter. 'Come on, Pauline,' he said, 'let's feed the ducks.'

Pauline took the bag, shoved her fist in and threw a cloud of crumbs into the water. A group of excited mallards came quacking over.

'Not all at once,' said Bible. 'A few at a time.'

He heard Shirley say goodbye to her friends before she came to stand beside him.

'You were very rude to Sylvia just now.'

'I don't know what you're getting into, Shirley, but I suspect I wouldn't like it.'

Pauline was digging into the bread bag again.

'We should have brought more,' said Shirley.

Across the pond the rowing boat hire was closed, the boats safely upside down on the island for winter. Beyond that was the spire of the war memorial on the slope down from the bowling greens. They wouldn't be playing now. Probably too late in the year.

'She was going to ask you to sign our petition, calling for an end to testing,'

'No thanks, 'said Bible, staring towards the bowling greens. In season or not, it was still where some of the old men of Chapel Heights liked to sit and smoke a pipe. Old men. They were still looking for the man who'd been in the audience at the school.

'Why not?'

'I don't feel comfortable with it.'

'I don't feel comfortable with the H-bomb. What's Pauline going to think when she grows up if there's an H-bomb war and she knows you supported it?'

'I don't support it. It's just with my job...'

'What's your job got to do with it?'

'I've got to be careful what I say. Politics.'

'You're just being difficult.'

'Watch Pauline for a bit, will you? I want to wander up to the bowls.' Bible could picture him clearly– a neat man, almost dapper, in a fawn coat with a green plaid scarf tightly muffled round his neck.

As Bible walked up the slope to the two bowling greens, he was surprised to hear the clack of wood on wood. So they were still playing. When he got there he realised it wasn't an out of season match, but a group of pensioners having a late year knock-up, enjoying the unexpectedly mild weather. A few others sat on the benches. They were not the most comfortable benches – two thick planks of wood for your bottom, another two to support your back, and thick knobbly metal arms at each end. Bible's memory of them when he stopped to watch bowls as a child was that they were usually wet, and soaked the seat of your short trousers.

A couple of the old men nodded at him as he went past. They looked wary; probably knew he was a policeman, though he tried to keep a low profile. Some would have known him as a child; some were even fathers of old school friends of his. None of them had that sleek look he remembered from the elderly man in the school audience.

Approaching the bowling hut, Bible heard voices. He looked in. The hut was dingy and smelt of damp wood. Three men were playing cards. He scanned them quickly. No, the man he was looking for wasn't there, but there was one he recognised, a short stocky man in a thick donkey jacket. Turner, the reservoir keeper.

'Chief Inspector Bible,' said Turner, hailing him like an old familiar. A couple of overcoats were hanging on hooks behind him, but they were all too shabby for the man Bible was looking for.

'Plain Inspector, I'm afraid.'

'Fancy a hand of solo? Albert here'll step aside.' One of the men looked up. Resentfully? Bible couldn't tell.

'No thanks,' said Bible. 'My family's with me. Off duty.'

'You lot are never off duty.' Bible scanned the faces. But apart from Turner, they weren't showing their faces.

The reservoir keeper slid a card across the table and took a trick. 'You after someone in particular?'

Bible wondered how much to give away. 'An old man. Quite smart.'

'Take your pick,' said Turner, gesturing to the men round the card table. They were dressed like gardeners.

'I saw a youngster in Teddy Boy get-up. Has he been round here?' One of the card players looked up, then quickly lowered his gaze.

'Doesn't sound like the sort of lad to play bowls,' said Turner. Albert and his companion studied their cards waiting for Bible to go.

'What about your friends?' said Bible. 'I saw him coming down from this direction.' Cannonball was someone Bible wanted to keep tabs on.

'Albert? Jed?'

The card players' mumbled denials were grunts rather than words, their head shakes minimal. Bible wondered what hold Turner had over them, that they were happy to let him hold court.

'They've been stuck in here with me.'

'They must enjoy your company,' said Bible, immediately regretting his sarcasm. He didn't want the chipper reservoir man to know how much he got on Bible's nerves.

He left the bowling greens and walked past the ice cream cabin shuttered up for winter.

'Daddy!' His daughter was running up the slope towards him between the dark rhododendrons. He was relieved to see she was laughing.

'Where's Mummy?'

'Talking to those women again,' sighed Pauline.

Shirley appeared around the bend in the path. 'We thought you'd disappeared,' said Shirley. 'Gone back to work.'

'I had a hunch,' he said. 'It came to nothing.' He bent down to Pauline and hoisted her onto his shoulders. 'Time for a ride.'

'I can see across the lake,' she said.

'Make the most of it,' said Bible. 'You'll be too big for shoulder rides soon.'

'There's a man rowing a boat.' She pointed.

Bible strained to see above the rhododendrons and glimpsed the man's coat. He quickly unhooked Pauline's legs from round his neck, planted her on the ground and ran to the end of the line of shrubbery.

'Hey,' he shouted. 'Stop.'

The oarsman looked towards him but carried on rowing.

Bible held up his warrant card. 'Police. Come over here.'

The rower shrugged, pulled on one oar a couple of times to turn the boat, and rowed towards where Bible was standing on the flat stones at the edge. As he got near he pulled in his oars and let the boat glide towards Bible.

'You should have said "Come in number twelve",' said the man in a dour West Riding accent as the boat bumped the stones at the edge of the lake.

The coat looked right; even the scarf tucked under the collar; but Bible could see this wasn't the man they were looking for. He had to make something of it, though.

'What are you doing with the boat?'

'I'm going to rob a bank and I need a quick getaway.'

Bible waited for a sensible answer, but none came. 'You'd better come to the station and put that in writing.'

'Give over, you daft 'aporth. I'm the boatman. I'm going over to get my stuff ready for repainting 'em over winter.'

'We're looking for someone about your age, with a coat and scarf similar to the one you're wearing.'

'Are you daft? Every man in t'city's a coat and scarf similar to the one I'm wearing.' The boatman mimicked Bible's posher version of Yorkshire.

'And he wears glasses,' said Bible.

'That narrows it down,' said the boatman. 'Can I go now?'

The oars made a dull rattle as he pulled them back through the rowlocks, the wood of the dinghy's hull acting like the soundbox of a double bass. The boatman lowered the blades into the water and began to scull away.

'That were a bloody performance, wa'n't it?' grumbled the boatman as he rowed towards the island and the quacking winter ducks.

Bible turned and saw Shirley and Pauline watching him from some distance away.

'Let's go home for dinner,' said Shirley brightly. 'I've got a pie ready to put in the oven.'

'Yummy,' said Bible, smiling at Pauline, and then at Shirley. 'Sounds great.' He was glad she hadn't said anything about the fiasco by the lake, but as they walked home, he still felt defeated. And he wondered why she hadn't mentioned talking to her friends again.

FOURTEEN

Logan looked at his wife sitting on the floor in the corner where he had thrown her. She hadn't even protested. He pointed to the kitchen door. It hung on one hinge, its glass panel smashed. 'I'll send Stanley round to mend that.'

But Jenny. He needed to know where she was. He left the living room and took the stairs two at a time. He was out of breath when he reached the top. He pushed open the door to his middle daughter's room. Wendy was sitting on the side of her bed. Her eyes widened. He grabbed her by the wrists and pulled her off the bed. 'When did you last see her?' He loosened his grip. She was frightened enough. She'd never had as much spirit as her sisters.

'Last night. When she came to bed,' she said, shaking.

Jenny's bed was separated from Wendy's by the small table between them. The varnish had worn off. On Wendy's side was a copy of *Woman's Weekly*. He let her have one if she was good. Jenny's side was bare. The top sheets of her bed were turned down, but the bottom sheet was hardly creased. If she'd slept in it, it hadn't been for long.

Logan pulled open the door of the narrow wardrobe. It wobbled as he swept the few clothes to one side and looked at the base. One pair of old dress shoes.

'How much stuff did she have in here?'

Wendy stammered a response. 'I don't know. Not much. More than that.'

'And a bag? Did she have a bag?'

'I think so.'

Logan cursed himself for not knowing. He'd let them have too much freedom.

'Have you got a bag?' he said to Wendy. 'Give it to me.'

'It's got my things in it,' she said. Logan felt himself go cold. He would do what was necessary.

'Give me your bag.'

Wendy was weeping. Silently. He stared at her. 'Your bag.'

Wendy got up and crouched to reach under her bed. She sniffled as she pulled out an old canvas shopping bag. Logan snatched it from her. 'Please, Daddy,' she said as he turned it upside down, emptying the contents over the quilt.

He looked down at the meagre belongings. A Peter Rabbit mug. A knitted doll an aunt had sent her before he had forbidden his wife all contact with her sisters. An elephant rubber. And a pencil on a spring he'd made her when she was five. She'd been able to attach it to her jumper, use it, and it would spring back. He looked at the small litter of memorabilia. He'd expected to find a secret supply of the forbidden: lipstick, cutout adverts for the A-line dresses he'd heard all young girls wanted. But he should have known. Not that for Wendy. No secret parading in front of the mirror or hankering after new fangled rock and roll. Just this memory of childhood. She'd never had any spirit. Jenny and Dawn were more like him; that was why he'd had to tame them.

Wendy was still on the floor, not whimpering audibly, but shivering. He knew she wouldn't be using the bag to pack and run away with. 'Put them away,' said Logan quietly. 'I won't be needing those.'

He left the room without looking back at her, remembering when the girls used to hold his hand.

*

Bible wondered where the dog was. It usually barked when he approached the gate to Carol's bedsit. As he stepped onto the short flagged path in the fading light, he realised why. A girl of not more than twenty in a blue duffle coat was sitting on the step, stroking the collie's neck. She looked startled to see him. Her hand stopped moving in the dog's fur.

'Hello,' said Bible. 'Who are you?'

'No one,' she said, frightened. 'I'm just going.' She stood up and grabbed the old army knapsack which had been hidden from view by the dog.

'No one?' said Bible.

'It doesn't matter,' she said, and hurried past him to the pavement. As soon as she reached the pavement she ran. The dog trotted after her for a few steps and then thought better of it.

'Hey,' shouted Bible. 'Come back.' But she carried on running into the fading light until he could no longer hear her footsteps.

The collie snarled as Bible thumped with the flat of his hand on the door. 'Open up. Police.'

No one came. He thumped again. He heard

shuffling on the other side. The door opened slowly. It was an old woman he'd never seen before. 'I'm sorry. Police,' he said, flashing his warrant card. He edged his way past and ran up the stairs to Carol's door. He knocked. 'Carol,' he shouted. He knocked again. 'Have you seen Carol?' The woman at the bottom of the stairs looked confused.

'Are you a real policeman?' she said.

The cat had come to purr round Bible's legs. 'Yes. I'm real.' He hadn't time to explain further. Since Holroyd's refusal to place a policewoman on the door, he was desperate to get Carol to a safer place. He tried her door. It opened without resistance. There was a soft meowing from the wardrobe, but apart from the kittens, the room was empty of all but the bare furniture which belonged there.

*

It was raining in Exeter. Logan sat in the Clocktower Cafe with an untouched pie in front of him. He used the cafe near the centre of town more as a headquarters than an eating place. He'd made Alfie sell newspapers all day on Fore Street watching for Jenny. He'd ordered Stanley, his runner, to ask after her among all the regular on-street punters. Stanley sat in front of him now.

'Are you eating that pie, Mr Logan?'

'Cheeky young bugger,' said Logan, pushing the untouched plate towards the boy.

'It's hard work, Mr Logan, running all round town.'

Logan slammed his hand down on the boy's left wrist, pinning it to the table just as the boy was about to use the fork to stab a mouthful of Logan's abandoned pie.

'Don't get too cocky son. I'm not at my best today.' Logan released his grip and used the stare he knew would terrify the boy. 'I pay you for running. I look after you for running.' Logan released Stanley from eye contact and sat back. 'Get me another mug of tea.'

Stanley pushed his chair back and took the mug up to the counter. Logan called after him. 'What about that father of yours? Is he back from his travels yet?'

'Came back yesterday, Mr Logan.'

'You should have told me.'

A blast of wintry rain came through the door as Alfie the newspaper seller came in, the clocktower monument behind him as grey as a tombstone.

'She's been seen, Mr Logan. Hitching a lift on the Heavitree Road. About an hour ago. Got into a Gumson's lorry. Removals.'

'I know what they do,' said Logan, going towards the counter. 'Give me the telephone,' he said to the boy in the apron, who was putting a new mug of tea in front of Stanley. 'Now.'

Logan dialled the operator. 'Gumson's. Harry Gumson's. Thank you darling.' He waited a moment to be put through. 'Harry. Tommy Logan here. You had a lorry heading out on the Heavitree Road this afternoon. About half past three. Where was it going?' Logan listened to the anxious-to-please voice at the other end. 'Address,' he demanded. 'Never mind customer privacy. Do you want customers in future? Remember who you're talking to.' Logan took the order pad and a pencil from the gaping top pocket of the boy's apron and scribbled down the address.

'Thank you.' He popped the notebook and pencil back into the boy's apron as if he were lobbing nuts into a jam jar. It was time to stop waiting.

'We're going on our holidays,' he said to Stanley. 'Birmingham. Your dad can drive.'

Half an hour later, the rain had stopped and Logan stood between the open boathouse doors, beckoning the yellow Bedford van as it backed towards him through the puddles in a series of jerks. 'Whoa.' He walked to the driver's door and pulled it open.

'Is that good enough, Mr Logan?' said Stanley. Logan could see the boy was looking for approval. He wouldn't get it.

'Hop out.'

Stanley slid from behind the steering wheel, looking sheepish.

'Driving is confidence and skill, son,' said Logan. 'You're having trouble with the skill bit.' Logan beckoned to the man in the passenger seat. 'Oi, Robbo, show your lad how to do it.'

The man with the pencil moustache and khaki overalls lifted his leg over the gear stick and took up position behind the large black steering wheel.

'Ronnie Robinson, you and your ideas.' Logan shook his head in feigned disgust. 'Major Robinson my arse. I heard you got arrested.'

'They couldn't pin anything on me, Mr Logan,' said Robinson cheerfully, stretching his moustache into a smile. Logan stared at him stony-faced. Robinson's smile died.

'You know I don't like people freelancing.'

Logan wondered if he was losing his touch. He was

used to having young bucks like Stanley test their mettle against him, but he thought he'd got his older staff trained.

'Let's have you out,' said Logan.

'I thought you wanted me to move the van...' His words withered like those of a man dying. He stepped down from the Bedford.

'Follow me,' said Logan. He turned towards the boathouse. 'I want to show you something.'

Robinson followed Logan for a couple of steps. When Logan knew Stanley's father was close behind, he span round and thumped the man hard in the stomach with his left hand. It was a short jab, the power coming from Logan's right foot planted firmly on the ground. Robinson sank to the floor, gasping. Logan looked at Stanley. The boy was scared. Good. It did a boy good to see his father humbled. Prevented false loyalties. False hero worship.

'You can back the van up now,' said Logan to the man on the floor gasping for breath.

Robinson pulled himself to his feet.

'What was that for, Mr Logan?' he said hoarsely.

'You know what you were up north for,' said Logan, taking his position back at the boathouse doors. 'And it wasn't for robbing banks. Get in and try not to run over your son.'

In the gloom of the boathouse, they could all pick out the figure in the chair, head lolling to one side.

'Is he dead Mr Logan?' said Stanley.

Logan was disgusted. He had more respect for the figure in the chair than for Stanley and his father. This boy had known and thought he loved his daughter.

That's why he was hard to break. Why he still had to use him.

'We could still drown him, Mr Logan,' said Robinson, looking down at the black water. Logan liked serious men with serious business. Family business. Fearless men. And Ronnie Robinson wasn't one of them. The small waves sucking at the posts beneath their feet echoed in the boathouse. Water dripped from the algae on the posts holding up the wooden walkway.

'Do you know what death is, Robbo? Stanley? Have you ever thought about it? You need to, if it's your trade. Look at that water. That blackness. How cold it is. Think what it's like to drown down there on your own. No comfort. No friends. Skeletons and stones and fish for company. And Heaven? That's not where you go. So don't play with murder when you don't know what it is.'

Logan looked at the two hopeless men before him, and squatted on his haunches in front of Larry.

'You're doing well, son.'

Logan ripped the tape from Larry's mouth. He ripped it because you had to do it quickly. It hurt less. 'We've got to go on a journey, Larry. Behave yourself and you'll be home soon.'

Larry gasped out a word. 'Why?'

Logan looked at him and spoke quietly so Robbo and Stanley would not hear.

'It's love, Larry. Love.'

FIFTEEN

Back from the bank - Menzies had accepted her excuse of 'fever' for Friday's absence - Carol lifted the net curtains and looked out at the garden and the moor beyond. It was the end of her first full day in the cottage. Even here, a couple of miles away from the mills and the muck, the wall at the end of the garden was almost black. Jagged lumps of gritstone capped the wall like knuckles. It marked where Miss Browning's neatness ended, and a rougher world began. The garden was tangled this time of year, as if giving in to the ragged moor around it, but the pretty living room in the cottage made no such concessions. Carol admired the antimacassars, the china dogs, the richly patterned deep red carpet. She wondered if Miss Browning would like a cat. She could bring the mother and kittens from the bedsit if she dared go back for them. And dared ask. She hoped Malcolm was feeding them.

Miss Browning wasn't back. It was six o'clock and already dark. Carol thought that was odd. Didn't schoolteachers finish work at about four, or even earlier in a school for little children? Miss Browning had said she was Headmistress of an infants' school in Chapel Heights, a stiff walk up the hill from Carol's old bedsit near the centre of town.

Carol went into the little kitchen, filled a large pewter-coloured kettle with water and put it on the hob. She found matches on a high shelf next to the Vim and Brasso tin and lit the gas ring. Miss Browning would probably like a cup of tea when she came in.

Half an hour later Carol was still sitting alone in the dark. The kettle had whistled long ago. She hadn't pulled the curtains. Although it would have made the room cosier, she wanted to know what was outside; didn't want anything creeping up on her unawares. The yellow glow of a streetlamp on the pavement at the front of the cottage gave her some reassurance.

Viewed in the gloom, the people in the pictures on the walls seemed more alive than when surrounded by daylight. They were mostly women from the first part of the century. Relations, she supposed. Grandmother, mother, aunties. Only one man struggled on his own for a place on the mantelpiece. Miss Browning's father? She must have liked him then. Carol wouldn't have wanted a picture of her father up. She looked nervously out of the window at the thought of her father.

Miss Browning's grandfather clock chimed the half hour. Half past six. Dark now. She didn't know any neighbours here in this little row. In the bedsit, she'd known Malcolm. Poor Malcolm. The life had gone out of him when she'd told him she was going to take the room. She looked at the clock again, though she knew what time it was, and decided to make a pot of tea anyway.

Carol emerged from the small kitchen with a tray, teapot and two china cups and put them on the oak table. The clock was chiming a quarter to seven. She hardly knew Miss Browning, and there was no reason why Miss Browning should have to explain herself and her movements. But her absence was unnerving. She found Miss Browning comforting, if a little fearsome.

Carol jumped when she heard someone trying the cottage door. Then she heard the rattle of a key, and the door opening. Carol rose quickly from her chair and stood with her back to the mantelpiece, facing the entrance to the tiny living room. Miss Browning came in out of breath, carrying a heavy leather briefcase in one hand and a paper carrier bag in the other. She stopped when she saw Carol standing.

'You locked the door, my dear.'

'Yes. I wasn't sure. It felt safer.'

'You're safe round here.' Miss Browning put her briefcase on a velvet-upholstered dining chair by the door, and the carrier bag on the floor beside it. 'Anyone who decided to make it unsafe would have me to answer to,' she said as she disappeared back into the little hallway to hang up her coat.

Carol sat down and picked up the teapot. 'Would you like a cup of tea, Miss Browning?'

'Very kind, my dear. I think you can call me Edith. And I might let myself sink down for once.' Miss Browning leaned back in the plush armchair on the other side of the fireplace from where Carol had been sitting. 'I'm not usually this late from school. Had a ticklish situation with a parent. No sugar, thank you.'

Carol began pouring tea. 'I was looking at the photographs.'

A crash of glass. The leaded window at the front of the cottage imploded. Carol jerked the spout of the teapot and poured tea onto the tray. She covered her head with her left hand, holding the pot in her right, as shards of glass fell into the carpet.

'Good heavens. We can't be having that,' said Miss Browning sternly and marched out of the room. Carol heard her wrench open the outside door. Someone was shouting. Something about an old dyke. You old dyke? It didn't make sense. She forced herself to go to the door, which was filled by Miss Browning's solid presence and booming voice.

'Mr Holmes, go home and comfort your wife. You have no business here.'

Over Miss Browning's shoulder Carol could see a small man on the pavement weaving his body this way and that as he raged at Miss Browning. 'You can't get rid of me. You're glad he's dead. You set me up with the police.'

'Mr Holmes, I spoke to you this afternoon, and I understand the police have not pressed charges.'

'You can't shut me up like that. Stone, that's you. Heart of stone.' Holmes was still twitching and jerking his body, but he seemed reluctant to set foot in the small garden.

Miss Browning boomed again. 'Carol, please telephone the police. The number's on the front of the directory. I'll stand here until Mr Holmes has calmed himself.'

Carol hesitated before turning. She had hoped the cottage would be an escape.

Miss Browning called after her without turning her head away from her fixed gaze on Holmes. 'Ask for Inspector Bible.' The name hit her in the stomach.

Holmes' voice came from the lane. 'That bastard'll only back you up.'

'That is rather what I am hoping, Mr Holmes.'

Carol slowly picked up the receiver. It was not something she wanted to do. And she felt guilty that she had not been honest with her new landlady about her past.

*

'Did you feel you were being followed?' Bible was sitting in the chair Carol had occupied and faced Miss Browning. Holmes had scarpered before Bible had arrived.

'This is not hocus-pocus land, Inspector. I do not have mysterious feelings in my bones or pick up messages. So no, I did not *feel* I was being followed. Nor did I sense it. My reason tells me he followed me.'

Bible was finding her irritating. More irritating than Holmes, a confused and weak man who'd felt like a victim all his life and wanted someone to blame.

'I know Mr Holmes is grieving,' said Miss Browning, 'but I also know what proper behaviour is.'

Bible wondered if she could sense or feel Carol watching them from the kitchen. She was taking an extraordinary length of time making a pot of tea. Carol had been introduced as the new lodger, and neither she nor Bible had indicated that they had met before.

'What do you want to do about the window, Miss Browning?'

'You're asking if I want to prosecute?'

'You've sensed my meaning,' said Bible. Miss Browning's pause told Bible she had noticed his dig. Not so insensitive then.

'I am not a cruel person, Inspector. And I can't

imagine what the local paper would think if I were portrayed as prosecuting the bereaved father of one of my ex-pupils.'

Bible winced inside. Ex-pupil? Ex-child? He said nothing.

'So no, I won't be prosecuting. I trust you will advise Mr Holmes on how to moderate his behaviour.'

Carol came in with a teapot on a tray and a plate of biscuits.

'I'd like to have a word with Miss Carlton, if I may.'

'Why? Carol knows nothing of Mr Holmes.' Miss Browning sat back in her chair. She showed no sign of moving. Having ousted her from her office a few days before, Bible thought he'd better not try to remove her from her own living room.

'Should I talk to her outside?' said Bible.

'Well her bedroom is out of the question.'

Bible reddened. 'Of course.' It was not something he expected someone of Miss Browning's age, or even his own, to mention so explicitly. But his embarrassment had caught him by surprise.

'Miss Carlton, shall we step outside for a moment?'

Miss Browning reached for a Rich Tea biscuit.

Carol followed Bible down the short path. Outside the air was brackish, haunted with smoke from the chimneys of Quarry Cottages. Across the lane, a field sloped away in the dark to the canal. She could just make out the shadow of the carthorse that lived there. Bible stopped at the gate, under the twigs of the rose bower. He turned to Carol.

'Rich Tea biscuits must be the most boring biscuits in the world,' said Bible.

The comment took her by surprise. She laughed but then her laughter turned to crying. Not just weeping, but deep sobs from her chest, from her past, from her fear. Bible waited patiently, but she couldn't stop herself. After the days of fear, the resolve to be tough, the tears came welling up. She wanted Bible to put his arms round her, just hold her to his chest, but she knew he wouldn't and that it would be improper to ask.

'I'm sorry,' she said. She shivered. She was still wearing the lightweight cardigan she'd had on in the house.

'Here,' said Bible, 'let me put my coat round you.' He began to take off his overcoat.

Carol wiped the tears from her cheeks. 'I'll be fine.'

'No, I insist,' he said.

He wafted the coat round her with a flourish, placing it gently round her shoulders and pulling it close under her chin. She gripped the lapels to hold it on and the base of her thumbs briefly brushed his. She dared not look up at him.

'Thank you,' she said. A crow squawked in the trees opposite. Another replied. Some sort of argument in the bare branches. 'I don't know anything about that man who came here shouting.'

'We know who he is. It wasn't anything to do with you.'

'Not everything is about me, I suppose.' Carol smiled.

'No, not everything is. But some things are.' Bible was being kind, but it was part of his job. It was foolish to think his kindness was personal. She didn't want to ask about the photographs. To talk about them made them seem more real. Here in the cosy living room she could pretend they belonged to another life.

'We went round to your bedsit. Why didn't you tell us you'd left?'

Because she wanted to be unknown. Because she wanted to pretend. And because she felt foolish.

'You should have told us. You're not safe. You need protection.' She felt like a schoolgirl being told off. Not that she had been told off much. Usually too scared to do anything wrong.

'I'm sorry,' she said meekly. She felt her eyes pricking. She feared she might disgrace herself by crying again. Bible put his hands on her shoulders.

'Look at me,' he said. 'We can protect you.'

She looked up at him. She felt herself going. The tears came again, and then Bible put his arms round her and pulled her to his chest.

'I can protect you,' he said.

SIXTEEN

Bible only held her for a moment before he let her go. Who was he fooling? How could he protect her? He wasn't even clear where the threat was coming from. Johnny Fraser? Cannonball seemed to have gone to ground. Photos at the reservoir? It was time to speak to that Water Board man, Turner, again. Carol's father? Ward was speaking to the police in Exeter.

The streetlight illuminated the side of Carol's face. Her eyes were downcast and she looked fragile. He hadn't mentioned what he most wanted to ask her about. The girl on the doorstep. But he didn't want to frighten her more. And it might not be anything to do with Carol.

'There was a girl at your old house. Sitting on the step with an old army knapsack. She ran away when she saw us.'

'I don't know anyone up here.'

'Blonde. Had a blue coat on.'

Carol's hand went to her mouth. 'How old was she?'

'Hard to tell. Nineteen. Twenty. Carol?'

'Nothing. It's silly.'

'Tell me.'

'My sister has a blue coat. But she's only seventeen.'

Bible pictured the face he'd seen. Perhaps it could

have been younger. She looked older than Ricky, but then girls did.

'She's the only one of us who's blonde.'

Carol rubbed her face. Bible wondered if she'd cry again, but she seemed determined to keep a grip of herself. 'I've got a school photo upstairs. My father never let us have photos of our own.'

The cottage door opened and Miss Browning appeared above them, silhouetted in the light.

'Inspector Bible, it's time to bring her in now. We don't want Miss Carlton to catch her death.'

Miss Browning stood holding the door open as they mounted the steps and went in. Bible thought she was glowering at him as he stepped past. Carol went upstairs to get the photograph of her sister. Once in the living room, Bible turned to face her.

'I'm afraid Carol is in some danger, Miss Browning,' said Bible.

'That's what it looked like, Inspector.'

So the old dragon had been spying on them. Well, he wasn't going to be put off his stride by a primary school headmistress who behaved as if she were prime minister.

'And I'm going to have to station a police constable at the gate.'

'I don't think I like that, Inspector. No, I cannot allow that.'

'You're not the only person being followed, Miss Browning.' They held each other's gaze. 'So I am afraid I have to insist.'

Carol returned with a small oblong, a black and white photograph of a girl framed in an oval of silky cream cardboard. 'He let us have our school photographs done so we didn't seem different from the other girls. That's Jenny.' She was about ten. Smiling. A big ribbon tied in a bow in her pale hair.

'I remember that ribbon,' said Carol. 'It was yellow, a daffodil yellow. Our mother tied it on for the photograph day. My father made her take it off as soon as Jenny got back home.' She looked up at him. 'You've got to find her.'

'If it was her. Have you a more recent picture?'

Carol shook her head. 'Nothing. He said girls got too fond of themselves if they saw themselves in photographs.' She paused. 'Not even a mirror.'

'Somebody should have been fond of you,' said Bible. He looked at the smiling face of the little girl with the ribbon, and wished she'd had more to smile about. It could have been the same girl he had seen on the steps. Something about the eyes, wide open, eager, and set more widely apart than usual. Carol's were a bit like that, but more guarded, particularly now as she looked up to him. Miss Browning was still planted in the middle of the room watching over them.

'Carol?' said Miss Browning. 'What is going on?'

Bible put the photo carefully into his inside pocket and locked eyes with Miss Browning. 'We'll pick up Holmes,' said Bible. 'Give him a flea in his ear.'

'I'll show you out, Inspector,' said Miss Browning, coldly.

His breath clouded in the chill November air as he stepped down the short drive.

The door was locked firmly behind him. Outside the gate he leaned against the stone of the garden wall, breathing in deeply. Smoke from the cottage fires mingled with the smells of a damp late autumn, and the muscular shape of the horse across the road faded into the blue-grey of the sky.

The silence was broken by footsteps. Holmes again? No, steady footsteps. The footsteps of a policeman who knew what it was to patrol a beat. Bible pushed himself off the wall. The pale glow of a trench coat emerged from the gloom and stopped under the street light.

'Evening, sir.'

'Bill?' What was Ward doing here? Bible waited for him to speak. There was a pause he didn't understand. 'Holmes has been here,' said Bible, 'making a nuisance of himself. We'll have to pick him up later.'

'I've been onto Exeter, sir. They know this Logan character. Don't think he's anything but a small time crook. Organises some kind of gambling racket and a bit of smuggling. They think he's still in Devon.'

'You could have radioed that, Bill. What's brought you out here?'

'Couldn't get you on the radio, sir. You've got it switched off.'

'I was in the cottage.'

'It hasn't been on since you left the station.'

Bible frowned at him. Ward's manner was stern. Awkward. Bible wondered how long he'd been there. He strode towards his car and pulled open the door. He could see the switch was off.

'I don't approve, sir,' said Ward.

'How long have you been standing there?' His sergeant must have seen him with Carol. But he'd make him say it. 'And you don't approve of what, Bill? Not locking the car door? Forgetting to switch the radio on?'

'She's a vulnerable young woman, sir.'

'For God's sake, Bill. For a no-nonsense copper you can sound like a pompous prick.' A gust of wind shook the skeleton of an elm and drops of water fell around them from the earlier rain. 'I know she's vulnerable.' Bible looked across the roof of the car towards the cottage door. The light was still on in the front room. What were they saying in there? Why had he put his arms round her? 'I thought she needed comfort.'

'Perhaps I'm old-fashioned, sir.'

'You saw what you saw. Make of it what you will. And the same goes for Holroyd.'

'He wouldn't care unless it got in the press.'

Bible jerked his head and eyed his colleague sharply.

'No one will hear about it from me, sir,' said Ward quietly.

'She's in danger, Bill.'

'I know sir. But Holroyd doesn't think so. Nothing's a case to him if the division can't get credit for solving it. We're on our own on this one sir.'

Bible reached into his coat pocket. 'Look at this photo.'

Ward took the small image and stepped sideways to hold it under the street lamp, angling it to catch the light. He squinted like someone who needed reading glasses. It reminded Bible that Ward was older.

'Is it Carol?' said Ward.

'Her sister. Jennifer.'

'She looks pretty with that ribbon.'

Bible wondered how Ward felt about not having children. 'I think it's the girl I saw on the step?' Bible hoped he didn't sound excited at the possibility. 'Something about the mouth looks the same.'

Ward peered at the photograph again and handed it back. 'I'll put pressure on Exeter. Get them to find out a bit more about the family.'

'We don't want them knocking on doors down there. Giving anything away to her father, wherever he is.'

'Always a model of discretion, sir.'

Bible smiled. 'Goes without saying, Bill.' He opened the door of his car and slid into the driver's seat. He was reaching for the handle to pull the door shut when Ward stepped close to the car and blocked the door with his hand.

'I should warn you, sir, Holroyd's talking about bringing someone up from Scotland Yard.'

'That's never been standard practice here.'

'We'll sort him out, sir.' Ward stepped back. 'I just wanted you to know.'

Bible drove away from Quarry Cottages, following the road as it led along the canal side before breaking away to wind up towards the city side of the moor. Where was his career taking him? His marriage? He felt like a man caught in a dark net. No faith. No freedom. Holroyd was trying to sideline him but he didn't care. He tried to substitute the memory of Carol with images of Shirley, forcing Carol out of his mind. He drove past an isolated pub with a faint light in the tap room window and at the crest of the hill he pulled onto a patch of moorland where the heather had been worn away. It was used as a car park and picnic stop in summer. He got out and pulled his collar up against the wind and looked out from the moor's craggy edge across the city, the lights laid out like jewels below him. It looked beautiful from up here, but it wasn't his. He didn't belong. He'd never felt at home in the city of his birth, among these Yorkshiremen with their certainties and self-belief. Ward, Holroyd, Turner. They belonged. They were at home with who they were. Shirley teased him about not having any friends. Mates. Well, it was as it was. He turned his back on the city, locked the car, and walked back downhill towards the public house, stumbling on the uneven ground in the dark.

He was the only one in a suit in the taproom. The only one under fifty. And the taproom was the only room there was. *The Lamb* seemed to have been hewn out of a boulder, its interior walls blocks of unadorned millstone grit. Three farmers in outdoor coats and battered trilbies sat by a cold fire agreeing in ever louder voices that anyone opposed to the retaking of the Suez Canal was a traitor. The sort of men who could control their wives. Perhaps his own father would have been like that, if he'd lived. But it didn't seem likely; his mother had been a spirited soul. Bible nursed his second pint and whisky chaser, and thought of his homely semi with its neat lawn and newly-painted front door. Pauline would be sleeping peacefully; Shirley would assume he was late at work. As he brooded on his daughter's face, he knew he wanted to go home. And that he didn't want to control his wife, however much her unofficial police work embarrassed him.

'So what do you think?' It took him a moment to realise the question was addressed to him.

'Sorry?'

'Eden. What's he so bloody weak for?' The speaker was the oldest of the farmers, a huge man too old to have seen active service in the last war.

Bible rose to take his empty glasses back. 'Well, that's politics for you.'

The farmer ambled over and banged his tankard on the bar. He looked down at Bible.

'We should tell the world why we still call it Great Britain, not bloody retreat.'

Bible ignored him and turned to leave. He knew the Prime Minister had accepted a ceasefire after pressure from America.

'Agreed?' said the farmer.

Bible stopped. 'If you mean Suez,' said Bible. 'We have no business being there.'

The farmer stepped in front of him and blocked his way to the door. 'We don't like traitors in here.'

'Then you'll be happy to step aside and let me leave,' said Bible.

One of the other farmers scraped his chair back and stood. 'Leave it alone, Isaac. He isn't worth it.'

Bible was excited by the freedom of feeling right. The man was a bully, fooled by his own size. Bible was ready for him and his stupid vanity. He felt like laughing, and realised he was drunk enough to want the farmer to throw a punch so he could take him down. They stared at each other for a moment before Bible pulled out his warrant card and pushed it into the man's face.

'Time for you to retreat, I think.'

The farmer's face twitched, but he stepped aside and Bible left.

*

Bible worked the key into the lock as quietly as he could, turning it delicately so there would be no clicks. His house was in darkness. Shirley usually left the hall light on when he was due back late, but tonight perhaps she had just forgotten.

He took off his shoes and tiptoed up the stairs. He gently pushed open Pauline's door. He could hear her soft breathing and make out a small mound in the bed clothes. It was easy to forget how small a child was. Ricky's door was at right angles to Pauline's. He thought of easing that door open too, but didn't want to risk a row if he woke the teenager. He heard a groan, and the bed springs creak. So his son was in. He was surprised at how relieved he felt.

In their bedroom Shirley was asleep. She'd left his bedside light on, and the light glowing through the pink shade with the fringes looked welcoming. He had thought he would be angry with her, that they'd argue about whatever she had been doing, but seeing her lying in the warm glow, he wanted to put his arms round her and say it didn't matter.

He carefully undressed, taking care with his trousers so the change in the pockets would not chink, and draped his clothes over the old utility chair in the corner. There was a chill in the air, so he put his pyjamas on quickly and slid between the flannelette sheets Shirley favoured in winter.

Bible was disappointed she didn't wake up. She had her back to him, curled in a semi-foetal position in her sleeveless nightie. He lay on his side and looked at her bare shoulder which glistened in the light from his lamp, and touched it gently with his fingertips.

'I'm asleep,' she murmured.

He lifted his hand. He hadn't meant to disturb her, but was glad she had woken. He lowered his hand again, and kissed her shoulder.

'Not now,' she said. 'Go to sleep.'

'Let's take Pauline into the country tomorrow,' he said. 'Have a family day.'

'You'll be working,' said Shirley.

'I'll take the day off.' He hadn't meant to say that, but now he knew he would. When Shirley was asleep again he'd slip downstairs and take the phone off the hook. And in the morning he'd sign her H-bomb petition. He lay back in bed wishing she had woken so they could make love. Then he realised it was putting his arms round Carol had got him thinking about sex.

SEVENTEEN

It was dark when Logan, Robinson and Stanley caught up with the removal van in Birmingham. Gumson's lorry was outside a row of terrace houses, its back open, the ramp down, and a light inside that must have been run off the battery. Two men were carrying out a bed and the lorry was nearly empty. Logan told Robbo to park about twenty yards away. The sawn-off shotgun was safely under Logan's seat. It could stay there. He wouldn't need it for this.

'Do you think she's still with them?' said Robinson.

'You'd better go and ask, Robbo,' said Logan. 'Catch them as they come out of the house.'

The two removal men were hoisting the bed over the doorstep into the brightly-lit terrace. The older man, feet firmly planted on the short drive, gave the orders to a younger one, who was bent awkwardly as he reversed through the doorway trying to keep a grip on the bed. All the lights were on, and through the uncurtained bay window Logan could see a young couple looking at their new home.

'Now,' said Logan. 'Take Stanley with you.'

Robinson and Stanley looked at each other.

'You know how this stuff works. Just do it, Robbo,' said Logan.

He watched Robinson and Stanley walk across the road. He waited until they reached the removal lorry before he slipped out of the passenger seat and opened the doors at the rear. Larry was lying on rugs, a gag in his mouth. His eyes were closed, but he was breathing. He was as comfortable as Logan had been able to make him. Logan clambered into the back, took a flannel from a bucket, and poured water onto it from an old pop bottle. He put it to the boy's lips.

'You'll be all right, boy. I'll look after you when we get there. You and me. We'll get them back.'

Larry's eyes opened. Logan could see no expression in them. He put his arm round the boy's shoulders and raised him a little, offering the water bottle to his lips. Larry spluttered and coughed.

'Easy boy. Easy. You're a brave one.' Logan put the pop bottle down, lowered the boy on to the rugs and slid out of the van into the road. Robbo and Stanley had stationed themselves on the pavement outside the house. Logan quietly took up position on the road side of the lorry, leaning against the rear wheel arch, hidden from view. He heard Robbo speak to the removal men as they came out.

'Hey up, pal. Did you pick up a hitchhiker just outside Exeter? Girl, about seventeen?'

'Who wants to know?' The voice sounded firm. The older man. A man sure of himself. A man about Logan's age.

'Someone important,' said Stanley from the pavement, where Logan couldn't see him.

'It can't be you, then.' The older man again.

'You'd better tell him.' Stanley trying to be tough. Sometimes Logan despaired of that boy. No technique. True to form, Robinson tried the conman approach. 'Sorry, mate, but she was just going up north to see a friend, and now her dad's been taken ill. They're not sure he'll last the night.' Robbo was smooth, Logan had to give him that. Smooth even when Stanley's bluster had thrown a spanner in the works.

Logan heard the older man's voice again. 'He'll be no loss to the world from what she told me and Arnie. If we see her again we'll give her the good news.'

Logan stiffened, but held himself still. He'd always known when to wait. The older man and Arnie came round the back of the van. Heavy boots plodded up the ramp ahead of a light clattering which Logan guessed belonged to Arnie. Logan twisted round from the side of the lorry and grabbed the young man's ankle with his right hand as he neared the top of the ramp. Logan's other hand pressed against Arnie's knee, forcing the leg against the joint and tipping the boy into the lorry. He thundered into the side of the empty van which rumbled like a drum.

'Hey what the fuck...?' said the older removal man, twisting round, but Logan was onto the ramp and into him before he could regain his balance. Logan put his hand over the man's face and kicked his legs away, sending him staggering into a pile of tarpaulins.

'So you were saying where you'd dropped the girl,' said Logan.

The man struggled to his feet. A big man, strong enough to lift a wardrobe on one shoulder, but not agile, and not used to professional violence. Logan only had to put medium pressure into a blow under the man's chin with the heel of his hand. He knew it would be enough to send him down again. He lay half sitting against the tarpaulins. Logan stood over him. 'Harry Gumson's a personal friend of mine. He'd be very upset if he knew you'd offended me.'

'Who are you then?'

'The name's Logan.'

Logan watched the older man's eyes flash as he considered fighting, but the spirit quickly went out of him. Logan was well known in Exeter.

The removal man looked exhausted. 'Dropped her on the A38 in Edgbaston. She was going to hitch from there.'

Logan kicked the sole of the man's boot. 'And?'

'That's all.'

Logan stood between the man's spread-eagled legs and stood with one boot on the man's right kneecap. The man yelled. Logan took his foot off.

'I don't know what you want,' gasped the removal man.

'Where did she say she was going?' said Logan patiently. He could hear voices on the pavement outside. Robbo and Stanley talking to someone.

Arnie shouted from where Logan had thrown him against the inside of the lorry. 'Yorkshire. She said she was going to Yorkshire. To see her sister.'

'Thank you gentlemen,' said Logan, turning from the van. 'Don't let me stop you working.'

He strode down the ramp, rattling the chains which attached it to the back of the lorry. The young couple who had just moved stood on the top step of their new house, silhouetted by the warm light in the hall. A small cocker spaniel snuffled curiously around the tiny patch of front garden.

'What's going on in there?' said the young husband. 'These two men wouldn't let us past.'

Robinson and Stanley stood at the garden gate, blocking the way. The new householder felt he ought to do something, but wouldn't dare; and he hadn't tried to force his way to the removal van because he didn't want to know too much. Logan could always assess weakness.

'They'll be fine' said Logan pleasantly as he reached the gate. 'Experienced blokes. You'll be all right with Gumson's.' The little cocker spaniel was snuffling around a small rose bush. 'Nice dog you've got there. A dog like that completes a home.'

Logan strode back towards the Bedford on the other side of the road, his hands stuffed in the pockets of his donkey jacket, hiding his anger. Someone had betrayed him. He heard Stanley and Robbo following, but he didn't want to speak to them. How had Jenny known to head for Yorkshire? He hadn't even told his wife where Dawn was when he'd made her write the letter. It was only luck that his eldest daughter's first lift had been with the *Express and Echo* van, delivering newspapers to the depot where Alfie Scadding picked up his batch. But Robbo and Stanley knew, and they could be blabbermouths if they wanted to impress.

He stopped by the closed door of the Bedford. Stanley watched him nervously. 'Shall I open the door, Mr Logan?' he said. Robbo hovered awkwardly behind him.

'Do you want to get in first, Mr Logan, if I'm driving? Stanley can sit between us,' said Robinson.

They waited for an instruction. Logan kept them waiting. 'Just remind me, Stanley, how did we know Dawn had gone up north?'

'Newspaper delivery man saw her get into a Yorkshire Dyers lorry.'

'And how do we know she went all the way?'

'Turner told you.'

Turner. His man in the north. Recommended by Robbo.

'So how come, knowing all this, no one has been able to find out where she actually bloody lives, but my daughter Jenny seems to be making a beeline for there?'

Stanley fingered his tie. 'We'd best get going Mr Logan, if we want to get there tonight.'

'Wait there.' Logan went to the back of the van and unlocked the rear doors. It was dark inside. Larry was awake and staring at him. Logan clambered in and pulled the gag from his mouth.

'You don't know where Dawn lives, do you?'

He saw Larry close his eyes and wait, wait for punishment. But Logan wasn't going to punish him again. 'Don't worry. I'm not going to hurt you anymore.' The boy didn't know; he'd asked him before and he always knew when people were lying, even in their silence. Logan untied Larry's hands and pulled sandwiches from an army haversack. 'Eat.' The young man took a sandwich. He ate slowly and warily. Logan could not tell what he was thinking. He respected that. He could read Stanley and Robbo as easily as odds on a racehorse, but this boy was different. And he hadn't told anybody anything. That was loyalty. Dawn hadn't deserved him.

'Give me your hands,' he said when Larry had

finished eating. Logan tied them together again, and slipped the gag back over the boy's mouth. He jumped out of the back of the van and went to Robbo and Stanley who were still standing in the road waiting for orders. Logan slid back the driver's door. 'Get in.'

Stanley shuffled into the middle seat and Robinson sat behind the wheel. 'So who else, in Exeter, knows where Dawn is and told Jenny?'

Logan saw Stanley panic. Robbo looked uneasy, but Stanley was afraid. 'It wasn't us Mr Logan. Dawn must have written to Jenny. Told her where she was. There must have been a letter.'

'Of course,' said Logan, and slapped his head to demonstrate his stupidity. 'The post. Now, why didn't I think of that?' He twisted in his seat and looked at them balefully. 'After years of making sure the post is only ever delivered to my hands?'

There was a pause. Logan knew Stanley would feel he had to fill it.

'I don't know, Mr Logan.'

'Because there wasn't any post, Stanley. Someone in Exeter has talked. Someone has found out where Dawn is and hasn't told me.'

'It wasn't me, Mr Logan,' said Stanley too quickly.

'I didn't think it was, Stanley,' said Logan smiling, leaving out 'until now'. He needed Stanley and his father with him. He'd expected Robbo to come up with a lie to get his son off the hook, but Robbo said nothing. Some fathers just weren't up to being fathers. Logan slid the heavy van door shut and walked round the front to get in the passenger side. They could have tried to run him over but he knew they were too afraid. Anyway, he was still carrying the ignition keys.

EIGHTEEN

As Carol closed the cottage door behind Bible, she paused for a moment to control her breathing. Her heart was racing. Her sister? Here in the city? Of her two siblings, she was closest to Jenny, but how could her baby sister know where she was? Had her father sent her as a decoy? Or had she run away too? Carol heard Miss Browning rummaging in the kitchen at the top of the cellar steps. She had never met a woman like Miss Browning before. So strong. So certain. Nothing like her own mother. But she wasn't going to apologise for letting Inspector Bible put his arms round her. Carol took a deep breath and turned. Miss Browning was emerging from the cellar head kitchen brandishing a dustpan and brush.

'Help me clear this up, would you, dear?'

'I'm sorry, I was just thinking,' said Carol, dutifully taking the broom.

'You sweep, I'll scoop.' The older woman's manner was brisk. Teacherly. Carol avoided her stare by dropping to her knees below the broken window. Shards of window glass lay on the strip of lino between the wall and the tassels fringing the edge of the carpet.

'We both need to think, my dear,' said Miss Browning, bending stiffly to kneel. She licked a finger and dabbed gingerly at a splinter of glass. For the first time Carol saw her landlady as vulnerable.

'I'll get some damp newspaper,' said Carol. She had seen a pile of *News Chronicles* under the sink. She ran one under the tap, and returned to kneel next to Miss Browning. 'This will pick up splinters.' It was a trick she'd learned in Exeter and had had to use many times after one of her father's rages. Except they never had been quite like rages. More like demonstrations to intimidate. But after those displays, amidst the broken plates and glass, she'd kept her head down, knowing she wouldn't get in any more trouble if she cleaned up like a good girl, pretending nothing unusual had happened. Carol kept her head down now.

'You're a very practical young lady,' said Miss Browning, watching, though she seemed detached from her words. She lay down the dustpan and brush, carefully, as if it were important not to make a sound with them. 'If you don't mind, my dear,' she said, 'I'll let you finish off. I think this little episode has affected me more than I realised.'

Miss Browning went to sit in her chair by the fire and poked at the red embers from the coals Carol had got going earlier. She felt the older woman wanted to say something, that she disapproved, but was not sure how to ask. Carol busied herself with the newspaper, parcelling it up and taking the damp bundle across the lounge and out of the back door to the dustbin.

Out in the garden, the charcoal sky was streaked with paler clouds. A few brave stars shone through. The dustbin was next to the privy in the small flagged area outside the back door before the stone steps up to the square of garden. Carol gingerly stepped onto the path next to the small lawn, hugging herself against the cold. She looked back at the rear of the row of cottages. There were a few lights on, shielded by curtains. But none of the neighbours had come out despite the shouting. Was this a safe community? Or were they scared? A world of people hiding from violence? 'Jenny, where are you?' she whispered, looking out to the empty moorland for an answer.

The only curtains not drawn were those to Miss Browning's cottage. Through the small living room window she could see her landlady huddled over the fire, doodling idly with the poker. Carol thought she looked lost, there on her own. But anyone could see her if they approached over the moor and down to the back lane. So this was how easy it was to be spied on. Carol shivered. She no longer felt safe out in the garden. She ought to tell Miss Browning to keep the curtains closed.

Back in the cottage Miss Browning was in the tiny kitchen putting another kettle of water on the hob. She struck a match and lit the gas ring. 'Well, my dear,' said the older woman. 'We've had quite an adventure this evening. Sit down and we'll have a talk.'

Carol positioned herself in the smaller chair by the fire, fearing what was to come, and looked again at the framed photographs on the walls. Most were formal portraits of people in what she assumed was their Sunday best. Posed in studios by the look of it, and standing in front of painted backgrounds. The women's gowns were extravagant, but the monochrome made it impossible to tell if they were aflame with colour. The solemn composed looks on the faces suggested not. Carol hoped their descendants had learned to smile.

The kettle whistled and a few moments later Miss Browning appeared with fresh tea and a plate of biscuits. Carol watched the older woman put the tray on the small drop leaf table. 'Sugar?'

Carol shook her head. 'No thank you.'

'I think you'd better have one.' She stirred Carol's cup. 'I'd rather you didn't stare, my dear.'

'Oh, sorry,' said Carol, startled by the directness of the comment. 'I was just surprised you weren't more shaken.'

'I was shaken. But that's no good, is it? We have to bear up and brace ourselves.' Miss Browning smiled as she passed the cup to Carol. 'Unless you have a better idea.'

'Who was that man who threw the stone? Why was he here?'

'That was Mr Holmes. And I'm not sure even he could tell you why he was here. He's the father of the murdered child. One of my children.'

Miss Browning looked away.

'I didn't know there was a murdered child.'

'My dear,' Miss Browning looked startled. 'It's all over the news.'

'I haven't been following it.' Her father had never allowed them to read the newspapers he brought home, inevitably folded to the racing page, and she hadn't acquired the habit in the few months she had been free. 'My father kept the newspaper hidden. Said it would give us ideas.'

'Some ideas are worth considering,' said Miss Browning, pouring the pale tea into the china cups. 'So why would your father not want you to have ideas? I don't think that is normal.'

Carol had little idea of what was normal, and regretted mentioning her father. 'He didn't want us to get into trouble.' That was true; it was a technique she had been developing – telling the truth without revealing anything so then she could never be found out lying.

'I hope that was not because you are a young woman.' Miss Browning nodded to the pictures on the wall. 'Who would remember my friends here if they hadn't been ready to get into trouble?'

'I thought they were relations,' said Carol, nursing her cup of tea with both hands.

'Oh my poor dear. Did they teach you nothing at school?'

Carol felt herself blushing.

'They're suffragettes, my dear, suffragettes. And where would we be without the enfranchisement of women? Biscuit?'

Carol declined. She wanted to ask what enfranchisement meant but feared revealing more ignorance.

'Gertrude Stein's there as well. Women who all knew themselves and what they stood for.'

'What about the man?' She looked at the picture of the young man in the wing collar. His thick glossy moustache looked as if it were moulded out of plastic and should belong to someone much older.

'He would have approved.' Miss Browning stirred her tea thoughtfully before speaking again. 'He was my fiancé. Died at Passchendaele.'

Carol nodded, but again she felt Miss Browning's words were leaving her behind.

'I thought he was your father.'

'No. 1917. Another year, and he would have been out of it. Such foolishness. And now I fear it's all starting again.'

'I'm sorry about your young man.'

Miss Browning smiled. 'It wouldn't have worked. But never mind that. What do you think of this Suez business?'

Carol didn't think anything about this Suez business. She'd heard the word mentioned at the bank, but that was all. She desperately wished she knew more.

'It just goes to show,' said Miss Browning. 'What fills our thoughts, what seems of vital importance to us, may not fill someone else's.' Miss Browning paused. 'I don't like saying this, Carol, but I didn't like what I saw outside. Inspector Bible is married, you know.'

Carol felt angry. 'It's nothing like that.'

'How do you know him?'

'Does it matter?'

'I think it does. I think I have a right to know who's in my house. And I don't know very much about you.'

'I was a witness at a cafe. There was some bullying. Some boys were bullying pupils from the grammar school.' It was true, up to a point. She hadn't lied.

'Does he always put his arms round witnesses?'

'I was cold.'

'These bullies. I hope it was no one I've taught. You do so wonder how they'll turn out.' Miss

Browning knelt to crack open the glowing coals with the poker. Carol rose to draw the curtains at the rear of the cottage where the window looked on to the back garden. There was a movement by the glass. A trick of the light, perhaps. But it had been like a face, a fleeting glimpse of a pale moon. She drew the curtains quickly and turned back to the window.

Miss Browning heaved herself up from the hearth. 'We're going to need some more coal.' She lifted the coal scuttle by the upper of its two handles. The few coals remaining rolled and echoed inside the grey zinc. 'Would you mind doing the honours?'

Carol hesitated.

'What's wrong?'

'I thought I saw something outside.'

'We'll see about that.' Miss Browning put the coal scuttle down, gripped the poker tightly and advanced to the window, lifting the curtain to one side as she leaned close to the glass. 'The imagination can play tricks, but we'll see.' She strode to the back door and went out into the garden. 'Anyone there?' called the older woman, stepping out into the dark. 'Come on, show yourself.' Her voice was more distant now. There was a clatter, the sound of a hollow drum rolling on stone as someone stumbled into the dustbin and knocked it over. A cry. Carol overcame her fear and rushed to the back door as, relieved, she heard Miss Browning's voice again, and the sound of the poker thwacking material.

'Leave off me,' said a protesting voice. A male voice. A voice she knew. Miss Browning dragged the figure from behind the privy, and into the light thrown by the glow from the sitting room.

'Hello, Malcolm,' said Carol.

NINETEEN

The wind was blowing sharply on the top so he led them down between dark outcrops of millstone grit towards Hebers Ghyll. Below them Ilkley was just catching the sun, and Beamsley Beacon gleamed in full sunlight beyond to the north. A train winding through lower Wharfedale towards the black stones of the industrial West Riding looked like a toy, but a grumpy Pauline kept asking when they could have their sandwiches. Bible was afraid the day had been a mistake.

'We'll find somewhere out of the wind,' he said as he led the way down the path popular with hikers walking over the moor from Eldwick. 'Have our picnic there. Watch your feet on this bit, Pauline.'

'I am watching my feet,' grumbled the little girl, bundled up in woollies and a zip-up jacket.

'Here, let me hold your hand,' said Shirley coming up behind her. 'This is a big step.'

Pauline ignored her, jumped down the rock step and walked past Bible who was waiting to see his wife and daughter safely down the scramble. Shirley took his proffered hand without smiling, and released it when she was down. She had been cold since they left home.

'Looks like she's leading the way,' he said to Shirley.

'Don't let her go too far on her own.'

'Wait there, Pauline,' he shouted. The little girl turned around. 'The wind's blowing up my clothes,' she said as a gust lifted her thick tartan skirt and she tried to hold it down. Suddenly she ran towards them and pushed her way in between. 'I want to hold hands.' They took a hand each as the clouds drifted southwards and the sunlight reached them.

'Swing me,' said Pauline. Bible and Shirley lifted their arms as they hoisted Pauline aloft and swung her across a stream that had carved a steep-sided channel in the sandy soil. Beyond the stream was a hollow in the bracken.

'What about here for sandwiches?' said Bible.

'All right by me,' said Shirley.

Bible dropped the sagging rucksack from his shoulder. 'Don't sit down till I've got the Pakamacs out. It might be damp.'

He looked up to the trees on the horizon below Doubler Stones and saw another walker up there. There weren't many at this time of year, though Ilkley Moor was a popular picnic spot in summer. Bible passed the rucksack to Shirley as he spread the macs out for them to sit on, taking care to avoid places where gnarled roots might poke holes in the plastic. 'You can sit down,' said Shirley to Pauline. Shirley unwrapped a neatly folded packet of greaseproof paper and gave her a sandwich. 'This is yours. Cheese and raisin.' Pauline held out a hand and bit eagerly into the bread. The concoction sounded horrible, but his daughter loved it, and it was healthy enough.

'What have we got?' he said.

'The same,' said Shirley. He tried not to look

disappointed. She laughed when she saw his face drop. 'Or there's potted meat.'

She held out the package and he reached for it. 'That's the first time you've laughed today,' he said quietly.

'I know you're angry with me for seeing Holmes,' said Shirley.

'Not any more. You did what you felt you had to do.'

'But I'm in the way.'

Pauline paused, her mouth full of white bread and cheese. 'What are you talking about?'

'Nothing, love,' said Shirley. 'And don't talk with your mouth full.'

'I signed your petition this morning,' said Bible.

They were interrupted by the tramp of feet pounding down the path. He stood up in the hollow to see who it was. It reminded him of being dug into foxholes in the jungle, anxiously looking for Japs. Pauline popped up too. He just stopped himself saying 'get down', but they must have looked absurd to the cheery-faced hiker striding towards them, his trousers tucked into his socks and his khaki rucksack joggling from side to side on his back.

'Now then,' he said as he bounded past.

'How do,' said Bible.

'Grand day,' added the hiker over his shoulder without slowing his pace.

Pauline tugged at Bible's elbow. 'Do you know him?' she whispered suspiciously.

'No,' said Bible.

'Why did he speak to you then?'

Bible shrugged. 'It's what grown-ups do.'

'He was scruffy,' said Pauline with finality, sitting down and ending the conversation. But Bible turned sharply. Scruffy. The same word she'd used about the man she'd seen outside school. 'Have you seen him before?'

'No,' she said, nervous now.

'Jim, sit down,' said Shirley.

'Yeah,' said Bible, after another glance towards the figure, who had just reached the edge of the trees where the ghyll tumbled down towards Ilkley in a sequence of woodland waterfalls. 'Sorry. It's just me. Let's find a bridge for Pooh sticks.'

The sun left them again as they entered the cool wood, and the sludgy leaves underfoot reminded them they were in the dead of the year. The ghyll fell in silver curtains over the rocks into brackish pools. Pauline slithered and fell on her bottom as they followed the twisting path downhill. She got up sullenly, rejecting all attempts to help.

'There's a bridge at the bottom,' said Bible. 'We can play there.'

Below them, near where the woodland reached the road, they could hear children playing and the occasional scream. But they were good-natured screams, playing screams.

'Who are those children?' said Pauline.

'I don't know, love,' said Shirley. 'Just children playing.'

'Are they bigger than me?'

'They must be if they're not with their mums and dads.'

'I don't want them there.'

Bible wanted to tell his moping little daughter that she'd have to get used to it, but instead he lifted her down a muddy step where a boulder had fallen out like a loose tooth. 'Let's not get your coat dirty.' He set her on her feet and waited for Shirley. As he gave her a hand down, he managed to whisper in his wife's ear, 'What's the matter with her? It's only children.'

'You know it's not just that. She knows something's wrong.'

Pauline was watching them, but he doubted she'd heard.

'Have we made her scared?' he said softly

Shirley paused and looked him in the eye. 'I hope not.'

There was a louder scream, then a shout. Shirley looked at him, startled. But then there was laughter. Children's laughter.

'It's nothing,' said Bible.

The white wooden bridge was deserted when they reached it. The children they'd heard were whooping upstream, but here it was quiet, the noise distant, and Bible reflected that the trickle of water made it seem quieter. Pauline stood on the footbridge with her mother behind her, ready to drop a spray of alder twig into the broken water as soon as Bible let go of his piece of bark.

'One two three,' said Shirley, holding Pauline's waist as she lurched forward to drop her Pooh stick. Pauline scampered to the other side to watch it reappear, but Bible stayed where he was, transfixed by a pair of shoes he saw in the stream, floating down like leather boats, twisted one way and then the other by the eddies. Small shoes. Children's shoes. He jumped round the end of the bridge and scrambled down the muddy bank, splashing into the water to catch them as they bobbed towards him. The water lapped around his ankles and filled his walking boots.

'What on earth are you doing, Jim?'

He grabbed for the shoes and caught them both, one in each hand, and splashed back up the muddy bank. They were girl's open shoes with a narrow strap across the top of the foot. 'It's all right, I've got them.' It didn't seem a good enough explanation. Shirley held Pauline's hand as they walked to him. His daughter looked at him suspiciously.

'Got you a new pair of shoes, love,' said Bible, trying to sound cheerful. He heard someone running towards them. A girl of about ten was stumbling down the path, wiping her eyes as she ran. Bible put his arm out to catch her as she rushed past.

'Here. Steady on a minute.'

Shirley was by his side in a moment. She squatted in front of the girl and held her hands. 'What is it, love?'

'They threw my shoes in the river.' The girl wore a faded pink cardigan grimed with mud, and a surprisingly clean tartan purse with a shiny plastic strap slung across her body.

Other children's voices sounded nearer, and two boys came into view on the muddy path by the stream. They wore grey short trousers and zipped up windcheaters. Brothers probably, thought Bible. One sported an imitation leather helmet with ear flaps, as if he were a Spitfire pilot. Bible left the shoeless girl to Shirley and stood in the middle of the path.

'Oi, you two.'

The boys stopped.

'Come here,' said Bible.

They moved slowly towards him. They were shorter than the girl, but the older one was probably about the same age, the younger one a couple of years younger.

'What do you want, Mister?' said the boy in the flying helmet. He seemed to decide he would take charge, and led them up to Bible. The younger boy had a runnel of snot dribbling from his nose to his top lip.

'Have you thrown this girl's shoes in the river?'

'We were only playing,' said the Spitfire pilot.

Shirley still stood next to the shoeless girl. 'She doesn't think you were playing,' said Shirley sternly.

'Are we in trouble?' said the smaller boy. Bible couldn't take his eyes off the yellow dribble of mucus running into the boy's mouth.

'Shut up, Billy,' said Spitfire pilot.

'Have you got a hanky?' said Bible.

'No, mister,' said Billy.

Bible reluctantly took out his own handkerchief and offered it to him. His attempt to stop suspected bullying had quickly turned into nannying. He looked towards Shirley. 'I think this is more your department.'

She smiled at him. 'I think you're doing very well.'

Billy held out the used handkerchief, his top lip cleaner but still glistening. 'You can keep it,' said Bible. 'What are we going to do about these shoes then?' Only one of the children knew what to do about the shoes.

'She can put 'em on wet,' said the Spitfire pilot decisively. 'It's nowt.'

Bible suspected the boy was right. He looked at the girl's muddy wet socks and the splashes of mud up her legs and thought wet shoes couldn't make much difference. 'Here, put them back on. And try to play nicely next time.'

The girl sat on a rock glowering at Bible. The shoes squelched as she pulled them on. So he hadn't turned out to be quite the knight in shining armour she'd expected.

'She's been with a man,' said the older boy.

'I have not,' said the girl, her cheeks colouring. 'Fibber.'

'You have so, Linda. He gave her that purse.'

'You were in there too looking at dirty pictures.'

'She's lying, mister. She got into a car with a man this morning. She were gone ages.'

'Is this true?' said Bible.

Linda backed off. 'I haven't done nothing.'

'Stop there,' said Bible. 'I can help you.' Linda turned and ran. 'Hey,' said Bible. She didn't stop. Bible pointed at the two boys. 'Are you telling me the truth?'

'He just dropped her at t'bottom o't'woods before we came up here,' said Billy.

'Look after Pauline,' shouted Bible. 'And you two, stay here.' As he ran off down the path after Linda, he noticed Shirley had put her hands over his daughter's ears.

TWENTY

Bible knew he'd scared her, and that running after Linda would scare her more. But he was running in the forlorn hope that the man who'd dropped her off would still be there. His feet were rubbing in his boots. They always did when you'd got your socks wet. He could hear the squeak as he ran.

But he couldn't see or hear Linda. Just his panting and feet slapping on the path. The girl must have been fast. He could just glimpse the tarmac of Heber's Ghyll Drive between the trees. There was a scrape above him, and he stopped. Sitting on the branch of an old oak which stood beside the path, he saw Linda, wiping her nose with her sleeve. The tree split into two barely four feet up, one trunk vertical, the other sloping out to the left creating a ramp up to where the girl now sat.

'I'll go higher,' threatened the girl, 'if you come after me.'

'Stay there,' said Bible. He had no time to deal with her now. 'Wait for my wife.' He didn't stop to see what the girl did.

The woodland path disgorged directly onto the pavement. He looked both ways. Nothing. No cars. But the hiker they'd seen earlier was there, sitting on a boulder by the bus stop, pouring something from a flask into the plastic top. Something hot. Steam was rising. The hiker looked startled.

'Hey up,' he said.

Bible nodded, and looked up and down the road again.

'Have you lost everybody?' said the hiker.

Bible walked steadily across the road. 'Excuse me, have you seen a car come down here? Or a man with a girl of about ten?'

'This sounds official.'

Bible pulled out his warrant card. He wasn't on duty, but he always carried it.

'What's going on?' The hiker drank from his plastic cup, and held it towards Bible. 'Want a sup?' It was tea. 'There's a spot of whisky in it.'

Bible declined. 'Have you seen anything, then?'

'Bloke drove off down there about half an hour ago. So you've missed him.'

'But you'll be able to describe him,' said Bible.

'I didn't see much. He didn't get out. But I think he was a neat sort of fella. Smart. But getting on a bit. Pulled up just over there.' He nodded to the gap in the trees where the path began.

'Was he by himself?'

'He was when he left. Not when he arrived.' Bible waited for a more helpful account. The hiker offered Bible the thermos lid again. 'Sure you don't want any?' Bible shook his head and waited. If this man was a hiker, why was he waiting for a bus? It wasn't that far down into Ilkley. The man methodically screwed the lid back on his flask.

'Dropped a little girl off. Pink cardigan she was wearing. I thought he must be her grandad or summat.'

'Didn't you think it a bit odd to drop off a young girl here, on her own?'

The hiker shrugged. 'Kids play out. There were some in t'woods as I came down.' He put the thermos back in his rucksack and started fastening the buckles. 'I thought she wa'n't wearing much. Just a cardigan on a day like today. Blows right through it.' The man pulled the last buckle tight and looked across the road, behind Bible. 'But you don't need to look for her anymore. She's there.'

Shirley appeared from the woods with Pauline holding one hand, and Linda the other. Billy and his brother each carried sticks and were whacking at the undergrowth. Billy was wearing Bible's rucksack, but the straps were so long it was bouncing on his bottom rather than his back. Somehow Bible was going to have to get them all back into the town and to the police station.

'What sort of car was it?'

'Who said it were a car? A van. It were a van. Like an old post office van. But repainted. A sort of mucky khaki.' The hiker finished buckling his rucksack. 'A bit odd, that. Smart fella and a scruffy van. And letting his granddaughter out with nothing on but an old cardy. Teks all sorts, that's what they say. Bus'll be here soon. Once an hour, on the hour.'

Shirley was now standing beside them. Billy and his brother were busy trying to poke each other's eyes out, fencing with sticks among bushes by the road. Pauline and Linda were watching quietly, still holding Shirley's hands. They'd have to find out where these stray children lived and take them home. And Bible's little Austin was in Ilkley where they'd left it before starting their walk. He took out his notebook. 'I'm going to have to ask for your name and address.'

'It's Ken. Ken Wigley.'

Bible tried to assess Ken Wigley. The name had come quickly; he was probably telling the truth. 'You seem to be very observant, Ken,' said Bible. 'We'll need to be in touch again.'

Ken gave an address in the city in Bible's patch. Useful. Here it was the West Riding force and Bible had no jurisdiction. That's why he ought to take the man to Ilkley police station. But instinct told him to leave it. He'd take a chance on Wigley having given him the correct address for when he wanted to talk to him again.

The bus came into view. Ken got up from the boulder he'd been sitting on and put his rucksack on one shoulder. 'Are you getting this?' said Ken.

'No,' said Bible. 'Our car's not far off.'

The bus pulled up so close to the kerb its dusty tyres dwarfed Pauline who jumped back in alarm.

'So what's it all about, then?' said Ken as he jumped onto the open platform at the rear of the bus. 'It's exciting. Like reading a book.'

'I'm glad we can entertain you,' said Bible quietly as the bus pulled away. Ken waved at them, holding on to the pole as if he were enjoying the ride.

'I think you've made a friend,' said Shirley as the bus disappeared.

Billy and Brian (the name Spitfire pilot eventually admitted to) lived near the Ghyll, but Linda lived on a farm up near the Beacon, Moor End Farm she called it, so Bible still had her in tow in her damp shoes when he walked up the steps of the small, stone-built police station on Riddings Drive. Shirley had taken Pauline to the market square, promising to buy her a milk shake, but Bible was doubtful if they'd find one on a Sunday. The desk sergeant took some time to weigh him up before he called his boss. Now Bible sat facing Inspector Daniels across a chipped wooden table that had once been varnished in a dark oak, but was now down to bare wood in places.

'Bit of a coincidence, you being a policeman and that,' said Daniels, doodling squares and circles on the pad in front of him. 'You after promotion?'

'Are you?' said Bible. 'We're the same rank.'

'Not in here, you're not. Not in those hiking boots.'

Bible had heard of Daniels, but never met him. Plodding, that's what they said. Got the job done, but slowly. He wore round glasses and was bald on top, with glistening black hair at the sides glued down with Silvikrin. Bible thought he looked more like an insurance man than a copper. He'd trust him to take books back to the library, but not much more.

'You need a WPC to interview the girl. She's called Linda. Get her to open up,' said Bible insistently. But he didn't mention the hiker. He'd keep Ken Wigley a secret.

'We don't need telling what to do by the city,' said Daniels, filling in one of the circles on his pad.

'We've got this murder case. A little boy. It may link up. We know there's a van involved.'

'Not solved it yet, have you?' said Daniels triumphantly.

'But if it's the same bloke...'

'Which it might not be.'

'He won't know we're looking for him here. He'll feel too secure. Make mistakes.'

'Ah, the strategist.' Daniels stopped doodling. 'I've been told about you. Clever, but so clever you can never decide what to do.'

'Have I done something to annoy you?' said Bible. Daniels was a disgrace. Bible felt the urge to smack him. The man was wrong. The man was a fool. Linda was sitting on the hard wooden bench in the entrance hall dangling her legs, and no one in the station showed any desire to comfort her, or do anything which might make her open up and tell them what had happened.

'I worked hard for my rank,' continued Daniels. 'I wasn't parachuted in after the war because I'd been an officer.'

There was a knock and the door opened. The desk sergeant. He seemed to belong to the same curmudgeonly culture as Daniels. 'Sir, that little girl's playing up. Trying to get out o't'door but O'Brien's holding her. Says she wants the man who brought her in here.'

'I'm coming.' Daniels threw down his pencil with disgust and left the room.

As they walked down the corridor Bible could hear Linda yelling 'Let go off of me.' An adult voice, angry, was shouting back. Daniels quickened his pace. In the entrance a young constable was holding Linda by one stick-thin arm as she tried to pull away. She kicked out at the policeman who grabbed her other arm, pulled her round like a rag doll, and lowered his face to her level. 'Stop it or I'll put you in the cells.' At which Linda kicked out again, and the youthful copper got redder in the face.

'Now, now, young lady. That's no way to behave,' said Daniels, trying to take command. He pushed the constable aside and pinned the girl's arms to her sides. Bible wondered at the misplaced confidence which allowed him to wade in like that. The girl was in a state. 'You should respect your elders,' said Daniels. Linda pulled her head back, then snapped it forward and spat in his face. Daniels slapped her across the cheek. Bible stepped between them, keeping his hands at his side and resisting the temptation to push the local inspector back. Daniels' eyes widened in disbelief.

'What in hell's name do you think you're doing?'

'That's not the way to talk to a child.'

'Do you know what sort of a child this is? What that lot are like up there?'

Bible looked at Linda, who was crying now and wiping her eyes. So this was Daniels' wild child from the moors. He was struck that she didn't say she wanted her mum. Pauline would have. But then Pauline was only six and Linda was about ten, though due to this station's interviewing techniques, they hadn't found out for sure.

'So you know her?'

'You can't believe a word she says,' said Daniels.

'Would you like me to take her off your hands?' said Bible. 'I don't mind being lied to.'

'I think we can handle her. Take her down the corridor.'

Linda was quiescent now. Resigned. She'd given in. Bible wanted to question her. Didn't trust Daniels. But he could hardly force his way back into the station and follow Daniels down the corridor. There were procedures, and he would stick to them, but he felt like smashing them down. He was left feeling foolish in the entrance area. 'I hope you're going to tell her parents,' Bible shouted after Daniels.

'Goodbye, Inspector Bible. I'll be putting in a complaint.'

That would mean another meeting with Holroyd.

Bible slammed the car door, sat in the driver's seat next to Shirley, and thumped the dashboard. He sounded the car horn with the heel of his hand and kept his hand pressed on it. Shoppers on Bridge Street turned to see what the commotion was.

Shirley pulled his hand away. 'What's wrong with you, Jim?'

'In there.' He nodded back in the direction of the police station.

A well-padded middle-aged woman with a shopping bag stared at the car fixedly.

'I think she's looking at the number plate,' said Bible.

Shirley clicked the passenger door open. 'I'm going to take Pauline home on the bus.'

Pauline was on the back seat, concentrating on her magic slate. Shirley got out on to the pavement, and was about to open the rear door to take Pauline when Bible jumped out, stood by his side of the car and spoke to her across the car roof.

'I'm sorry.' A scene in the street was not what people were used to seeing in Ilkley, but, blast it, what the hell. 'It was the coppers here. No bloody sympathy. It's them needs a posse of mothers on their backs.' Bible took a deep breath. 'It's all right. I feel better now.'

Shirley opened the passenger door and got back in. Bible returned to his place behind the steering wheel. Shirley fixed her gaze on the glove compartment.

He engaged first gear and pulled out into the street.

'Do you still think it's Teds? After this?'

'I don't know,' said Shirley.

Pauline was busy on the back seat. He hoped she hadn't heard.

'How's the drawing going, love?' he said over his shoulder. Pauline pulled out the cardboard slide to erase what she'd just drawn and pushed it back in again.

'Going to draw a crocodile,' she said.

Bible glanced at his wife and mouthed quietly, 'I bet it's the same bloke.'

'Just take us home,' said Shirley.

'And he'll hang if we find him.'

As he turned right to connect with the road back towards the city, a uniformed policeman on the beat noticed the car, and stepped into the road with his hand out, palm towards them. Bible stopped the car. It wasn't a policeman he'd seen in the station. Bible wound down his window.

'Now then, sir, we've had reports of some bother with this car you're driving.'

'It's all right, officer...'

'It may not be all right. Have you been sounding your horn and making a nuisance of yourself? It's an offence to sound your horn if you've nothing to sound it about.'

Bible smiled at him and showed his warrant card. 'There were some boys larking about and running into the road. I was just warning them. I'm not on duty. I'm just here with my family.'

'Sorry, sir. I'll let the governor know.'

Bible put his warrant card away. 'I shouldn't bother him. It was nothing serious.'

'As you say, sir.' The policeman stepped back. As Bible pulled away he could see the policeman in his rear view mirror, staring at their car. Shirley looked at him now.

'You lied to him,' she said.

'Yes,' he said.

'I've never known you lie before.'

'No,' said Bible. Lying had been easier than he thought. But when the complaint reached Holroyd, he'd probably be taken off the case.

TWENTY-ONE

The rain came on as they left Birmingham and drove north towards Manchester in the dark. They pulled into a woodland track, out of sight of the road, for a brief sleep. Winter light was dawning as they turned east towards Yorkshire and Logan stared grimly at a bleak watery landscape.

'Saddleworth Moor,' said Robbo. The spindly wipers thrashed against the sheets of water pouring down the windscreen. 'I ought to pull over till this has passed.' Robbo leaned forward in the driver's seat and peered through the glass as if he were looking into a fish tank.

'Keep going,' said Logan. He shouted into the back of the van. 'Not our sort of country this, Larry.' Perhaps it was as well the boy couldn't see it. It would only make him more miserable.

'It's like Dartmoor,' said Stanley.

'I've never been,' said Logan. But he did know the soil around Exeter was red. This earth was black. Some of it looked like it had been burnt. And the tussocky grass he could just make out was an ill-looking green. Why had Dawn come here? Anyway, he'd come to rescue her. Via, it now seemed according to Stanley's irritating chatter, Huddersfield. What bloody stupid names.

The water hissed under the tyres as they entered the city. The stones were so black he thought they'd been painted to match the moors. Men with rain dripping off their flat caps and carrying army knapsacks waited at bus stops for the journey to work. Old women with bandy legs lurched from side to side with shopping bags, their hands full, leaving them defenceless against the rain. The men looked tough, Logan's sort of men, but defeated; the women looked tougher.

'Let's find Turner,' said Logan. He didn't like being dependent on Robbo.

As they neared the city centre Logan noticed newspaper placards about a murdered child, and policemen on the pavement watching cars and stopping pedestrians. Too many policemen.

'What's going on here?' said Logan.

'Search me,' said Robbo.

'Looks like you might get taken at your word,' said Logan. A man with a heavy moustache and a pale trench coat stained dark on the shoulders with rain stepped into the road with his hand out. A policeman in plain clothes – you could tell them a mile off. Robbo pulled the van over to the side. Logan could feel Stanley's leg go tense on the seat in between them.

'Excuse me, sir,' said the policeman in a flat northern voice Logan hated at once. 'We're stopping all van drivers. Can you tell me where you've come from?'

Robbo wound down the passenger window. 'Why, what's up 'ere then?' he said in an accent Logan hadn't heard him use before. Sometimes it was useful to have a conman on your payroll.

'You can't be from round here, else you'd have

heard,' said the detective, putting his hands over the bottom of the open window. Logan hoped it was too dark to spot Larry lying in the back.

'Nah, we're just up from Dewsbury, like.' Robbo should have gone on the stage. Logan knew he had to keep his mouth shut. His accent would give him away. But Dewsbury. What sort of place was that?

'Going where?'

'Doing some tiling for a mate.'

'So you'll have tiling gear in the back, then?'

'Still waiting for t' shops to open, aren't we?'

'But you won't mind if we check.' The policeman pushed himself away from the door and beckoned to a couple of coppers in uniform to come over. Logan didn't like the way this was going. The policeman looked in again, ranging his eyes over Logan and Stanley. 'You all from Dewsbury then?' Logan nodded curtly. Stanley followed his lead and nodded too. The copper with the moustache stared at them intently. 'There can't be much conversation down there if you two are anything to go by.'

'Aye, they're no good at nattering,' said Robinson, a touch too merrily. 'You'll have to come dahn for a quiet pint.' Logan feared Robbo was overdoing the accent, but it drew the copper's attention from him and Stanley. The policeman stared hard at Robinson.

'Haven't I seen you somewhere before?'

Logan saw Robbo finger his recently shaved upper lip. 'I don't think so, Sergeant.'

'Did I say I was a sergeant?'

There was a shout from somewhere round the back of the van. 'You'd better come round here, Sarge.'

'Wait there,' said the sergeant. He prised himself

away from the door and walked to the back of the van.

Logan, still leaning back, murmured to Robbo and Stanley. 'Get ready to move if he starts opening that door.'

'Do you know him, Dad?' whispered Stanley.

'Ward,' hissed Robbo. 'He's called Ward. He's a bastard.'

They could hear voices behind the van, the constable's first.

'This number plate, Sarge. It's not from round here. Somewhere down south, I think.'

'Right, let's search it.' Ward's voice. The sergeant shouted. 'Switch your engine off, sir.'

'Now,' said Logan. Robbo slung the gearstick into first and put his foot down. Stanley was tossed back like a doll and then lurched forward as his father wrenched the stick back into second. There was a thump in the back of the van where Larry was tied lying on the floor. A uniformed policeman standing near the front jumped aside quickly and Logan, his forearm braced against the front pillar of the open window, turned round to see a helmet rolling in the road. The coppers' shouts faded as the van picked up speed.

Robbo was good at some things. He had to be kept in his place, but he was good. A skilled driver was worth keeping, and it left Logan free to think.

'I'm not dodging down any of these little roads yet.' Robbo moved the long pudding spoon of a gear stick like a rapier as he went from second to third. 'This'll do.' He swung the van round a wider corner, and then took a right down a road that led off at an angle of seventy degrees rather than ninety. 'Choose your corners carefully,' he grinned.

'You'd better be right,' muttered Logan. Stanley was squashed between them, and Logan was pushed into him as the van swayed downhill through a canyon of Victorian mills, tall dark buildings with batteries of windows in uniform rows. Larry's body rolled in the back again, but when Logan turned to look, it was too gloomy in the rear of the van to see clearly.

Robbo slapped Stanley's thigh. 'Look and learn, my son, look and learn.'

Yes, too cocky. Needed taking down a peg or two.

'We're going to have to get rid of this crate,' said Logan.

'Turner knows places.'

The bell of a pursuing police car tinkled in the distance. Ahead a flatbed truck had pulled across the road to reverse into a delivery bay. It was piled with tightly packed bales of wool, bulging in hessian sacking. Robbo pulled the van to a halt. None of them spoke. Logan could hear the police bell getting nearer. A man on the pavement was shouting instructions to the lorry driver. 'Right hand down a bit.' Robbo stuck his head out of the Bedford.

'How much longer mate? I'll be in right shit if I'm late wi'this,' he shouted in his adopted Yorkshire accent, jerking his thumb towards the back of the van.

'Keep your hair on. We've all gorra job to do.' The speaker signalled to the lorry driver with his hand up. 'Whoa. Tek it forward a bit, then right hand down again.'

Robbo drew his head back into the cab and looked at Logan. 'What do you want me to do, boss?'

Logan knew Robbo was looking to him for action. Perhaps violence. In Exeter, he'd have been known. The mill owner would probably have been in his pay. Certainly the haulage company paying the lorry driver. But here...not his patch. And violence would only get them noticed. He should have made connections. More connections than Turner. The police bell sounded nearer. The lorry had moved forward. The heavily treaded front wheels pointed out more sharply and, with a crunch of gears, the driver threw it into reverse again.

'Should we get out and run?' said Robbo.

'Dad?' said Stanley anxiously.

Logan looked into the back, where Larry had tumbled against the rear doors. They couldn't run with Larry. Logan reached under the seat and pulled out the shotgun. He'd cut it down and polished the stock himself, as well as the barrels.

'We can't kill a cop, boss,' said Robbo.

'Stay where you are.' Logan adjusted the wing mirror of the Bedford so he could see down the road behind them as it sloped uphill to where they had turned off. He couldn't see the police car yet. The lorry slowly eased its way into the archway of the mill. In the mirror Logan saw a black car flash across the top of the street, sticking to the main road, the sound of the bell dying as it moved away.

'He's missed us,' said Logan. The lorry was finally nestling into the loading bay. He slid the heavy gun into the long pocket he'd had sewn into the inside of his jacket. 'Keep going.'

Robbo moved the van forward. 'You had me worried, there, boss.'

Logan looked at Robbo and risked a smile. 'Trust me, Robbo. Trust me. Let's go see Turner.'

They stopped at a wooden gate across the track: *WATER BOARD VEHICLES ONLY*. Ahead of them, Logan could see a bleak stone tower like a godforsaken military outpost, the sharp line of fortification along the top of the reservoir embankment, and beyond that an expanse of grey water. He didn't like reservoirs. The River Exe was all right, enclosed by the city. He understood cities. But this wilderness...not enough people. No one to manipulate. And in manipulation lay his safety. He looked out at a sheep tugging at the tussocks of coarse grass.

'Well,' said Logan. 'Frightened of the Water Board are we? We've become very law-abiding all of a sudden.'

'Someone needs to open the gate,' said Robbo. 'Stanley?'

'I can't get out. I'm in the middle.' There was a pause.

'I'll do it,' said Robbo and jumped out of the van. Robbo's town shoes skidded in the mud as he approached the gate. He turned to shout towards the van. 'It's padlocked.'

Logan grabbed the crowbar he always kept near him in the Bedford, and slid the door back roughly. The shotgun in the special pocket was heavy against his ribs as he stepped down. He splashed through the mud, put one of the crowbar's blunt forks behind the metal plate the padlock was attached to, and levered it off, the wood splintering. He swung the gate towards Robbo so forcefully that he was knocked off balance and almost left sprawling in the grass. 'Let's see what the Water Board make of that.'

Logan shouted to Stanley. 'Get behind the wheel and bring it through.'

The Bedford jolted down the track for three hundred yards before it got to the pumping station, the lonely castle Logan had viewed from the gate. Turner appeared out of a primrose yellow door, buttoning up his donkey jacket.

'Hey, you shouldn't have brought that up here.' Logan thought Turner looked scared.

'Get rid of it for us. Robbo says you know places.' Logan went round to the rear of the Bedford and banged on the door. 'Journey over, Larry.' He threw open the rear doors. Larry was there all right, lying on his side with his hands tied behind his back. But across his forehead was a deep red gash, and his face lay in a pool of vomit. Logan clambered into the van and knelt by the young man. He cradled the boy's face between his hands. The eyes flickered and Larry moaned. Not dead.

Turner appeared standing by the open rear doors.

'I'm not having him here.'

'I'll decide that,' said Logan. 'Help me get him inside.'

'Not into the pump house. Bring him round to the boiler room.'

They laid Larry on the cold floor of a cellar-like room built into the dam wall where it joined the pumping station. Logan covered him with a blanket.

'I want something softer under him,' said Logan.

'I've nowt down here,' said Turner.

'Give me that coat.' Logan pointed to the mackintosh hanging where Stanley was sitting astride an old 500 cc. BSA.

'I might need that,' complained Turner. Stanley lifted the coat off the hook and passed it down to Logan. 'What if it rains?'

Robbo helped Logan spread out the raincoat and lift Larry on to the check lining. 'And that scarf as a pillow.' Logan, kneeling by Larry, pointed to the hook where a knitted scarf hung. It started raining, a hard rain, rattling against the one small window. Logan watched Robbo reach for the scarf and stare at Turner as he took it. Turner did not protest. Logan, Stanley and Robbo were a gang now, asserting their power over the natives in this strange land.

Larry groaned. 'Have we any water here?' said Logan in a murmur. He knew the men around him would pick up every word he said.

Turner laughed. 'Nay, there's no water here. It's only a reservoir.'

Stanley went up to Turner and pushed him in the chest. 'You're getting a bit too chipper, mate.'

Turner knocked Stanley's arm away. 'Don't try that with me, son.'

Logan knew Stanley was trying to impress him. It was pathetic. 'Stanley' he said. It was a warning. 'Somebody find some water.' Stanley looked around. Robbo tried a cupboard on the wall.

'You'll not find anything in there,' said Turner, proud of his secret knowledge, and standing his ground.

Logan had had enough. He pointed at Turner. 'You get it.'

Turner paused, then went out of the door. Logan busied himself with Larry.

'What are you going to do with him, boss?' said Stanley. Logan felt the anger rise. It was not a question he liked. Use Larry to get Dawn back was what he intended. But he knew what Stanley was really after. He wanted to know if Logan was going to kill Dawn's young man. And no, he wasn't. He was going to talk him round. Get Larry to see how important it was for Dawn to stay true to her father. And for Larry to realise what a mistake he had made.

'That's for me and Larry to sort out, isn't it, Larry?' said Logan.

The door opened and Logan looked through the rain to the grey moor beyond and a spiky plantation of conifers blurring into the sky. Turner came in with a cup of water, and more water in an old pop bottle. Logan took the cup from him, raised Larry's head, and forced him to take a sip. Then he laid the boy's head down and let him rest.

'You're going to have to move that van before it gets bogged down,' said Turner.

'Hide it,' said Logan. He pushed his bulk up from the floor and stood looking down at the ailing boy.

Turner hesitated. 'What do you mean, hide it? Stands out like a bloody ice-cream van stuck up here in the drizzle. Might as well have bloody tunes playing out o' t'top of it.'

Logan twisted to grab Turner's arm, kicked his leg away, forced him to the floor and used his hand like a claw around the reservoir keeper's face as he kneeled on his chest. 'I don't think you understand,' said Logan. 'I've bought you. Remember who was coming after you before I paid them off? You're mine now. Get it?' Logan could see Turner got it. But he hadn't got it properly. There was no gratitude there. Just resentment. He couldn't be relied on. But Logan needed him for now. Later, though, it would be another matter. 'Now you know your way around this godforsaken bog you northerners live in, so go and get rid of the van.'

Logan relaxed his grip on the reservoir keeper and eased himself up. Robbo and Stanley were watching. Logan knew he'd got their attention. Turner raised himself from the floor and pulled his donkey jacket straight. 'You can't treat me like that.'

'Yes I can,' said Logan. He'd never trusted Turner, and wondered why Robbo had insisted he was the man for them in Yorkshire.

'Best move the van, Jack,' said Robbo softly.

'What about the boy?' said Turner sullenly, his hands stuffed in his jacket pockets.

'He stays here,' said Logan. 'We're going to look after him, you and me, aren't we?'

'What if the police come round?' Turner murmured.

'And why should they do that? High crime rate round here, is there? Sheep rustling among you sheepshaggers?'

'They were round here the other day.'

'And why would that be, Jack?'

'Someone's killed a kid outside a school. There's police everywhere and all t'local mums are panicking.'

Logan fixed Turner with his eyes. 'And the fathers?'

Turner shrugged. He was, Logan guessed, a man without a family.

'Go and hide the van,' said Logan. 'Larry stays.'

Robbo pulled at Turner's sleeve. 'Come on Jack. Best do as he says.'

Turner stumped out of the boiler room, up the two stone steps onto the half-paved track. Logan called Robbo back.

'Watch him, Robbo. He's a man who feels nothing.'

Stanley was watching, his back against the wall. A few days ago he would have been watching and learning; now, Logan thought, the boy was watching and scared. Best to keep him guessing for now.

'Go with them, Stanley.'

Alone with Larry, he raised the boy's head and reached for the mug of water. He put it to the boy's lips and let a drop trickle in. Larry's tongue moved and his eyes half opened, but looked dull and barely comprehending. Logan cradled the young man's head and lowered it back on to the improvised pillow.

TWENTY-TWO

When Bible threw back the heavy oak door of the police station next morning, Ken the hiker bounced up from the wooden bench on which he'd been waiting, but then sat down again. Holroyd was approaching purposefully from his office. Swann glanced down before he caught Bible's eye. Word had got round then. Holroyd fixed on him with his eyes.

'Follow me, lad.'

In Holroyd's office, Bible closed the door behind him. Holroyd was staring out of the window. 'I hear you've been mixing it with the County boys.'

'Have you had a complaint, sir?'

Holroyd turned towards him, startling Bible with a broad smile. This was hard to trust. 'Don't worry about that prick. Getting a bit above himself, chucking his weight around with someone his own rank.' Holroyd flashed open his silver cigarette case, the Capstans lined up like incendiary bombs. 'Daniels says you attacked him. I wish I'd seen it. Here, have a real smoke.' Holroyd pushed the cigarette case towards Bible.

'No thank you, sir.'

'Don't be eccentric, Bible. Have a fag. We're on the same side now.'

'Not this time, sir.' It wasn't worth explaining that he'd stopped smoking after shooting a Jap in Burma. The cigarette he'd tried to smoke afterwards as he looked at the blood seeping from the poor bloke's mouth had made him sick, and every cigarette he'd smoked since had done the same.

'Suit yourself,' said Holroyd, taking a cigarette for himself before snapping the case shut and returning it to the top pocket of his tunic.

'What do you know about Daniels, sir?'

Holroyd tapped the side of his nose. 'You don't need to know, Bible. I'll sort him out. So what was it all about?'

Bible told him about Linda, but he could see Holroyd was barely listening. And Holroyd's smile when he'd finished told him that his boss had some game plan of his own.

'Now this murder. Struggling a bit, aren't you?'

Bible knew Holroyd had a point. 'We have a few leads, sir.' It wasn't a convincing defence.

'I've called the Yard in,' Holroyd announced. Well, Ward had warned him. 'It's not unusual,' continued Holroyd. 'I've always resisted it, but we can't afford a failure. What with our Chief Inspector being off long term, it falls too much on you.' He leaned forward, dropping his voice to a rough whisper. 'And if we can't bottom this bloody murder, it'll be his failure, not ours.' Holroyd winked and picked up the phone on his desk. 'Tell Wallace to come through, will you.'

Bible waited angrily. It was all about how the force looked. Not about protecting the public or, in this case, children. 'We mustn't fail, sir. Children are in danger.' Bible knew he sounded pompous. But if

Holroyd had seen Linda, he might have felt more urgency. Or would he have reacted like Daniels? 'Even if a Yard man takes over, I want to be active on this case.'

'You will be. He's a fat bloke, six months from retirement. Won't want to do much walking.'

Holroyd lit up another cigarette as the door was pushed open without a knock. A large man in double-breasted suit, and maroon waistcoat stretched across his stomach, waded into the smoke holding out a hand.

'Inspector Bible? Superintendent Wallace. Pleased to meet you.'

Bible left Holroyd's office angrily, hunting for Ward. Wallace had been patronising, smug, only after a case which would end his career in a blaze of glory.

Swann glanced up as Bible passed the desk. 'I thought you wouldn't like him.' The desk sergeant nodded towards Ken on the visitors' bench. 'He's been waiting to see you since eight this morning.'

'Where's Bill?'

'He's briefing the coppers on the beat.' Swann swivelled the occurrences book round so Bible could read it. 'Things were happening whilst you were having your day off.' Swann thumped a finger onto a line of Ward's writing. 'Bedford van. Got away somewhere off Thornton Road. Everyone's looking for it.'

Bible read the report. Someone had looked up the number of the Bedford. Exeter. He leaned in to Swann. 'Do you know why Holroyd would have a grudge against a copper called Daniels over the border?'

'I might have heard something.'

Bible waited. 'Don't tease me.'

'Something to do with Holroyd's daughter. She worked on a farm there in the war with a load of other lasses. Rumour was, some copper too old for her wouldn't leave her alone. That was Daniels.'

'Get hold of Bill for me, will you,' he said to Swann, and glanced towards Ken Wigley, who stood up eagerly. 'Follow me.'

Ken sat in the interview room facing Bible and Ward. He had abandoned his hiking boots and zipper in favour of a worn sports jacket and flannels. Monday to Friday clothes, Bible assumed, wondering what his job was.

'I thought I'd better come and see how you were getting on. You know, two heads better than one. Three heads with your assistant here.'

'Sergeant Ward knows enough to run this enquiry himself.'

'The thing is, I've been thinking, why would whoever it was bring that girl back to where he picked her up? What if her parents were out looking for her?'

Ward interrupted. 'We need information.'

'Yes well I'm coming to that. When I got home I put a tin of beans on and I started thinking.'

'Have you remembered something, Mr Wriggly?'

'Wigley. It's like I were saying, I started thinking...'

Bible could hear Ward breathing heavily beside him.

'...and it were the van I were thinking about. The one that dropped the little girl off. I thought, now then, that van. I've seen it somewhere before.'

Ward held his breath.

'And then I thought, now have I? And I have. It were on t'moors. Down a track somewhere. 'Appen Queensbury way.'

Bible glanced at Ward. He could feel his sergeant's impatience. They waited.

'I'm trying to think.' Bible watched Ken struggle with his memory. 'No, it's gone.'

'Perhaps you could describe the van again, Mr Wigley,' said Bible.

'Well, it were a sort of mucky colour. Mucky green. Not shiny. Like someone had painted it themselves.'

'Make?' asked Ward.

'Come again?'

Ward sighed.

'Make? Model?' Ken still looked puzzled despite Ward's brusque promptings.

Bible said more softly. 'Who manufactured it?'

'Small,' said Ken, enlightened. 'It were small. Not big.'

Bible stood up to signal the end of the interview. 'Thank you, Mr Wigley, that's very helpful. We'd better go and see if we can find it.'

Ken got to his feet. 'I'm sorry. I'm not very good at cars. Never had one.'

'We'll do our best.' Bible held the door open. 'If you could sign out at the desk. I don't want you to be late for work.'

'I've got it covered. Lady round the corner minds the shop for me first thing. I'm a newsagent, you know. That's how I keep up.'

'Good,' said Bible. 'We like to keep on the right side of the press.'

'I think you've disappointed him,' said Ward when the door had closed behind Ken.

'I'm getting used to disappointing people,' said Bible. 'Why have no men on the beat seen this van, then?

'Because it's not being driven around the city,' said Ward. 'And everybody's on the look out for the Bedford that got away yesterday.'

'Vans. It's all about vans.'

'Find the van, you've got the man.'

'Yes Bill, very droll.'

There was a knock and Ken's head reappeared round the edge of the door as he opened it.

'It's just come to me. High Gill Moor. Where I saw it. Near the reservoir up there.'

Bible and Ward looked at each other, and stood up.

'Can I come with you if you go to have a look?'

'If you could just sign out at the desk.' Bible stepped after Ken. Wallace was filling the end of the corridor.

'Should I go and tell them at Ilkley?' said Ken.

'Save your bus fare,' said Bible. 'We'll let them know.'

Wallace stood next to Bible as they watched Ken leave.

TWENTY-THREE

Mist smudged the skyline and the jagged line of conifers that stood like a battlement half a mile away across the moor. Ward held the steering wheel firmly as he and Bible rocked from side to side on the rough track down to the reservoir, a dull grey mirror in the middle distance. The turrets along the reservoir wall and the tower of the pump house made Bible feel they were approaching a medieval castle. He caught glimpses of the car behind in the mirror. It too rocked from side to side, but seemingly on an opposite pendulum swing to them.

The gate was open, so Ward drove through and stopped the Wolseley on the cobbles by the pump house. Bible got out into a fine drizzle. Higham pulled up the following car on mud. He and three uniformed constables stepped out gingerly onto the oozing moorland track. A watchful sheep shied away from Higham as he clapped his hands to frighten it.

'What's that poor thing done to you?' shouted Ward, slamming the driver's door. Higham grinned.

'You'd better crack out the wellies,' said Bible.

It was a bleak scene. The yellow door to the pump house looked incongruous – not cheerful, just ill-matched; not suited to the muted colour scheme. There was a tug on the door from the inside, and

Turner emerged, pulling an oilskin over his donkey jacket. Bible saw Turner's face register surprise when he saw the police, but he guessed it was a feigned surprise.

'Hail, friends,' said the squat reservoir keeper, raising his open palm. 'I was just coming out to do my round.' Bible looked at the window in the side of the pump house. Turner could easily have seen them coming.

'A word with you inside, please, Mr Turner.'

Turner looked round in mock astonishment. 'What, not enjoying the fresh air, the Yorkshire wind through your hair?'

'Not today, thank you.'

Ward was organising his small team of constables, now in wellingtons. Two were walking slowly back up the moorland track, and Higham and another were following it down past the reservoir.

'Have you got a search warrant?' said Turner.

'I don't want to talk out here, Mr Turner.'

Turner shrugged and pushed open the yellow door. Despite the soft humming of the pumps, the room felt cold. There was one chair by the small table. Bible gestured towards it and Turner sat down on its edge, as if ready to spring up.

Bible leaned against the wall. 'When someone says "have you got a search warrant" it makes me think they have something to hide.'

'Nay, I were just joking. I've never seen a search warrant. I'd like to have a look at it if you've got one.'

Bible looked around the floor. And most of the watercolours had gone. 'You've moved your paintings, Mr Turner,' he said.

'Once I've got used to what they're like, I start afresh. And I haven't had much time for painting lately.'

'What's kept you busy?'

'This and that.'

'Have you got a van, Mr Turner?' said Bible suddenly.

'A van? Me, no.'

'Don't you drive a van for work?'

'You didn't say, "do you drive a van", you asked if I'd got one. Well I 'aven't. But drive one. Yes, I drive one sometimes. For t'Water Board. But it's not here now.'

'You're a long way from town.'

'Yer what?'

'Still got a motorbike?'

Turner shifted on the edge of his seat. 'Motorbike?'

'You said you had a motorbike. That's how you get here. Where is it?'

'Safe out o' t'rain. It'll be all right.'

'I wasn't worried about its condition, Mr Turner. I want to see it.'

'I'll bring it round to t'station sometime.'

'I'd like to see it now.'

Turner looked uncomfortable.

'Or are you going to insist on a search warrant?'

Turner got up from the chair. 'Suit yourself. It's a bit slithery. Won't do your shoes any good.' He opened the door out onto the track. Bible was glad of the fresh air. Something about Turner made him feel creepy. Ward was about a hundred yards away back down the track from the road, talking to two of the constables. Higham was returning from where the track petered out by the side of the reservoir.

'Nothing down here sir. I'll go and see what Sergeant Ward's found.'

'Shall we go and have a look?'

'You don't want me to see your bike, do you, Mr Turner?' It was odd. It was as if Turner were deliberately wanting to make himself suspicious.

'Come on then,' said Turner, resigned, it seemed, to being found guilty.

The steps from the yellow door led down onto a hump of grass which fell away sharply to one side. Turner led the way down earth steps in the grass to a paint-blistered door set into the dam wall. He pulled out a heavy key, unlocked the door, and waved his hand inside. 'There she is'.

Bible stood looking at a powerful BSA, spattered with mud. He stepped into the cramped cellar, and looked down at the concrete floor.

'We'll need to wheel it out,' he said. 'And you need to get this tyre seen to.'

'I was hoping you wouldn't see that. Are you taking me to court then?'

'Not this time.'

Turner seemed relieved. 'That's what was bothering me.'

Bible didn't trust him. Could Turner really believe they'd bother with a bald tyre in the middle of a murder enquiry?

Ward had returned and stood by the open door as Turner kicked the stand up and pushed the machine out into the open. Ward obviously wanted to tell him something, but Bible's eyes were drawn to a dull brown stain on the floor. He beckoned Ward in.

'Tyre tracks sir.' Ward spoke in not much more than a whisper. 'Not ours. Fatter than a van would make. Going back to the road. And there's another thing. That open gate we came through – a padlock has been rived off with something like a crowbar. The wood's freshly splintered. Must have been done recently.'

'We'll see what Turner has to say. First though, what do you make of that?' Bible pointed to the stain.

'Oil?'

'Perhaps.' Bible squatted down and ran a fingertip over the stain. It was dry. 'I think oil would just be a dark grey. I'm thinking blood.'

Turner reappeared in the doorway and peered into the gloom.

'What have you found?'

Bible rose to block his view. 'Tyre tracks. So you've not seen a van or something bigger up here, then?'

'Rabbiters,' said Turner. 'They drive up. You'll find shotgun shells all over that slope up to the plantation.'

'And do they always have to break the lock off the gate to get through?'

*

Logan sat among the pine trees in a cradle of broken branches he'd fashioned into a makeshift shelter for Larry who lay with his head on Turner's old coat. Stanley was whittling a stick with a big flick knife. Robbo was stamping out the fire they'd made. The reservoir was a quarter of a mile below them, at the bottom of a hillside of sodden, yellow tussocky grass. Logan wondered if the forlorn sheep wished they'd been born somewhere else. Somewhere like Exeter, perhaps. Or Dartmoor. He'd never bothered with the place, but he bet it was nicer than here.

Logan watched the two black cars bounce down the track towards the reservoir. Police. He glared at Stanley, who stopped his carving. Two men got out of the first car, four from the second. One of them looked like the one who'd wanted to search the Bedford the day before. Ward, Robbo had called him. Why so many, and how could they be on to him? His hand gripped the shotgun in his lap.

Two of the uniformed men started walking slowly back towards the road, eyes fixed to the ground. The man from the roadblock pointed down by the side of the reservoir. He saw Turner appear from his yellow door, seeming to wave at the other policemen.

'What's going on here, Robbo? Why are there cops all over the place?'

'Search me, boss. No one followed us.'

Larry groaned. The boy was in a bad way. He put his hand against the boy's head. It was hot.

'What you going to do with him?'

Logan reached out and grabbed Robinson's jacket and pulled him towards him. 'I'll tell you that if you tell me what Turner's been up to?'

'Nothing.'

Logan let go of him and Robbo straightened his clothes. Logan's hand tightened on the stock of the gun. He trained his eyes on the pumping station again. Turner was wheeling a motorbike out.

'That bike's too big for him,' said Stanley. 'He's only a little fella.'

'Shut your noise,' said Logan.

The plain clothes policeman from the second car was working his way up the slope towards them, looking down at the vegetation. He stooped to pick something up and shouted down the slope, cupping his hands around his mouth.

'Shotgun cases, sir.'

A faint answer from below was lost in the wind. The policeman turned towards them again. Thirty yards away.

'He should stop about there,' murmured Logan. Stanley froze with the knife in his hand, the bare wood of the shaven stick pointing at the ground. Robbo held his breath. Logan kept one hand on his gun, the other on Larry's chest. Logan would protect him like a son if he had to. Robbo and Stanley too. The policeman waded nearer through the tussocks. His trousers were stained dark to the knee with the wet grass. They knew he wouldn't find any more empty shells up here. Turner hadn't planted any this far up when he'd concocted the story about the rabbit hunters to cover anything the police might find. A cunning bastard, thought Logan, up to more than he let on.

The plain clothes man sank to his ankle in a bog. Logan heard him swear. He calculated that if the copper came up to the edge of the wood he'd be able to reach out and grab the poor bastard. No need for the gun.

The policeman was pulling his foot out of the mire when Larry gave out a groan. The policeman looked up and peered into the forest. He wouldn't see anything if they were still, but Logan knew he couldn't grab him from here. Logan was ready to move with the gun if he had to.

234

There was a call from down by the reservoir. The young copper turned.

'Nowt here,' he shouted.

Logan couldn't catch the reply from down below, but he could see them beckoning. They were waving the copper back. He watched the policeman take long strides back down over the grass and his hand relaxed on the gun. But when he turned to Larry, the boy was dead.

TWENTY-FOUR

'You won't need to get home tonight, will you, Mr Turner?' said Superintendent Wallace, taking a pinch of snuff and pushing it up each nostril.

'Are you arresting me?'

Wallace snapped the snuff box shut, returned it to his waistcoat, and pulled out a pocket watch. 'Not yet,' he said. 'We've got time. Plenty of time.'

Bible was uneasy. Wallace had demanded they bring Turner in, but they should have kept him under observation. Bible didn't like the overfamiliar reservoir keeper. His stories of night-time rabbit hunters were not convincing, but the Water Board had confirmed Turner's story of using an officially marked vehicle that was usually kept at a reservoir north of the city. If Turner did know something, they'd only succeeded in putting him on his guard.

It was cramped in the little room, and Wallace smelt of sweat. Bible didn't trust Scotland Yard. Their vanity. Their contempt for provincials. He had been offered a chance to start in the Met when he joined the force after the war, but his wife's illness, his reliance on Shirley's help as the girl next door, had made it impossible. Perhaps that's why he resented them, thinking they were above an ordinary cop when he could have joined them.

Wallace clasped his hands in front of his belly and looked at the cocky reservoir keeper. 'Don't try and fool us – you're not bright enough. The Inspector here has enough to put you away for a very long time. Fire away, sir.'

It wasn't true. They had nothing. The tyre tracks and damaged gatepost were just circumstantial. The possible bloodstain would help, but even that could be explained away by a cunning defence.

Turner sat opposite them with a self-satisfied smirk on his face. 'I want to help you,' he said. 'That little lad. It's terrible. Someone should be hanged for that.'

Wallace took another pinch of snuff. 'Go on, Bible. Sort him out.'

'The tyre tracks, Mr Turner,' said Bible. 'Two sets, recent, at the entrance to the track where they turn into the road.'

'I've told you about them. After t'rabbits. Always out there when they know I won't be.'

'How do they know you won't be there, Mr Turner? You told us yourself. You're there all hours.'

'Aye, well, I were 'appen boasting a bit. We're all entitled to a pint.'

'Where do you go for a pint?'

It should have been an easy question to answer, but Turner ignored it. 'You saw the shells. Someone had been there.'

'And the broken gatepost, Mr Turner?'

'Aye, these poachers. They're hooligans. Stop at nothing.'

Bible saw heads at the window. Ward had returned from the reservoir. Holroyd opened the door for Ward, and looked urgently at Bible. Ward leaned down and whispered into Bible's ear.

'Tell me, lad, tell me,' said Wallace irritably.

'Inspector Bible will explain, sir,' said Ward.

'No, you'll explain, Sergeant,' said Wallace, heaving himself out of his chair. 'Follow me. Both of you.' Wallace listed from side to side as he lumbered towards the door. Ward looked towards Bible, shrugged, and followed the Superintendent. Bible stayed where he was and sat back in his chair. Wallace turned and glowered at him.

'I'll stay where I am,' said Bible.

'Do I detect dissension in the ranks?' said Turner cheerfully as Ward closed the door on the scene in the corridor. Bible could hear Ward's murmur, then footsteps receding. He avoided eye contact with Turner in the silence that followed, though he knew the reservoir man was smirking. He heard the familiar clack of the metal reinforcements on Holroyd's shoe heels as his footsteps returned.

A moment later, Holroyd opened the door. 'Detective Inspector Bible, step outside please.'

'Oh dear,' said Turner.

Bible rose. It wasn't often Holroyd gave him his full title.

'I thought Turner was about to give us something,' said Bible as he joined the men in the corridor, trying to make his excuse for refusing Wallace sound defiant rather than lame.

'You need to get your men in order, Holroyd.' Wallace, Bible reflected, had no sense of tact. That would annoy Holroyd. 'Right, Sergeant Ward,' said Wallace, 'spit it out.'

'Everything at the reservoir, sir, seemed very clean.

The banks round the side. No rubbish. No litter. That deflated inner tube had gone. The pump house was empty, apart from his motorbike.' Ward looked at Bible. 'And those paintings sir. The ones he had all over the floor, leaning against the walls. They've all gone now.'

'Paintings?' said Wallace.

'Watercolours,' said Ward. 'He fancies himself as something of an artist, our reservoir keeper.'

Bible got an image of Turner strutting around like a bantam cock, crowing about his achievements. Showing off about his daubed chocolate box paintings.

'I think we should check his name,' said Bible. Wallace and Ward looked at him for explanation. Holroyd paused, his cigarette halfway to his mouth.

'Turner. J M W Turner, the artist, early last century. Our reservoir keeper joked about the coincidence of names. Perhaps it isn't a coincidence. He's a boaster. Cheeky and too fond of himself. Perhaps he's changed his name.'

'Let's see what he's hiding,' said Wallace. 'Puzzle him out.' Wallace led the way back into the tiny interview room. As Bible was about to follow, Holroyd grasped his arm and leaned towards him with a whispered growl: 'Don't worry, son. I know what I'm doing.'

Bible feared Wallace would go for a frontal assault. Wallace and Holroyd's version of subtlety made even Ward look like a sleight of hand magician. But the Yard man seemed more engaged with the case now. Perhaps he had been a real policeman once. Wallace settled himself in the chair in the interview room again and took out his snuff box from his waistcoat.

'Now Jack.' He paused with the snuff box held above his belly. 'Mind if I call you Jack?'

Turner looked uneasy, but nodded.

'Snuff?' Wallace held out his box. Bible noticed it was wood inlaid with mother of pearl. Turner declined.

'So Jack... a local man.'

'I am.'

'Born in...'

'1902. Second of September.'

'I meant place, Jack. Place.'

'Oh right. Cleckheaton.'

Wallace looked at Bible and smiled. 'Cleckheaton. Sounds like the noise my wife's knitting machine makes. These northern names. You couldn't make 'em up, could you? ' Wallace looked at Bible, proud of his pleasantry. But Bible could see that the man knew what he was doing.

'There's Heckmondwike as well. You'd like that,' said Turner.

'So as you know the area, you'd know where someone could hide a van.'

'Garages, lock-ups. Could be anywhere back in town. The city's a big place.'

Bible interrupted. 'No vehicles came back into town, Mr Turner. We have checkpoints throughout the city.'

'Let's give the man time to think,' said Wallace. 'We need to use his local knowledge. We'll have to take you for a pint, Mr Turner. In that pub you mentioned.' Here it came. Wallace trying to set up a good cop/bad cop routine.

'I didn't mention a pub.'

'No, funny that,' said Wallace leaning back expansively, thumbs in his waistcoat pockets.

'I go in t' Cock and Pullet sometimes. I didn't want to say, like. I knew what you'd think.' Turner grinned. 'But there are some honest men in there.'

The Cock and Pullet was on the edge of town, on the bus route down from the reservoir. It made sense that Turner would go there for company from his eyrie on the moors, but it wasn't a pub where the police were popular. It was a place where a good deal of stuff was fenced.

'And you didn't see any van out there?' said Bible.

'There's never anyone out there.'

'No one? Hikers? Picnickers?'

'Only in summer. And the lampers at night.'

'Lonely.'

'Suits me.'

'Not even your paintings to keep you company.'

Turner shifted in his seat.

'You've had a big clean up. Where are all your paintings?'

'Ah, well, I decided they weren't much good. I burnt them.'

'And what did you do with the stuff you cleared up from round the banks of the reservoir?'

'Only litter and that. Paper. A few bottles. Binned it or burnt it.'

Bible thought of the missing inner tube.

'But wasn't there a smell of burning rubber?'

They had to let him go, but smuggled him out of a side door as Swann on the desk sent word that the main entrance was blocked by a crowd of reporters. 'There's guys up from London,' said Swann, looking up from his paperwork. Bible and Wallace stood by the desk to watch the commotion outside.

'We'll stay back here,' said Wallace. The steps were blocked by Holroyd's back as he faced a crowd of men brandishing notebooks and pens. 'There's Higgins from the *Express*. He's like a fox round chickens when there's a big story on.'

They could hear Holroyd's voice muffled through the wood and glass of the door. 'I can assure you things are fully under control. We have the best police minds in the country on the case. Superintendent Fred Wallace is the best man at the Yard.'

'Send for Fabian,' shouted someone.

'Fabian's a bloody poser,' muttered Wallace to Bible about the famous Yard detective, 'getting himself on television.'

Holroyd's voice again: 'I'll be happy to meet you all at nine tomorrow morning, when I hope to have more to report.'

There was more jabbering and waving of notebooks. Bible thought he heard his own name mentioned. Hidden in the gloom of the foyer, Bible saw Holroyd raise his hands in a quieting gesture.

'I'm sorry gentlemen, that's all I have for you.' Holroyd turned on his heel and flung back the double doors into the station. There was a louder gust of shouting before they swung shut behind the furious Chief Superintendent.

'I suppose you're used to putting up with this pack of hounds,' he said to Wallace.

'Get them on your side, they can be very useful,'

said the bulky Yard man.

'Well I'm not having it. They can see me properly. On my terms. Follow me.'

When Bible and Wallace got to Holroyd's office, the Chief Superintendent was already filling the place with smoke.

'Well?' he said, waving his Capstan behind his shoulder and letting ash drop to the floor 'Turner?'

Wallace sat down heavily in the wooden chair with arms facing Holroyd's desk. Bible hesitated, before sitting down in the upright chair purloined from the information room.

'He did it,' said Wallace, prising his snuffbox out of a tight waistcoat pocket.

'So you'll be charging him then?' said Holroyd.

'Not yet. We need to get some evidence first.' Wallace took a pinch of snuff. 'And we'll get it, when we've decided what he's done.' There was something ominous in the way Wallace said it. Something Bible didn't like. Wallace tucked his snuff box away. 'There's an art to finding evidence.'

In the silence that followed, Bible saw Holroyd's face working. He wanted a conviction, perhaps at any cost to the truth. Bible forced his mind to think of what they did know. He knew they were after a child killer, and Ken Wigley had brought the reservoir into the picture, and that meant Carol could be connected in some way.

'Turner said he hadn't seen anyone out there,' said Bible, 'Round the reservoir. But that can't be true.'

'And?' Holroyd leaned forward across his desk.

'We know the girl, Carol, went there regularly. She

said so. He must have seen her, so why hasn't he said so?'

'What girl's this?' said Wallace.

'Another case the Inspector is following. Could be something and nothing,' said Holroyd.

'There's a girl Turner hasn't seen who says she's been there?' said Wallace. 'So your evidence against him is that he hasn't seen something? Dearie me.'

'We know Carol was chased by a van at the reservoir.'

'Is that van A, B or C?' chuckled Wallace. 'But this Turner. He's not got any kids, has he? Not even married. So what was he doing round the school that afternoon?'

Bible wondered if Wallace had read the file correctly. 'No one saw him round the school.'

Wallace turned his head to Bible slowly. 'So let's make sure someone did.'

The implication was clear. Wallace wanted to fix the evidence. Holroyd took a pull on his cigarette, and only the rumbling cough that followed broke the silence. When he recovered, he spoke. 'Let's keep it all above board, Fred. We like to do things a bit differently up here.'

Bible was relieved. He hadn't been sure how Holroyd would react. He was a hard man to fathom.

Wallace laughed mirthlessly. 'Suit yourself.'

'You'll join me in the press conference tomorrow, won't you, Fred?'

Wallace heaved himself up from the chair. 'If I'm going to be facing that lot, I'd better do some thinking, then.' He looked down at the still seated Bible. 'You'd better come and join me in the canteen, lad. Let me in on your alternative theories about evidence.'

'He'll be down in a minute,' said Holroyd.

Wallace shrugged. 'I'll get you a tea in.'

When he'd gone, and they'd heard his feet tramp down the corridor, Holroyd leaned back in his chair and grinned broadly.

'I think we're in the clear, Inspector Bible.'

'I don't understand, sir.'

'The Man from the Yard will be at the press conference. The expert. So who gets the blame if progress is slow? He does. I'm getting a lot of flak over this case, Jim. This gets you off the hook, and it gets me off the hook. For a while anyway.' Holroyd stubbed out his cigarette.

'We do still want to get someone, don't we, sir?'

Holroyd lit another cigarette. 'Of course we do, lad, of course we do.' He leaned back in his swivel chair, hands behind his head. 'This is just insurance. But this girl, Carol, and the van that chased her. Could be seeing things, couldn't she?'

'Someone's watching her, sir.'

Holroyd blew smoke into the air and watched it rise. 'You're sweet on her, aren't you?'

'No sir. But she's vulnerable.'

'Just be careful. Everybody's watching us now.'

As Bible left Holroyd's office he was thinking about Turner. The man did have a passing resemblance to Mr Potato Head.

TWENTY-FIVE

The tip of Beamsley Beacon caught the sunlight as he nosed the car uphill past the monastery and Middleton Woods. Motoring. Going for a drive. How innocent it sounded. Open-top car. Driving gloves. He could imagine the poster. *Wonderful Wharfedale*. But this wasn't carefree motoring. There'd be hell to pay when Holroyd found out where he was, unless his vendetta against Daniels was such that he just didn't care. And the motorist Bible was after wasn't innocent and didn't spin along in an open-topped car.

He was driving along the edge of the moors now. Spikes of moorland grass were sharpened yellow by the sun. Sheep lifted their heads and considered the intruder, then lost interest. Another rambler. Another farmer. Another cop. The police Wolseley would have looked too conspicuous out here, a place more used to tractors and trailers, Land Rovers and old motorbikes, so Bible was driving his Austin. He braked as a sheep ambled across the road unperturbed. Perhaps it didn't know he was a cop. Or perhaps he just wasn't scary enough.

A farm was coming up on the left, down the slope from the Beacon. The gate was closed so he stopped the car, avoiding the ditch which ran between the road and a drystone wall in need of a bit of dental work.

He shut the car door, stood on the road and listened. Quiet. Or quiet for the sort of sounds he was listening for. A flock of lapwings wheeled and tumbled over the stubble field next to the farm buildings; sheep baa-ed reassuringly as they had done for hundreds of years. The November sun reminded him there was still warmth in the world. He wondered if Carol had seen anything of the Yorkshire countryside other than that bleak reservoir. He knew she only went there because it was easy to get a bus, but he'd like to take her somewhere fresher, a place where people enjoyed themselves.

'What are you after then?' The blunt question came from a farmer leaning on the wooden gate across the farmyard entrance. Bible walked towards him.

'Good morning.'

'If you say so. You're not a bloody hiker are you, come here to leave all t'gates open?' The gate was off at one hinge, leaning against the gateposts at seventy degrees and held loosely shut with a loop of rope. A rich smell of cow dung wafted across the yard.

'Is this Moor End Farm?' said Bible.

'Might be.'

Bible hadn't meant to antagonise the man who was probably Linda's father; he'd hoped they were both on the same side.

'Is there a girl lives here called Linda?'

'Do you want me to fetch the police?'

Bible noted the word 'fetch', not 'phone'. He glanced upwards. No telegraph pole. No wires. The farmer seemed to read his thoughts. 'I don't need them anyway.' He called. 'Ramrod! Joker!' A pair of border collies tumbled barking out of the cowshed and towards the gate. 'I can look after my own.'

'I was down Heber's Ghyll on Sunday with my wife and we came across a girl who seemed to be upset. Said she was called Linda.'

'Kids get upset.'

'This got an adult upset. Me. She some stranger had picked her up in a car. There were two boys with her. Brian and Billy.'

'So why have you come all this way to tell me?'

'I've got children of my own. I was worried.'

'Stay there,' said the man. He turned and walked across the muddy farmyard towards the house, disappearing through the door. Another door in need of repainting.

The farmer reappeared, squatting by the side of a young girl, his arm round her waist. He pointed towards Bible. 'Have you seen this man before?'

'No,' said the girl sullenly.

'This man says you 'ave.'

'I've never seen him before.' Linda was trying to pull away from him, but the farmer held on to her arm.

'He says you were with Billy and Brian. And you were with a man.'

Linda squirmed in his grip. 'I didn't do nothing.'

'All right love.' He let her wriggle away and stood up. 'Appen you'd best open t'gate and tell us what you saw. Dogs'll not hurt you.'

The square wooden table in the large farmhouse kitchen was laden with mixing bowls, flour and milk. The room was warm with the smell of baking. 'We don't have much cause for entertaining up here,' said the woman Bible guessed was Mrs Sugden. She was moving her rolling pin across the flattened dough with a firm, muscular action. She put the rolling pin on one side and dusted the flour off her hands. 'But I'll mek you a cup o' tea. It's not long since boiled.'

'That's very generous of you,' said Bible, hoping he didn't sound sarcastic. He hadn't meant it sarcastically. Sugden was peering at the warrant card Bible had felt obliged to show once he was in the farmhouse. The farmer didn't look like a man who'd want to be tricked.

'If you're the police, how come I've never seen you before?'

Mrs Sugden's hand paused over the gas ring. 'I'll warn you now,' she said before lighting it, 'we don't take too kindly to the police up here.'

'Lily,' warned the farmer.

'It needs saying,' she said, 'So we won't clear you a space on t'sofa until we know what you're about. You can stand.'

Mrs Sugden warmed the teapot with water from a battered silver kettle, rinsed it round and poured it out. She scooped fresh tea out of a black caddy, with images of Chinese temples picked out in faded white. Bible wondered if she ever thought about that as she made a brew. There was one picture on the wall, squashed above a sideboard where no one could see it clearly: a montage of Tower Bridge and Big Ben. Whatever was going on here, it didn't feel like the feckless family Daniels had warned him about.

'So what's this about our Linda?' She lifted the kettle from the ring and poured water into the pot. 'Linda!' The power in the farmer's wife's voice took

Bible by surprise. 'I sent her to feed the hens,' she said.

'I'd like her to stay feeding the hens if you don't mind,' said Bible. 'It's better if your daughter's out of the room.'

'Has Daniels sent you?' said Sugden roughly.

Bible decided it was time to gamble. It was unlikely that Sugden and his wife knew the niceties of police jurisdiction, or would realise he had no right to talk to them at all. 'I'm not from round here,' he said. 'I'm from the city force.'

Sugden grunted. He reached for a pipe from the high mantelpiece made of thick oak. He pulled a tin of Ogden's from his jacket pocket. Bible could see he was buying thinking time. 'So you don't know Daniels?'

'I've met him once,' said Bible. He watched Sugden blow through his pipe to clear the stem, knock the bowl on his heel, and flick the loosened ash towards the fireplace. Mrs Sugden thumped another ball of dough on to the floured kitchen table. 'And he wouldn't like to know I was here,' added Bible.

'What do you think, Lily?' said the farmer to his wife.

Mrs Sugden stared directly at Bible. 'I can see you're not Daniels.' She paused her rolling pin. Bible waited for her verdict whilst she returned to her rolling. 'So we'll listen to what you've got to say.'

Bible sat facing Sugden. The farmer had put his pipe back in the rack on the mantelpiece and cleared a place for Bible on the sofa, shifting a thick paper bag of dogmeal on to the floor, and a pile of *Farmers' Weeklies*. Now Sugden stood in front of the fire.

Awkwardly. Bible could hear Mrs Sugden's voice in another room and occasionally, protesting, Linda's. Then it went silent. There was a wooden radio perched on a stool at the end of the sofa. Bible found himself reading the stations listed on the glass rectangle below the grill over the speaker cloth: Hilversum, Athlone, Minsk, Luxembourg. He wondered where they all were. He knew more about Burmese geography than places nearer to home.

'Do you use the radio much?' said Bible.

'Nah. Wife does. Likes "The Glums". Daft if you ask me.' He fished a squashed packet of Senior Service from his pocket. 'Smoke?'

'No thanks. I don't,' said Bible. Sugden shrugged. Bible guessed Sugden and his wife were in their forties. But farmers sometimes looked older than they were. Mrs Sugden's weathered face meant she could have passed herself off as Linda's grandmother. A late child then. But probably a wanted child, despite what he'd first thought. Perhaps her husband had been away fighting, like Bible had, but that would have been unusual for a farmer.

'Were you in the war, Mr Sugden?'

Sugden lit his cigarette and threw the spent match into the fire. 'What are you getting at?' Bible realised he'd put the man on his guard again and that his train of thought had betrayed him.

'I've got a six-year-old daughter. But I was away for four years so having a child had to wait.'

'Aye, well, it weren't that with us. I were here. Reserved occupation. Your friend Daniels used to taunt me with it. "Cowards like you'll lose us the war" he used to say.'

'Daniels isn't my friend,' said Bible.

'I didn't see him doing any fighting. He had his own thugs.'

Bible waited for Sugden to expand.

'That's why the dogs...well, they're not just sheep dogs. I'll say no more.'

Bible felt lonely. Sick of his colleagues. Sick of the police. Holroyd. Wallace. Daniels. He was afraid of finding out what Daniels had been up to because he'd have to act on it, but he wanted to find out too. He swallowed, and spoke quietly. 'We're not perfect, but we shouldn't be corrupt.' Sugden stared at him. Bible knew he was being assessed. 'So what's he been up to?'

'Black market. He wanted all us farmers round here to give him summat. Said he'd look after us. They all did, except me. He's had it in for me since the war.'

There were footsteps coming down the stairs.

'And then there were a to-do wi' t'land girls. Dirty bugger, that Daniels.'

Bible stood up as the door opened. Mrs Sugden came in, and looked back up the stairs.'

'Come on, Linda.'

Her daughter slipped in, head down, holding a screwed-up handkerchief at her lap. She didn't look at Bible and the dark patches under her eyes told him she had been crying.

'You can sit there, Linda,' said Sugden, pointing to a small wooden stool at the side of the fireplace. It could have been a milking stool, but Bible didn't know much about these things. Mrs Sugden went over to her daughter. She knelt beside her and held her hand.

'Linda, tell him what you told me.'

'You tell him, Mum.' The girl wiped her nose upwards with the hanky, making her look like Andy Pandy.

'I think he'd like to hear it from you.'

He could hear Sugden breathing heavily. Then the farmer spoke.

'We're on your side, Linda. Whatever it was, it won't happen again.'

'Linda.' Mrs Sugden cupped her daughter's hand in hers. After a moment, she looked towards Bible. 'She said there was a man. He took her, Billy and Brian with him in a van.'

'Why did you go with him, you silly girl? We've told you,' said Sugden. Lily looked at her husband, warningly. He seemed to accept her managing his domestic affairs.

'It was Billy. He wanted to go,' said Linda, sniffing. 'He's allus been daft, that Billy.'

Linda was going red. Bible felt for her embarrassment.

'Linda?' said the girl's mother. The girl twisted her handkerchief.

'He said he'd show us some magazines.'

The adults waited for more.

'There were pictures of people with no clothes on.'

'Aye, that'd tempt little Billy,' said Sugden.

Bible sat forward on the sofa. 'I'm sorry. Do you mind? '

Mrs Sugden nodded, giving him permission to go ahead.

'Where did he show you these pictures?' said Bible.

'I didn't look at 'em. It were Billy.'

'It doesn't matter. Just tell us where he took you. What sort of place.'

'It were in his van. He just drove us round in his van.'

Bible didn't want to accuse her of lying; she was like a nervous deer edging close to a fence. But Billy and Brian had shown no sign of nervousness. 'The boys said only you had been in the van.'

'They didn't want to get in trouble, did they?' The girl coloured again. 'He let them go before me. He made me stay and do things.'

'What things Linda?' said Bible. Linda shook her head and looked down.

Mrs Sugden trapped his gaze. 'Photos, Mr Bible. Photos. She says he took photographs of her. You know.'

Bible wasn't sure he did know, but he didn't want to ask again with the girl there.

Sugden threw his cigarette end into the fire. 'I'm going to that Billy. He'll know more than he's let on. Smutty little tyke.'

Bible jumped from the sofa. 'I think you should leave it to us, Mr Sugden.' But Sugden was out of the farmhouse door. Mrs Sugden had quickly stepped towards him and caught his arm. 'He's a peaceable man, Mr Bible. But he's had a lot to put up with.'

When Bible got to the farmyard Sugden was already in the driving seat of his Land Rover. Bible ran towards it, but the vehicle was moving off as he grabbed at the handle of the passenger door, lost his footing in the farmyard mud and stumbled to the ground. The wheels of the Land Rover sent a spattering of mud into his face.

'Mr Sugden,' he yelled, but the farmer was heading for the gate. As Bible heard the driver engage first gear to take the slope up to the road, a large Austin Princess pulled up in front of the tumbledown gateway, blocking the entrance. Daniels got out of the passenger side holding open his warrant card, the sun catching the bald dome of his head. 'Mr Sugden,' he said. 'You're under arrest. What have you been doing to your daughter?'

TWENTY-SIX

Logan sat with Larry's body, his hand on the dead young man's chest. He nursed his shotgun and watched the watery daylight fade to late autumn gloom. The forest floor was cold, the twigs and branches a leathery brown. Larry's cheek was cold when he touched it, the few creases in the pale young flesh looked like moulded plastic. Logan stirred for the first time in some hours and gathered branches from the ground. From each branch smaller feathery twigs fanned out so that when he lay them across the body they looked like palm leaves.

Stanley and Robbo had inched away from him shortly after the moment of the boy's death, and he had let them. When the police convoy had left with Turner, he'd watched the father and son pick their way down the boggy moorland towards the reservoir. Down at the reservoir they had walked along its edge and disappeared round the far end. At midday he'd seen Turner return, walking down the track from the road. They could do what they wanted. Logan didn't need any of them. He'd find his daughters himself.

Logan looked at the mound of branches. He was on his own now, and the boy couldn't help him. He was thinking tactically again. He didn't need Turner, could not trust Robbo and Stanley. Larry was OK.

Larry was safe now. And Larry was a man. It wasn't as if he'd let a child die. He could be buried later. Somewhere safer, where he wouldn't be found.

Logan stood up straight and dusted himself down. He picked up the shotgun from the forest debris of pine cones and needles, and stared towards the reservoir below. He wouldn't find Dawn there; he'd have to go into town. And if he were doing that, he'd have to stop Robbo and Stanley running around like mavericks. Stanley. He'd thought he was a bright boy. Smarter than his father. Logan was sorry if Stanley was going wrong.

The light had not yet gone. The day was in that slow wintry decline, so different from the sudden darkness he'd seen in North Africa. Military Policeman. That was a laugh – but it had taught him how to be boss. Logan buttoned his donkey jacket against the chill, and trapped his shotgun in the crook of his arm. The pump house stood darker now, like a photo he'd seen of Urquhart Castle on Loch Ness, a silhouette against the silvery water. He believed in the Monster of Loch Ness, and he'd like to go and look for it some time. You couldn't fake something like that.

As he pulled his collar up he saw Turner emerge from behind the pump house with something under his arm wrapped in cloth. Logan watched the strutting Yorkshireman walk down the path at the side of the reservoir embankment towards where Robbo and Stanley had disappeared from view.

It was time to move.

Logan worked his way down the slope at an angle, hoping he wouldn't be seen in the dwindling light.

Turner was walking beyond the reservoir to where the path narrowed, crossed a stream, and went uphill. Logan let him get three hundred yards ahead, then followed, pleased with his own agility and energy. Anger had always given him power.

Turner left the path to cut across moorland towards an old barn. Logan watched the reservoir keeper clamber over a drystone wall. That gave Logan a chance to cover ground quickly, up the slope, his movements hidden if Turner looked behind him. Logan ran the final hundred yards, crouching low, and looked over. Turner had reached the barn. It wasn't isolated in a moorland waste, but at the end of a rutted track which marked the edge of the fell. And there, outside, was a vehicle. A van. And a van Logan knew but hadn't seen for some time. An old post office van he'd resprayed in a dull khaki and used to take Larry to the boathouse. A van he'd told Robbo to get rid of, or else. As twilight faded into darkness, he could just make out the heads and shoulders of two men – Stanley and Robbo. Logan watched as Turner joined them and they disappeared inside, closing the double doors behind them. He glimpsed the radiator of the Bedford in which they'd come up from Exeter. Robbo and Turner must have hidden it here, reversed into the darkness of the barn. Logan climbed the wall, walked stealthily to the barn door, and took a deep breath before reaching for the heavy metal ring on the door sneck and twisting.

Logan crashed Turner against the radiator of the Bedford, pushed the shorter man's head back with his forearm, and rammed the muzzle of the shotgun against the reservoir keeper's upturned chin. Turner's bundle dropped from beneath his arm and hit the ground with the sound of breaking glass. Robbo and Stanley stood frozen barely six feet away. They could have rushed him, but Logan knew they would not. He pushed the muzzle further into Turner's chin, forcing his head back further.

'I think I'm owed an explanation.' Logan fixed his gaze on the threatened man, but he was speaking to them all. He lowered his gun and grabbed a fistful of Turner's jacket with his left hand. He pulled him away from the bonnet of the Bedford and thrust him into Robbo.

Stanley watched. He looked surprisingly calm. Logan noted fleetingly that he might have to reassess the boy. He didn't like that look.

He pointed the gun at all three of them, keeping his anger down, where it was useful and ready to spring.

'You got any light in here?' said Logan.

'There's a paraffin light,' said Turner hoarsely.

'Be my guest.' Logan stepped back so none of them could rush him as Turner went to a cluttered shelf by the door, pulled down a metal storm lantern, struck a match and lit the wick. The flame brightened and illuminated their faces.

'Put it back on the shelf,' said Logan. Turner obliged. Higher up, the lamp cast more light over Robbo, Stanley and Turner, but Logan knew he remained in darkness. 'And you'd better fetch that petrol can down, Turner. It's not good to have it up there next to a flame.'

Turner lifted a rusting jerry can from the shelf. Logan heard the petrol slosh inside.

'We can't see you, boss,' said Robbo.

'You don't need to see me, Robbo. You don't need to know more about me than you know already, but I need to know about you.'

Turner was holding the petrol can.

'Better bring that to me. For safe keeping,' said Logan.

Turner placed it at his feet and Robbo licked his lips.

'Mouth dry, Robbo?' said Logan. 'You must be scared of something.' Logan glanced behind him, and saw an old oil drum. He reversed and sat on it. 'I'll just settle here for a bit whilst you think of something I might believe.'

'It's not what you think,' said Turner.

'And what do I think?' Logan glanced down at the earth floor of the barn, where Turner had dropped his bundle. Broken glass and picture frames lay among the folds of the old blanket Turner had carried them in. 'Any chance of a cup o'tea in here?'

One of them would have to explain something, but Logan didn't know what he wanted the truth to be. Turner the lone betrayer, or all three his enemies now?

'I didn't know Turner still had the van,' said Robbo.

'Why did he have it at all? I told you to get rid of it.'

The barn door was hanging open, one of the rusty hinges at the top broken from when Logan had wrenched it open. The cloud had cleared, and the moon was full. Moonlight glinted on the old post office van outside.

'Looks good in the moonlight, doesn't it, that van,'

said Logan. 'But the thing is, it shouldn't be here, should it?'

Turner felt his throat and spoke hoarsely. 'He sold it to me, Mr Logan. He didn't tell me you wanted rid of it altogether.' Then the reservoir keeper tried to laugh it off. 'I mean, it's a useful little runabout, is that. You don't want to go getting rid of it too easily.' Turner looked round for agreement, but no one nodded.

'You can't trust him, Mr Logan,' said Stanley. 'How can he have been looking for Dawn all this time and not found her?'

Logan looked at the three men – or two men and a boy. All of them liars. Not like Larry. He'd been true. He could have made something of Larry.

Logan pointed the barrels of the shotgun down towards the blanket that had fallen from Turner's grip. 'What's all this junk you've brought with you?'

'Nothing Mr Logan, just a few watercolours I do. Landscapes. Scenes.'

'Enough.' Logan levelled the shotgun at Turner. 'Stanley, what's your eyesight like? Get grubbing among that lot and see what you can find.'

Logan kept his gaze fixed on the reservoir keeper as he heard the boy rummage among the broken glass.

'There's a photograph here as well as paintings, Mr Logan,' said Stanley.

'To me,' said Logan, holding out his left hand. His right was still on the shotgun.

'And there's an envelope.' Stanley handed them over.

'Back over there, lad,' said Logan, indicating with his gun.

Stanley joined the others against the wall of the barn. Logan moved to where the storm lantern cast a light from its high shelf. He could hardly make out the photograph in the gloom. A grey reservoir scene. And perhaps a figure, but in this light it could have been a post. He looked up. The three men were still standing against the wall. He used a thick finger and thumb to push apart the sides of the dirty envelope. There were more prints inside.

'Stanley,' said Logan. 'Look through these. Tell me if there's anything of interest.'

Stanley took the envelope and reached up for the hurricane lamp

'Leave that. Use the moon.'

Stanley moved into the open doorway, and fingered through the contents of the envelope. He pulled out two small square prints and angled them to catch the moonlight, but when he looked to check the position of the moon, he paused.

'Mr Logan.' Stanley spoke quietly. 'There's someone out there.'

Logan levered himself from the oil drum, reached up for the lantern, and stepped towards Stanley. Up on the hillside, he saw a light moving, a long way off, but it was where he'd left Larry's body.

'Can we go, now, Mr Logan?' Turner's voice.

'And where would you be going, Jack?'

'That's a no,' said Robbo. Logan could feel Turner's fear, but Robbo was relaxing too much.

'Don't forget the van, Robbo. There's still the van,' murmured Logan. The light seemed to be moving across the tree line, keeping to the high ground. 'Any idea why there'd be a light, Turner?'

'Poachers. Lamping for rabbits,' said Turner. 'They'll not come down here.'

Logan hadn't seen any rabbits as he'd come down from the plantation of pines, but he wasn't a countryman, and as he looked at the dark mound of moorland, he wasn't sure which bit of the hillside he'd stumbled down. How did anyone find their way around these places?

'We'll wait,' said Logan. He turned the knob of the paraffin lamp so the wick only supported a faint glow. 'Keep looking, Stanley.'

No one moved in the barn for fifteen minutes. 'There's no light now,' said Stanley. 'I think he's gone.'

'So let's have a look at those photos.'

Logan turned the lamp up again as Stanley showed him the photographs.

The first was of a street. A northern street. Stone terrace houses, and walking along a pavement in front, a young woman in a headscarf seen from the side. Logan breathed deeply. He didn't want to betray himself with any display of emotion. He had to keep in control of the situation and the three men around him. But the woman could have been Dawn.

'And there's this, Mr Logan.' Stanley held out another photograph. The same street, but a closer view. And a woman in the same headscarf coming out of a house, shutting the door behind her. How had Turner managed to get so close? But you could see the face this time. And the face belonged to his daughter Dawn. Logan felt weak with love and angry with need. He turned over the photograph, and on the back saw someone had scribbled an address: 29 Sebastopol

Road. He raised the shotgun and pointed it at Turner's head.

'Hey, wait a minute,' said the Yorkshire man. He seemed genuinely indignant.

'How long have you known?' said Logan quietly.

'Yesterday. I took those photos yesterday.' Turner was covering up. And he probably knew that Logan knew it. 'I was going to show you.'

Stanley held the first photograph so Logan could see it. It was the reservoir, and a woman in the same headscarf gazing across it. The photograph was grubby. Like the envelope. And like the man before him.

Logan tucked the stock of the shotgun firmly into his shoulder and pointed it at Turner. 'That wasn't taken yesterday.'

Something came into the barn and sniffed around his legs. He looked down and Turner rushed him. Logan fell back over the dog. The shotgun he was holding went off into the roof space, sending down a shuttering of stone and dust. Turner scrambled to the open barn door. Logan rolled with his fall as Robbo slipped out past Stanley. He stumbled to his feet, keeping a grip of his gun, and moved into the doorway to find himself blinded by a light in his eyes. But it was held too close, and a quick sideways block with his forearm knocked it aside and to the ground, and he found himself looking into the eyes of a skinny untidy man, who backed away pointing a shotgun at him.

'I've got one of those too,' said Logan, raising his gun and pointing it safely to the sky. The man looked like someone who wouldn't use his shotgun unless he was panicked.

'I'm going to kill you,' said the man. The lurcher that had tripped Logan stood patiently by his owner's knee. Logan realised that the man was crying.

'Now why is that?' said Logan. He wondered where Robbo and Stanley were, but he needed to keep his eyes on the man in front of him. Turner, he was sure, had escaped.

'I've seen your van. I know what you've done.'

'What have I done?'

'Killed my son.'

'Not me.' Logan was puzzled.

'Donald Holmes. Six years old.'

'Holmes. That your name? Holmes?'

'What's it to you?'

Logan remembered the newspaper placards about a dead child as they'd driven into the city, the police all over the place, and Turner's later explanation.

'I didn't do it, Mr Holmes.'

'That van was outside the school. And it's the same van that's outside now.'

Logan calculated that he had to persuade the angry little man of his honesty. And that was easier if he was honest.

'Yes it was my van.'

Holmes raised his gun again.

'And I can help you find the driver.' Logan called into the darkness. 'Stanley.'

'They've all gone,' said Holmes. 'There's only you. I've only got you.'

So Stanley had let him down too. Skedaddled with his dad. Both weak. Logan knew the man in front of him was weak too, but desperate. And desperation got rid of fear which made people harder to control. If there was a child killer on the loose, Logan wouldn't mind finding him himself. Fear and anger and a hand on a gun were a dangerous combination.

'Well, are you going to shoot me?'

Holmes took his right hand away from the trigger, wiped his eyes, and quickly grabbed the gun again. But Logan hadn't moved. He'd only make a move when he was certain of success.

'You could shoot me,' said Logan. 'But what if I'm not the right man? You'd never know for sure.'

'My dog was sniffing round your van. Whining.'

'The man you want is called Turner. And you've just let him get away.' Logan could see the man was thinking. He also saw that a figure was moving against the drystone wall behind Holmes. But the dog sensed it too, and with an elastic bound was barking round the shadow. Stanley shouted as Holmes spun towards the commotion. Three strides launched Logan onto Holmes, who fell face down with Logan's knee pinning him to the ground, and his gun arm trapped uselessly by the weight of Logan's hand on the man's wrist.

'Grab the dog, Stanley,' shouted Logan, but the dog was bobbing and side-stepping every move and ran off into the dark.

Logan smashed Holmes' knuckles against the stone cobbles, and loosened his grip on the trigger guard. Stanley kicked the shotgun away. The move took Logan by surprise, but he smiled. So Stanley had stayed.

'Quick thinking, Stanley, but I'd have got it off him.'

Stanley quickly stooped, snatched the gun from the

ground and stepped back, away from the two men on the ground. Logan was puzzled.

'It's all right, Stanley. He won't do anything now.' Logan held his hand out for the shotgun. Stanley took another step back and pointed the gun towards his boss, holding it loosely at his waist.

'Stay back, Mr Logan.'

Stanley looked nervous, his grip on the gun insecure. Logan was aware of the pathetic figure crying on the muddy stones at his feet, but his mind was fixed on Stanley. He'd underestimated the boy, and his loyalty to that fool of a father.

Logan raised his hands, palms towards his protégé. 'O.K., son, O.K..' Stanley looked unsure. 'I knew you were like me. Know what you want and how to get it.' It was a lie. The boy was uncertain, and Logan decided to increase his uncertainty. 'What you going to do now?'

Stanley turned his head from side to side, as if looking for an answer.

'Find my dad and take him home.'

'Good, Stanley, that's good. Family loyalty.'

'I'm not going to let you kill him, Mr Logan.'

Logan laughed. 'Kill him? I need him, Stanley.' Logan made sure he didn't move forward. He wasn't going to rush the boy; he'd make Stanley come to him. 'I was cross with him, but you know what Robbo's like. I have to think for him. Not like you. You can think for yourself.'

'He's looked after you, Mr Logan.'

'I know, Stanley, I know.'

The boy looked frightened. More frightened than he'd seen him before. Stanley looked over his shoulder. 'Dad?' Stanley looked to Logan appealingly. 'Where is he?'

'Out there somewhere.' Logan inclined his head towards the darkness around them. 'Perhaps I was a bit harsh. Here…' He reached inside his donkey jacket a little too quickly. Stanley fumbled with the gun and flicked the safety catch off. 'Easy, Stanley,' said Logan, 'if you're going to take Robbo away from me, you'll need money. You can't use the Bedford. They'll be looking for it.'

Logan eased his wallet out of his pocket. Stanley levelled the gun at him. 'Put it on the wall.' Holmes was still lying on the cobbles between them, twisting his head from side to side as he looked at Stanley, then Logan, seemingly terrified at what was unfolding. Logan realised, sadly, that he was going to have to deal with him. Logan removed a five pound note and three green one pound notes from his wallet and held them out at arm's length.

'You'd better take them before they blow away.'

Stanley stepped gingerly round Holmes towards Logan. As Stanley lowered the gun to take the money, Logan engulfed the young man's hand on the trigger with his own, pulled the boy sharply towards him, and twisted the gun sideways and upwards so it discharged into the night sky. The stock kicked into Stanley's side.

Holmes leapt to his feet, but it was an awkward move and Logan reached out with his free hand and grabbed his coat. There was a moment when Holmes cycled on the spot before Logan dragged him to the ground, and stepped back. He levelled the gun at Stanley, who was nursing his bruised ribs, and looked down at the defeated figure at his feet. Holmes made no attempt to get up, but lay on the ground crying angrily. 'You killed my son,' he said, wiping his eyes and smearing mud across his face.

'Get up,' said Logan. Holmes went silent, but stayed where he was. 'Up.' Holmes rolled over onto his back, and sat up in the dirt.

'I know you're a killer,' he said. 'My dog found a body on the hill.'

Logan felt sorry for the man. He had just made a fatal mistake.

TWENTY-SEVEN

The hills were dark now, rising from the road towards the grouse moors. Bible was tempted to go and walk among them. He'd be anonymous there. There weren't many good people he'd met during this investigation. Sugden was probably one of them, but Bible was sure that he himself was not. Sugden was under arrest and there was nothing Bible could do to help him. Trespassing in another force's patch, he was in too weak a position.

He wound the car window down. A windless night. Silent, apart from an isolated bird call which told him a lapwing was having a restless night in the secret life of the fields. The lights of the town were below him, scattered down the valley like sinking stars fallen to ground. On the other side of the valley, another black hogsback of moor against the gunmetal grey sky. Beyond that, the city. His city. But it didn't feel like his city, or his police force.

A van near the school. A van dropping off Linda. And the same van near the reservoir if Ken the hiker was right and his certainty not simply an eagerness to please. So were the hounding of Carol and the killing of little Donald Holmes linked? The answer was lurking somewhere in that dark hump between him and the city. He had to remind himself he didn't believe in evil, only the deep fallibility and squalor of people.

He glanced towards the horizon. There was a glow on the skyline. A dab of bright yellow. A fire probably. Must be a farm there. A farmer burning something. Bible looked at his watch. Six thirty. He couldn't hide out here in his muddy suit. Shirley would be waiting for him. He needed a callbox to tell her he'd be late for tea. And he had to see Carol to see how she was. Was that for her sake, or his own? He'd just see Carol, and then home. He turned the ignition and engaged the gearstick. His little Austin wasn't used to such adventures, just family outings.

He parked outside the cottage. The light was on in Browning's living room window. He stepped outside into the smoky air and instinctively stepped round the pool of light created by the sole street lamp. He knocked on the cottage door and waited. Nothing. He knocked again. A few moments later he heard the inner door open, and Carol's voice.

'Who's there?'

'Inspector Bible.'

A bolt was pulled back and a key turned. Carol stood before him dressed simply in dark blue slacks and a pale, round-necked nylon jumper. She didn't have to try hard to look attractive.

'I'm glad you're being careful,' he said. Carol looked past him down the short path. 'I'm on my own,' he added.

'So am I,' said Carol. 'Miss Browning is out for the evening.' She showed him into the living room and sat primly on the edge of the two-seater settee. Bible stood looking at her.

'You can sit down,' she said.

Bible hovered. He sat in the chair opposite. 'I want to make sure you're protected.'

'There's nothing you can do. It isn't a crime for a father to want his daughter back.'

'Perhaps it should be in some cases.' Bible realised he ought to think of a better reason for coming. 'I wondered if Miss Browning had changed her mind about having a watch on her house?'

Carol shook her head. 'She says the beat bobby will do. We're not a special case.'

'I think you are,' said Bible. Carol was looking at the carpet. He wanted her to catch his eye. 'Do you know if your father had a large van? A Bedford with sliding doors?'

'I only ever saw a small van. A bit like the one I thought was chasing me at the reservoir.' She looked down. 'Sorry about that.'

It struck Bible that Carol didn't know what her father did for a living.

'He took us out in it once when I was little. A picnic. The only one we ever had.'

Bible wanted to jump across the room and put his arms round her. Instead, he stepped across and sat next to her on the edge of the little settee.

'A Bedford jumped a police inspection yesterday. It had an Exeter number plate.'

He heard her sharp intake of breath.

'It doesn't mean he's here,' said Bible. He put his arm round her and she folded into him.

'It does,' she said. 'I'll never escape him now.'

'You don't have to,' said Bible. 'We'll catch him.' He could feel her body warm under her jumper, and knew he shouldn't be there. 'I need to be getting back,' he said. Carol pulled away, breaking his one-armed embrace.

'Thanks for telling me,' she said.

'I should have kept quiet. Shouldn't have worried you.'

Carol started laughing. Bible was puzzled. She twisted towards him on the settee and stroked his cheek. 'You poor thing. You don't understand, do you? I've been worried all my life.'

Bible took her wrist, gently pulled her arm down, and held her hand between his palms. He knew he wanted to kiss her, and he leaned towards her, but she pulled her hand free of his and put it lightly over his lips. 'No,' she said. 'I don't want that.'

At the doorway she kept a short distance from him. He raised his hand awkwardly, as if to touch her arm, but then let it drop.

'I know you mean well,' she said.

'You need looking after,' he said.

She smiled. 'I think I need to look after myself.'

*

He pulled up outside his house. He normally turned straight into the drive, but the chunky wooden gates were closed. It could have been Shirley being security conscious, but he feared he was being shut out – or that he was shutting himself out. He left the car on the road. The gates were sticking when he opened them, swollen with damp, so he made more noise than he intended. He wondered why he was being so quiet. It wasn't late – about eight o'clock – but it felt late.

As he stepped into the hall, he could hear Shirley upstairs reading to Pauline. The television was on in the front room. Ricky was sprawled on an armchair staring at the wooden cabinet with its small rectangle of illuminated glass. They'd only had it a few months, but Bible thought it looked quite smart. The valves projected a silhouette of the TV set's rear grill on to the wall behind.

'What you watching?' said Bible.

'*What's My Line?*' His son didn't look round, but he wasn't hostile. There was a gust of laughter from the television following some remark from the smooth-tongued Irishman who presented the show. Bible pulled the door to so the noise wouldn't disturb Pauline, took off his shoes, and padded upstairs to his daughter's bedroom.

Shirley was tucking the blankets around the little girl. 'She's just dropped off.' An open copy of *The House at Pooh Corner* was lying on the pink eiderdown. 'She hoped she'd still be awake when you got back.'

'I am awake,' murmured his daughter without opening her eyes. 'Hello daddy.' Bible was proud of her long black lashes. She would be a beauty all right, and he knew he didn't want to risk losing any of them – Shirley, Pauline, Ricky. He knelt beside his wife at the bedside and put his arm across her shoulders. They watched until Pauline was breathing deeply in a calm sleep.

'I love you,' Bible whispered to his wife.

Shirley smiled. 'What's got into you?' He nuzzled her ear. She giggled. 'Stop it. That tickles. I've got a chicken stew to warm up for you.'

'Not hungry.'

'And the station's been ringing.'

'Tell them to go hang.' Bible looped a lock of hair round her ear and kissed it. 'Shall we go to bed early?'

'With Ricky downstairs?'

'He'll be all right,' said Bible. 'He seems calmer.'

'I was nice to him.'

He took her hand in his and she kept it there as he led her from Pauline's bedroom. He closed Pauline's door behind them and called down from the landing.

'Ricky!'

There was a pause, and then the front room door was pulled open.

'What?' said his son.

'I've had a tiring day. We're going to bed early.'

There was a pause before Ricky responded. 'What's it got to do with me?' he said and closed the door.

Bible put his arms round his wife and they kissed. It felt like it used to feel. Warm and mutual. They moved into the bedroom and lay on the bed. He undid the buttons of her frock one by one all the way down the front and slipped his arm inside.

*

Logan leaned back on the drystone wall where the moorland ended and watched the distant blaze glow and crackle. The smaller van on the lane was a dark skeleton inhabited by jumping yellow tongues of flame. The barn doors were ablaze and as the rafters inside ignited, the big yellow Bedford that had brought them from Exeter was consumed in a furnace.

'You shouldn't have done it, Mr Logan,' said

Stanley. He was sitting on the ground with his back to the wall, drawing his knees into his chest.

'It was necessary,' murmured Logan, as he slid the shotgun into the secret compartment inside his jacket, and buried his hands in his pockets against the cold. 'He knew too much.'

TWENTY-EIGHT

The early morning light was a wash of watery grey and melancholy. The barn dripped and the acrid smell of charred timbers and burned-out vehicles made Bible want to heave. A few wisps of smoke or steam eddied from piles of ash. A fire officer was coiling the flattened canvas hose they'd run up from the stream, but he avoided eye contact when Bible gave him a nod.

'We did our best,' said the fireman. 'Couldn't get near.' The fire engine was parked in the lane, blocked by the burned-out Bedford.

'You couldn't have done more,' said Bible. The fireman shrugged.

Bible walked to the burly figure in uniform standing near where the barn door had been.

'First here, Tom?'

The policeman nodded. 'I've secured the scene, sir. Duggan's taken photos. Pathologist's on his way.' Tom Best was a homely man. A beat bobby with a bicycle, known and liked by the scattered inhabitants on this rural outskirt of the city. But this morning his friendly manner had been replaced by a more sombre bearing.

'What do you know about Turner?' said Bible.

'He's a rum'un, sir.'

'He's not at the reservoir. And he's not at his cottage.'

Best took his helmet off and wiped his forehead with a handkerchief.

'You all right, Tom?'

'Bit of a shock, sir, you know. What with the kid outside the school, and now this. Perhaps I'm getting too old.' He nodded towards the empty shell of the old Bedford, in what Bible recognised as a gesture of delicacy. 'Poor lad, whoever he is.'

The body was in the driver's seat, but the previous inhabitant of the blackened bones and melted flesh had not been going to drive anywhere. His wrists, her wrists – it was impossible to tell – were bound to the steering wheel. Bible removed his trilby as a mark of respect. The smell of burned flesh coming through the shattered window took him back to Burma and the ambushed ammunition convoy. There was little hope of fingerprints after a fire, but he pulled out his handkerchief and wrapped it round his hand before trying the driver's door. Locked. Ward appeared beside him, but said nothing.

'Looks like he was locked in,' said Bible.

Ward breathed out heavily. 'Do you believe in evil, sir?' he murmured.

'I believe in less and less, Bill.'

'I've met some villains, but only an animal could do this.'

Another car pulled up down the lane. Ward glanced out.

'Wallace.'

'Let's find something to show him. See what's survived the fire.'

They trod delicately through the damp ash which crunched softly underfoot. Water from the fire hoses still dripped from the charred roof beams as they eased their way inside. Bible stooped to a pile of singed cloth and broken glass, and poked at the debris with a pencil. He heard Wallace grumbling as he marched through the yard.

'Tell me when I can go back to a place where you don't need wellies all the time.'

The superintendent rooted his heavy frame next to where Bible was crouching. 'Someone's barbecue's gone wrong,' he said, sniffing. 'What's going on, then?'

Bible stood up. 'The burned out van in the road fits the description of the vehicle seen by the hiker, and near the school, sir. And this Bedford is the one that got away from Ward on Sunday morning.'

'It shouldn't have got away, should it?' said Wallace curtly.

Ward shouted from the dimness at the rear of the barn. Bible and Wallace squeezed down the side of the van, rubbing against the blackened stones of the wall.

'I'm going to claim for a new coat after this,' said Wallace. 'You should do the same.'

The fire had been less intense at the back, where they found Ward tugging at something on the earth floor and trapped under sacks. A piece of cardboard, its sides shaped in curves. Little daylight reached this part of the barn. Bible picked up Ward's torch as his sergeant heaved up the board.

'It's quite damp, sir,' he said.

'That's not surprising,' said Wallace. 'Fire Brigade squirting their piss all over the place.'

'It's been wet longer than that, sir.' Ward leaned the board against the wall. It was shaped as a figure, life size. 'And it's weighted at the bottom.'

Bible shone the torch beam up the figure. A plastic Brownie camera pointed at them from the figure's waist. A narrow tie formed a neat line between the lapels of a smart suit.

'It's a Kodak advert,' said Bible. 'One of those you see standing outside a chemist's.'

'I'd rather have the bird in the bathing suit,' said Wallace, pulling his snuff box from his waistcoat.

The image was crinkled with water, the cardboard softening at the edges. But when the torch picked out the head, Wallace's fingers gripping a pinch of snuff paused in mid action. The face was not that of a happy snappy new camera owner. It was of a young man who did not look happy, whose face was dirty and tear stained, his mouth open and shouting soundlessly.

'My God,' said Ward.

'This isn't an advert, Bill,' said Bible. 'This wouldn't tempt you to buy anything.'

*

Logan held the lurcher on the chain he'd taken from Holmes, and looked from the graveyard towards the factory chimneys of the city, ghostly in the early morning mist.

'What are you going to do now Mr Logan?' said Stanley.

'I can tell you what you're going to do, Stanley,' said Logan slowly. 'You're going to take me to Dawn.'

Logan had been thinking, ever since he'd forced Stanley to pour paraffin over the vehicle and Holmes screaming in driver's seat, and they'd taken off across the moor, through the pine forest, to where the houses of the city began. And now he knew Stanley had betrayed him. They were sitting with their backs against a solid slab of gravestone, blackened with soot. It had offered some immediate camouflage, as the city would, but he wanted to wait for the streets to fill up with people before he tried to lose himself among the crowds of men trudging to the mills.

'I don't know where she is, Mr Logan,' said Stanley.

Logan smiled. He was taking it slowly. He'd time to take it slowly. If Jenny had followed Dawn to the West Riding, Dawn had got a message to her somehow. And he knew all his daughters' contacts.

Logan grabbed hold of Stanley's neck and thrust his face into the soil of the newly dug grave next to them. 'Yes you do, son. And you're going to tell me.'

'I can't breathe, Mr Logan.' Stanley lifted his head a fraction and spat out soil.

'How did Jenny know her sister was up here?'

'Dawn must have told her.'

'How? Telephone? We don't have one. Post. No, I control it. So how, Stanley? How? Who did she use to pass a message on?'

'My dad. It must have been my dad.'

Logan put a knee on Stanley's back, whipped the lurcher's chain round Stanley's throat, pulling the squealing dog over onto its side and dragging the dog's muzzle near to Stanley's ear. Stanley tried to reach the chain with his hands, but his position made that impossible. He choked hoarsely, as if he was going to retch.

'She wouldn't trust him, Stanley. But she'd trust you.' Logan relaxed the pressure of the chain on the boy's throat.

'I hardly know her. You don't let anybody near her.'

'Are you criticising me for looking after my children, Stanley?' Logan was angry now. He didn't want to be angry.

'No, Mr Logan, no. You've looked after them proper.'

'But you'd like to get near her, wouldn't you Stanley?' Logan tightened his grip on the chain. 'That day you pretended you couldn't remember her name when she'd been to the pictures. I saw through you, lad. I've seen the look you gave Jenny when you came to our house. You fancy her. You've been having dirty thoughts about my daughter.'

Stanley could not speak, his throat gagging like a football rattle. Logan relaxed the pressure.

'But that's all right, lad. She's a very attractive young woman.'

Stanley gasped. 'Please, Mr Logan.'

Logan released the chain and pulled it through like mooring rope so the lurcher stood up relieved and shook itself. 'But you're not having her.'

Logan leaned back against the gravestone and pulled out the small black and white photo of his daughter Dawn in the drab city street. 'So where is it?'

'Sebastopol Road. Number 29.' Stanley was gasping. There was no more danger from Stanley. He had destroyed the boy. He was back in control. 'And she calls herself Carol now.'

Logan tensed. But it wasn't Stanley who had found

out where she lived and kept it from him. That was someone up here in Yorkshire. Robbo. Or Turner. His money was on Turner. What game had he been playing? Logan felt the energy go out of him. He looked at the exhausted boy and laughed. 'I knew you were lying about not knowing her name. You were at school with her since she was five.'

Stanley massaged his throat. His cheeks and forehead were stained with graveyard soil.

'We're going to have to get cleaned up before we go and see her,' said Logan. He watched a cat stalking along the top of the graveyard wall. It dropped down onto the grass at the edge tangled with dirty leaves. The lurcher's ears pricked up and it jumped to attention. Logan unhooked it from its collar, and it was gone, flashing across the gravestones like quicksilver in defiance of the death beneath.

'When you watch an animal, Stanley son, you realise how feeble we are.' He put the shotgun on the ground and grabbed Stanley's wrist. 'See the way it chased off, covering the ground. How long would it take you to cover that ground?'

'You should have shot it,' said Stanley. 'It'll give us away.'

'You're a cruel bastard, Stanley. That's why I don't trust you.' He quickly pulled the boy's wrist towards him and trapped it between his knees. 'Humans aren't strong, Stanley. That's why we need brains and cunning.' Logan wrapped the links of the dog lead round Stanley's wrist. 'You're safe with me, Stanley,' he said. He stood up and pulled on the lead. 'Come on, we're going to get washed.'

The church echoed. Logan listened. It was still early; most people would only just be getting up for work, and he could not hear anyone. The fight had gone out of Stanley and the chain hung loosely between them. The boy kept his head bowed. 'Feel uncomfortable, boy?'

'It's a church.' Stanley spoke in a whisper.

'It's a building.'

Logan led the boy down the aisle, past the altar, to where he hoped there would be a vestry. He'd been forced to Sunday School as a child. He remembered the layout of the church he'd been marched to whenever his parents decided it was their duty to instil a bit of godliness into their recalcitrant child. The vestry room itself was meagrely furnished – a table and a rack of coathangers with clerical robes.

'What about these for a disguise, Stanley?' He unhooked a surplice and held it against his sullen accomplice. 'Quite the choirboy.' Stanley said nothing. Logan knew the boy wanted to get away. No loyalty. Only Larry had had loyalty and now he was dead. Only Larry and Logan had been true to Dawn.

At the back of the room was a toilet. Whereas the vestry had dark wood panelling to chest height, the toilet had plain plaster walls painted in lime green. There was a sink with a small mirror above and two toilet cubicles next to a window. They were clean and smelt of disinfectant. Someone cared for them. Logan shut the door of the washroom behind them and was surprised to see a bolt on the inside. He smiled. He was used to luck being with him. And he could feel he was getting close to Dawn. He slid the bolt across.

He gestured towards the washbasin. 'Get yourself

cleaned up. We're going into town. We don't want to look like farmers.'

The moors, the escape, the struggle with Holmes, the fire, had left their mark. He could smell smoke on his clothes and his hands were grey with dirt. But the boy was not moving. 'Do it, Stanley.'

'I'm still chained up.'

'You'll manage.'

Sluggishly, Stanley turned the taps and ran the water, picking up the sliver of green soap, and working up a thin lather on the palms of his hands. Perhaps he'd overdone it with the boy. Made him too afraid. He should have softened him up more. Flattered him. Kept him loyal. Still, he only needed him to take him to Dawn's. He could be done with him then. Stanley stepped back from the washbasin. 'Don't forget your face, Stanley. You look like you've been Guy Fawkes on a bonfire.'

When Stanley was done, Logan followed suit and looked at himself in the mirror above the basin. A rough face, but clean enough. A working man's face. He'd blend in with the northern crowd provided he didn't speak much.

'What about our clothes, Mr Logan?' They were both mud stained. Trying to wash it off would only smear the dirt further. Logan cast around. There was usually a solution. It was a confidence which had got him to where he was. That and a lack of fear. He pulled Stanley towards the toilet cubicles – they were attached by three feet of chain, so Stanley was obliged to follow. Logan reached in and pulled a toilet brush out of its holder. It was clean enough and fairly dry. He shook it to get rid of any excess drops. 'There's always something, Stanley,' said Logan proudly. His brain was clear as a bell. He was cruising now.

There was a distant bang. An echoing door. Logan stopped brushing and listened. He looked at Stanley and put a finger to his lips. He heard a dragging sound, like someone moving a piece of furniture, but still some way off, beyond the vestry. Stanley looked at him in panic. Logan smiled.

'There's a window, Stanley. Never get locked in a room without a window.'

Bumping in the vestry was followed by a metallic clang. It sounded like a cleaner with a bucket. Well, he could sort out cleaners.

'Come on, Stanley. Out you go.' Logan lifted the bar which held the window shut, and Stanley climbed onto the heavy iron radiator below it. This pulled the chain leash taut.

'You'll have to untie me, Mr Logan.'

The door was rattled on the outside. A voice. 'Anyone in there.' An old man's voice, croaky and unsure. He could be dealt with if necessary.

Logan unwrapped the chain he'd wound round the boy's hand, but paused before he let go and stabbed a thick finger at Stanley. 'Wait for me.'

Stanley nodded, threaded his legs through the casement and jumped. The door was shaking. 'Who's locked this door?' said the old man's voice. Logan ignored him, pulled his bulk onto the heater, and squeezed himself out. But Stanley had gone.

*

Bible sat at his desk, looking at the life-size two-dimensional figure propped against the radiator. It didn't need forensics to see that the crinkled photograph of a face crudely wired on to the head of the image was a late addition. The suit and tie were neat, the camera held at its waist an invitation to join the Kodak snapshot club. Although there was dirt and oil smeared across the picture, it looked like the shirt would once have been white and sunlit. But the head was screaming in darkness. Even under grime, it looked to belong to a different light. And the picture was damp, clearly soaked at one time, the cardboard edges softened, the surface of the picture wrinkled. It could have been the fire brigade with their hose, but the dummy had been at the back of the barn, away from the main seat of the fire. No, this had been submerged in water. And for a reason he didn't understand, it had been strengthened from the waist down with lead piping down the legs and wired to the feet.

Bible knew he'd have to see Carol.

TWENTY-NINE

Carol was back at work at the oak desk below the clock and the portraits of Menzies' formidable predecessors. It was comforting adding up figures, pressing her pen onto the thick paper of the leatherbound ledgers, everything neatened by the blue horizontal lines and the pretty pink columns. The previous day's figures were in order. She blotted her final entry, and pulled open her drawer. She'd be needed at the counter soon.

She was aware of raised voices. Or one raised voice. Menzies squeakily protesting, and another voice, firm. The girl on the desk opposite looked up too. Carol smiled at her.

'He's not panicking enough for it to be a robbery,' she said. The girl smiled back. Shared jokes about their nervous boss kept them amused at tea breaks, and helped persuade Carol she was sane after all. She saw a shape, two shapes, appear behind the frosted glass of the door to Menzies' office and the door swung open.

'Carol, Inspector Bible is here to see you again.' Carol felt both pleased and nervous. And she was embarrassed to find herself blushing. She got up quickly and took short quick steps towards Menzies, keeping her head down as she passed him.

'I'm not happy about this, Carol,' said Menzies.

'I didn't ask him to come, sir,' she said. Bible was standing in Menzies' office, a charcoal overcoat over his arm.

'Miss Carlton had no idea I was coming, Mr Menzies. A police enquiry follows where its leads take it.'

'A bank has a reputation to keep up.'

'But not one for helping police with their enquiries?' Good old Inspector Bible. Carol hoped Menzies would carry on making his peevish objections so Bible could deliver more verbal jabs. She was beginning to realise that her nervous boss had it in him to become a bit of a bully if given the upper hand.

'We know our duties,' said Menzies coldly. He stood holding the door. Bible remained standing. Carol wondered if she'd been called to witness a jousting match. She hoped the victor would be Bible and, when she realised what she'd just thought, hoped that she hadn't blushed.

'You'll need your coat, Carol. I need to show you something at the station.'

'Oh really,' said Menzies. 'Very well.'

'I know,' said Bible. 'Some of you have work to do.'

*

Logan never used the bus in Exeter. He walked and liked to be seen. But this city was bigger, and he'd no idea how far he'd have to go. He didn't like it, wedged in with a lot of women and shopping bags, the hidden gun pressing against his ribcage and weighing his jacket down on one side. The men had all gone upstairs for a smoke. But Logan wanted to be able to get out early, and hear the driver when he called his stop.

They seemed to be getting near the town centre. The buildings were tall and ornate, window ledges and surrounds carved by stonemasons. This place had escaped the bombs, unlike Exeter, gutted by Hitler to destroy morale. But not Logan's morale. He'd find Stanley somewhere. He was keeping his eyes open for Stanley. People looked so miserable. Off to work in the mills, he assumed. Heads down. Good boys. Victims. He hated the north, from what he'd seen of it. Dawn needed rescuing.

The buildings here were grand. Pompous. Full of importance. Department stores which looked like they'd make you dress up to go into them. Banks designed to frighten people. Logan had never bothered with a bank account. He was man enough to look after his own money.

On the pavement a man in a dark coat looked too smart for the people around him. He was showing a young woman into a car.

Logan was forcing his way out of his window seat in an instant.

'You could say excuse me,' complained the woman next to him. There was confusion. Commotion. People standing in the aisle were squashed over people sitting down as Logan fought his way to the open platform at the rear of the bus. A young man in spectacles with thick black frames tried to block his way. 'I'm sorry, but you should say excuse me.'

'I need to get out,' he heard himself say as he

squeezed past. He hadn't meant to speak. That Devon accent. But there were a number of flatter, Yorkshire voices.

'Appen he's ill.'

' 'ad a funny turn.'

'Come over all queer.'

The bus conductor held his hand out, blocking the way. 'Steady on there, mate, remember your manners.'

Logan stopped. 'I'm getting off,' said Logan simply and stared at the man. He didn't want to draw any more attention to himself. Voices grumbled behind him.

'He's not from round here.'

'Doesn't know how to behave.'

The conductor was a big man, but Logan knew he was not big enough. The conductor stepped aside and pressed the bell. 'All right, all right. I've told t'driver to stop. But just wait...'

Logan jumped off the moving bus before he heard the end of the sentence. He was breathless by the time he got back to the spot outside the bank where he'd seen Dawn, but the car had gone, and with it the man who had taken her away. He rounded on a council worker pushing a dustcart up the gutter, sweeping the streets. 'Did you see a car here? Young woman and a man getting in?'

The street cleaner slid sweet papers and dust from his shovel into the bin. 'And who are you to be asking?' he said.

Logan looked around him, at this unfamiliar place, with its black Victorian buildings and miserable people, and he knew he was working alone.

*

Carol felt looked after, but fearful. Bible guided her out of the car gently, reaching round to put his hand on her shoulder. As they climbed the steps of the central police station, he went ahead, then leaned down and held his hand out solicitously and touched her elbow. It was as if she were an honoured guest. She felt his uncertainty when they reached the entrance. Who should go first? She decided to end his misery by pushing open the heavy doors and letting him catch them before they swung shut.

'See, I'm not as delicate as you think,' she said.

Bible frowned. 'I don't know what you mean.'

'You've been handling me like porcelain all morning. And you hardly spoke in the car.' Carol thought she'd raise a smile from him, but she felt her own smile fade as Bible looked at her solemnly.

'I need to show you something,' he said, and led her down the long empty corridor to his office, the metal caps on her low heels echoing noisily.

As Carol sat crying quietly on the hard chair in his office, Bible was ashamed to find himself feeling jealous and excluded. He stood awkwardly and pulled the clean handkerchief from his jacket pocket. Bible reached for the life-size human cut-out with the face of the missing Larry and began to turn it towards the shelves of box files.

'No,' said Carol. 'I want to look at him.' She dabbed her eyes with Bible's handkerchief, and screwed it between her hands. 'Why does he look like that?'

'We don't know.'

'Someone is making him suffer, aren't they?'

'We'll try to find him.' He didn't tell her about the charred body tied to the steering wheel. And that Turner was involved. Bible was angry with himself for his failure to acknowledge that Turner had been fishy from the start. But Turner acting alone, tying a body to the steering wheel of the Bedford? Unlikely. So who were the three men in the vehicle that had got away from them in town? Ward thought he knew the driver from somewhere, but couldn't place him.

'I'm not in love with him, you know.' Carol's words startled him. 'But I am fond of him. We see things the same way.'

'Why has no one reported him missing?' said Bible. The look on Carol's face surprised him. It was as if she'd never thought of it before. 'His family? His parents? We've all got parents.' Bible felt stupid and clumsy. 'Surely somebody knew him.'

'I don't know,' said Carol. 'He never mentioned his family. I thought, perhaps it was like mine.' Bible felt her eyes look at him squarely. 'What's happened to him?'

He wanted to help her. Too much, he realised. He pulled a chair beside her. He put his arm round her and she leaned into him.

'You think he's dead, don't you?' Carol murmured into his shoulder.

'I don't know. But someone knows.' He pulled her closer. He hoped it reassured her. It didn't reassure him.

*

Logan stood opposite 29 Sebastopol Road and took the photo out of his pocket. The image was grainy, and so many of these streets looked the same. But when he looked closely, he could see that the door panelling matched, and that the grey patchiness on the photograph was peeling paint. So this was the place he had been looking for.

Logan walked across the road towards the house. A border collie came running up the pavement towards him, but turned back when he glowered at it. He walked up the short path to the door. The bell had been painted as well as the door, and the button was clogged with gloss. He felt like smashing his way through it. It was the only enemy he could see. He could control his anger when faced with someone who was afraid, but with this emptiness…He took a deep breath. A pensioner sucking on a pipe was walking past, and stopped to knock the dottle out on the low stone wall. Logan glared at him.

'Now then,' said the pipe smoker. Logan guessed it was a sort of greeting. He nodded. Move on, old man. But the pipe smoker was patiently refilling his briar. 'Not so bad for t'time o' year.'

Logan shrugged. He didn't want to risk revealing his accent.

'Bit o' sun allus 'elps,' said the smoker, drawing his cheeks in as he sucked on the pipe, pulling the flame of the match downwards as the new tobacco ignited. 'That your house?' said the man between the pops of his breath as he sucked and smacked his lips together. Logan realised he must look odd standing there, neither going in nor coming out.

Logan shook his head. 'Debt collector.'

'That explains it. I've seen t'beat bobby banging on t'door a couple of times.' By now the pipe smoker had created a small bonfire which seemed to satisfy him. 'Any road, be seeing you,' he said, and stepped on his way leaving drifts of St Bruno wafting towards Logan.

Logan turned and hammered on the door with the flat of his hand. He heard movements inside. He hammered again. A latch was turned and the door opened. An old woman stood there leaning on a stick. She wore a stained dress that looked as if it were made of dark sacking. He forced the door open wider and stepped in.

'Have you got my daughter in here?'

The old woman stepped back, gawping. Chin going up and down. Mouth opening. Silly old bat.

'Dawn,' he demanded. 'Young woman.' He sighed. His anger was subsiding. He could see his enemy. And for now it was a stupid old woman. 'Wouldn't sound like she was from round here.' She didn't look like she was going to tell him anything. He paced into the hall. An open door to his right led to a dimly lit room. That must be where the old woman hibernated. In front of him a flight of stairs, a gloomy corridor at the side leading to a dark brown door with panes of frosted glass. That must be a toilet. A cat litter tray which needed its sand changing lay next to the hall stand.

'There's Carol,' he heard the old woman say behind him. She leaned on her stick, and lifted a wobbling hand towards the stairs. Logan looked up and saw one white door at the top of the first half flight of stairs where it moved into a dogleg. He grabbed the banister and hauled himself up to it, two steps at a time.

*

Bible watched from the information room as Higham ushered Carol towards the car outside the police station. He wished he could have driven her back himself, but she'd been anxious to return to the bank and Ward was waiting to speak to him.

'I'm glad she's got someone to look after her, sir,' said Ward drily as Higham's arm lingered across Carol's shoulders as he guided her into the car.

Waiting alongside Ward was the young constable who had taken the photographs at the scene of the fire. Duggan was a short young man who'd barely made it into the force – seemingly too small and too shy to be a policeman. But his patience and technical knowhow had proved invaluable. He held some large manila envelopes.

'Show him what you've found,' said Ward.

Duggan laid one of the manila envelopes on a wooden table, sliding out the contents, a mixture of glass, paper, and photographs. 'I've been looking at the rubbish that was in the blanket sir. The glass and broken picture frames.' Duggan produced a pair of tweezers. 'I thought they were just watercolours, landscapes, but there were photographs behind the paintings, like they were hidden. These.'

He pulled out two black and white photographs. Each featured a child of about twelve, naked. One a girl, one a boy. 'And then there's this.' Duggan reached into the second envelope and pulled out a thick piece of heavily textured watercolour paper, soiled and singed on one side. He laid it on the table next to the photographs. It was a painting of the boy, in the same pose.

'And there's one of the girl, as well, sir. Like he's been taking photos and copying them.'

Bible looked closely. 'Who are these children?'

Ward shrugged. 'We don't know sir. No one has reported anything.'

Duggan held out a magnifying glass. 'I've been looking at them through this. Looking at their faces. Do you want to try sir?'

Bible took the magnifying glass reluctantly. It didn't feel right, looking at naked children through it. But although the children looked watchful, wondering, they didn't look frightened.

'Any younger children?' He was thinking of young Donald, lying dead in the grass opposite the school.

Duggan shook his head. Bible bent over the photographs again. They were sideways on, hands on the backs of chairs, leaning on them, showing their bottoms towards the camera. There was a drape behind them, the same drape, with the same creases; it looked as if the photos had been taken on the same day.

Bible straightened up. 'You can't see where they were taken.'

'Not from the background, sir,' said Duggan. 'But if you look at the floor, it's concrete. Sergeant Ward says it's like the floor of the pump house.'

'I think he's our man, sir,' said Ward softly.

'Any more photos?' said Bible. It bothered him that these children were older than Donald had ever been. Ten or eleven.

'Look at the next one, sir,' said Ward. 'Duggan?'

The young PC produced a print from a cleaner envelope and laid it on the table. 'This wasn't as dirty as the others. Probably more recently developed and printed.'

'Taken in the back of a van, sir. A small van.' Ward waited for the connection to be made, enjoying the drama. But there was a connection Bible hadn't yet told Ward about.

'I know her,' said Bible. 'She's called Linda.'

*

He could smell her. See her. Nearly reach her. Dawn had been here. The room was abandoned. But neatly. That was Dawn. He'd trained her to be tidy. The sheets on the bed he sat on were pulled back, the bottom one straightened – no imprint of a body. He pulled out a pair of high-heeled shoes moored under the wardrobe side by side like fishing boats. He'd always insisted she wore sensible shoes. Whores wore fancy shoes. The higher the heels....he threw them to one side so they drummed against the wardrobe door. A tart. That's what she must be. A common tart. She was living on something. Kept by someone. He'd find him. She'd looked like a tart in that photo with the headscarf and sunglasses. A wardrobe door was ajar, and he felt a tingle as it moved. It was a cat. That was all. The tabby moved paw by paw towards him, unsure, but came to his leg and purred, rubbing its head against his old flannels. Logan reached down to pick it up, put it on his lap, and held its face between his heavy palms.

'Where has she gone then? And what's she been doing with you?'

The cat trusted him. As everyone should. He knew how to look after people when they let him. He put the animal down gently. He'd nothing against animals. It was people who couldn't be trusted. He got up to look in the wardrobe. At the bottom the cat's bed, a neatly folded woollen skirt he'd made Dawn wear. Ingratitude. Underneath it was newspaper dated August two days after she'd left. And an envelope, simply bearing the name 'Dawn' in copperplate. The letter he'd made his wife write, and given Turner to deliver if he ever found her. The door to the room opened. Logan stood up and stuffed the envelope into his pocket. The old woman doddered in. 'Carol's gone, you know. Malcolm said.'

'And who's Malcolm?' said Logan.

THIRTY

'You can tell he lived alone,' said Ward. 'The smell.'

Bible felt Turner hadn't opened a window in his squalid cottage for more than a year. The stench was more than stale air. It was a sour smell, like something rotting. And although there was sun outside, the high wall of the weaving shed across the cobbled lane blocked any of it from reaching this ground floor room.

Ward poked among the clothes scattered on the floor and over the old leather sofa, cracked in places and losing its stuffing. It was the only seating accommodation in the room. Turner cooked in the corner on an old gas stove. It had seen a good deal of spillage, now burnt on hard. Bible's eyes were drawn to the old Belfast sink, white with a pattern of blue veins discolouring it, and showing its age. Below it was a bucket.

'We've got a reservoir keeper who can't manage his own plumbing,' said Bible. 'No waste pipe.' The bucket was directly under the plughole of the sink and full of water. Bible squatted down. The liquid had a green tinge. The smell made him feel sick. 'I think he's been boiling cabbage and pouring the water in here.'

'Look at these, sir,' said Ward. Under the clothes was a dog-eared scattering of *Health and Efficiency* magazines, each depicting a woman enjoying the benefits of nature with no clothes on, though the genitals were smoothed out and featureless. 'Dirty bugger.'

'Those'll be the pictures he tempted Linda's friends with. No sign of his rabbiting gun anywhere,' said Bible. He pulled the bucket from under the sink. 'I'm going to chuck this.' He carried the slop bucket to the back door, hoping to find a drain in the yard at the rear. A mound of coats suspended from a hook hid the door knob. He pushed them to one side revealing another coat, hanging neatly from a coat hanger. A fawn coat, with a woven scarf snuggled securely into the neck as if someone were wearing it. Bible put the bucket down and patted the pockets. He put his hand in one and pulled out a pair of tortoiseshell glasses. The lenses were plain glass, useless as an aid to sight.

'I think I've found something interesting here, Bill,' said Bible. He tried to picture the old man in the school hall who had never been seen since. The neatly pressed coat and the delicately arranged scarf carefully placed on the hanger were a contrast to the chaos in the rest of the room.

'Imagine Turner in those,' said Bible.

He watched Ward spread the coat as wide as he could by pulling out each side near the pockets. 'Isn't Turner a bit of a fatso?'

Bible smiled. Ward was lithe as a whippet. 'He's always been padded out against the cold. You wouldn't make do with a mac like that up at the reservoir.'

The picture of the elderly gentleman in the school hall was re-forming in his mind. Turner was somewhere in middle age but not what you'd call elderly. But now he thought of it, perhaps the skin of the man in the school had not been that of an old man. He was afraid he was now making the image of the man fit Turner.

'Have we ever seen Turner without his flat cap?'

'I don't think so, sir. Still had it on when you were questioning him.'

That was normal. No one asked if they could take their jacket off before they were charged. Clothes were a form of defence. And Turner was a defensive man.

Bible picked up the bucket. 'Let's get rid of this cesspool and take a look upstairs.'

The single upstairs room was bright, the window high enough off the ground to catch the winter sun. It dazzled in the small panes and cast a waffle shadow over the pale wallpaper.

The bed was unmade. Next to the bed, an upturned orange box served as a makeshift table. On it, a tobacco tin and cigarette papers. Accumulations of junk had gathered along the skirting board like flotsam at high tide. But Bible would look at that later. His eyes were fixed on the small washbasin in the corner. On the shelf above it, the tools of male grooming were laid out neatly. Safety razor. Spare blades. Shaving brush. Everything spaced out equally along the shelf. And at the end of the row, a jar of Brylcreem, its opaque white glass shining like a small sculpture. He heard Ward come into the room behind him.

'You can tell a lot about a man from the state of

his shaving equipment,' said Bible without turning, thinking about the neatness, and its contrast to the chaotic squalor elsewhere in the cottage. 'But the Brylcreem. Does he strike you as a man for Brylcreem under his flat cap?'

'No sir.'

'Me neither.'

'The old man's hair was neat. Newly cut and combed. We'd better have prints off this lot. We know it's his, but we don't want him saying we planted it.'

'Nor this,' said Ward. He held what looked like a piece of card in his hand. Ward put it on the bed. It was a piece of stiff watercolour paper. And on it, a delicate painting of a naked girl with slim hips and the breasts just beginning to bud. Bible felt ashamed for looking at it.

'Another girl, Bill. And in the photos Duggan showed us, all girls.'

'He's a nasty piece of work, sir,' said Ward. 'And they say art civilises people.'

As they drove back Bible raised Swann at HQ and told him to put out a call for Turner.

'I'll do my best.'

Bible heard shouting in the background.

'It's a bit chaotic down here, sir.'

Bible continued. 'And I want someone going round that barber's near Turner's cottage.'

'But he's a cunning bastard,' said Ward. 'I think he might have his hair cut where no one knows him.'

Bible nodded. It was good to have Ward thinking with him. 'Get the beat bobbies onto all the barbers in the city.' He waited for Swann to answer, but there was just crackle. 'What's going on, Bill?'

Swann came on air again. 'Sorry, sir. I think you'd better come back in.'

Bible glanced at his watch. 'Ten minutes.'

As Bible and Ward walked into the police station, Wallace was standing in the foyer in his coat and trilby, waiting for him. 'We've got him calmed down a bit. Follow me.' Wallace waved a finger towards Ward. 'And you.'

'Got who calmed down, sir?' said Bible. They strode after Wallace as he rolled down the corridor.

'Holroyd. Someone's taken his granddaughter.'

Holroyd's office was crowded and thick with smoke. Half a dozen of the uniformed force were there and all of the detective constables from CID. Holroyd was standing and shouting at them from his desk, waving a lit cigarette in his right hand, and the next one ready to light in his left. Bible wondered if Holroyd ever tried smoking two or three at once, sticking out of his mouth like bad teeth.

Holroyd harangued Bible as soon as he came in. 'At last. Where the fuck have you been? I want every last man in this station looking for Turner.'

'What about the fraud case at Lorrimer's?' The speaker was a detective sergeant looking into funny goings on at a mail order firm.

'Drop it.'

'With respect, sir, we've got to look like we're in control,' said a uniformed inspector.

'I don't care what it looks like, I want my granddaughter found.' Holroyd went red in the face and started coughing, an eruption of throat-raking explosions which threatened his ability to breathe as he steadied himself on the desk. Bible feared his boss was about to have a heart attack and stepped forward to catch him, but Holroyd recovered and said hoarsely, 'Take them away, Bible. You know what to do.'

Bible murmured to Ward, 'Stay with him a while, Bill. Check he's all right.' He looked at the men crowded into the office, and then at Wallace, who stood impassively behind Holroyd's chair staring at Bible.

'We'll start in the information room,' said Bible, and the assembled policemen shuffled out.

Wallace caught up with him as Bible waited for his team to sort themselves out with chairs or perch on tables. 'And what's this about a crowd of mothers doing their own door-to-door around the school, asking about that bloody van? Seems your wife's one of them.'

Bible hoped his alarm didn't show. The van. He hadn't told Shirley they'd found it. Ward came in and nodded at him. Did Bill know about Shirley's activities? His face was inscrutable as he sat on a chair facing his two superiors.

'You'd better get this right, son. He's counting on you,' said Wallace. It sounded like a threat. He wondered if Wallace would want to take charge, but the London man must have read his mind. 'You know the area. You'd best get on with it.'

'Is that a compliment, Superintendent?'

'Take it how you like, son. But don't try anything

like that cowboy stunt over the border. I don't like mavericks.'

You never knew how people really saw you. He looked at the assembled faces. The men were ready, plain clothes men near the front, uniformed officers at the back. He thought they saw him as steady but slow. But perhaps he wasn't. Perhaps he was changing. He tried to put Wallace's report of Shirley's activity out of his mind.

Higham looked impatient. 'Shouldn't we just pick Turner up, sir? You had him in yesterday.' Other heads nodded vigorously. Voices. 'He finished young Holmes off. Now he's got Holroyd's lass.'

'You're right, Turner's a suspect and he hasn't been seen since the fire. But we don't know it's him. We're not just here to make arrests.'

'I am,' said Higham, laughing and looking round for approval. Bible was glad no one else laughed.

'Other children are in danger if Turner's not the culprit and we don't look any further. So we'll stick to procedure.' So much for the maverick in him. 'You know the routine. She disappeared on her way to the sweet shop after school. Her grandma had given her some money for spice. Start from the shops and work outwards. Higham, find out who was shopping there this afternoon. Bill can take a team to search all the gardens, garages and sheds within a mile.' He looked towards Ward. 'Is the police box flashing for the beat bobby?'

'Done sir. He'll call in as soon as he sees it.'

'Where's the girl's mother now?'

'Holroyd's daughter? She's at home. WPC's with her.'

'I'd better go and see her,' said Bible.

'Any point?' said Wallace. 'You know who you should be picking up.'

'I'm going to be a maverick, Superintendent,' said Bible, picking up his coat, 'and stick to routine.'

*

Logan thanked the old woman politely, asked if his daughter owed any rent, said he was sorry to have troubled her, and let her close the door behind him. It paid to be polite which was why he always insisted on it with his daughters and his wife. You needed people on your side. He let the door close quietly behind him, and stood on the top step.

'Got a light, mate?'

The voice came from a youth with a Teddy Boy quiff looking at him over the scraggy privet hedge. Logan stepped down to pavement level and patted his pockets for the rattle of the box he always carried. He struck a match, and held it for the boy as he leaned towards the flame. The youth puffed a couple of times to make sure his cigarette was going, then took it from his mouth with an exaggerated sweep of the hand.

'You're not from round here, are you, mate?'

'You'd know, would you?' said Logan.

'It's the way you talk. Gives you away.'

'But you hadn't heard me say anything,' said Logan. He'd got the boy on the defensive. Good.

'Looking for your daughter?'

Logan froze. His impulse was to grab the boy's fancy jacket in his big fists and pull his foxy little face towards him nose to nose.

'I might be able to help you,' piped up the youth.

There was no 'might' about it, thought Logan. If the boy knew something, Logan would make him tell; but for now he'd let him think it was voluntary.

'So who are you?' he said.

'People call me Cannonball.'

'Is that what your dad calls you?'

The boy looked truculent. 'Doesn't matter what my dad calls me.'

Logan laughed. 'All right. Cannonball it is. And whilst I've got you here, who's Malcolm?'

'He's a poof your lass hangs around with.'

Logan put a heavy arm round Cannonball's shoulders. 'I think it's time you and me took our friendship a bit further.'

THIRTY-ONE

Holroyd wanted publicity. As far as Bible could see, Holroyd wanted the whole country looking for his granddaughter. The local press men – the City crime reporter, and men he hardly knew from *The Yorkshire Post, Leeds Evening News* and *Halifax Evening Courier* – were outnumbered by men with trilbies and notebooks from London: *Express* and *Mail*, *News Chronicle*, *Times* and *Telegraph*. Only the man from *The Manchester Guardian* seemed a match for the men from the south, as Wallace – sitting at the centre of the table with Bible on his left – played to his familiar London audience.

'I thought you were going to retire, Superintendent,' said a London reporter on the front row, waving a yellow pencil.

'Not till I've got my man,' said Wallace smugly. Bible was getting fed up of Wallace's grandstanding. The Superintendent pointed to a tubby figure in the front row who looked like Alfred Hitchcock. 'Percy.'

'Is it true you've already had a local man in for questioning?'

'The local boys have had a few people in. I'm helping them sort wheat from chaff.'

'But is it true that you personally interviewed your chief suspect, and let him go before the Chief

Superintendent's granddaughter went missing?' The voice came from three rows back. Bible recognised the familiar figure of Graham Rose from the local *Argus*. Bible had no idea where he had got his information from. Wallace ignored the question, and nodded towards another of the London men.

'Are you connecting this girl's disappearance with the murder of the little boy at the school?'

Bible butted in. 'No one was killed at the school gates. His body was found some distance away.'

'We're confident it's the same man,' said Wallace, and then delivered a murmured growl to Bible. 'Let me do the talking here, Bible. You do the detecting. ' One of the London men left his seat at the front and squatted by the end of the third row, talking to Graham Rose, before holding up his notebook. Wallace ignored him and turned to a reporter on the other side of the room.

'How is morale in the force when an incident touches on one of your own?'

'It makes us more of a team.'

Another voice from the back. 'Is that what the county force thinks?' It was the man from *The Yorkshire Post*. 'Haven't they arrested a farmer for a similar offence?'

This was getting dangerous. Bible didn't want Sugden's arrest getting out. He feared for Sugden among the locals out in the country. There was a clamour of voices at the back.

'No shouting, boys,' said Wallace, wearily. 'Keep it in order, gentlemen.'

Rose from the *Argus* raised his hand again. 'Is it true Inspector Bible has been to a cottage in Chapel

Heights that belongs to the man you let go?'

Bible felt a flash of anger. Who had spoken to the *Argus*? Bible was ready to answer questions, but the press only seemed interested in Wallace. The London man now squatting by Rose stood up.

'With respect, Superintendent Wallace, you haven't answered my colleague's earlier question about a link with the murdered six-year-old? Would Chief Superintendent Holroyd's granddaughter have been safe if you hadn't let a man go yesterday?'

Bible could see Holroyd in the corridor, watching through the open door. He was in full dress uniform, adorned with medals, but looked drawn. He needed time off, but couldn't let go. When he walked stiffly into the room, the hubbub decreased. He stood on the other side of the seated Wallace, his hands clasped behind his back holding a brown manila envelope. For once, he did not have a cigarette with him.

'Gentlemen, I am grateful for your attendance, but I want to speak to you now not as Chief Superintendent Holroyd of the City police, but as Albert Holroyd, a grandfather, fifty-five years old. My lovely little granddaughter is missing, a girl who played like a fairy in my garden on a Sunday, and sang like an angel. I would like to ask for your help in finding her. In particular I'd like to ask for your help in locating this man.' Holroyd produced the envelope from behind his back and extracted a quarto-sized photograph. 'Jack Arnold Turner. Keeper of High Gill Reservoir. Now missing from both his place of work and his home. Jane...' He called into the corridor, and a female police officer came in with more photographs. 'My WPC will distribute photographs which I would personally like you to publish.'

The assembled press men passed the photographs along the rows. Bible was surprised more questions weren't being fired at them now Holroyd had appeared, but perhaps they were reluctant to break the sombre mood the Chief Superintendent had introduced. It was hard not to respect a man under threat of personal loss as Holroyd was. Holroyd carried on. 'Few cases of this nature are simple, but I hope your questions about how we have handled this case can wait until my granddaughter is found. But yes, we did have Mr Turner in for questioning before we had hard evidence. And it is true a farmer was arrested by the County Force at the weekend, but I understand from my opposite number there that he has now been released after we have supplied them with our information.'

'I meant to tell you,' muttered Wallace.

It was the first Bible had heard of Sugden's release. It must have been the photographs of Linda in the back of the van. Voices were shouting from the floor of the room. 'So why was the farmer arrested in the first place?' 'What can you tell us about the county case?' 'Will someone be disciplined?'

Bible could only see Holroyd's back, but he felt his boss was struggling. Wallace leaned into his ear. 'There's a man needs a fag if ever I saw one.' Wallace fished his snuff box out of his waistcoat pocket and took a sniff. Bible wished Holroyd would get this man off his back. Bible left his table, went to Holroyd, and touched his elbow. Holroyd looked at him. Bible could see he was holding a lot back.

'Would you like me to take the rest, sir?' Holroyd

nodded, and stalked from the platform. More voices from the floor. Bible held his hands up and addressed the assembled newspaper men. 'No more questions, gentlemen. Ten o'clock tomorrow morning, we'll speak to you again.' Bible turned and walked out quickly, after Holroyd. He heard Wallace push back his chair. The Superintendent caught up with him in the corridor.

'What the fuck do you think you're doing, son?'

Bible faced his superior from London and found himself despising his fancy waistcoat, his snuff, and all the mannerisms which told him Wallace was only in it for personal glory. 'There's no need for that language, sir.'

'You left me sitting there like a bloody toilet attendant. I'm the Superintendent here. All you've got to do is find out who's been fiddling with little boys and girls. And get that wife of yours sorted out before she thinks she's Sherlock Holmes.'

'I'm not her keeper,' said Bible, turning his back. A few steps further down the corridor took Bible to Holroyd's office. He knocked on the door and opened it. Holroyd was sitting at his desk and spitting at a piece of paper in his hands. Bible didn't think the Chief Superintendent had noticed him, but Holroyd looked at him with glazed eyes and held up the picture. It was a photograph of Turner. 'Find him, Bible. Find him.' Bible closed the door gently. Wallace had followed him in and was standing behind him. 'Even if it means you have to interview sheep to find him.'

Swann was bustling along the corridor towards them as they left the office. 'You'd better come to the interview room. Ward's got an old friend he wants you to meet.'

The cramped interview room smelled of fire and smoke. Ward stood looking down at a dishevelled figure in trousers stained with mud, and a face daubed with ash. 'Major Robinson has come to see us, sir.'

'We haven't time for this, Bill.' Bible felt annoyed. The bank fraud was a trivial matter now, and he needed to phone Shirley. 'You deal with it.' He was turning to go when Ward called him back.

'He was driving the van we tried to stop, sir. And he knows where Turner is, don't you, Robbo? Come on Major Robinson, let's hear your voice.'

The bedraggled conman looked up, and wiped his face, smearing it with ash. His voice was not much more than a husky whisper. 'I need protection.' Only a whisper, but enough for Bible to hear that this was not a northern voice, nor one with the plummy tones he'd heard from the conman in the bank. It was a voice like Carol's, with rolled West Country vowels.

'We don't offer people like you protection,' said Ward.

'Arrest me then.' The former Major Robinson looked at his soiled hands clasped in front of him on the table.

Bible gave a single nod of his head to Ward.

'We can oblige with that,' said Ward standing up. 'Ronald Robinson, I'm arresting you for the murder of Larry Cole...'

Robinson looked shocked. 'No.'

'What Mr Robinson hasn't told you, sir, is that he's best friends with a gentleman called Logan. And they couldn't wait when we stopped them because they had an appointment with Turner at the reservoir. Busy men, sir.'

Bible sat down, leaning over the table to close the distance between himself and Robinson. He kept his face impassive, though he wanted to grab hold of the weaselly little man and shake out of him everything he knew.

'There's a child's life at stake here, Mr Robinson. We need Turner and you're the missing link.'

'I don't know anything about a child.'

'What do you know?' said Bible. The miserable individual before him shrugged. 'Where's Turner?'

'I want you to find my son. Turner hasn't got him. Logan has,' said Robbo. He was almost crying.

'And how old's your son?'

'Eighteen.'

Bible slapped the table so it shook. 'We're looking for a missing seven-year-old girl, and the killer of a little boy, so your son can take his chances. Now you tell me about Turner.'

'I haven't seen him since he cleared off.'

'Tell me how you started the fire.'

Robinson looked startled. 'I didn't start the fire. Nor did Turner. We'd both scarpered before then.'

'So stop smearing ash over your face,' said Ward. 'Convince us.'

'I was behind a wall. Logan didn't know I was there.' Robinson wiped his face with the heel of his hand, and looked at the grime on the palms of his hands. 'I heard a scream, and Stanley shouted, "Don't do it, Mr Logan." I looked through a gap in the top of the wall. Logan was possessed. He'd wired that poor bugger's hands to the steering wheel and was sloshing petrol around from an old jerry can. You don't cross him when he's like that. The man in the driver's seat was screaming, but he just set him alight and watched. Stanley tried to stop him. I heard him say they'd see the fire down in the city. But Logan said they had to do it. I couldn't watch any more.'

'They?'

'Him and Stanley. But it wasn't Stanley. Logan always says we have to do stuff. Even when he's doing it all.'

As Bible listened to Ronnie Robinson's story he could hear echoes of Carol's voice in his soft Devon accent. Hard to think that so much evil could come out of a place with such soft sounds.

'If that had been my son, I wouldn't have hidden behind a wall,' said Ward quietly.

'You don't know Tommy Logan. You never know what he'll do,' muttered Robinson.

'So you watched a young man burn, a man not much older than your son?' said Ward.

Robinson looked shocked. 'He wasn't a young man. Old. Older. Scrawny fella. Came out of nowhere. Accused Logan of killing his son. None of us knew what he was talking about. But he was mad. You couldn't reason with him. Had a dog with him. Lurcher.'

Bible glanced over his shoulder to where Ward was standing, grim-faced. Ward nodded. They didn't have to say it. Holmes.

'I hid. Turner ran off over the moors somewhere. Logan took Stanley with him.'

Bible sat back in his chair. 'Get a search team out.

I want someone at every track leading off High Gill Moor.'

'Will do, sir,' said Ward, reaching for the door.

'And send someone to Holmes' cottage, Bill.' said Bible. 'Someone sensitive.'

Ward closed the door quietly behind him.

'I'm not a bad man,' said Robinson hoarsely.

'Not you who did all this stuff, then?' said Bible.

Robinson shook his head. 'Why would I burn a man to death?'

'Don't fool yourself. You're just another villain, but you all think you're justified in some way.'

'You have to do what Logan says. He takes over your mind. You don't know who you are. That's why his daughter ran away. Did you know that? Did you know that's why he's up here?'

Bible waited. He wanted Robinson to talk. Let him think he could deflect blame.

'No,' said Bible. 'We didn't know that. Tell me about this Logan.'

'You don't want to meet him,' said Robinson, looking down.

'I think I do,' said Bible into the silence Robinson had left.

THIRTY-TWO

The city was an ugly place. The streets of blackened stone houses made Logan long for the openness of the river, and the green fields you could see beyond the edges of his small cathedral city. He wondered who the real villains were in this town, as Turner wasn't up to much. An early winter smog had descended on the city as the youth with the fancy jacket led him down streets and alleyways.

'I hope you know where you're going, boy,' growled Logan.

'Yeah well, you've got to trust me, haven't you?' said Cannonball with a chirpiness that made Logan want to grab him by his velvet lapels and explain who was boss, but for now he felt he had to keep this young streak of piss sweet. A trolleybus wheezed by, barely visible through the fog but for the lighted windows illuminating homebound workers who gazed out glumly on the streets of stone and soot. Logan had never been a wage slave and didn't intend to start. 'How do you cave dwellers breathe in this place?' he grumbled.

'We're just hard,' said Cannonball, flashing Logan a grin. Logan wondered what he was doing following a lippy kid round a town he didn't know. But he knew he'd have to bide his time. The cocky Ted would find out how hard Logan was if it became necessary.

The alleyway opened out on to a main road. Cars crawled by slowly, their headlights casting conical shafts of light filled with motes of dirt as if they were in the cinema. He could make out a glow across the road, yellow lights in a large window gauzed in fog.

'We're going to that pub over there. Watch out for cars. They can hardly see us in this.'

'I know how to cross the road, boy.'

'I didn't know you had cars in the sticks.' Logan grabbed the boy's arm from behind and pulled him back.

'It's time you gave me some information if our friendship is to continue.'

Cannonball smirked. 'You're a bit old to be chucking your weight around, aren't you?'

'Not old, boy. Just experienced.'

Cannonball tried to pull free, but Logan closed his fingers round the youth's other arm and backed him against the wall, guarding his crotch against a sudden knee in the groin. This kid might just have the bottle to try it. 'See,' he said. 'Just remember I reward people well if they're loyal.' Logan released his grip, and Cannonball straightened his jacket.

'You're not a big shot round here, you know. Turner knows people.'

Logan laughed. 'Turner. Yeah. Let's find Turner.' He was in an unfamiliar city, but perhaps there was no opposition. 'Is he over there?'

Cannonball shook his shoulders in his jacket, put his collar up, and stepped into the road. 'Follow me. Got summat else to show you first.'

They crossed the murky river of fog towards the lights of the public house, a block of stone that looked more like a church than a pub.

'We're going in here,' said Cannonball.

'Want me to buy you an orange juice?' Logan wondered at the boy's age.

The pub was not busy. The velvet-covered bench seats around the walls had clearly seen better days. The small round tables were dark and thick with layers of old varnish. Empty stools, capped with mock leather fixed by brass studs, were neatly arranged around them, like children expecting a story. Logan looked at his watch. Early. Perhaps the pub would fill up later.

'What you having?' said Cannonball. Logan sensed the boy was showing off.

'Nothing.' Logan didn't drink much, and he certainly didn't want to drink now. He had to keep his wits about him. Drink would only make him brood, and get angry. But this boy offering to get him a drink? What was he after? Time to stop being so friendly.

Cannonball shrugged, strolled to the bar.

Logan chose a seat next to a wood-panelled partition. He didn't want to be too noticeable. Cannonball returned with a dark drink, fizzing in a glass.

'What's that? said Logan.

'Coca Cola. American.'

Logan didn't like Americans. He hadn't liked the GIs during the war, talking loudly and chucking their weight about.

Cannonball took a swig. 'We all drink it now.'

Logan grabbed the glass, took a sip and smiled. 'Who are you kidding? That's dandelion and burdock.' He put the glass down as Cannonball glowered at him. 'He didn't like you up there at the bar.'

'Nah, he doesn't like us Teds. Frightened we'll cause trouble.'

'And why would he think that?'

'We don't like the people who come here. You'll see.' Cannonball grinned as he lifted his glass. 'He let me stay when I told him you were my dad.'

The boy had a cheeky appeal, but he was a villain. Logan could see that. He wondered how much rope to give him. 'Stop your prattle and tell me why we're here. Where's Turner?'

'Here, let me show you summat.' Cannonball reached inside his jacket and pulled out a paper bag. He took out a photo and put it on the table. It was a small black and white picture of a girl wearing very little and watching the camera with suspicion.

Logan looked at it with disgust. 'What's this?'

'I can get more. For a price.'

'Where did you get this?'

'I'm not saying unless you...'

Logan jerked Cannonball from his stool by putting his hand round the boy's neck and pulling his head down towards him. He could feel the grease on the boy's hair and it repulsed him. 'Where's Turner?'

'Gerroff me,' said Cannonball, his voice muffled by his head being held low beside the table. 'You don't have to have 'em if you don't want 'em. They're Turner's. He doesn't know I've got 'em.'

The landlord, a burly man in his forties, called

across from the bar where he was polishing a beer glass, and addressed Logan.

'Hey, none of that in here else you're out.' Logan released his grip on Cannonball, and raised his other hand in apology. 'Sort him out when you get him home,' said the landlord. 'He must drive you mad.'

No one in Exeter would have talked to him like that, but Logan smiled at Cannonball. 'So behave yourself son. He knows what a dad should do with a snotstreak like you.'

'Bloody hell,' said Cannonball, getting out his comb to reshape his hair. 'You take liberties.' The boy looked flushed and embarrassed.

'Just so you know where you stand,' said Logan. 'So they don't know you here?'

'It's not my sort of place,' said Cannonball sullenly.

'What is your sort of place? One of these milk bars?'

'Might be.'

Logan laughed. 'Nothing wrong with milk. I'm partial to a nice milk pudding myself.' But as he said it, he felt a sense of loss. Jenny gone now. He wouldn't let Dawn take his family away from him.

The pub was busier. Men from work, but not the grey men with knapsacks and sludge-coloured coats he'd seen trudging round the pavements. There were three men in suits with colourful ties, laughing at the bar and joking with the barman. Another young man came in and hesitated by the door, but smiled when he saw the trio at the bar and went over to them. They were nearly out of Logan's view as he sat partly hidden by the partition.

'Get the idea?' said Cannonball.

'Don't play games.'

'You going to pay for information?'

Logan nodded. He'd lost Turner, Robbo and Stanley. He needed this boy's help. He hated to feel he needed help.

'This is a pansies' pub. And that kid that's just come in, that's Malcolm.'

Logan stiffened. He knew why he hated this city. It was an evil place. It had taken two of his daughters. Turner's photos belonged to a world he didn't understand. Perverts ran free and, according to this boy, one of them knew his Dawn.

'He'll see me in a minute,' said Cannonball. 'Watch his face when he does.'

Logan rose from his dark corner by the partition. 'Get in there. I don't want him to see you.' Logan stood where he blocked the sightline from the group at the bar to Cannonball. 'Move.' The Teddy Boy shifted round to the corner Logan had vacated.

'He's scared of me,' said Cannonball. 'I don't have to hide.'

Logan put his fists on the small round table which rocked slightly with his weight, and leaned over the boy. 'And what's he going to do if he sees you and gets scared. He's going to run, isn't he? And he'll run out of the back, but we're over here, so we'll lose him, won't we? But all I'm doing now is leaning over to ask what you want to drink, cos I'm going to the bar, and you're going to keep your face hidden whilst I do it.' Logan waited. Cannonball looked down.

Logan put one foot on the brass rail and looked down the length of the bar. The four young men looked happy. They made him feel sick. He ordered a pint of bitter which had a thick foam on it you didn't see in Devon, another dandelion and burdock for the boy and carried them back to the table.

'I thought you weren't drinking,' said the boy.

'Blending in, son. Blending in.' He sat hunched over his pint, his back to the bar.'

'He may be queer but he's got himself a girlfriend.'

Logan twisted his head towards Malcolm's group.

'Get ready to move,' said Logan quietly. The girl who'd just come in was Jenny.

THIRTY-THREE

There were times when the job made Bible want to cry.

'It's definite,' said Duggan, arranging dental charts on the table in the information room. 'You can see the fillings there.' He pointed at the teeth chart. 'It's Holmes all right.'

'You ever meet him?' said Bible.

'Just a name to me.' Duggan yawned. It was almost midnight, and Bible guessed they'd still be up when it got light. 'It's fascinating,' said Duggan, skimming through the charts on the table. 'He went to the dentist every year until ten years ago, and then didn't bother. Just let his teeth rot.'

'Yes, O.K.,' said Bible.

'It's a painful way to die. That'll teach him to go poaching.'

Bible guessed Duggan was in his early twenties. Too young to have been in the war. It made a difference. A clever young cop. Logical. Probably came from a good home, where they'd have photos of their son in smart police uniform on display. And why not? It was wrong to be angry with him for being heartless.

'He wasn't poaching. I think he was just trying to be a family man,' murmured Bible. 'Go and get that cardboard dummy from my office and bring it to the interview room.'

Holroyd appeared in the doorway and leaned against the door jamb as Duggan left. He looked waxen. 'Is this Robinson our man?' asked the Chief Superintendent, weakly.

'He's implicated,' said Bible.

Holroyd doubled up with coughing. A sequence of harsh raking growls which racked his body so he had to steady himself on his desk. 'I want to see him,' he gasped.

'With respect sir, he's only just started talking to us,' said Bible. 'If you go in…' He did not know how far Holroyd trusted him. Bible watched his boss's need for answers wrestle with his judgement. 'It must be very distressing for you sir. Perhaps you need to get some sleep.'

'Do whatever you need to,' said the Chief Superintendent. 'I'll be in my office.' Holroyd turned and walked stiffly down the corridor.

Robinson had his head in his hands when Bible returned to the interview room. He told Duggan to wait in the corridor with the cardboard dummy which was almost as tall as he was and still bore the ragged image of Larry. It was dark outside and Wallace had his back to him, bulky in his overcoat and trilby, watching the fog press against the window. Bible would rather have had Ward with him, but his sergeant had gone to organise the search for Larry.

'Home from home, for me, this,' said Wallace. 'The smog.' Wallace was ignoring their argument at the press conference and Bible's disregard of his rank.

Bible wondered what that meant. The man from London was subtle. Cruel. And Bible feared he wanted convictions more than the truth.

Bible sat down. Wallace took a pinch of snuff. 'I'm feeling quite relaxed up here now.' He stepped behind Robinson and looked down at him. 'What about you? It'll be cold in that cell tonight.'

Robbo licked his lips. 'I just want you to find my son.'

Wallace grabbed the back of Robinson's neck and forced his face down so his forehead banged onto the table. 'First there are other children to account for.'

'The photographs. The paintings.' said Bible softly.

'I don't judge other people's habits,' mumbled Robinson. 'Get him off me.'

'The inspector can't see anyone doing anything, can you, Inspector?' said Wallace, relaxing his grip and letting Robinson sit up. 'Mind you don't bang your head again.' Wallace looked at Bible and smirked.

'Photographs,' said Bible.

Robinson flicked a finger towards Wallace. 'He's as bad as Logan.'

Bible stared at Wallace. 'He won't do anything now. I just want you to talk.'

Robinson massaged the back of his neck. 'Turner was always taking photographs. Good at it. Not like Logan. His were tripe.'

Bible beckoned to Duggan. The young policeman carried in the heavily weighted two-dimensional dummy and leaned it against the wall. 'This one of his?' said Bible quietly.

Robinson quickly looked away. 'I've never seen it before.'

Wallace slapped Robinson round the back of the head. 'Now now, it's naughty to tell lies.'

Bible remained impassive. He didn't like what Wallace was doing, but they needed information.

'Logan took it,' said Robinson. 'Turner made it bigger – he's good at stuff like that - and pasted it onto an advertisement board from outside a chemist's. Got this Ted he pays to pinch it for him.'

There was silence. Robinson studied his hands. He winced when Wallace bent to whisper in his ear. 'I think we need more.'

'What's the name of this Teddy Boy?'

Robinson swallowed. 'Calls himself Cannonball. Don't know his real name. Have you got a fag?' he said weakly. Bible felt in his suit for cigarettes and matches, and slid a tin ashtray across the table. He didn't smoke, but always carried a pack of ten. Useful when you wanted someone to talk. Robinson's hand shook as he tried to steady the cigarette between his lips and Bible held a match to the tip.

'Where's Larry now?' said Bible.

Robinson exhaled a cloud of smoke. 'Dead probably. He got injured in the van when we drove away from you lot. I last saw him with Logan in the woods above the reservoir. He was unconscious. Not in good shape.'

Bible thought of the stain on the floor of the pump room. Wallace moved from behind Robinson and went to the door. 'I'll let Ward know. Get the dogs sniffing in the right place.'

Robinson tried a weak smile when Wallace had left. 'He's a bit of an animal, that one.'

Bible snatched the cigarette from Robinson's lips.

'And he likes a good hanging.'

'I haven't killed anyone. Logan kept him prisoner in his boathouse. Took pictures so Turner could show Dawn if he found her. He thought it would flush her out. Make her come back. That's what he wanted, not having to come up here to get her himself. Hurt his pride. He didn't know Turner already knew where she was.'

'Why didn't Turner tell Logan he'd found his daughter?'

'Turner wants to be a big man. Resents Logan.'

Bible thought of Turner strutting by the reservoir, wanting to be noticed. And going to the school in disguise – he must have been boasting to himself. 'Go on,' said Bible.

'He knows Logan despises him, so he likes to cheat him a bit. Get one over on him. Likes to feel he knows more than Logan. He's a fool. But he's scared now. Can I have that fag back?'

Bible passed over the cigarette. 'Tell me what went on at the reservoir.'

'The dummy's weighted, see. In the legs. So it sits upright in the water. I went up there a couple of days before you caught me in the bank and he'd stuck it in an inner tube and tied a rope to it. He knew Dawn would be coming up, so when he saw her he got me to float it out and haul it back in.'

'Where was Turner?'

'He went back to the pump house.'

'To take photos?'

Robbo stubbed the cigarette out in a little tin ashtray. 'Probably. I was on the far side. I saw him jump into the van I'd brought up and chase after her.

He laughed about her running away. Thought it was a game.' Robinson appealed to Bible. 'I said he should have told Logan.'

It was pathetic. The man thought he was in trouble for double-crossing Logan.

'Are these Turner's?' Bible took a wallet of photographs out of his pocket and spread the prints on the table. They were the photographs of Carol, at the reservoir and in the street outside her bedsit. Robinson nodded.

'Why did Logan trust him?' said Bible.

'He didn't. He just thought people were too scared to cross him.'

'And where might Turner be?'

'He knows places. He knows the moors. That's how he knew where to hide the Bedford. He always knows somewhere else.'

'So the small van we've been looking for was yours?'

'Logan's. I was supposed to get rid of it, but Turner offered me fifty quid so I let him keep it. I should have known you can't double deal with Tommy Logan.'

'Where do you think we'll find Logan now?'

Robinson shrugged. 'Wherever his daughter is.'

THIRTY-FOUR

Logan sat with Cannonball in a grassy hollow, the midnight bulk of the fell rising behind them. He was used to the moors now as a place of invisibility, a dark shroud of hill and timelessness. No one would see them from the cottage, where the light was on in the small living room. He watched his two daughters embracing and he felt lonely.

'You knew she was here?' said Logan. He nursed the shotgun in the crook of his left arm.

'Like I said, I keep an eye on people. Followed her, didn't I?'

'And Turner? He knows?'

'There's only you didn't,' smirked Cannonball. 'Why are you bothered about your daughter if she's a bitch?' Logan twisted and smacked Cannonball on the cheek with the back of a closed fist.

'Clean your mouth out,' growled Logan.

'I only asked.' The boy fingered the spot where Logan had hit him. 'You might have broken my jaw.'

But Logan wasn't listening. There was an old woman in the cottage as well as the young queer they'd followed from the pub. He could have gone in to rush them, but he wanted the young man to go. And he wanted to catch each daughter alone.

'That's my old headteacher,' said Cannonball. '

331

"The witch" we used to call her.'

'And what did she call you?' murmured Logan. He could hear a car approaching on the road at the front of the cottage. It stopped, and the engine was cut. The place was getting busy. The old woman disappeared from the room.

*

The light was on in the cottage sitting room as Bible took the steps to the door in one stride and knocked. He ignored Browning's look of displeasure and didn't wait to be asked in. Once in the living room, he was relieved at what he saw. Carol, Malcolm, Browning, and the girl he'd seen on the step. Carol's sister. She was smaller, but there was something about the set of the lips and nose that meant they must be related. At least Logan hadn't got here.

'Things seem to be getting out of hand, Inspector,' said Miss Browning, closing the living room door and nudging the draft excluder back into place with her foot. 'Increasing numbers in my house, but none yet in prison.'

Bible wondered what she was trying to prove. Why she took everything in her stride. If this was a woman who could always cope with what life threw at her, he'd like to know her secret.

'And you seem out of breath. Have you come on your bicycle?'

He was out of breath. It was anxiety, and then relief. He spoke directly to Carol. 'I need to station a policeman outside. Your father's on the loose in the city. We don't know where, and we don't think he knows where you are. But...'

'...you think he's resourceful enough to find us,' said Carol, completing his sentence.

'Did you ever meet a man called Robinson in Exeter?'

'Robbo? Whatever my father did, he did with him. But we didn't see him much. My father liked to keep his business separate.'

Bible saw Jenny's eyes were darting everywhere. Anxious. Cornered. 'You must be Jennifer,' he said.

Carol took Jennifer's hand. 'He's all right. You can trust him.' But despite what she'd said, Bible felt Carol look at him sharply. 'Why do you want to know about Robbo?'

'He's been talking to us,' said Bible. He examined their faces. Startled but not panicked.

'Is he here?' said Carol. 'In Yorkshire?'

Bible nodded.

'He came into the station. A frightened man.'

'I know his son,' said Jenny. She looked down shyly. 'He...I met him secretly once or twice.'

'You never told me,' said Carol.

'Dad would have beaten me if he'd known. And Stanley.' Jenny gripped her sister's hand more tightly. 'I didn't want you to have to keep a secret.'

Carol clasped Jenny to her. Bible turned away and studied the china in the glass-fronted cupboards attached to the bureau. 'Oh Jenny,' he heard Carol say.

'That's how I knew you were up here. Stanley told me. Is he with Robbo?'

Bible went to the back window of the cottage and looked out through the darkness towards the lowering hills and the quarry which gave the cottages their name. 'Robinson's worried about his son. He thinks he's with your father. There was an incident at the reservoir.'

'You have to find Stanley,' said Jenny. Stanley, Turner, Logan, Holroyd's granddaughter - there were a lot of people out there he had to find.

'I've brought a uniformed man. PC Johnson. I'm going to have to leave him at the door.' Bible looked towards the headteacher, who was sitting on a hard chair, watchful and tense. 'Miss Browning?'

She raised her hands helplessly. 'If you think it best. These people...you look at the faces in the classroom, but you never really know who you've got in there. What they'll turn into.'

*

Logan breathed heavily. His two daughters were no more than thirty yards away, on show through the lighted cottage window like dolls in a doll's house. He could break through the door and take them, but he wanted them to come to him. He'd brought them up. Taught them right from wrong. Kept them safe.

'I'm fucking freezing,' said the callow youth beside him.

Logan reached out and cuffed him round the side of the head without looking at him. 'Shut up and don't swear.'

The old woman reappeared in the warm room with a man in his thirties. He was young and athletic looking.

'Cop,' said Cannonball.

'You know him?'

'He's called Bible. If it's cops, I'm off.'

Logan caught the boy as he sprang up, and pulled him to the ground. 'You find me Turner. Here.' He fumbled in his pocket and pulled out a leather wallet so softened with use it seemed to be returning to animal form. He let go of the boy and pulled out a couple of pound notes. 'There'll be more if you find him for me.'

The boy took the money and grinned. Cocky. They were all cocky. Stanley had been cocky until he'd sorted him out.

'I know where he is,' said Cannonball. 'Or I can guess.'

Logan grasped the boy's lapel and pulled him towards him, but the grin remained. 'Mind me jacket, mate. I'm not going to give you information for nothing, am I.'

Logan hoisted the boy closer. 'Loyalty doesn't just depend on payment.' He released his grip.

Cannonball straightened his jacket. 'You're not on your home turf now, you know.' The inspector in the cottage was looking out at them. Logan was confident he couldn't be seen. Not whilst there was a light on in the cottage. The cop spread his arms and closed the curtains.

Logan eased the hidden sawn-off shotgun to one side where it was digging into his body. 'So where?'

'It's a fair walk.'

'How far?'

'About a mile up there. There's an old house he uses. The White House, they call it.'

Logan looked behind him to the swelling belly of the moor.

'Take me to him.'

THIRTY-FIVE

Bible had been uneasy about leaving PC Johnson at the door of the cottage. Johnson was a lazy young man who'd been in the force about three years. He grumbled about his shifts, the uniform and his beat. He'd obviously rather be with his mates at the billiard hall on Tyrrel Street. But Johnson would have to do; all the other bobbies were deployed on the moorland search.

He'd looked into Johnson's plump face as he delivered his instructions. 'You stand on this step, Johnson. You take a turn round the back every ten minutes. And you stay polite. Only go in if you're called, or if you hear anything unusual.'

'She's a very attractive young woman, sir, that Miss Carlton.'

'There are three women to look after in there, Johnson. Make sure you don't even fancy a cup of tea.' He hated the idea of other men eyeing up Carol, but one day she'd find a husband. He didn't like to think of it. He feared it was jealousy.

The headlights caught Ward stamping his feet at the gate across the track that led up to the burnt out barn. Bible ratcheted up the handbrake. They stretched. Ward had one uniformed policeman with him shining a torch across the moorland either side. They had High Gill Moor surrounded, but thinly. Four radio cars were not enough to cover an area eight miles long, and three wide. Even on foot Turner could have crossed the moor in any direction by now if he were alone. But if he still had the little girl with him, and if she were alive...Bible thought of Pauline. He knew his anger was as useless as Holroyd's desperation.

'We've been up to the barn, sir. Nothing up there. Should we move on to the Friars' Gate path?'

It was a gamble. How likely was Turner to go back to the places the police connected him with already? 'We can't do much in the dark. How many buildings are there on the moor we haven't checked?'

'More than you'd think,' said Ward. 'Abandoned barns. Old Mary's cottage. Green Lodge. And then there's The White House. I think it's been locked up ten years.'

The radio crackled in the car. Bible reached through the open window for the receiver. It was Higham at the reservoir. 'No sign of him here, sir. But that twelve bore's gone from the pump house. Do you want me to come back? Over.'

Bible wondered if Higham had looked thoroughly. Then he remembered his doubts about Johnson guarding Browning's cottage. He had to trust people. He couldn't do it all himself.

'Lie low there for a bit. In case he turns up. Over.'

'Roger that.'

Bible put the receiver back and scanned the treeless horizon. Searching streets was easier. The curves of High Gill Moor, scarred by becks and bracken-clad valleys, hunched over their secrets in frozen tranquillity. Somewhere out there…

*

Cannonball shivered against the cold, shoulders hunched, hands deep in the pockets of his drape jacket.

'You want to get a decent coat,' said Logan. His donkey jacket was stained with mud from the graveyard, and stank of smoke from the fire, but he couldn't feel the cold even though they'd been out all night. And he was carrying his gun now they were away from the town.

Cannonball had led him up a stony track criss-crossed above their heads by a latticework of tall bare trees. The track was bounded by drystone walls at the top of a grassy bank on the left, and woodland sloped downhill away from them on the right. Cannonball stopped where the grass bank was broken by a muddy chute leading to a gap in the wall.

'You'll find him up there,' said Cannonball.

'Lead the way then.'

'I'm not wrecking these shoes for you. Friars' Gate they call this lane if you get lost.'

Logan's grunted laugh was what he used when he admired someone's cheek, but was about to keep him in order. He raised the barrels of the gun, but kept it low against his waist.

'You're not going to use that,' said Cannonball. 'You don't want everybody to hear.'

'I bet they've heard shotguns round here before.'

Cannonball sneered, though started backing off. 'You'd have it at your shoulder if you were serious.'

Logan pointed the gun at the sky and pulled the trigger. The rooks roosting in the trees above exploded in a panic of flight and coarse croaking. Cannonball ran down the track and turned when he was a hundred yards away.

'You're mad, you.'

Logan laughed. He felt in control again. 'I want Turner to know I'm coming for him.' He watched the boy run down the track out of sight. Perhaps he should have shot him. But no. Cannonball wouldn't tell the police. He had too much to hide.

THIRTY-SIX

Logan wheezed as he stumbled over the tussocks in the dark to the house at the top of the slope. It was an old house, painted with thick whitewash which coated the Yorkshire stone like icing. It looked empty, but not derelict. It was a quarter of a mile from where he'd left Cannonball. The lad might raise the alarm, but Logan knew he'd be gone by the time anybody got here.

At first he thought there was no light on, but then he saw a faint glow from a room above the porch and to the left. Logan walked heavily, struggling to control his breathing. He wondered how Turner had access to a house like this, but when he stepped into the porch he saw splinters of wood where the heavy wooden door had been forced. But the exposed timber was yellow and damp; Turner could have been using this hideaway for some time. Logan picked up a handful of soil and stones from the mud beneath him. Yorkshire was a dirty place and he felt stained by its landscape. He threw the stones so they clattered against the dimly illuminated window and backed himself against the wall of the house. He'd be hidden by the porch if Turner came out. The stones bounced off the window and rattled down onto the porch roof. He waited. He'd expected a window to open or, better, Turner to come out and look. He listened for movement. There was nothing. Only the rooks down in the trees on the lane.

Logan stepped quietly into the porch and nudged the inner door. It opened easily, the hinges creaking, revealing a staircase. He held the shotgun ready, waiting for Turner to appear. Nothing. He wanted to see his enemy. He was never afraid of a physical confrontation, but faced with nothing he wondered if what he felt now was fear. He trod stealthily up the stairs and turned onto a landing. He could see light leaking out underneath a door at the end. He kept his gun trained on it as he tried the handle of a door at his side. Locked. If Turner were hiding in there, the lock would make a noise if he opened it to attack Logan from behind.

He took three steps forward and kicked the end door open with the flat of his boot. It swung back, crashing against the inside wall of the room. Logan stood in front of the doorway.

'Turner,' he shouted. Silence. He had to risk it. A moment he couldn't control. He'd frightened Turner too much and that made him dangerous. He fired one barrel. The plaster on the wall opposite sprayed up into a fountain of dust. Logan ran into the room and swung his gun in an arc. No one. He'd spent the last ten minutes stalking a phantom.

Against the wall was a carved chest. In front of it, a wooden chair draped with loose rope and on the floor a red neckerchief he remembered Turner wearing. It was knotted now, and lay in a ring, thin and wet at the front, like it had been held in someone's mouth. It was a gag. The ropes suddenly made sense.

Someone had been tied to the chair, and gagged. Someone small. The circle of neck scarf was too small for an adult jaw. He thought of the pictures Cannonball had shown him. He kicked the chair over, and wrenched open the window, breaking the rusty arm of the catch, and yelled into the darkening moorland sky: 'Turner, I'm coming to get you.'

He turned sharply at a sound behind him, but could see nothing. Then he heard it again. A whimper. His eyes were drawn to a pile of blankets thrown into a corner. He put his gun on the floor and squatted down, picked up the edge of a blanket and pulled it gently towards him.

The little girl underneath backed away, her eyes wide.

'There's no need to be afraid, love,' said Logan, holding his hand out. 'I've got girls of my own.'

*

Bible had left Robinson to stew overnight in a cell whilst he was out on the moors. Now he was back at the station with Ward. Robinson knew what had happened in the past, but nothing that would help them find Logan or Turner now.

'Powerless and waiting,' said Bible to Ward, sitting opposite him. 'Turner must have another bolthole we don't know about. And Logan...all we know is that he's obsessed with his daughters, so he might turn up at the cottage.'

'Every beat constable is on the lookout. Johnson's on the door at the cottage.'

'Do you trust him?' said Bible sharply.

'He knows his job.' It was a lukewarm

endorsement compared to Ward's usual defence of the rank and file coppers.

'His job and nothing more,' said Bible.

There was a tap on the door and Swann from the desk put his head round. 'I think you'd better come, sir. That Ted's at the desk demanding we look after him. Says he's been threatened by a madman with a gun. Sounds like Logan.'

*

It was a struggle getting the three cars up Friars' Gate. Bible and Ward swayed from side to side as the Wolseley pitched in and out of the ruts. Cannonball sat in the back, handcuffed. 'Here,' he said, 'where the wall's broken down.' Bible stopped the car. 'That's where I told Logan to go. Takes you up to The White House. Turner's taken me there before.'

The White House. It had once been a place where the well-to-do went to take the waters. Reputedly it had a well inside with revitalising power.

'You can tell us why afterwards,' said Ward.

'Likes little girls, doesn't he, Turner?' sniggered Cannonball. 'That's where he does the photos.'

Bible took the keys out of the ignition and threw them to Ward. 'Take the car up another hundred yards. There's a gateway you can turn round in.' He saw Ward looking puzzled. 'I was up here with the family in the summer,' explained Bible, stepping out into the stony lane. Behind him, six constables clambered out of a police van.

'Through the wall,' said Bible. His wellingtons were in the boot of the car. No time for them now. Bible stepped onto the grassy bank, the pistol he'd signed out from the armoury heavy in his pocket. He slipped on the gritty earth, leaving a line of mud down the front of his calf, and scrambled up the embankment.

When they reached the house, the grey winter light was just breaking. The White House looked grey, but a faint light glowed in an upstairs window. A candle? Turner and Logan huddling together like cavemen? But they hated each other, according to Robinson. The uniformed men had fanned out behind him like a flock of ravens.

'Logan! Turner!' he shouted. 'You're surrounded.' There was nothing to be heard but the plaintive bray of sheep and the rooks down on the lane.

The window above the porch, where the light was, moved gently in the breeze. Bible could see a broken window stay hanging down.

'Throw your weapon down.'

Only the silence of the wind. Bible took out the Webley and held it out in front supporting his wrist with his right hand as he approached the porch. The door was open. He stepped into a whitewashed corridor leading to a staircase. He kicked at a closed door to the left. It swung open into an empty room. He reached the foot of the stairs and shouted up. 'Logan?' He paused. 'Turner? You're surrounded by police.' He took the wooden stairs as quietly as he could. At the top he twisted to look down the landing. The door at the end was open and led to the room with the light above the porch. He guessed by now there was no one there, but guesses could be wrong. He walked slowly down the landing, trying a door on his left. Locked. He quickly paced into the room ahead and swung the pistol in a two hundred and seventy degree arc around the bare walls. No one. He kept his gun raised and returned to the locked room, braced himself against the wall and kicked hard against the handle. The wood splintered. In the room was a tripod and camera, and nailed to the wall, a crude grey cloth drape. He thought of the chair, ropes and neck scarf he'd seen in the other room. It was all beginning to make sense.

He stepped out into what was now daylight. Ward was coming up the slope, trying to run but defeated by the tussocks, his pale coat open and flapping, and he was waving an arm.

'Go and radio the station, sir. Your wife's had a telephone call. Someone threatening your daughter. '

Home had totally gone from his mind as he'd focused on the house. But Ward looked serious. And when Ward looked serious, it was serious.

'You'd better get home sir,' said Ward, panting as he reached the house.

Bible ran and stumbled down the slope. He felt the same sick fear he'd felt in Burma, running away from the Japs after they'd swarmed out of the jungle and overrun him and his young Welsh private in the arms dump. He'd zigzagged through the trees dragging Winterburn, but the boy had fallen, and a lone Jap had come upon them. Bible had turned and jabbed both fingers into the Jap's eyes until the eyeballs popped back, gagging the soldier's mouth with his other hand to stifle his scream. Winterburn had been sick, but Bible had dragged him into a leech-filled pool, hiding their heads under overlying grasses. The same anger was in him as he reached the car, opened the back door and pulled Cannonball out of the back seat, knocking the youth's head on the door frame and leaving him sprawling in the lane.

As he engaged gear, the image of Winterburn filled his mind, not killed by the Jap but by bullying and misery. The poor sod had pulled the pin on the grenade himself. You needed anger to survive.

THIRTY-SEVEN

The little girl clung to Logan's neck as he worked his
way down through the woods. If he kept going
downhill he was sure he'd come to a road. His back
was killing him. Carrying the shotgun and the girl
reminded him that he wasn't used to physical work
anymore.

'I'll have to put you down, my bonny,' he said,
disengaging her arms and setting her down on a dry
tree root.

'When can I go home?'

'Soon, darling, soon. When we get to a road.' She
looked like an elf, sitting among the fallen leaves. 'I'm
just resting for a moment.' The girl trusted him. She'd
told him her name. Judy. And he could protect her. It
had once been like that with Dawn and Jenny. Small
and trusting, both of them. It was when they grew into
women…

'Has that man gone now?'

'Yes, that nasty man's gone.'

'How do you know?'

Logan smiled and crouched in front of her.
'Because he isn't here.'

'Are you going to shoot him?'

'Don't you be thinking about shooting, my lovely.
You be thinking about home.' He hid the gun in his

jacket, thinking he should have done it sooner.

'I want my mummy.'

'Come on. Can you walk for a bit?'

The little girl nodded and took Logan's outstretched hand, hers soft and tender in his. Shooting wouldn't be good enough for Turner.

*

Carol sat with Jenny in the cottage sitting room, its cosiness belying what she and her sister felt. Miss Browning had gone to the door. Her irritation at having a policeman on her front step was making her find more and more reasons to move him. The landlady's trenchant orders were barely muffled by the porch door.

'Not here,' she heard the headmistress say. 'I will not have cigarette ends left on my doorstep.' Miss Browning returned to the room in full headmistress armour, tie flowing over her bosom and held in place by a tie clip. 'I have to talk to him as if he's still at school.' Poor Johnson, thought Carol, never allowed to forget he once wore short trousers. The headmistress bent to pick up her briefcase. 'I have to go to school now. We can't have any more uneducated policemen. You two will be safe, I'm sure.'

'My father's a dangerous man,' said Carol. 'I'm glad there's a policeman outside.'

'If Mr Logan comes here, he'll have me to deal with.' Miss Browning closed the inner door as she left, her voice booming back into the room as she passed PC Johnson. 'Go on, off you go. Set fire to those nasty cigarettes where people can't see you.'

'How can you stand her?' said Jenny as the headmistress's voice faded.

'She's been nice to me,' said Carol. 'She's softer than she sounds. I think she's just showing us who she'd like to be.'

'I need fresh air,' said Jenny. 'I bought some cigarettes.' She took a slim packet of ten out of her rucksack. 'Do you want one? We can go in the back garden.'

'No.' Carol was sharp.

Jenny rattled a box, and laughed. 'I've got matches.'

'Put them away.'

'Are we going to be afraid all our lives?'

Carol didn't want to tell her how terrified she felt. How she hoped Miss Browning really was as tough as her words. 'I've lived up here by being careful.'

'Always the big sister.'

Carol looked at her sister. 'And you always the wild one.'

'No,' said Jenny, putting the cigarettes and matches back in her bag. 'We never had a chance to be wild.' She smiled a mischievous smile Carol remembered her using as a child until it was knocked out of her.

'Stay there,' said Carol. 'I'm going to check our policeman's still in place.'

*

The path through the woods led them to a village on the outskirts of the city. Milky cloud. A chilly day. Logan held the little girl's hand as they left the woods behind and walked past low one-storey cottages. Then the houses became larger. Small terraces with an upper floor. One had had its front window enlarged to make it a small shop. A general shop. Cigarettes and tea. Bread and milk. It was early morning and the shop had just opened. He was hungry. The little girl must be hungry. But he couldn't risk it. His accent would give him away.

'I'm hungry,' she said, tugging at his arm. Logan pulled back.

'Steady on, my lovely.'

'I want sweets.'

Judy began to cry. Logan could see she wanted her home. He bent to her height. 'I'll give you some pennies and you can go in and get some.'

She shook her head. 'You.'

Logan stood up, his knees stiff. He felt in his pocket and jingled change. Dammit, he felt sorry for the little thing. He'd known how to be firm with his own kids, but with this little waif, left alone with Turner... He ushered Judy before him as he went in. The bell inside the door tinkled. The shop was cramped, the working space on the counter crowded with a glass case containing bread. The shelves either side of him were piled with dried groceries: Heinz Beans, Saxa Salt, Typhoo Tea. But his eyes were drawn to gleaming jars of sweets paraded on the shelves behind the counter. Pineapple chunks, bonbons, mint imperials. What did little girls like? A tiny old woman in a knitted shawl and wearing a headscarf shuffled in from the back room. She was only about five feet tall and the counter came up to her chest. She stared up at him.

'Well,' she said after a pause, 'do you want summat or are you just sightseeing?'

Logan pointed to a jar on a high shelf and grunted

in a way he hoped would disguise his accent. 'Humbugs.'

The woman tutted. 'Allus the same, people wanting stuff from high up.' She shuffled to a corner where there was a stepladder.

Judy gripped Logan's hand and whispered. 'She could put things people want at the bottom.'

The woman turned her head sharply. 'Oh, you're a cheeky monkey.' She looked at Logan. 'You should give her a good slap.'

'She's done nothing wrong,' said Logan. He reached over the little old lady's head, clamped his hand round the jar and lifted it down to the counter.

'Here, you can't do that.'

Logan slammed down a few coins and unscrewed the lid of the jar. He shook out a small pile of sweets, their cellophane wrappings glistening like they'd just come out of the sea. He pointed to the coins. 'Enough?' The old woman nodded. Logan gathered up the sweets, and unbuttoned the purse with bobbles the girl wore round her. 'For you, poppet,' he said. He took her hand and led her towards the door. The old woman snarled after him peevishly as they left.

'I know you're not from round here.'

He turned and froze her with his stare. 'I've been accused of worse, my lover.' He opened the shop door, holding the girl back. Logan looked carefully up and down the street. Ahead, in the distance, he saw what he wanted and stepped onto the pavement.

'You see down the road, there. That's a policeman. I want you to go to him and tell him who you are.'

'You come too,' said the little girl.

'No, not me, my bonny. No need to tell him about

me.' He could tell the girl was unsure. 'You can trust a policeman more than me. Go on.'

He watched the girl walk uncertainly down the pavement, looking back for reassurance. But when she fixed her eyes forward again to the policeman on his beat, he slipped down the alley next to the shop and out of her life.

*

Carol opened the cottage door on to the pale morning, the branches of the elm opposite sketched in thick black lines against the paper-thin cloud. A crow croaked for its mate from the crown of the tree, and flapped away easily over the field towards the canal. But Johnson was missing. Miss Browning had already gone to work. Carol felt a gurgle of anxiety in her bowels, and wanted to retreat back into the cottage. Then she spotted Johnson down the road about four doors away. He held his hands behind his back, but two trails of smoke rising from his nostrils betrayed him. Carol waved her hand, beckoning him.

'It's all right. You can come back here to smoke.'

Johnson looked around furtively before slinking down the road towards her. 'Not supposed to smoke on duty anyway,' he said, nipping the end of the partially smoked cigarette between his fingers. 'Your landlady was my teacher at school. She didn't like me then and she doesn't like me now.'

'She isn't your teacher any more,' said Carol. 'And I'm saying we need you. Are you cold out here?'

'I'll survive. We looking for this Turner bloke to show up here, then?' said the young policeman.

Carol was puzzled. 'Turner? No. A man called Thomas Logan.'

Johnson grinned. 'Ready for anyone, me.'

A man. It didn't explain much really. She looked down. 'He's my father. Was my father.'

'We see a lot of trouble in families. Mine's rubbish too.'

'I think you ought to come back inside.'

Johnson grinned. 'I'll look after you, love, don't you worry. Any chance of a cup of tea from you ladies?'

Carol paused, unsure. Then nodded. 'But you can't smoke in the cottage.'

Johnson followed Carol into the cottage, but the sitting room was empty. 'Jenny?'

'Just us two, is it, then?' said Johnson. 'Where's your sister?'

Carol strode through the room to the back door, and went out into the yard. 'Jenny?' No answer. She ran to the gate at the end of the garden and stepped onto the cart track which ran along the back of the cottages. She was aware of the cold, the moors, the sheep watching her in the glow cast by light from the cottage. She shouted as loudly as she could. 'Jenny! Come back!' Johnson was behind her now.

'She should be here. I told her to stay.'

'Appen she's got a boyfriend.'

'You don't know what you're dealing with,' she said angrily, and made for the back door.

'Hey up, love. Steady on.' He reached out his arms to catch her, but she thrust them aside.

'Has no one told you what's going on here? Get Inspector Bible.'

'Bible. He's as much use as a paper truncheon.'

'I'll telephone him.' Carol went past him into the cottage.

'Here, I should be doing that.'

As she reached out her hand for the receiver, the phone rang. She snatched it up, and heard the rattle of coins as someone pushed button A in a call box. It was a rough voice, a voice she had not heard before.

'Tell Logan I've got your sister. And if he comes after me, he'll not see her again.'

'Who is that?'

Johnson snatched the telephone from her. 'This is the police,' he said firmly. 'Tell me your name.'

Carol heard a distant laugh crackle through the receiver before the line went dead on her police protection.

THIRTY-EIGHT

Bible wrenched the steering wheel of the Wolseley, almost smashing the headlight onto the gatepost of his narrow drive as he turned in. The front door was locked, top and bottom. He scrabbled with the keys. The hall was empty. He called for Shirley and Pauline. There was a faint voice upstairs.

'We're here, Daddy.'

The bathroom. Bible grasped the banister and took the stairs two at a time. He pushed the handle on the bathroom door. Locked.

'Shirley, it's me.'

There was movement inside the bathroom, and the bolt clicked back. The door opened as Shirley was turning away, Pauline held on her hip. His wife sank to the cold lino between the bath and the washbasin and began sobbing.

'Shirley?' said Bible as he bent to put an arm round his wife. His suit trousers were tight on his knees as he crouched. She gripped his arm fiercely.

'What happened?' said Bible.

She took a deep breath and shook her head. 'I can't tell you here.'

She meant in front of Pauline. But Turner, or Logan? Who had threatened his daughter? As the fury rose within him, he didn't know how to manage his anger and be caring at the same time. They needed him, but he wanted to thump the bath and get out after – well, Turner, he guessed.

'Was it a Yorkshire voice?'

Shirley nodded. It made sense. A kind of sense. He knew Turner wanted power and was full of resentment, however futile his plan. Bible had felt it, and Robinson had provided confirmation.

'Was he the man seen with a van in Ilkley?'

'Yes.' Bible put his hand comfortingly against his wife's cheek. 'I'll get someone round here. I'm going after him.'

'Will you take me with you, Daddy?' said Pauline.

'I'm taking you both with me,' said Bible.

*

The call box at the end of the row of cottages was empty, but the receiver dangled on its cord and the directory was open. Carol knew this was where the call must have come from. There had been no time for whoever had taken Jenny to get any further before ringing. But where would he go from here? Not back to the road, surely, dragging a struggling nineteen-year-old; it would attract too much attention. But how could he drag her anywhere? Unless he'd done something to her. Threatened her to make her move. She looked at the hillside swelling to High Gill Moor and the path to the quarry she'd seen when she first came with Malcolm. It rose steeply, so she could not see far. But the bracken didn't hide it as much as she remembered. She ought to tell Johnson, but there was no sign of him following her down the lane. He'd said he needed to telephone the station for reinforcements, but she had to go after Jenny. Carol waded up the hillside, the rough stalks tearing at her nylons and scratching her legs.

*

Bible pulled up behind the police station, opposite the statues of kings and queens which stood like sentries carved into the masonry of the town hall. Shirley and Pauline were in the back of the car as he drove. Shirley hadn't spoken during the drive. He'd made a few remarks, commenting on things they passed, but felt he was chatting foolishly, the main weight on their minds remaining unspoken between them.

Bible twisted round in the driving seat. 'It'll be over tonight.' It was a foolish promise.

'Don't promise if it's not true, Jim,' said Shirley. It was a fair comment, but it was all he could offer, and he needed to offer her something.

Shirley waited on the kerb with Pauline as he locked the car. As he guided them to the main doors of the police station in the town hall a line of police cars swept away from the front of the building. Ward was driving one, Holroyd in the back, squashed by the bulk of Wallace. Their faces were determined.

*

Logan peered through the bracken at the back of the cottage. It was the first time he'd seen it in daylight. Calm. Peaceful. But no smoke from the chimney, though there was from other cottages in the row. There was no sign of anyone and the curtains were still drawn, though it was mid-morning now. He eased himself from his hiding place and skidded down the steep slope to the track along the cottage backs. A policeman minus his helmet rushed out of the gate looking bewildered and glancing in all directions.

'How do,' said Logan, keeping his shotgun hidden behind him.

'Who are you?' said the policeman.

Logan's fist caught him just below the sternum.

*

'They've found her,' said Swann, squinting over his half moon reading glasses and fiddling with the arrests ledger. 'She's safe, and so,' he slammed the heavy blue ledger shut, 'we're safe from Holroyd for a bit.'

'Who's safe?' said Shirley, gripping Pauline's hand tightly.

'The boss's granddaughter. Found wandering round Upper Carr village by the bobby on the beat there. Some bloke dropped her off.'

'Turner?' said Bible.

'We'll know when she comes in with her mother.' Swann pulled a square of paper from the pile of notes on the spike beside him. 'And this came in about an hour ago. Call from that woman with the Devon accent. Pretty garbled. Something about her sister being kidnapped.'

'Why didn't you tell me about this?'

'Johnson took the phone off her. Said he'd got it in hand.'

Bible spun towards Shirley. 'I've got to go,' he said. He crouched to Pauline. 'You need to stay here for a while, love. Just for today.'

'I want to go to school,' said his daughter grumpily.

'Mummy will look after you.' He stood up and pecked Shirley on the cheek. 'It'll be all right,' he said, and left the police station hoping it was true.

*

Logan had made the uniformed copper handcuff himself to the legs of a heavy oak table. Now he was binding his ankles together with a washing line cut down from the back garden.

'Please,' begged the young copper, eager to comply and probably about to lie. 'He can't be far ahead. We can go after them.'

'Hold your legs still.' Logan pulled the knot tight. 'Tell me.'

'Turner must have used the call box at the end cottage. Carol went to look.'

Logan pulled the knot tighter. 'She's called Dawn.'

The copper winced. 'I'd better phone the station or they'll come looking.'

Logan reached across from where he was kneeling and tore the phone from the wall. The policeman whimpered. 'Please. We need to go after Carol.'

'Dawn,' said Logan, and trained his shotgun at the policeman's head.

*

The cottage door was ajar, and the top step where Johnson should have been on guard was empty. Bible stepped into the porch and nudged open the inner door. Then he saw the police boots, and ankles tied with thin rope. He was quickly in the room, kneeling by Johnson, relieved to hear a groan that told him the young PC was alive. Johnson's eyes flicked open sharply when Bible felt for his pulse. Normal. And no signs of visible injury.

'Get me an ambulance,' groaned Johnson. '999.'

'I know the number,' said Bible. He was angry with Johnson for being overpowered. There were no signs of injury or struggle. The keys to the handcuffs were on the table. They were soon unlocked and the constable rolled onto his side, breathing heavily. Bible suspected it was all a show. 'Who was it?'

Johnson leaned to one side and pretended he was going to be sick. Bible wrenched him round and looked him in the face. 'Who?'

'Carol's dad. Logan.'

'So he's got Jenny as well.'

Johnson gasped. 'No. Turner.'

'Where have they gone?'

'Out the back somewhere. I think I'm going to be sick.'

Bible reached for the young bobby's helmet. 'Get up, put your uniform on, and phone your own ambulance.'

'He could have killed me.'

'I'm surprised he didn't.' Bible left Johnson protesting and went out of the back door.

He envied the uniformed branch their boots as he slipped in shoes designed for city pavements. At the top of the slope opposite the cottage he looked at the moorland plateau in front of him. The yellow grass was catching the sun. Sheep were scattered like boulders. A nearby ewe watched him scornfully, recognising he wasn't dressed for the part. He scanned the horizon. Carol, Jenny and Turner would be long gone by now, if they were together. But what had happened? Which way should he go? The reservoir was two miles away across the moors. Beyond that the blackened barn where Logan had started the fire. The White House was nearer, but surely Logan wouldn't go back there? He looked down the slope. Johnson was standing in the lane. Turner? Logan? He needed to know.

'Johnson, remember you're a copper and tell me what happened.'

'Big bloke came up the lane. Hit me. I'd been in to phone HQ.'

'Not what happened to you. The girls.'

'Carol went after her sister. Turner phoned to say he'd got her.'

Bible didn't understand. Carol wouldn't have let Jenny out by herself.

'So where were you when Turner took Jenny?'

'I'd gone down the road for a smoke. Carol came looking for me.'

'Damn you, Johnson.' Bible ran along the back of the cottages looking for the phone box. Where would Turner take somebody? Not The White House. He'd guess the police would be round there. Back to the reservoir? Possible. The barn? Perhaps. That was his area, but for now they'd finished searching there. Then he saw the path up to the moors, the broken stalks, and the signs of recently disturbed earth.

*

The heather was like a mattress. Logan lay on his stomach and spied over the edge of the hollow. The figure in the distance was a woman. She ran and stumbled over the rough terrain. So he'd guessed right. He was a city man, but he'd read the landscape well and followed the track someone had forced through the bracken. He could have been an Indian scout in another life, like in the westerns. He felt his old strength come back. He knew he'd win.

THIRTY-NINE

Carol gasped when she reached the quarry. It had been hewn into a long escarpment of millstone grit and its jagged craggy outline stood against the sky like battlements. The sun had been in her eyes as she struggled up the hillside to where the bracken gave way to heather, but as she entered the amphitheatre of the abandoned workings, the sun was blocked and she felt a chill. She prayed under her breath, a childish chant she and Jenny had shared in their beds at night: 'Please, Lord, keep me well, keep me from the mouth of hell.' She'd seen Turner dragging Jenny in the distance when she'd crested the slope behind the cottages, but now they had disappeared. The crevices and cracks around her had swallowed them.

'Jenny!' Her voice echoed off the bare stone walls, mocking her with her own ghost.

Then a male voice chased her own around the rocks. 'Come and join us, love. We've been waiting for you a long time.'

Carol ducked under an overhanging ledge, breathing heavily and flattening herself against the rock. She didn't know the voice. It could have been the voice on the telephone. So who had got Jenny? Someone her father had sent?

Then another male voice, an angry roar she knew

too well. 'Turner!' Her father. Above her, on the rim of the quarry, a silhouette against the sky with his gun pointing up towards the clouds. Carol trembled. She edged out of sight, but he must have heard her shout. She felt sick. She heard rocks falling, clacking like bowls against one another, and when she peeked round the sharply cut edge of rock she saw her father slithering down a gully, leaning back to keep his balance, rocks and soil rolling down in front of him. He looked rough. His trousers were torn, and there was blood on his hand. He reached the base of the quarry and limped into the middle of the amphitheatre.

'Turner. Show yourself.'

Boots scrunched on the ledge above her head. Dislodged soil trickled in front of her face. Then the voice she hadn't heard before. 'You won't get me Logan, unless you want to kill your daughter first.'

Carol ran into the clearing. Logan had his back to her, twisting and looking up at the grassy ledges, holding a short gun. She screamed at her father. 'He's got Jenny!'

*

Bible squelched through the bogs careless of the water seeping into his shoes. It was Turner he was after now, the man who'd dared threaten his daughter. He wanted to forget the violence of the war, and make a home, a family. But it was a false ideal. He was at war again, with two men who threatened the people he loved.

He knelt by a moorland stream, and scooped up a handful of water from where a miniature waterfall filled a clear pool. A little world of clarity amidst the mess. Pauline would have loved playing here if she were safe. He stood up and breathed deeply. The quarry was still a quarter of a mile away, its entrance lit by the sun rising towards its zenith. On the open moor, Bible would be visible to anyone watching.

*

Logan swung round to face her. He was thirty feet away, but there was a look in his face she'd not seen before. Something softer. He reached his hand out and stepped towards her. Carol shrank back. How dare he look softly on her now?

There was a rumble overhead. Rocks rained down and a heavy object like a sack blocked out the sky as it descended. Logan threw himself at her and they fell in the dirt together as a dead sheep landed where Logan had been standing. Its ribs were red and exposed, its eyes pecked out by crows. Logan's arm was round her, holding her down. She thrust it away in horror and scrabbled free.

'That's what your daughter will look like,' mocked the voice above them.

Logan was on his feet and clawing his way up a steep grassy slope to the ledge above them from where the sheep had dropped. His gun slipped from his grasp and slithered towards Carol. Turner appeared fifteen feet above them, his shotgun pointing towards Logan, who was at full stretch, one hand gripping a clod of earth and grass, the other folded over a sharp edge of stone. Carol recognised the face. She'd seen him at the reservoir she no longer dared visit. The reservoir keeper. He glanced down at her, smirking.

'You look prettier than you did in the photos, love.'

Logan roared and lunged at the squat reservoir man, digging his boots into clay and grass as he floundered onto the ledge. Turner swivelled wildly, throwing himself off balance. He stumbled, and fell from the ledge with a yell, landing on his shoulder. He scrambled to his feet, glared at Carol, and limped away, pointing his gun at her as he went. Logan slithered back down the slope. She grabbed her father's gun from where it had come to rest, pointed it towards him, and backed away, but he hardly seemed to notice.

'I'm coming back for you,' he shouted, as he crashed across the sandy floor of the quarry after Turner.

Carol was frightened of the weapon she was holding, but she hung on to it as she scrambled up the bank to the ledge. Her feet slipped so she had to dig her knees into the dirt for additional purchase. The gun was an encumbrance. She threw it onto the rock shelf and trusted to handfuls of grass to haul herself up. A trail of drag marks and bootprints in the yellow clay of the ledge led to a wide crevice which made a narrow cave. Jenny was at the back, her eyes wide, a gag around her mouth and her hands tied behind. Carol knelt beside her, pulled the gag from her mouth and hugged her. Jenny sobbed.

'Here. I'll undo your wrists. Twist round so they're in the light.' There was only a glimmer of light in the back of the cave, but just enough to see the knots.

'What are we going to do?' said Jenny. 'He'll find us wherever we go.'

Carol eased one of the loops on the knot, using her concentration as an excuse not to speak. She didn't know what they could do.

'Where is he now?' said Jenny.

'He went after Turner.' She didn't add that he'd said he'd be back for them.

'Dawn!' A shout from outside. The girls froze. Carol felt that lurch in her stomach again, that sudden lightness of fear. She threw her arms round Jenny and hugged her close.

'I'll not let him get to us.' Carol hurriedly undid the rope around her sister's wrists. 'I'm going out to him.'

'I'm coming with you,' said Jenny.

Logan stood below them. 'I've seen him off.' He was out of breath. 'I'll get him later. But you're safe now.'

'We've never been safe with you,' said Carol.

'I'll come up and get you,' said Logan with a smile.

*

As he felt along the slabs of millstone grit towards the entrance to the amphitheatre, Bible felt the temperature drop. A ewe ragged with dung on its backside lolloped down the slope from the quarry. He listened. It was a few minutes since he'd heard the pop of a distant shotgun. He edged along with his back rubbing against the rock to within a yard of the sharp edge of stone which marked where the quarry opened out. Then he heard someone coming towards him, heavy-footed but irregular. Bible prepared to pounce, but the reservoir keeper saw him too soon and raised his shotgun.

'Stay where you are, Inspector Bible.' He stood,

swaying slightly, holding the double-barrelled weapon with one arm - but Bible was near enough to present an easy target. And the Webley was tucked too securely in its holster under his jacket for him to reach it. Empty moorland stretched across towards Widdop and Calderdale. Bible had no support, but Turner might not realise that if he hadn't looked down the hill.

'We've got you for everything, Turner. The photos. The paintings. Kidnap.' Bible took a step towards him.

'Stay there.'

'The little boy outside the school.'

Turner looked shocked. 'He was nowt to do with me.'

'So why were you in the school hall the day after?'

'I'm a concerned member of the public,' sneered Turner.

'You can't get away. Look down the hill.' It was enough to distract the reservoir man. Bible jumped at him and swept the gun from his grasp, gathering Turner's arm in a lock against the joint. It broke with a crack as he put his knee on Turner's chest and smashed his fist into Turner's face. 'That's for my daughter.'

'Lovely, i'n't she?' said Turner with a smile through the blood on his teeth. Bible picked up the shotgun and rammed the double barrel into Turner's cheek, wanting to destroy that leering face forever, but as his finger touched the trigger he found himself saying, 'Jack Turner, I'm arresting you for the murder of Donald Holmes, anything you say will be...' The blast above their heads drowned out the rest.

*

Carol was standing on a rock ledge when Bible reached them, Jenny was beside her. Carol's eyes stared down at the wounded man on the ground below. There was a large red patch on his chest, and he was propped against a rock. Bible knelt beside him. Logan coughed.

'Did you get Turner?'

'We got him,' said Bible.

He spluttered and blood dribbled down his chin. 'The little girl,' he gasped. 'Judy. Is she all right?'

Bible nodded. He thought there was a half smile on Logan's lips.

'Good. A man has a right to his daughters.'

Logan's eyes glazed over and his laboured breathing went still. Bible looked up at Carol and Jenny, standing on the ledge.

Jenny raised her head. She spoke eagerly. 'He shot himself. Dawn had just taken the gun out of his hands and we ran up here to be safe.'

Bible shook his head, and Jenny's voice tailed off. It was a story any prosecution counsel could destroy in a minute. No one shot themselves in the chest. When you didn't want to miss, you put the muzzle in your mouth. He thought of Ruth Ellis. Over a year now since the last woman had hanged, and he hoped that was the end of it. Self defence. Perhaps Logan had gone for her. Turner was down below, stunned but alive, and in a place where he'd seen nothing to contradict that. And Logan had been attacking his girls for years.

'I could have protected you,' he said.

'You didn't protect us,' said Carol. 'He came. I stopped him getting us.'

Her defiance had saved her, unlike young Winterburn in Burma, a victim of bullying who hadn't survived. Logan groaned and his body fell to one side.

'It's just the air escaping,' said Bible. He'd been this dispassionate in Burma, when he'd lifted Winterburn's body, drained of anger when it was too late for sympathy to be of any use. And too late to do anybody any good.

'Come on, let's get you both down to safety.' He was the first officer on the scene. He needed to secure the site, and find telltale signs of Logan trying to attack his daughters. Carol was a survivor; she'd know when to stay silent. The truth would lie somewhere in the gaps of unknowing.

FORTY

Holroyd was standing in front of his window below the town hall clock when Bible answered the summons to the Chief Superintendent's office. The April sunlight caught the tawny liquid in Holroyd's whisky glass.

'Gwen, pour the gentleman a wee dram,' said Holroyd. The young policewoman obliged, waitressing now part of her duties, thought Bible. She wasn't offered one herself. Chivas Regal. Man's stuff. And Holroyd's idea of high-class hospitality.

'Come on Bible, let yourself go for once. This is all down to you.'

Ward stood holding a glass awkwardly. Johnson looked down when Bible entered, but Higham looked smug, basking in the sense of privilege. PC Best had declined, citing the demands of his beat even though Holroyd also deemed him part of his 'first eleven', the team that had uncovered Turner's activities.

'Gangster from Devon got his comeuppance, that lass you fussed about got off, Turner's going to swing, so everyone's happy.'

Happy. Bible pondered the word. There was Holroyd, smoking himself to death, but claiming to be happy. The prospect of a hanging seemed to have stopped him coughing.

'I won't have a drink, thank you,' said Bible.

'Give the lad an orange juice, Gwen.' The WPC held a glass towards him, and Bible let himself take it. Holroyd looked at the grandfather clock standing against the wall. 7.59. The deep rhythm of the pendulum was the only thing to break the silence until the clock in the town hall bell tower boomed its Westminster chimes and Bible felt sick. Holroyd lowered his head as the deep bell bonged eight times. Then he raised his glass.

'That's him swinging,' he said with a smile. 'To justice.' Higham and Johnson voiced an embarrassed cheer. Ward mumbled something. Bible thought of Turner's body hanging in Armley Gaol, put down his untouched orange juice, and left the room.

Outside he drew his coat together as he walked down the stone steps and put the station behind him. The town centre was quieter than normal. The Easter holiday meant no children with blazers and leather satchels were dragging their way to school. It was Pauline's birthday and Bible had an hour to kill before meeting his family. He found himself drawn to the railway station. There were a couple of black taxis outside, but he went in through the echoing ticket hall to the platforms. He loved the acrid smell of coal and oil. He sat opposite an engine that had just pulled a chain of carriages from Scotland; steam hissed from between giant wheels. Perhaps there were fresh places he, Shirley and Pauline could go to. Even Ricky might come. Along the wall behind him, brightly coloured posters boasted of coast and countryside. *The Devon Riviera. Skipton: Gateway to the Dales*. A cartoon fat sailor skipped along a sunny beach. *Skegness is so bracing*. Perhaps it would be. As Bible rose from the bench, an engine driver in oily overalls climbed down from the footplate. They nodded at each other. Working men. Travel was a dirty business too.

At nine o'clock his wife and daughter were waiting on the pavement in front of Baines the sports shop. Shirley watched him as he approached, searching for his mood.

'I'm all right,' said Bible. He picked up Pauline, a hand under each arm, and suspended her in the air. She giggled as he bounced her up and down. A green metal badge pinned to her coat announced 'I am seven'. The sun caught the daffodils in front of the town hall. It had been a spring day like this when Pauline was born, though Bible had not been allowed to see, told off by the ward sister when he skulked around the doorway. 'Policeman or no policeman, you're not allowed in here. Be off with you.' One of the Miss Brownings of this world, plaguing him with their bossiness. Or like Holroyd and Wallace with their simple certainties.

'I'm hungry,' said the little girl.

'We're going to have breakfast and buy you some roller skates.'

Bible had booked the day off for his daughter's birthday. He set her down on her feet and she looked into the sports shop window.

'Can I have those?' she said, pointing at a pair of gleaming silver skates standing on their cardboard box.

'We'll see,' said Shirley. 'It depends what the choice is. You don't just buy the first ones you look at.'

Pauline pressed her face against the display window, leaving a cloudy imprint of her lips on the glass.

'I think she's lost interest,' said Bible. 'I thought Ricky was coming?' He watched his daughter rub out her lips and breathe on the glass again.

'Still in bed,' said his wife.

Bible's barely buoyant spirit sank. 'He said he'd come. I was hoping he meant it.'

Shirley put her hand on his. 'He's been a lot better. It was a shock his friend going to Borstal.'

'Dad!' A thin figure hurried towards them in a suit that was too small for him. 'I got up late,' said Ricky. 'Forgot to wind my clock up.'

'Nice of you to wear a suit for your sister,' said Bible, trying not to smirk at the luminous socks that showed between the bottoms of the trousers and Ricky's shoes. It was a suit they'd bought him for a wedding when he was fifteen.

'Got an interview, haven't I?' said his son. He was still sporting his Teddy Boy quiff despite the interview.

'Why didn't you tell me?' said Bible. He looked to Shirley and Ricky and back to Shirley, but neither spoke. Then Ricky looked at his feet. 'In case I don't get it,' he mumbled.

'Come on,' said Bible. 'Let's get breakfast. Pauline, come on. Don't do that.' She was breathing on the glass of the shop window and drawing with her finger in the condensation.

'Why not?' said Pauline. And as Bible took her hand in his, he realised he didn't know why not.

*

Carol was shocked when she saw Bible's face peering in the café window from the street. And she knew he'd seen her too.

'What's wrong?' Malcolm had his back to the window, but turned to look. A little girl had her face pressed against the window too, but Bible quickly ushered her away. Malcolm turned back to her. 'He's gone.'

Carol pushed her empty plate aside and smiled at Malcolm. 'You'd have ducked your head down a few months ago.'

'No point hiding,' he said, picking up the teapot. Malcolm had a new confidence about him since he'd got the bookstall job in Swan Arcade. He had friends now, and dressed in neat suits. And he went to mysterious meetings, though he never said what they were. 'And he helped you.'

'Yes,' said Carol, studying the refilled cup Malcolm slid towards her. She had never explained to him what happened in the quarry. The Judge had accepted self-defence after hearing Bible's account of seeing her father lunge towards her. 'And I'm grateful.' She looked up. 'But he wouldn't want me to say so.' Just as he wouldn't want her to thank him for lying. 'I saw it just as I got to you,' he had insisted.

'I'm glad you didn't go back to Exeter,' said Malcolm.

She thought of her sisters. Wendy never acknowledged anything she sent. Jenny had mentioned Stanley in a letter; she seemed to have a soft spot for him now his father was in Dartmoor. And her mother had written asking Carol what she expected them to live on now she'd killed her father.

'It's a dark place for me,' said Carol, lifting her cup.

*

'Not worried about the interview then?' said Bible as his son set about polishing off a plate of sausage, egg, bacon and beans. The restaurant was on the first floor, the aroma of roasting coffee beans wafting up from the tea and coffee shop below. A raised dais near a potted palm was where a violinist would play at lunchtime.

'This place is like the olden days,' grumbled Pauline.

'The first place was full,' said Bible.

'It wasn't,' said the little girl.

'Don't contradict your father,' said Shirley. But Bible had hardly noticed. He was trying to forget Carol. He didn't think Shirley had seen her, though she'd been surprised when he'd hurried them away from the café.

'I'm going to burp,' said Pauline.

'No, darling,' said her mother.

'But it's my birthday.'

'Go on then,' said Ricky. 'If you can't burp on your birthday, when can you? My mate Cannonball was always belching.'

'He should have gone your route and applied for a job.'

Ricky fiddled with his knife and fork. 'He wouldn't get an interview. He can hardly read and write. I reckon that's why he was a bully.'

'Who did he bully?' said Shirley. Bible was afraid of her going into protective mother mode.

'It doesn't matter. Ricky's shot of him now.'

'So who did he bully?' repeated Shirley.

'I was never with him, like,' said Ricky, spiking a chunk of sausage. 'Not when it was kids from the little school. I'd have stopped him.'

Bible remembered facing Cannonball in their hallway. His eyes. There was a look he'd seen before. Eyes that didn't connect to a conscience. Eyes that weren't afraid. Ricky wouldn't have been strong enough to stop him.

'How do you know he bullied them if you weren't there?' he said.

'Well, sometimes it was just, you know, like, teasing a bit.' Ricky was edgy now. No, he wouldn't have been strong enough. 'Breaking up their football games. Taking the ball off them.'

'That sounds like bullying.'

Ricky pushed the remaining egg around his plate. 'I didn't stay when he did that. He used to do it with that Donald who got killed, and his little mates.'

Shirley looked alarmed. 'Ricky!' She flicked her eyes towards Pauline.

'Oh, yeah.'

'Why don't you go along with Mummy and look at those skates? I'll be along when he's finished,' said Bible.

'But your plate's empty,' protested the little girl.

Shirley stood up and grabbed Pauline's hand. 'Daddy's still got to pay.'

Bible waited till they'd gone.

'What do you know, Ricky?' He should have questioned his son earlier. He'd let family life get in the way.

'He hated Donald. Told him he came from a scummy family.' Ricky looked up. Defiant. 'Which he did.'

'He was a little boy.'

'His dad's scummy.'

'What's Cannonball's dad like?' He hated glorifying the young thug as Cannonball, though he knew the name had stuck.

'Not much better.'

'Were you with him the day Donald died?'

Ricky shook his head. 'But he told me he'd been messing with Donald the day Turner killed him.'

'What do you mean, messing?'

'Shoving him around on the field.'

'Why didn't you say anything?'

'He was a mate. I wasn't going to help you when you'd just pushed us round in that cafe.'

Bible slid his plate to one side, thinking of the football found near Donald's body, Turner's vehement protestations of innocence, and the man's fondness for little girls.

'You think Cannonball did it, don't you?'

'It could have been an accident. Banged his head on a rock. That Donald, he was a tough little get. He'd fight you to get his ball back. It was always a crap one, half deflated.'

'You know Turner hanged this morning?'

Ricky was looking down at his lap. Tears were beginning to ooze down the sides of his nose. 'He was a twisted bastard.'

'But he didn't kill anybody, did he?'

Ricky wiped his eyes with his sleeve and shook his head. 'I need to go to my interview.'

'Were you there, Ricky?'

Bible's son nodded his head dumbly. Bible passed him a handkerchief to wipe his eyes.

'Go on. Tell me' said Bible. But Ricky pushed his chair back and walked out of the café.

It wouldn't be Ricky's last interview that day. Bible knew he'd go through the rest of Pauline's birthday like a hollow man.

*

Pauline clutched her skates, having been denied permission to wear them on the bus. Bible wished the stop were not opposite the police station. He felt a hand tugging at his sleeve.

'Daddy, do you like my skates?'

'Lovely, darling.' He'd have to speak to Shirley, too. Bible could see activity around the station entrance. He wished the bus would come. He'd speak to Ward. Bill could handle it. He'd pass it all over to Bill.

Shirley stood close to him. 'You're not saying much, Jim.'

'Excited about Pauline's party.'

Shirley laughed. 'No, you're not. Are you worried about Ricky?'

'Yes.' At least it was true. He could see Holroyd across the road in the entrance. And people with notebooks. He seemed to be giving an interview.

'He'll be all right. Or if he isn't, he'll get another chance. And National Service'll help him.' Shirley took his hand and squeezed it. 'But now all this is over, I am going to look for a job.'

'That's fine love. Fine. You were right all along.'

The Teddy Boys. He hadn't listened. He'd wait until Pauline's birthday was over before telling Shirley about Ricky. Someone in the crowd outside the police station was pointing in his direction. It looked like Higham.

Pauline pushed between them. 'Why isn't the bus here when it's my birthday?'

'That's not how they work out the timetables love,' said Shirley.

Holroyd had seen him. So where was the bus? The Chief Superintendent was coming over, the press photographer from the local *Argus* after him. And there was Ward, hanging back, knowing how Bible would feel.

'Jim!' The Chief Superintendent hailed him from the middle of the road. 'Man of the moment!'

Holroyd was soon at the bus stop with his retinue. He wrapped an arm round Bible's shoulders. 'Come on, Jim. Join in the fun. We need a photo.'

Shirley held Pauline's hand and stood in front of Holroyd. 'Can't you let him enjoy his daughter's birthday?'

Holroyd looked at her in shock, as if she were a blank space that had just spoken. Then he grinned. 'But he's a local hero, darling.' Holroyd pulled Bible round to face the press photographer. 'Say cheese.'

Bible ducked away as the shutter clicked. 'Hey, I need another,' shouted the reporter, but Bible had already taken his wife and daughter's hands and was stalking away.

'We'll get a taxi,' he said, leading them towards the railway station.

He heard Holroyd laugh. 'I told you he was shy.'

Bible heard someone running behind him. Ward.

'The guv'nor wanted you to know,' Ward paused to catch his breath, 'he understands.'

'Does he? Does he really?'

'He's told the pressman to lay off. He's still grateful you got Turner for what he did to his granddaughter.'

'I don't deserve any of this, Bill. Any of this praise.'

'I know you don't like hanging, sir. I'm not sure I'm with it anymore.'

'He didn't kill anyone, Bill.' Ward looked puzzled. 'It wasn't Turner.'

'With respect, sir, there's no need to feel guilty.'

Yes, there was. Turner, Carol, Ricky. He was aware of Shirley and Pauline watching him, Shirley annoyed, Pauline simply impatient. He had to get something right. It could wait until after Pauline's birthday.

'I'll see you tomorrow, Bill.'

* * *

Author's Note

If you enjoyed *Stone and Water,* please consider leaving a review on Amazon.

To be kept up to date with news on further novels and stories in the Jim Bible series, and, in time, a free download, please contact me on mail@davidjamesbuckley.com or visit my website http://www.davidjamesbuckley.com.

I can also be found on Twitter @djbuckley_ and on my Facebook page at Facebook.com/davidjamesbuckley.

Acknowledgements

I would like to thank the three retired policemen who gave me a good deal of their time when I was in the early stages of this novel. I have not named them to protect them from any blame for the undoubted liberties I have taken, probably unknowingly, with police procedure in the 1950s.

I am also grateful for the support I received from my lecturers and tutors when studying for the MA Writing at Sheffield Hallam University, and the feedback from my fellow students in our regular workshops.

Finally I need to thank my army of proofreaders. Any errors and typos which remain are entirely my responsibility.

About the Author

David was born in Bradford, West Yorkshire. He has had plays produced on Radio 4, and BBC Radios Leeds and Sheffield. For a number of years he reviewed fiction regularly for *The Observer*. He also wrote for *The Independent, The Guardian, New Statesman and Society, The Yorkshire Post* and *The Times Educational Supplement*.

David has also had short stories and poetry published. He turned to crime fiction and novel writing when studying for the MA Writing at Sheffield Hallam University. His first novel, *Stone and Water*, is the outcome of that.

He is currently working on his second novel in the Inspector Bible series, *Surviving Angel,* and a short prequel to *Stone and Water*.

David and his wife live in Sheffield and have three grown up children.

Printed by Amazon Italia Logistica S.r.l.
Torrazza Piemonte (TO), Italy

12748944R00223